ST. MAR
MINOTAUR
MYSTERIES

PRAISE FOR BEN REHDER AND HIS BLANCO COUNTY MYSTERIES

GUILT TRIP

"As memorable and funny as [Rehder's] previous titles."
—*Austin Chronicle*

"Ben Rehder has found a way to keep the laughs coming even when the bodies start to litter the countryside of Blanco County, Texas. Lots of distinct characters ensure the novel never lags, and John Marlin is a happy combination of ecologist and eccentric."
—*Dallas Morning News*

"Rating: A. Would I move to Blanco County? No, but I'm happy to visit."
—*Deadly Pleasures*

"Rehder has jumped to a new level, and *Guilt Trip* just might grab a chunk of the outsize Hiaasen crowd."
—*Booklist*

"One of the genre's rising talents."
—*South Florida Sun-Sentinel*

FLAT CRAZY

"Intriguing and entertaining. Rehder's characters may be outrageous, but they are never boring."
—*The Dallas Morning News*

"Outrageous fun."
—*Kirkus Reviews* (starred review)

"*Flat Crazy* is Texas at its twisted best. Ben Rehder throws open the gates, shoots his pistols in the air, and unleashes a stampede of comic madness."
—Tim Cockey, author of *Backstabber*

More...

"You'd have to be *Flat Crazy* to miss a Ben Rehder book. This guy is the funniest, freshest voice in Texas mystery writing today. His work stands out like a DayGlo parka in deer season."

—Rick Riordan, author of *Southtown*

"Rehder's clever storytelling skills, his expert comic timing and flair for characters have made this series shine. Rehder doesn't just write niche mysteries, he's proving to be one of the genre's rising talents with his twisted tales." —*South Florida Sun-Sentinel*

BONE DRY

"An over-the-top-tale of sex, mayhem, and murder in Texas's Hill Country. Readers will get a wild ride." —*Publishers Weekly*

"You don't need an invite to the Bush ranch to have fun in Texas. Ben Rehder, whose *Buck Fever* earned him an Edgar nomination for Best First Mystery last year, is back." —*Chicago Tribune*

"More funny adventures of John Marlin, amiable, estimable game warden of Blanco County, Texas...[a] winning sequel to *Buck Fever*....Characters to chuckle at, yes, but Rehder never forgets he's got clues to furnish and a story to tell." —*Kirkus Reviews*

"A humdinger. Funny, sardonic, and filled with clever metaphors and similes, *Bone Dry* is as cool and satisfying as a Lone Star beer on a hot Texas afternoon." —*Sports Afield*

"Lots of twists and turns and authentic police procedures...[a] fast-paced romp." —*San Antonio Express-News*

"Weird, wild, and wacky. One of the funniest mysteries of the year. [This] fast-paced novel has a variety of peculiar plotlines that all converge in a wild and memorable ending. Rehder's first book was a finalist for the Edgar Award and the Lefty Award (for the funniest crime novel of the year). His latest effort is in the same category—it's a nifty, hilarious romp that's tough to put down."

—*Lansing State Journal*

"Funny...much like Carl Hiaasen's gore-spattered howlers."
—*Field & Stream*

"The pace of [*Bone Dry*] is steady and swift, the tone wry and playful."
—*Drood Review*

"Take a novel about hunting, throw in some unforgettable characters, and add a dash of ribald humor." —*Abilene Reporter-News*

BUCK FEVER

"This fast-paced comic thriller comes within shooting distance of Hiaasen and Leonard territory...a promising debut." —*Booklist*

"This debut novel is a complete success. There's sure to be a long career for this wacky, happy series."
—*Publishers Weekly* (starred review)

"A hilarious debut. *Buck Fever* does for Texas what Hiaasen does for Florida."
—*Clues Unlimited*

"A deserving, character-rich atmospheric crime novel that is deserving of the Edgar nomination." —*Deadly Pleasures*

"Imagine Carl Hiaasen with a Texas accent. *Buck Fever* is a laugh-filled riot."
—*Denver Post*

"Briskly paced, amusing, spiced with deftly drawn good-old-boy portraits; an altogether promising debut." —*Kirkus Reviews*

"A wild and crazy first novel." —*Library Journal* (starred review)

ALSO BY BEN REHDER

Flat Crazy

Bone Dry

Buck Fever

AVAILABLE FROM
ST. MARTIN'S/MINOTAUR PAPERBACKS

GUILT TRIP

A BLANCO COUNTY MYSTERY

BEN REHDER

St. Martin's Paperbacks

This is a work of fiction. All of the characters, organizations and events portrayed in this novel are either products of the author's imagination or are used fictitiously.

GUILT TRIP

 For information address St. Martin's Press, 175 Fifth Avenue, New York, NY 10010.

Library of Congress Catalog Card Number: 2005047016

ISBN: 0-312-94094-7
EAN: 9780312-94094-2

Printed in the United States of America

St. Martin's Press hardcover edition published 2005
St. Martin's Paperbacks edition / October 2006

St. Martin's Paperbacks are published by St. Martin's Press, 175 Fifth Avenue, New York, NY 10010.

10 9 8 7 6 5 4 3 2 1

For Liz and Karl.

Better read this one.

&

For a good man named Ed Fanick.

ACKNOWLEDGMENTS

MOST OF THE names are becoming familiar by now. These are the people who answer my countless questions with endless patience, knowing that I'll probably make all kinds of mistakes anyway.

Special thanks to Lieutenant Tommy Blackwell (retired from the Travis County Sheriff's Office); David Bailey, Chief of Investigations with the Austin Fire Department; Lampasas County Game Warden Jim Lindeman; Blanco County Game Warden Bobby Fenton (retired); Director of Wildlife Enforcement David Sinclair; Natural Resources Specialist Trey Carpenter; and Detective Trey Kleinert of the Austin Police Department.

Thanks also to John "J. B." Barber, Martin Grantham, Mary Summerall, and Jeff Strandhagen for their valuable input and assistance.

Much appreciation to my early readers, Helen Fanick, Becky Rehder, and Stacia Hernstrom, and to copyeditor India Cooper.

As always, thanks to Ben Sevier for more things than I can possibly list here, and to Nancy Love for keeping me on track.

1

ON FRIDAY, MAY 7—a beautiful spring morning fairly bursting with promises of hope and renewal—Texas state senator Dylan Herzog received a phone call that grabbed him by an extremely sensitive part of his anatomy and yanked him to a place he definitely didn't want to go.

Before the unwelcome interruption, Herzog had been minding his own business, thumbing through a copy of *Esquire,* contemplating the possibility of cheek implants. A senior aide named Rusk was in Herzog's office with him, both of them moving slowly, sort of easing into the morning. They were seriously hung over, having spent the previous afternoon on a cabin cruiser with a couple of hard-drinking lobbyists and their bikini-clad dates. These were young ladies with scruples; their tops hadn't come off until the third round of margaritas.

"You seen this yet?" Rusk asked, hefting a document three inches thick.

But Herzog was too distracted by the article, a somewhat facetious piece on cosmetic surgery. For a price, you, too, could look like a Hollywood hunk! There were before-and-after shots: some loser who'd spent a cool twenty grand for a complete makeover. Hair plugs to give him a thick mop like Hugh Grant's. Liposuction for the trim waist of Russell Crowe. Cheek implants for the Brad Pitt look. But now, in Herzog's opinion, the patient simply looked like a hairier, skinnier, cheekier loser.

Rusk repeated his question, and Herzog glanced up. "Seen what?"

"The prelim report on the red-necked sapsucker."

Herzog tossed the magazine aside. Cheek implants? The very idea. He was a devastatingly handsome man as is, even if he was approaching fifty. "The red-necked . . . ?"

"Sapsucker."

"What about it?"

"They want to move it from endangered to threatened, but they need more funds to continue the study."

Screw the sapsucker, Herzog was about to say, but right then Susan buzzed in on the intercom.

"Senator Herzog, there's a call for you on line one," his executive assistant said, sounding somewhat less chipper than normal. Herzog frowned at the phone. He had asked her to hold all calls unless it was important. And for God's sake, he'd told her, don't put the wife through.

"Who is it?" he snapped, running a hand through his hundred-dollar haircut.

"Well . . . he didn't say."

"Didn't I tell you—"

"You need to take this one, Dyl."

Herzog shot a quick look at Rusk, thinking, *Jesus, how many times have I told her not to call me that in the office?* He lifted the phone from its cradle.

She whispered, "Sorry about that, but it's some guy . . . he didn't give his name. He says he has photos—"

"Aw, Christ," Herzog said, wondering why she would interrupt with a call from a person he didn't even know. And why was she whispering? "Just take a message, Susan, and tell him—"

"Of us!" she hissed. "He says he has photos of us."

Just like that, everything changed.

Herzog sat up straight. His forehead suddenly felt like a furnace. A million invisible pins pricked at his scalp. The hair on his neck would have stood on end if it hadn't been meticulously trimmed with a GroomRight Deluxe. He tried to smile at Rusk, who was looking more curious by the minute. *Everything okay?* the aide mouthed. Herzog nodded.

"I wasn't going to put him through," Susan said gingerly, "but when he said that, well . . ."

Herzog stared down at the red blinking light on the phone's base. The caller was waiting patiently. "What were his exact words?"

"He said he'd been watching us . . . and he has photos. He sounds pretty creepy, Dyl."

"Okaaay," he said, drawing the word out, giving himself time to think. But it most definitely was not okay. He covered the mouthpiece. "Can you give me a few minutes, Ken?" Rusk gave him a questioning look, but nodded and left the office.

Herzog took a deep breath, then pushed the red button and mustered up as much bravado as possible. "Who the hell is this?"

There was a moment of silence, then a harsh backwoods twang. "Mind your damn manners, Herzog, or every newspaper in the state's gonna know you cain't keep your pecker in your pants."

Play it tough—that's what his instincts told him. Herzog had dealt with his share of blowhard rednecks before, and they usually backed down when he got firm with them. Besides, the caller might be bluffing. "I don't know if this is a sick joke or what," he said, "but if you think—"

"Have you checked your mail this morning?"

"No, I haven't, but I have no intention—"

"Just shut the hell up and check with your secretary. She seems to take care of all kinds of little things for you, know what I mean?" There was a taunting quality to the caller's voice.

With one hand, Herzog began to rummage through his overflowing in-box. "You leave her out of this," he demanded. "My relationship with Miss Hammond is purely professional." He meant to issue the words in a bark of indignity, but they came out in a frantic squeak.

" 'Purely professional,' " the caller mocked. "I wish I had me a setup like that. Now you just find them photos and we'll all see how professional it really is. I sent you a little care package on Wednesday. Would've been in yesterday's mail, today's at the latest."

It was. Herzog found it buried in the middle of the pile: a plain manila envelope, Herzog's name and address in block letters, with the word PERSONAL below that. The return address said "Kimberly Clark." Why did that name sound familiar? "I've . . . I've got it right here," Herzog said.

"Well, hell, boy, don't be bashful. Take a look."

Herzog swallowed hard, tore the envelope open, then braced himself and pulled the contents out.

Oh my God.

He felt an iron fist grasp his balls and squeeze. Sweat was beginning to trickle from every perfectly exfoliated pore.

The photos were grainy and of poor quality, but they did the job. They had been taken through the rear windows looking into the living room. His stomach went queasy. Someone had been spying on them from Susan's backyard!

The first shot wasn't too troublesome—just him and Susan kissing, fully clothed. He even remembered the night, Friday of last week, when his wife was out of town.

Herzog flipped to the second shot, and a wave of nausea churned in his abdomen. Much more incriminating. Now they were undressing—Herzog unbuckling his belt, Susan with her blouse off, her skirt at her feet. The important question was, how long had the photographer hung around? Was the last shot worse than the first two? After all, Herzog had certain, well, "predilections" that the average constituent simply would not fully understand. He might be able to survive a run-of-the-mill infidelity scandal, but if these photos ventured into—

His thoughts were interrupted.

"That gal's sure got some nice titties," the caller said. "Them store-bought or what?"

Herzog couldn't answer. He was beginning to hyperventilate. Everything depended on the third shot, and he couldn't bring himself to look. His hands were trembling, and his eyes had watered up. Why was this happening? He played golf with all the right people, greased all the right palms, followed the code of the modern-day politico. For God's sake, he was supposed to be governor some day! "Who are you?" he managed to mumble. "Why are you doing this?"

"We'll get to that. But first, have you seen 'em all yet? That last one's a beaut."

Herzog summoned up his courage, what little was left, and flipped to the final photograph. He almost passed out at his desk. A bolt of pain stabbed from temple to temple.

The shot was from later in the evening, after they'd both had plenty to drink. Susan was wearing her black leather outfit—corset, thigh-high boots, and a G-string. A riding crop completed the fetching ensemble. But that wasn't the worst part. Not by any stretch of the imagination. What Herzog was wearing made the photo an unmitigated disaster.

Dylan Albert Herzog—the distinguished representative of Senate District 32, chairman of the Natural Resources Committee—was now on foreign soil. Rather than being the one in power, the one who commanded others to jump through hoops, he was at the mercy of a stranger at the end of a phone line. It was his worst nightmare. "What . . . what do you want?" he chirped.

"Oh, I see I've got your attention now. Okay, listen up." The caller's tone had gone from chiding to militant. He spat each word out like curdled milk. "I'm sick of laws that favor the rich folks and screw small landowners like me. I'm sick of the government meddling where it don't belong. I'm sick of letting a bunch of dirtbags screw me out of a dollar every chance they get. And it makes me sick when I know the chief dirtbag"—here there was a diabolical cackle—"is a guy who likes to wear a friggin' diaper."

Herzog pulled his trashcan from under his desk and neatly launched his breakfast. *Kimberly Clark.* Now he got the joke.

"What do you want?" the senator croaked, with much more sincerity this time.

Late Sunday afternoon. Annie and Horace Norris, retirees who proudly hailed from Madison, Wisconsin, had just left the Snake Farm & Indian Artifact Showplace (an attraction they had found rather odd, to be honest) when they spotted the drunk driver.

"No doubt about it, the guy's smashed," Horace growled, stooped over the wheel of his Winnebago, heading north on Highway 281 toward Johnson City, Texas. "A regular menace, that's what he is."

"Oh, dear," replied Annie, his wife of forty-six years.

Horace didn't like it. No sir, he didn't like it one bit. It was hard enough to maneuver his RV in a safe and prudent manner under ordinary circumstances, but when you had to share the road with a drunk driver, well, that was entirely unacceptable. He hadn't survived four decades in the dog-eat-dog world of actuarial analysis to be killed by some hotshot in a flashy red Corvette. Looked brand-new, judging by the temporary dealer plate in the rear window.

"This fruitcake is all over the road," Horace grumbled. And the sports car was, too—floating from lane to lane, forty yards ahead of the Winnebago's massive front grille. He glanced down at his speedometer, which was sitting on *30*. A measly thirty miles per hour. Horace couldn't believe it. Not only was this joker weaving, he was doing it at roughly the same velocity at which Horace could break wind.

Horace had seen enough.

"Climb back there and grab the video camera," he said. "I wanna get some tape of this guy."

Annie was perplexed. "Why . . . what for?"

"To show to the cops!" Horace barked. "I'll flag one down if I have to. Show him what kind of lunatics are using the roads nowadays. Evidence, that's what for!"

Annie unbuckled (she never sat in the front seat without buckling up), and as she made her way toward the rear of the vehicle, Horace continued to rant. "In all my sixty-six years," Horace proclaimed, "I've never seen a guy drive like this. But come to Texas and what do we get? A friggin' demolition derby. Well, we may not be Texas taxpayers, but we pay our federal taxes, for Chrissakes. And since this is a U.S. highway, we got our rights! We have a right to be safe on our freeway system!"

"Oh, dear," Annie murmured again, opening a storage compartment above the Formica-topped dinette.

Horace was good and angry, boiling really, now a mere twenty yards behind the Corvette, breaking his own strict tailgating rule. He wanted the driver to notice him back here and know that his appalling behavior wasn't going unobserved. "What we'll do—you find that camera yet?—what we'll do is stop at a pay phone and report this nutcase. Show him what's what, this guy. And when the cops pull him over, we'll—"

Horace's train of thought was interrupted by movement in the Corvette. Until then, Horace had seen only one occupant in the car. But now a woman's head popped up—*from the driver's lap*—and she returned to her place on the passenger's side. She appeared to dab her lips with a tissue and then buckle her seat belt.

Horace couldn't believe his eyes. The man driving the Corvette wasn't drunk at all. No sir. Horace knew exactly what was going on. Hanky-panky! On the open highway! Right in front of Annie, for God's sake!

Horace was shocked. He was outraged. He was envious.

The driver, finally glancing in the rearview, gave a small wave to Horace out the window, then goosed the vehicle up to highway speed, leaving the Winnebago behind.

Horace could only watch it disappear on the horizon.

"Here's the camera," Annie said, returning to her seat and buckling in. She glanced out the windshield. "Wha— Where did he go?" She looked over at her husband. "Horace?"

"Never mind," Horace mumbled.

2

BLANCO COUNTY GAME warden John Marlin was two miles from Lucas Burnette's house when it exploded late Sunday afternoon.

Before that, he'd been sitting in one of his favorite stakeout spots, high on a hill above Ranch Road 1623, listening for the sound of shotguns, watching a massive wall of rain clouds lumbering in from the west. Turkey season was in progress, and he'd been eyeballing one nearby ranch in particular, owned by a man with a teenaged son who was a fledgling poacher.

Last fall, Marlin had caught the punk shooting deer at night on a stretch of county road that was always thick with whitetails. It had been about 3:00 A.M. on a Saturday, a time when mostly drunks and poachers (and sometimes drunk poachers) were out, and Marlin heard a shot on Sandy Road. Sitting in his green Dodge truck on a nearby hillside, he could see headlights as the vehicle stopped; a door slammed, then the vehicle came roaring his way. Marlin came down the hill, lights off, and waited by the side of the road. When the Chevy truck made the curve, Marlin was waiting, red and blue strobes flashing.

Problem was, there was no passenger, no rifle, and no deer in the back of the truck. But Marlin knew from years of experience: Roadside poachers *never* hunt alone. It's like a social activity for them—a big hunting party on wheels, often with alcohol involved, maybe a little pot. So Marlin pulled the skinny teenager out of the Chevy, took his driver's license, and asked him where his partner was.

"Who?" the guy replied, his eyes as wild as a penned steer's. "What're you talking about?"

"Son, what exactly are you doing out here?"

"Just out driving."

"Alone?"

"Yeah."

"In the middle of the night."

The kid shrugged.

Marlin didn't bother to argue. It was a common poacher tactic: One guy would shoot the deer, then jump out and track it down. Meanwhile, the driver would take off—figuring it was smarter not to leave a vehicle idling at the scene of the crime—then return in ten minutes or so if the coast was clear.

So Marlin tried a favorite tactic of his own. He cuffed the kid and said, "Where are your keys?"

"My, uh . . . my *keys*?" The boy's voice had a slight tremble to it.

"Yep."

"In the ignition."

"Hang loose. I'll be back in a few minutes."

Marlin climbed into the poacher's truck and did a U-turn. He drove slowly, lowering it to a near crawl when he reached the vicinity where the shot had been fired. Sure enough, the other poacher—who by now had located the eight-point buck and dragged it closer to the road—saw his friend's Chevy coming and emerged from the brush to wave him down. When Marlin pulled over, the kid swung the carcass into the bed of the truck and hopped in, failing to notice who was driving. He said, "My house, man!"

Marlin said, "You mind if we stop by the county jail first?"

The boy nearly pissed in his pants.

Back then, Marlin thought both boys had learned their lesson. Lately, though, he'd been hearing things about the kid who had done the shooting, and he suspected the delinquent-in-training was back at it again.

Moments earlier, sitting in his truck, Marlin had been thinking of making an unannounced visit to the ranch, just to let the boy know he was watching.

That's when he heard it—a huge, quick boom, sounding like a cannon being fired in the Blanco town square. The resulting chatter over the radio told Marlin something big had just happened, but nobody seemed to know what.

Marlin cranked the engine, dropped it into gear, and bounced down onto the road. He cut the wheel to the right and floored it toward the small town of Blanco. As he headed east, it seemed every deputy in the county was on the air—but it was a full minute before anyone came through with an explanation. Deputy Ernie Turpin, his siren screaming in the background, said, "Dispatch, be advised we've got a house fire at the end of Heimer Lane. Flames out every window. This place is going up quick, y'all."

Lucas Burnette was another local problem child, and had been since the age of fourteen. Now he was twenty years old and on a first-name basis with every cop in the county. The short version was, Lucas had a drug problem, and it dominated his life like a stack of overdue bills. His list of infractions was long. Breaking and entering. Possession of stolen goods. Possession of marijuana. Driving under the influence. Marlin had even busted him a couple of times for poaching.

Despite all of Lucas's problems, most of the officers couldn't help but like the kid. Not all that bright, but funny as hell, affable, easygoing. He'd make jokes at his own expense when you were arresting him, and then, riding in the cruiser, he'd ask, with sincerity, how your family was doing. He was respectful and courteous, and he never resisted. Lucas hadn't seen state prison time yet, just county jail. Each time he was paroled, released to a halfway house in Austin, those who knew Lucas would hold their breath and cross their fingers. *Grow up, kid!* they'd think. Disappointment always followed. Lucas would do fine for a couple of months, working steadily, staying clean, keeping out of the system. Then one day he'd skip out—just walk away from his best chance at redemption. Invariably, he'd come back to Blanco County, an hour west of Austin, and lie low, enjoying his freedom until the deputies happened to cross his path and pick him up again.

This last time, though, it looked like he was finally shaping up. He'd been meeting the terms of his parole, including drug testing once a month. He'd been working full-time at the feed store, earning enough to move out of his parents' place and make the rent on a small house on Heimer Lane.

The same house—Marlin realized as he arrived on the scene—that was currently on fire.

Ernie Turpin was right; the place was completely engulfed in flames, and the throng of emergency workers and curious onlookers was pushed back by the heat. Marlin knew there wouldn't be any putting this inferno out, not until there was nothing left but the house's charred skeleton. Regardless, Marlin spotted several firefighters in turnout gear dragging a hose from the only pumper truck on the scene. If nothing else, they could go defensive and knock down grass fires to protect the neighboring homes, the nearest of which was two hundred yards away.

Marlin parked behind a cluster of deputies' cruisers, an ambulance, and a dozen volunteer firefighters' vehicles. As he climbed from his truck, Marlin saw two deputies—Ernie Turpin and a new woman named Nicole Brooks—working traffic control, keeping a path clear for emergency vehicles. Ernie and Nicole working closely together—no surprise there. Marlin gave them a wave, signaling his intentions, and proceeded in a wide arc around the home. For fifteen minutes, he walked the perimeter of the property, five or six acres, working his flashlight, searching for victims—people who might have staggered from the house and then collapsed—or for evidence of what might have caused the explosion. He'd once seen a water heater with a faulty relief valve turn a garage into kindling. Gas leaks, too, were a major problem, so Marlin scanned the backyard to see if the house was fed by a propane tank. There wasn't one, which was just as well. Now the only question was whether anybody had been trapped inside.

Coming around the front, Marlin spotted Senior Deputy Bill Tatum near the road, finishing a conversation with the fire chief. Marlin walked over.

"You bring the weenies?" Tatum asked, nodding toward the flames.

Marlin grinned. Somebody always broke down and used that corny line. "Any word on Lucas?"

"Nope. We called his friends, next of kin. Nobody knows where the hell he is."

There wasn't much to say to that. Now it was a waiting game, and the firefighters would give them their answer in a day or two when they sifted through the extinguished rubble.

"No cars," Marlin said, noting the empty dirt driveway. There was no carport or garage. Lucas drove a crummy little import, and it was nowhere to be seen.

Marlin could barely stand the irony. It would be even more of a tragedy if Lucas had died right when he was getting his life straightened out.

Neither man spoke for several minutes, transfixed by the fire, listening to pine knots popping like fireworks, watching the firefighters do their job.

Tatum said, "I heard you took a trip up to Dallas last weekend."

Sparks flew high as the west wall of the house buckled and collapsed inward.

"Just visiting an old friend," Marlin said, as fat marbles of rain began to fall.

Senator Dylan Herzog was sitting in front of a rancher named Chuck Hamm, and he felt like a kid called to the principal's office for shooting spitwads. Hamm was leaning back in a leather chair behind an obscenely large desk made from burnished walnut.

"You know it's a goddamn impossibility, don't you?" Hamm said.

Herzog nodded. He continued to stare at the calfskin rug on the floor. Sunday evening now, and his insides were still jelly. One phone call. Hard to believe that's all it took to drop his life into a blender and hit PUREE. He'd been reluctant to take his troubles to Hamm, but Herzog hadn't been able to think of any alternatives.

Hamm said, "Even if we did what he's asking—and we damn sure ain't—it wouldn't make no difference anyhow. Didn't this moron realize that?"

Herzog shook his head, noticing, of course, the rancher's presumptuous use of "we" instead of "you." "I tried to reason with him," Herzog lied, "but he wouldn't listen. You know how those guys are. Like rabid dogs."

Hamm grunted, a sound that befitted his personality. "I mean even you—the all-powerful senator—you can't do it all on your own. Didn't you point that out?"

Herzog hated Hamm's smug sarcasm. "I'm afraid this man couldn't grasp the fundamentals of legislation."

"And you got no idea who he is?"

"Unfortunately, no."

"Someone you know, maybe? Someone you met already?"

"Could be, Chuck, I really don't know. You have to understand, this fencing issue makes people angry as hell. I get letters, phone calls, e-mails."

"You think it was one of them?"

"I guess it's a possibility, but the point is, there are plenty of people it could be. That's what makes this such a difficult problem."

"You didn't get a number off your caller ID?"

Herzog shook his head. "Came through as unavailable."

Hamm eyed Herzog over the rim of a bourbon glass. It made the senator squirm. Hamm was tall, like Herzog, but older and heavier. Most of the extra weight was stored in a belly that strained the lower buttons on Hamm's shirts, but underneath the flab one could still recognize the hardened musculature of a rural working man. He had a weathered face, eyebrows that looked as if they might crawl off his forehead at any moment, and a square jaw that was just getting jowly. His skin was the color and texture of a pancake left too long on the griddle. "What's he got on you?" Hamm asked.

Herzog sighed. "I told you already. Photographs."

"Yeah, but of what? Snorting coke, pissing in public, what?"

Herzog desperately wanted to avoid this issue—but he knew he'd have to share the basic facts eventually. Otherwise, Hamm might not comprehend how dire the situation really was.

Hamm gave Herzog a skeptical look and said, "I've wondered about you, Herzog, to tell the truth. The way you dress, your aftershave, all that. Maybe you was chasing some tail in one a those special nightclubs in Austin?"

"I'm not sure I follow you."

"I think you do."

"No, Chuck, I really don't."

"Fine, then. Are you a fairy? That's what I'm asking. Or maybe you swing both ways, like that governor up in New Jersey."

Herzog rolled his eyes. It had been obvious to him for quite some time that Hamm had little, if any, respect for him. Just because Herzog didn't get a little dirt under his fingernails now and then? Just because he didn't have a farmer's tan from repairing a fence on the back forty? Just because—*yeehaw!*—Herzog had never milked a cow? It was damned unfair. Herzog worked hard, too—hell, he exhausted himself—but he did it with brainpower, not mindless manual labor.

Herzog noticed that Hamm was waiting, indeed expecting an answer to the whole gay question. "Of course not," he huffed.

"'Cause that kinda scenario could fuck things up real bad," Hamm said quietly, a grimace on his face, as if the room were suddenly swarming with prancing homosexuals. Hamm lifted one boot onto the desktop and stared at the ceiling, thinking. "Maybe it's something you could, you know, just ride out. Hunker low in your saddle and see if it'll pass. Hell, most folks aren't even surprised by what you people do nowadays. Guy gets a bee-jay right in the Oval Office and what do we do? Elect his wife to the U.S. Senate, that's what. Damn pitiful, if you ask me."

Herzog wasn't sure if he was supposed to comment or not, so he remained silent. He let his gaze roam upward to a Cape buffalo mounted high on the wall behind Hamm's desk. Fierce-looking animal, with eyeballs that seemed to penetrate Herzog's very soul. Underneath the ferocity, though, there appeared to be a touch of embarrassment on the animal's part at finding itself displayed above a credenza that held a combination scanner/copier/fax machine.

Herzog realized Chuck Hamm had just said something. "Excuse me?"

"I said if I'm gonna help you out—and that's an *if* at this point—you gotta give me some idea what we're dealing with. The photos. It's not like you robbed a liquor store or something, right?"

Herzog shook his head. If only it were something that respectable.

"Jeez, gimme a clue, here," Hamm snorted, sitting up, losing his patience. "What ballpark we're playing in, something like that."

Herzog grasped for the right words. This was all so humiliating. Finally, he took a deep breath and just said it. "The photographs *are* of a sexual nature, but I'd rather not go into details." He could feel his face flushing a deep red. But deep down, it felt good, unexpectedly good, to share his burden with someone. Even a troll like Hamm.

The rancher didn't smirk or leer or make sophomoric comments, as Herzog expected, but rather seemed to be contemplating the implications. "Not your wife?" he asked.

"Uh, no." It pained Herzog deeply to admit that to another human being.

Hamm nodded as if he understood completely. "Just one woman?"

Herzog emitted an exasperated breath. "Well, yeah, what else?" *Jesus, what does this guy take me for?*

Hamm grinned, showing tobacco-stained teeth. "Some guys, you know, they like a coupla gals at a time. You oughta try it."

Herzog fought hard not to form a mental picture of Chuck Hamm in a threesome. "I'm sorry to disappoint you, but no, it was only one." He was already revealing far more than he had intended to.

"And what? They caught you coming out of a hotel room? Playing a little grab-ass at her car door?"

Herzog closed his eyes and said, "It's worse than that."

Hamm laughed unexpectedly, a big booming rumble that made Herzog's cheek twitch. "Shit, don't tell me. Are you nekkid in the pictures, Herzog? Is that it?"

Nearly, Herzog thought. "I . . . I fail to see why that's funny."

Hamm continued in a merry chuckle, and Herzog was beginning to get angry.

Hamm said, "Hell, son, when you decided to have yourself a scandal, you dove in head first, huh? Just went straight for the big leagues."

Herzog was not amused. *If I ever get out of this,* he swore to himself, *I'll never again do business with a man like Chuck Hamm. I don't care how large his campaign contributions are.*

The rancher finally regained his composure. "Tell me this. Was she a hooker?"

Now Herzog had to wonder if Hamm was merely having a little fun at his expense. "No, she was *not* a prostitute."

"Porn star? Titty dancer?"

Herzog refused to dignify that line of questioning with an answer.

A look of sudden panic creased Hamm's leathery face, and he set his bourbon glass down deliberately. "For fuck's sake, we are talking about a white woman, ain't we?"

Herzog wanted to lecture Hamm on the racist undertones of that remark, but he simply nodded instead.

"Well, Christ, why're you getting so damn uptight?" Hamm asked. "She sounds like a perfect angel."

3

THERE'S AN OLD saying in Texas: If you don't like the weather, just hang around a few minutes; it'll change. And while Texas weather is notorious for its unpredictability, the natives know that its sheer intensity is a force to be reckoned with, as well.

The infamous Galveston hurricane of 1900 decimated the island and took with it more than eight thousand lives—the deadliest natural disaster in U.S. history. Texas is plagued by more tornadoes than any other state, and in one year alone, 1967, suffered through 232, more than half of those coming in a single month. In the early fifties, the state was gripped by a drought so severe and unrelenting, most of Texas was classified as a disaster area. When it finally ended, the pendulum swung wildly in the other direction and the rains came hard.

Tucked between the state's coastal plains and the southern rim of the Edwards Plateau is the Hill Country, with its limestone and granite peaks, box canyons, and spring-fed rivers and creeks. The area includes Blanco County, and all of it is prone to flash flooding, more so in the springtime than other times of the year.

So when John Marlin woke in the middle of the night to the heavy roar of rain on his metal roof, he was naturally concerned. It had been pouring all evening—which had been a boon to the firefighters at Lucas Burnette's house—but now it was really coming down. The kind of storm that can quickly swell waterways to three or four times their normal width.

Marlin's dog, Geist, a pit bull who was terrified of thunderstorms, had sought refuge under the bed hours ago. Marlin could hear her panting nervously.

Marlin flipped his bedroom TV to the weather radar channel and saw a massive storm stretching from Waco to Uvalde, shaped like a boomerang as it struggled to move eastward. The problem was, this damn storm was lingering in place, rebuilding upon itself. For Marlin, this was cause for alarm.

In addition to enforcing hunting and fishing laws, game wardens are often tasked with leading water-rescue and victim-recovery operations on Texas lakes and waterways.

And Marlin had been on the job long enough to know: The water would rise, and somewhere in the county, for some reason, some half-wit would try to drive through it.

"Think we oughta chance it?" Red O'Brien asked, staring through the windshield of his old Ford truck. The wipers were having a tough time keeping up with the amount of rain coming down. Hell, his headlights could hardly penetrate the curtain of water.

His longtime friend and poaching partner, Billy Don Craddock, gave him a look. "You plumb outta your mind? This ain't no submarine you're driving. The road's gotta be four feet under."

That's about what Red had expected. Billy Don was a huge, scary-looking ol' boy, but he had no gumption at all. Never willing to take risks.

"I'll just back it up and get a running start," Red offered. "We'll scoot across like we're on damn water skis."

"Yeah, water skis made from two tons of steel."

Red tried to reason with him. "Planes weigh a bunch, too, but they can fly, can't they? Hell, the principle's the same here. There's all kinds of complicated formulas and variances involved, but I'm telling you, it would work. I saw something just like it in *Popular Mechanics.*"

"Include me out."

At this point, Red was thinking he ought to leave Billy Don behind to fend for himself. "You know what's gonna happen if we get caught again?" he asked.

Billy Don didn't answer.

"Do ya?" Red repeated.

"No, what?"

Red snorted. "Well, now, I ain't exactly sure, but it won't be pretty, I'll tell ya that much."

"I say we stay right here till the river goes down. If that means we gotta ditch them hogs later, well, we'll just ditch the damn things."

Red was stunned. That was crazy talk, plain and simple. Here they'd just spent the better part of the night poaching wild pigs, popping them behind the ear with a quiet little .222, and now Billy Don was prepared to just leave them all behind.

"You know how much time I spent putting this operation together?" Red was angry, feeling unappreciated. Why, he had even bought a new set of bolt cutters for this little excursion. Earlier in the day, he'd overheard a rancher at the café saying he'd be spending the night in Austin—and when God lays an opportunity like that at your feet, you don't let it pass you by. If they could just get off the damn ranch, they'd have enough pork to last a year. But now the weather had gone and made things all complicated. Red could never get a break.

The thing that made him nervous was, they didn't know when the rancher would be back. Might be first thing in the morning.

By the time the water dropped, the rancher might be waiting on the other side, wondering who in the hell was on his ranch.

Both men sat in silence, Red trying to find something decent on the radio. He was wishing his eight-track player still worked.

After a few minutes, Billy Don said, "Lord, it is *raining*. I mean it is really coming down."

"I can see that, Al Roker."

"Red, if I was ever drownt, would you give me mouth-to-mouth?"

"Jeez, you gotta be kidding." The dumb questions this guy asked. It gave Red the heebie-jeebies, the thought of his lips anywhere near Billy Don's cavernous mouth.

"Some kinda friend you are," Billy Don huffed.

"Hell, Billy Don, half the time your breath smells like Vienna sausages."

"On account of that, you'd just let me die?"

"Can you think of a better reason?" Red was tired of this conversation already. He couldn't imagine sitting here all night. "Do me a favor, will ya? Just shine the spotlight down there and let's get a good look. See what we're dealing with."

"I think that's a fine idea," Billy Don grumbled, rolling down his window, letting the rain gush in. "Then you'll ree-lize what kinda fruitcake you are."

He grabbed the spotlight, with its intense million-candlepower beam, and stuck his massive arm out the window. The light cut a swath through the rain—and the men saw that the narrow, shallow river they had crossed earlier was now a raging torrent of whitewater. The surface was littered with tree limbs and branches and other debris. Red even saw a cow carcass whiz past.

"There now, you happy?" Billy Don hollered, his face soaked with rainwater.

As Billy Don pulled the spotlight back into the window, Red saw something else floating downstream. Just a quick glimpse—but this particular item was so large it convinced Red, absolutely and without question, to stay on high ground. Billy Don was too busy glaring at Red to have seen it.

"Shine it downstream, Billy Don!"

"What?"

"Right there!"

Billy Don swung the spotlight to his right, and then he saw it, too. The object looked so odd and out of place, getting pushed along by millions of gallons of rushing water, that neither man spoke for a moment.

"Jesus, ain't that a Ford Explorer?" Billy Don finally said with awe.

"Yep," Red replied. "Eddie Bauer edition, if I ain't mistaken."

"We ran the plate," Senior Deputy Bill Tatum said the next morning. "Owner's name is Vance Scofield." Behind him, a group of deputies and rescue volunteers were donning rain gear, preparing for a search. Several had brought four-wheelers, and a couple of volunteers were on horseback. Across the river, a similar crowd had gathered, awaiting instructions via handheld radio. The TV news crews hadn't shown up yet, but it was only a matter of time.

"That's Phil Colby's neighbor," Marlin replied. Scofield was a local real estate agent who owned a small ranch to the east of Colby's place.

Tatum snapped his fingers. "I thought I knew the name. The Wallhangers Club. The big lawsuit."

Marlin nodded as he studied the black SUV beached on the bank of the Pedernales River, half a mile down from the Mucho Loco subdivision. The Explorer was lying on its side, every window broken, the interior filled with muck and sediment.

It was ten o'clock Monday morning. Twenty minutes earlier—just as Marlin had decided that the rainfall wasn't going to be a problem after all—he had received a phone call from the dispatcher. *Vehicle in the river, John.*

The bulk of the storm had moved on an hour ago, but it was raining lightly, and most of the creeks and river crossings in Blanco County were still impassable. The water was high and moving fast, though beginning to recede. The phone call to the sheriff's department had come in from a landowner who had walked down to the river to see how high it had risen.

Tatum said, "Ernie drove the long way around to Scofield's place, but nobody was home. From what we can gather, he lives by himself. We got hold of his father, but he wasn't any help. Couldn't remember when he'd seen Scofield last. About half senile, I think. No other family members."

"The father lives alone?"

"Yeah. He's got a nurse that checks on him. She couldn't tell us anything, either."

"What about Scofield's friends?"

"We're working on it."

Marlin stepped over to his truck and began removing several items from the backseat of the extended cab. A rain poncho, neon orange surveyor's tape, binoculars, a small camera. Tatum stayed with him, waiting for Marlin to form a plan. As he gathered his equipment, Marlin asked, "What's the latest on Lucas?"

"The state fire marshal is sending a team to overhaul the house tomorrow," Tatum said, referring to the slow, methodical removal of debris during an investigation. "But no sign of Lucas. None of his friends or family have a line on him. Nicole is pulling his phone records."

Nicole Brooks, the new deputy, had joined the department just six weeks ago, coming from the Mason County sheriff's office. She'd replaced Rachel Cowan, who had signed on with the Austin police department. Cowan had been an outstanding deputy, and the sheriff, Bobby Garza, had tried to convince her to stay. But Cowan had an interest in crimes involving computers and the Internet, and that sort of thing was seldom seen in Blanco County. Marlin could understand Rachel's decision; he considered the Austin police force to be one of the finest in the nation. Cowan had called Garza just last week, excited, describing how her unit had nailed a pedophile trolling for teens online. They were all happy for her.

The good news was, Brooks had stepped right in and filled the void seamlessly. She was knowledgeable and friendly, excellent at dealing with the public, worked well with the other deputies. A great addition to the department. But there was one thing about Nicole Brooks that could have been a problem, especially among a sheriff 's staff that was largely male. She was gorgeous. In a double-take kind of way. Thick auburn hair that she wore in a braid while on patrol, curves that her khaki uniform couldn't quite conceal. The sort of looks that made the locals crack jokes about getting speeding tickets on purpose. So far, the other deputies, to their credit, had behaved like gentlemen. Marlin had heard no improper remarks, no locker-room innuendo. It was like ignoring an elephant in the coffee room.

"So we still don't know if he was in there or not?" Marlin asked, referring to Lucas.

"Nope." Tatum lowered his voice. "It's looking like arson, John. Ernie said he smelled gas real strong when he first got there. And some of the guys smelled ammonia."

"You're kidding me. As in *anhydrous?*"

"Yeah." Tatum leaned in closer. "We're thinking he was running a lab."

Marlin shook his head in disgust. *That damn Lucas.* "Well, that's just great." He had more questions, but they'd have to wait. It wasn't his case, anyway.

Marlin closed the truck door and nodded toward the river. "No chance of getting out on that water." He had brought a small flat-bottomed outboard on a trailer, but navigating the river right now was just short of impossible. He'd be swamped in seconds.

"I don't guess so," Tatum said.

"We'll treat it as a rescue," Marlin said quietly, "but at this point, I think we're looking at recovery."

Tatum nodded.

It was obvious to both men: Given the conditions, they'd likely be searching for a body rather than a survivor. But they could be wrong. Scofield could be stumbling along the banks, disoriented, or in the middle of the river, clinging to a tree.

Marlin lifted his handheld unit. "Ernie?"

"I'm here."

Turpin was now on the other side of the river after visiting Scofield's home.

"Here's how we'll tackle this thing. I want your group to split into two smaller groups. One searches upstream, one downstream. The nearest crossing is the low-water bridge into Mucho Loco, and that's the same road to Scofield's ranch. For the time being, we'll assume that's where the SUV went in. So your upstream searchers don't need to look any further than that. Tell everyone to work in pairs—no solo efforts. Tell 'em to find a buddy and stick with him. If anyone sees something in the water, tell 'em not to grab it unless they can reach it from the bank. I want everyone clear on that. Nobody is to enter the water. Just mark the spot. Are you with me?"

"Ten-four."

Marlin continued. "We've got a DPS chopper coming, but it'll be an hour or so. We don't know how many people were in the vehicle, and we don't know when it happened. Any questions?"

"No, we're all set, John."

"Let's get after it."

Marlin and Tatum approached the crowd on their side of the river. Marlin recognized most of the faces—chiefly lifelong county residents, but a handful of newcomers as well, each of them waiting eagerly for instructions. The crowd quieted down as Marlin and Tatum neared.

Marlin spoke loudly. "Okay, folks, here's what we're gonna do."

"I suppose y'all have heard about Scofield," Chuck Hamm said.

It was seven in the evening. He was seated behind the desk in his den, a generous glass of Crown Royal in front of him. Filling the room—some seated, some standing—were the other seven board members of the Wallhangers Club. All of the men were Blanco County residents, and they had gathered because Hamm, the club's president, had called an emergency meeting.

"Damn shame," Tyler Hobbs said.

Lance Longley said, "A deputy called me this afternoon, wondering if I knew where he was."

"Me, too," someone added.

As it turned out, all of the men had been called.

Longley had a sarcastic grin on his face. "I imagine it's tearing you up inside, huh, Chuck?"

Some of the men laughed softly.

Hamm smirked and said, "Yeah, Lance, it's breaking my heart."

More quiet chuckles.

"Okay," Hamm said, "we'll say a prayer for Vance and all that crap, but that's not why we're here. Herzog came to see me yesterday, and it looks like we've got a little problem." As he began his tale, he studied the faces of the men around him. Like most of them, Chuck Hamm had come by his Hill Country ranch the old-fashioned way: He had inherited it. His great-grandfather had purchased the ranch at the turn of the twentieth century, and now Chuck Hamm was the fourth generation to steward the rolling land in eastern Blanco County.

Much as it had been a hundred years ago, the two-thousand-acre Hamm Ranch was still dotted with thick copses of oak and elm, prickly pear, sycamore, and cottonwood. The clear water of Yeager Creek still ran as cold and pristine as the day Chuck's daddy was baptized in it as a boy.

But one thing had changed dramatically.

Whereas the three Hamm men before him had managed a comfortable lifestyle by raising cattle, Chuck Hamm had found that that particular well had run dry in the past decade. With the price of beef nowadays, the profits were simply no longer there. No matter how many backbreaking hours he put in each day, it was a losing battle. So, in the early nineties, Hamm came to a conclusion many of his ranching brethren had already reached.

He could make a hell of a lot more money off white-tailed deer than cattle.

Deer hunting was a two-billion-dollar-a-year industry in Texas. Hunters bought rifles and ammo, camouflage clothing, blinds and feeders, boots and knives. They built hunting cabins and financed shiny new trucks to get there. And—the most important thing, the part that interested Hamm—the hunters were willing to plunk down thousands of dollars in hard-earned cash for a shot at a trophy deer.

Hamm, despite his rural upbringing, hadn't done much deer hunting. Never had the time for such things. But he had plenty of friends who hunted, and they were quick to fill him in on the basics. One of the first things they told him was, there are two types of deer hunting in Texas: behind a "low" fence made of regular barbwire, or behind a "high" fence, meaning a game-proof eight-footer.

Now, the low-fenced properties, they said, those are for your average Joe, a guy looking for some affordable hunting. Place like that might have some big deer on it, and then again it might not. You take your chances. The place might've been overhunted in years past, or it might be that the neighbors blast away at every buck they ever see, leaving you with slim pickings. There's just no way to know for sure.

Then you got your high-fenced places, they told him. And *that's* where you're more likely to find yourself a trophy deer. With a high fence, Hamm learned, a rancher can carefully control the deer herd; he can practice "game management," which was a big buzzword in the hunting world. The term implied a lot of things, but chiefly it meant the landowner could contain "his" deer within the fence while keeping other deer out. That way, the rancher could cull the bucks with lesser antlers and let the larger trophy bucks do all the breeding. As the years progressed behind a high fence, if you worked things right, you just naturally wound up with bigger, better deer. His friends assured him: When a high-fenced buck reaches maturity—with a big ol' rack of antlers sprouting from its head—there were hot-blooded hunters all across the state who couldn't wait to get a crack at it. For an enormous price.

Long story short, boy, were those guys right. After hearing all the facts, Hamm decided that high fencing was the way to go. First, though, he had to grin and bear the high price. At two dollars per linear foot, and nearly four miles of exterior fence line around Hamm's ranch, it was a hell of an expense. But it was an investment that eventually paid off handsomely. Whereas a low-fenced ranch in the area might bring a thousand dollars per hunter for an entire season, Hamm's high fence allowed him to command anywhere from two to five grand (and sometimes more, depending on the size of the deer taken) from a hunter who might be on the property for *a single weekend.*

In the end, no matter how you looked at it, it was deer hunting, not ranching, that had made Hamm a reasonably wealthy man. Sure, Hamm still ran cattle, but whitetails were the cash crop.

For obvious reasons, then, Chuck Hamm was an enthusiastic proponent of high fences, as were the board members of the Wallhangers Club, a hunting organization formed by Hamm ten years earlier. Each and every board member was in a position similar to Hamm's, meaning they all made a small fortune off deer hunting. Each of them had a stake in the future of property rights in Texas, and those rights included putting up a fence however high the landowner damn well wanted.

Now, as Hamm described his meeting with Herzog, the room was beginning to buzz. These men were sharp; they knew something bad was coming. Hamm simply laid it all out for them—Herzog's entire sordid tale, ending with the photographs.

Jaws dropped. Faces contorted in disbelief. Heads shook in amazement. Groans were heard all around.

Hamm set his glass of Crown Royal down and raised his hands for absolute silence. When everyone had grown quiet and Hamm was certain the news would be received with the gravity it deserved, he spoke again. "What the blackmailing sumbitch wants," he said through clenched teeth, "is a goddamn law against high fences."

4

FOR A MOMENT, nobody spoke. They were all too shocked. Then Lance Longley muttered, "You gotta be kidding," voicing the thought on each man's mind.

Other comments simultaneously filled the air.

"The guy's lost his mind."

"Not that horseshit again."

"I'm not believin' this."

Hamm let the babble run for a minute; then he raised his hand again. "Now, understandably, our boy in Austin is a little upset by this nasty bidness. And I can't blame him for that. But the question is, should we help him out?"

Seventy-year-old Dexter Ashby, seated in front of Hamm's desk, said, "What, there's an option?"

"The way I see it, yeah, there is."

He took a long pull of Crown Royal as everyone waited.

Then he said, "I know this sounds a little cruel, maybe a little risky . . . but we could always just let him deal with it." Hamm paused as everyone pondered that possibility. He knew there would be discussion and debate, and when it was over, he could steer them in the direction he really wanted them to go. He knew he shouldn't start out with a plan as abrupt as the one he was going to suggest.

"Let the photos come out?" someone asked.

"I don't see why not. These types of things seem to be losing their shock value. It'll be big news for a day or two, then it'll pass. Chrissakes, even that blow-job queen in the White House is ancient history. And Herzog, hell, he's nothing but a state senator. Low profile. Trust me, he could get through it no problem."

"But hold on a sec," Tyler Hobbs, one of the younger men, said. "What exactly is in these photos? You said Herzog's been fooling around on his wife, but don't you think we need to know exactly what we're talking about here?"

Heads nodded in agreement.

Barry Yates, another old-timer, said, "Yeah, Chuck, I don't know about this. We've sunk a lot of money into that boy over the years. He's on the right committee and all. Hate to see it go to waste."

"I understand that perfectly, Barry. I'm just saying it's one way we could go."

Lance Longley said, "Didn't Herzog try to reason with this scumbag? I mean, shit, he might as well try and make it illegal to wear cowboy boots. Ain't no way something like that'll ever pass. We've been through all of this before."

"Herzog said he told him that."

"But what about the photos?" Hobbs asked again. "Do we know what they show?"

All the men looked to Hamm for an answer.

Hamm knew this was a delicate topic. "Well, no, not exactly."

"What's that mean?"

"Far as I can tell, there's some nudie shots of Herzog and the woman. But, hey, at least it *is* a woman. Beyond that, he wouldn't tell me."

"Oh, man," Longley said, shaking his head, "this could be brutal. For all we know, the guy's into S and M or something weird like that."

Barry Yates leaned toward Dexter Ashby. "S and what?"

Ashby shrugged.

No one spoke for several moments as they all pondered the predicament.

Then Longley said, "You think this has something to do with Scofield? You gotta admit, it's pretty weird. Herzog gets this phone call, and then one of our former members—"

"Christ, Lance, don't let your imagination run away with you," Hamm said. "It was just an accident. Vance got stupid and tried to cross. So let's get back to the original issue. What are we gonna do about the photos?"

The room got noisy as some of the men began to argue, offering differing opinions on the right course of action. Hamm decided the time was right, so he said, "There is something else we could try."

Again, the men all went silent.

"Well . . . what?" Longley asked.

"It's simple, really," Hamm said. "We find out who the blackmailer is."

Now the room was still. Nobody wanted to voice the next question, the obvious one. Hobbs finally spoke up. "Okay, so maybe we get lucky and track him down. Then what?"

Everyone looked at Hamm.

"Then," he offered, "we firmly point out that he's playing dirty pool." Hamm gave a broad grin. "We convince him to be a nicer man."

"We?" Longley asked, a trace of concern on his face.

"Well, to get technical, no, not us. But I happen to know a guy who can handle this kind of thing just fine."

Longley said, "Someone you can trust? I mean, we don't want this thing getting out of hand."

"I agree," Hamm said, nodding. "No, the man I have in mind is perfect. He has a delicate touch."

* * *

Buford Rhodes hoped they wouldn't have to turn the surgeon's hand into a mangled stump, but you never could tell. Buford's partner, Little Joe Taggart, was right there egging him on, but Buford knew he had to play it cool. Disfigure the guy, and then what? Guy can't earn. Can't pay back the money he owes. And then Buford's client Emo—Fort Worth's top bookie—would be pissed as hell. Yeah, there's a certain satisfaction in enforcing the rules—especially when the client turns out to be a prick, like this guy—but you can't lose your head in these situations. End up with a reputation as a hothead and then you're screwed. Clients like Emo no longer want your services. Even the bail bondsmen Buford worked for on occasion wouldn't want a guy who brings the skips back on a stretcher every time.

They were in the surgeon's kitchen. Guy named Winsted. Buford didn't know if it was the man's first name or last, but he didn't care. The critical fact was this: Winsted owed Emo seventeen five, and it was way overdue. According to Emo—telling Buford things he didn't need to know—Winsted had had a nasty run of luck, but it was an over-under on a Cowboys/Eagles game that did him in. Dumb old Winsted had gone with the over, meaning the combined score had to total more than forty-seven. A late field goal by the 'Boys brought the total to forty-five, but that was all she wrote. Game over.

"I know what this is about," Winsted had said earlier, grinning, when they were still in the living room. Mr. Nice Guy at first. Invited them right in, like they were there to fix his toilet or something. He even made a pleasant comment about Buford's suit, the light blue one with the silver studs. Then: "You're here about the money, right?" Winsted said, all smiles. House like this—small mansion, really—the man could afford to be in a good mood.

"Yeah, we work for Emo," Buford replied. Big smile right back at him. Not playing the hard-ass just yet.

"Damn straight," Little Joe said, already swaggering, his eyes all jumpy. Buford gave him a quick glare. *Settle down.*

"Yeah," Winsted said, "good ol' Emo. I wanted to talk to him about the situation. I was gonna call."

Buford tipped his Stetson back, then made a gesture, spreading his hands, like *Hey, what's there to talk about?* "It's pretty simple, really. You owe him some money. We're here to collect it."

"Hell yeah," Joe said.

Winsted frowned. Buford didn't like that. Then Winsted said, "See, about that last bet. I'm not so sure I really owe anything for that one."

Buford raised his eyebrows. *Explain, please.*

"I was drunk when I placed that bet! That's what I told Emo, but damn, he wouldn't listen. He knows I drink too much sometimes. We talked about it." Winsted was raising his voice now. Not a good thing to do. Buford figured, the way the surgeon was slurring, he was pretty smashed right now, too. And to think this boozer actually operated on people. Kind of shook your faith in the American health care system, such as it was.

"Your drinking habits are not our problem," Buford said.

"Hell no, they ain't," Joe added. "Want me to pop him one?"

Buford shook his head.

"Maybe we can work something out," Winsted said, keeping an eye now on Joe. But he was starting to get a tone, like this was all a big inconvenience. "Damn, I need a drink," he said, and proceeded into the kitchen. Never even offered his guests anything, which was downright rude. Buford and Little Joe followed right behind him.

In the kitchen—a room as large as Buford's apartment—Winsted poured himself a glass of scotch. His eyes were still watery from the first gulp when he said, "Here's the deal. You run on back and tell Emo I'm willing to pay half. I think that's fair."

"Run on back?" Buford said, not liking Winsted's choice of words. Man had no negotiating skills at all.

"Yeah."

Joe looked at Buford, a pleading look in his eye. "I could break his finger."

Buford shook his head. "You'll pay half? That's your proposal?"

The surgeon nodded, his eyes still on Joe, but talking to Buford. "Better than nothing, right? Emo should be damn happy with it."

Buford was thinking, *Don't these shit-heels know they shouldn't bet if they can't afford to lose?* Now it was clearly time to put a scare into the guy, make it plain that his offer was completely unacceptable.

Buford liked kitchens because there were all kinds of handy devices in there. Interesting implements you could use to put pressure on a guy. Knives and forks, of course. Blender. Stove. Hell, even a cheese grater could do the trick if you used it right.

Buford chose the disposal.

In one swift move, he grabbed Winsted's left arm and twisted it behind the man's back. Then he took Winsted's right hand and plunged it deep into the drain hole in the sink. Winsted had slender fingers and a narrow wrist. It was an easy fit. Little Joe was whooping and hollering. Winsted's glass of scotch was on the floor now, ice skittering across the expensive tile.

"Christ! What the fuck're you doing!" Winsted cried, groaning, straining to get away. But it was no use.

Buford nodded to a wall switch on the right side of the sink, and Joe eagerly covered it with his hand. "I'm gonna tell you how this is gonna go," Buford said, "and I want to be absolutely clear on it just so there's no confusion. So here's the deal. I'm gonna ask you again, and you're immediately gonna answer me. No lies, no bullshit, and no reason for me to turn your hand into hamburger. 'Cause believe me, I'm prepared to do that. In fact, it really don't make much difference to me either way. The only thing on the plus side is, I get paid more if you give me what I want. You follow me?"

Winsted grunted in pain.

"Good, then," Buford said. "We have an understanding. But I should tell you—I'm not gonna ask twice. You get one chance, and one chance only. We clear?"

"Yeah, we're clear."

"That's what I wanted to hear, Winsted. You're doing real good so far. Okay, now, the big question. Where is our money?"

"I . . . I don't have it!"

Buford knew bullshit when he heard it. Guy like this had to have access to cash somehow. Maybe not right here in the house, but somewhere. Bank account, safe-deposit box, something like that. "Don't lie to me, Winsted."

Winsted was stupid enough to say, "Fuck you."

The man had balls, that's for sure. "Pardon me?"

"You dress like a Nashville retard."

Little Joe snorted and said, "Oh, mister, you done it now."

Buford didn't even have to think about it. He nodded to Joe again, and his partner immediately flipped the switch.

The light above the sink came on.

"Assholes," Winsted giggled through the pain. "Disposal's broken, anyway. Coupla fucking goons."

"That's quite an impressive vocabulary," Buford replied.

"Daniel friggin' Webster," Little Joe added.

Buford didn't have the heart to point out that Joe meant Noah, not Daniel.

He noticed another switch on the left backsplash, farther from the sink than the first one. He'd seen that before—some builder putting the switch more than an arm's length away to prevent your average pinhead from accidentally maiming himself. "Try that one," he said to Joe, nodding, ready to watch Winsted suffer, not caring about the money so much now.

Winsted's body immediately tensed up.

"No, don't!" the surgeon said. "I'll pay. Just turn me loose."

"All of it?"

Little Joe had his hand on the switch, all bright-eyed and ready to go.

"Yeah, I promise, all of it."

"Where?"

"In a shoebox. Upstairs."

"Okay, now we're getting somewhere."

"Let me go."

"One last thing. Do you like my suit or not?"

"Jesus, what?"

"I mean, first you said you liked it, and then you call me a retard. Which is it?" Buford gave Winsted's left arm an extra twist, the bone no doubt just millimeters from breaking.

Winsted wailed in agony. "Goddamn, I like it! I like it!"

"You think it's snazzy?"

"Yeah, snazzy as hell."

Buford eased Winsted's hand out of the drain hole and patted him on the back. "That wasn't so hard, was it? A wise man makes wise choices, Winsted, and I think you just made a good one. Trust me."

As Winsted led the way to the staircase, Buford's cell phone chirped. A familiar number on the caller ID.

"Uncle Chuck," Buford said. "How's it going?"

Driving home in the dark, eleven o'clock, John Marlin tried to remember Vance Scofield's face. He had only met Scofield one time, in passing, at the hardware store, and that was before Phil Colby had filed a lawsuit against him.

Phil Colby was Marlin's closest friend, and had been since grade school; both of them were Blanco County natives. Colby owned four thousand acres in the center of the county, a small spread compared to the original thirty thousand acres of prime ranchland purchased by Samuel Colby six generations ago.

Pieces of the ranch had been snipped off and sold over the years, a huge chunk auctioned during the Depression, and Phil Colby had actually lost the remainder for several years due to a problem with property taxes in the late nineties. He'd been struggling financially, beef prices in the basement, but now he was back on his feet. What he'd done was, he'd finally opened the gates to deer hunters willing to pay a fair price. That income boosted Colby's bottom line considerably and kept the ranch solvent. He wasn't wealthy—far from it—but he was able to live without the fear of losing the land on which he was so deeply rooted.

Then came the question of high fencing.

Colby knew he could charge the hunters higher fees to hunt

behind a deer-proof fence—but Colby didn't believe in high fences, feeling that they gave the hunter an unfair advantage on all but the most immense ranches. He went so far as to remove the high fence that had been erected when his ranch was temporarily out of his hands. It wasn't just a personal decision; it was Colby's opinion that ranchers with high fences were violating the law, restricting the movement of animals owned—according to the Parks and Wildlife Code—by "the people of the state of Texas."

He felt strongly enough about the issue that when Scofield announced plans for a high fence the previous fall, Colby decided to take his neighbor to court. Marlin had warned Colby that he was fighting a losing battle, that his lawsuit would be tossed out.

"Screw 'em," Colby said. "It'll make a statement."

"And what would that statement be?" Marlin asked.

"High fences suck," Colby replied, grinning wide.

That was Colby—just as ornery as hell and willing to take a stand.

It turned out Marlin was right. Colby hired an attorney, the attorney filed the suit, and it was dismissed the first day in court. Vance Scofield's lawyer had pointed out that current law allowed a property owner to erect a fence of any reasonable height. The judge saw no reason to disagree. It was all a fairly civil proceeding, until afterward, when Colby and Scofield exchanged some words and nearly got into a fistfight in the corridor.

In the end, Colby felt that he had achieved his goal—to draw attention to the topic. In the eyes of the press, Colby was the common man against the wealthy, David versus Goliath. He practically had folk-hero status in some of the blue-collar hunting camps around the state.

Now, just a few months after the whole spectacle, Vance Scofield was missing. So, as Marlin maneuvered up his long caliche driveway, he wasn't surprised to see a familiar blue truck parked in front of the house. Phil Colby was sitting in a rocking chair on the porch, drinking a beer, Marlin's dog, Geist, sleeping at his feet.

As Marlin mounted the steps, Colby called in falsetto, "How was your day, dear?"

Marlin plopped into a chair next to the swing. He hadn't been this tired since the end of deer season. "Oh, your average nightmare."

"Just got back into town," Colby said. "I heard about Scofield."

"Yeah, where the hell were you? We could've used you out there." Colby was a member of the Blanco County Search and Rescue Team. Marlin couldn't imagine that Colby's feelings about Scofield would have kept him away from the river.

"Went to the cattle auction in Fredericksburg," Colby said. He tilted his beer bottle. "You look like you could use a cold one."

"That'd be nice."

Colby shook his empty bottle. "Well, grab me another one while you're at it."

Marlin glared at him. Colby had a key to the house, and he was known to make himself right at home. That suited Marlin just fine, although he occasionally gave Phil some grief for leaving the beer supply low.

"All right, then, allow me," Colby said, rising. He returned with two fresh bottles and said, "So give me the details."

Marlin summarized the day's events, concluding with the fact that there had been no sign whatsoever of Scofield. There had been no calls reporting any other missing persons, so Marlin was reasonably certain Scofield had been alone in the Ford Explorer.

"You pretty sure he was in the vehicle?" Colby asked.

"Man, I don't know. If he managed to get out, you'd think he would've called us by now. Somebody would know where he is."

"You talk to any relatives?" Colby asked.

"Deputies reached his father, but he wasn't any help. Ex-wife in Austin, same thing."

"What about his hunting buddies? That club they're all in."

"None of them had a clue."

"So what's the plan?"

"Get back out there in the morning and start over. The water'll be lower and I can use the boat."

"How about a cadaver dog?"

"Too early for that. Maybe the third or fourth day."

"Guess he could be hung up underwater. Caught on a tree stump or something."

Marlin nodded.

"Or way downstream," Colby added. "Didn't one ol' boy make it all the way to Lake Travis once?"

"Yeah, a family in a boat found him four days later."

That victim's body had traveled more than thirty miles on the Pedernales River, over dams and low-water crossings, to the large lake just northwest of Austin.

Marlin studied the moon, just past full, hanging low in the sky like a tomato on the vine. The storm system was long gone, and no more rain was expected anytime soon.

"What time're you gonna get back out there?" Colby asked.

"First light."

"Can you swing by and pick me up?"

"Yeah, that'd be great." Marlin knew from experience, there were usually fewer volunteers on the second day. It stood to reason. The sense of urgency was no longer there. No emergency services would be needed; the body would be found when it wanted to be found.

Marlin took a swig of beer, and both men sat without talking for quite some time, listening to the chatter of crickets and the scrape of limbs against the rain gutters.

"You haven't told me much about Dallas," Colby said.

Marlin made a gesture with his hands. *Not much to tell.*

"How was it?" Colby persisted.

"You ever been to a wedding before?"

"Well . . . yeah. Plenty."

"It was just like all of those."

The only difference, Marlin thought to himself, was that he should've been up there instead of the groom—some guy named Scott, who worked in the world of advertising of all things. Wrote copy or slogans or whatever you call it. Marlin had formed a mental image right from the start: a slick, schmoozy guy who dressed all in black and said things like "Let's do lunch." Christ.

Colby chuckled to himself. "So you don't want to talk about it."

"Nope."

Three months ago, Marlin had received a call from Becky Cameron, a woman who had spent a year by his side and later blew a hole in his heart by leaving. On the phone, she had told him she was getting married, and she would be honored if he could attend. She would also understand if he chose not to. The news filled him with a wistfulness so intense it dulled his senses for several days afterward. But yeah, he had gone, and Becky had looked so damn beautiful standing at the altar, all he could think during the ceremony was . . . *What if?*

What if I had moved to Dallas to be with her?

"You got a bum deal with Becky, that's all it was," Colby said quietly.

Marlin didn't reply.

"She was a big-city nurse, she needed a big-city hospital. Nothing you could do about that."

Marlin remained silent.

"Lots of good women in Blanco County."

Marlin looked at him. "You think so?"

"Hell, yeah."

"That girl you've been seeing lately—"

"Melinda."

"Where's she from?"

"Austin."

Marlin nodded, making his point.

"Yeah, but it's worth the drive," Colby said. "Every minute of it."

"If things got serious between the two of you, where would you live?"

"I haven't thought that far in advance."

"Think she'd want to move out to the ranch, live more than an hour from the nearest decent mall?"

Marlin could tell from the expression on Colby's face that his friend now had something new to worry about. "How many people live in Blanco County, Phil?"

"I don't know. Little over eight thousand?"

"Right around there. So we've got about four thousand females. How many of them are roughly our age?"

"Maybe ten percent."

"Okay, four hundred. How many of them are single?"

"Not that many."

"Probably ten percent again, right?"

"Yeah, probably."

"Forty women."

"You've really thought this through, haven't you?"

"Why not? I didn't have much else to do while I was sitting in the church."

Phil drained the last of his beer. "Forty women. You're right, that ain't many to choose from. Some of them are probably pretty ugly, and I bet the rest wouldn't find a redneck like you all that appealing."

After Phil left, Marlin stepped inside, Geist at his heels, and began to strip off his filthy uniform. He sat in the kitchen in his underwear and ate some cold fried chicken, barely able to keep his eyes open. He put some food out for the dog, then checked his answering machine. There were two messages.

Hey, John, it's Max Thayer returning your call. The message you left on my voicemail—I think it's a great idea, and I'll support you however I can. Give me a call back.

A beep, then:

Uh, yeah, this is David Pritchard calling. I don't know if you remember me, but I'm Vance Scofield's attorney. Anyway, I understand you're leading the search, and there's something I think you need to know. I'll give you all the details when we talk, but here's the short version. I'm the president of the Rotary Club in Blanco, and we're raffling off a new Corvette. Each ticket is a hundred dollars and . . . well, I guess you don't need to know all that. Anyway, Vance is the treasurer, and he had the Corvette stored in a metal barn on his property. So I went over to his place just to check on things. Here's the problem. The Corvette is gone . . . and, uh . . . Vance was the only one who had the keys.

5

JUST BEFORE EIGHT o'clock on Tuesday morning, a seventy-year-old man named J. D. Evans was clerking at the Exxon outside Minneola, Florida, when a couple of youngsters came into the store. Both were about twenty, maybe twenty-one, the boy tall and skinny and pale, the girl looking like a pin-up with long blonde hair.

"Morning," J. D. said, holding his fifth cup of coffee, just one more hour to go on his all-night shift.

The boy nodded and headed down the candy aisle toward the cooler in back. The girl skedaddled right to the bathroom, like most of the women do, but not before J. D. got an eyeful. She was a sight, all right. A real looker. Enough to make J. D. remember one or two just like her, back when he'd sown a few wild oats of his own.

J. D. went back to the newspaper on the counter.

"You got any Snapple?" The boy was calling out from the back of the store.

"Any what?" J. D. hollered back, squinting.

"Snapple." The kid shrugged, maybe a little embarrassed. "It's what she drinks," he explained.

J. D. said, "If we do, you're in the right spot."

The boy looked again. "Don't see any."

"Guess we're all out."

That seemed to satisfy the kid. He turned back to the cooler, and J. D. went back to his sports page, keeping tabs on the Braves.

He heard the bathroom door swing open, and a minute or two later both of the youngsters were at the counter. Now the girl was front and center, busting out of a low-cut top, her shorts riding low enough to give J. D. a heart murmur if he wasn't careful. He tried not to stare.

The boy plopped a liter of Mountain Dew and a bag of Cheetos on the counter, followed by a package of hair coloring and a twelve-pack of Miller High Life.

"Y'all doing all right this morning?" J. D. asked, giving himself an excuse to run his eyes over the young lady.

She smiled back at him, the kind of face that draws men like birds to fresh-mowed grass. "Real good. And you?"

"Can't complain."

The boy was grinning at him, too, kind of an I-know-what-you're-up-to expression on his face. J. D. winked at him and rang up the first two items. "Awful early for a cold one, ain't it?"

"Doctor's orders," the boy said. "He told me to get lots of fluids."

J. D. gave a polite chuckle.

"You got some ID? All you young'uns look like babies to me."

The boy slipped a wallet from his hip pocket and produced a driver's license.

J. D. eyeballed it, working the numbers in his head. "Now, my 'rithmetic is a little rusty," he said, "but I believe this here says you're twenty. Drinking age is twenty-one."

The boy, cool as you please, reached into his wallet and

dropped a sawbuck on the counter. J. D. shook his head. The boy dropped another. J. D. scooped them up and tucked them into his pocket, then added the beer to the total on the register. "What brings y'all over from Texas?" he asked, bagging everything up.

"Selling Bibles," the kid said, pulling hard on J. D.'s leg, all three of them knowing it. "The holy word of Jesus."

Now they were all smiling. These kids spreading the gospel was about as likely as J. D. cleaning the toilet twice per shift. "What, like missionaries?" J. D. asked, playing along.

"Yeah," the girl said. "You interested in that kind of work? We could use some help."

Damn, the girl's voice was like honey on a biscuit. Flirting with him, too, all part of the joke.

"I'll have to pass," J. D. said. "Can't you see I'm making a solid fortune right here?"

The boy grabbed the bag and said, "Well, if you decide you *are* interested in a missionary position, just talk to ol' Stephanie here. She knows all about that stuff."

The girl giggled and swatted the boy on the arm. *"Lucas!"*

Then out the door they went, and J. D. watched through the glass as the girl sashayed her fine little butt out to the Corvette parked at the curb.

In Red O'Brien's way of thinking, hiring illegal aliens was about like poaching deer. That is, he didn't want anybody else to do it, no sir, but he didn't see the harm if he did it now and again himself. If a large job came Red's way—say, clearing a thousand acres of brush or building a rock wall or putting up a deer-proof fence—Red was more than happy to round up a crew of wetbacks and get after it. Those boys worked hard and cheap, any day of the week, and you didn't have to hassle with insurance, Social Security, FICA (whatever the hell that was), or any of that other shit.

Then there were the other times, the lean times, when Red wasn't the boss but was working for somebody else. Instead of hiring the crew, he was *on* the crew. All at once, Red would be in direct competition with the illegal immigrants, and his attitude would change considerably. Red would suddenly realize that the same men he'd hired just last month were now taking jobs away from regular old white boys like himself.

"Them border-crossing beaners are causing the downfall of American society!" Red had proclaimed to Billy Don one day, pointing toward two illegal aliens laying bricks.

"Who, Manuel and Tony?" Billy Don replied. "Naw, they wouldn't do that. They're nice guys."

That certainly didn't make Red feel any better. When he saw work slipping through his hands because of the illegals, it made him wonder—Lord have mercy on him—what good it was to be a native-born American anymore.

And that's exactly how Red felt when he pulled up to the job site on Vance Scofield's ranch Tuesday morning and noticed a couple of extra Mexicans working the fence line. This was what Red had been afraid of.

"Uh-oh," Billy Don said. "They's three of 'em now."

"You always was quick with numbers," Red replied, throwing his truck into park. He spotted their boss, Jack Chambers, pulling ten-foot T-posts off a trailer. "I'll do all the talking," Red said.

Billy Don groaned. "Then we're screwed for sure."

"You wanna keep this job or not?" Red snapped.

"Jeez, Red, I was just kidding."

"Then let me handle it."

Both men got out and walked over to the trailer, where Jack was wiping sweat off his forehead, smiling as they approached. "I was wondering if I was gonna see y'all again," he said. "Where were you boys yesterday?"

Red played it innocent. "Flooded in at home. You mean you was working?"

"Me and Jorge got out here right after lunch. Put in a good six hours, just the two of us. I left a message for you."

"Yeah, sorry 'bout that. We was outside cutting up a pig," Red said. It wasn't a lie, either. Yesterday morning, they'd made it back to Red's trailer with the truckload of wild hogs just fine, crossing the river as soon as it got low enough, no sign of the rancher. But since most of their night had been wasted sitting in the truck, waiting for the rain to stop, they'd had to use the afternoon to butcher the hogs before they spoiled. "Besides," Red said, "we kinda figured the job was on hold, what with Mr. Scofield being drownt and everything."

That brought a frown to Jack's face. "Well, yeah, he might be, but he already paid in advance. That means we gotta finish it up."

Red kicked the mud with the toe of his boot. "I see you got some new boys working."

"When you didn't call me back, even last night, I had to do something. Jorge brought a couple of his cousins along."

Red glanced over at the trio of Mexicans, busy as bees, unloading tools from the bed of Jack's truck, ready for a long, sweaty day. "We sure could use the work, Jack," he said.

Jack removed his cap and scratched the crown of his head. "You'll show up when I need ya?"

"You know we will. It was just that damn rain the other night. A misunderstanding."

Jack appeared to think it over. "Listen," he said, "I promised them two new ones a full day's work. But you come back tomorrow and I'll get you back on the job, okay?"

Red figured that was a reasonable proposition, so he shook Jack's hand and he and Billy Don turned for the truck.

"Hey, Red," Jack called. "I saw Loretta last night."

That stopped Red dead in his tracks. Billy Don, too. They both turned around.

Billy Don said, "My ex-wife?"

Jack shook his head. "No, I said *Loretta.* Red's ex-wife."

"Yeah, she's mine, too," Red said.

Jack was puzzled. "Wait. You saying you was both married to her?"

"It's a long story," Red said. "Where'd you see her?"

"I was married to her first," Billy Don said.

* * *

Lucas knew he should feel different about the whole situation—nervous or scared or that remorseful thing they were always talking about on cop shows—but he didn't. It was damn near impossible. He was tooling along the roads of Florida in a brand-new Corvette, the girl of his dreams by his side, and all he could feel was great. If there was hell to pay later, then that's what he'd do—pay it later. For now, he was going to see how long he could make it last.

"What you got in your suitcase?" Stephanie asked, after she'd drained her third beer. She'd been tossing the empties—hers and his—out the window at cattle-crossing signs, making a game of it. Hit the cow, win a prize.

" 'Bout forty pounds of black-tar heroin."

"Shut up."

"You asked."

"No, seriously."

"Clothes, mostly."

"What else? Anything special?" She said it all singsongy, like she was angling for something. He knew what it was, too.

Ecstasy.

She loved the stuff. Lucas, well, he could take it or leave it. He did, however, enjoy the effect it had on Stephanie. Made her a wildcat, all sexed up and ready to go. And he had half a dozen tablets in his suitcase.

"Steph, you know we oughta hold off on that. Least while we're on the road."

"I don't see any reason why *I* can't do some. *I'm* not driving."

The thing was, she had a point.

He cut a glance at her from the corner of his eye and it made his heart thump. God, what a wonderful face she had. There were times when Lucas felt he could stare at it for hours, just get lost in it and forget all his troubles. He almost expected to hear harps playing when he was around her, like she was an angel straight down from heaven.

She belched and said, "Where the hell are we, anyway?"

"You know how, when you're looking at a map, Florida hangs down into the ocean like a big ol' dick?" he asked.

"You're so gross," she said, giving him that look where she was trying to frown but was about to laugh.

"Well, we're about halfway down it."

She yawned and lit a cigarette, and they bounced along the narrow county road for a few miles. Staring out the passenger-side window, she said, "Lucas, you really think we're doing the right thing?"

"Hell yeah. You know how you love the ocean and everything? Well, Key West'll be a hell of a lot nicer than Port Aransas, I promise you that."

She looked at him with no expression at all. Lucas had dealt with her mood swings before. Just a few days ago, she was thrilled about this spontaneous adventure.

"What's wrong?" he asked.

"Nothing."

"You miss your mama?" he asked.

She scrunched her face up, thinking about it. "Not really."

"What, then?"

"It's just riding in this car. I'm gettin' sick of it. When the hell we gonna get there? You told me two damn days."

"Don't snap at me, Steph. It's only *been* two days."

"And we're not there yet, are we?"

"Yeah, but we've been mostly sticking to the back roads, and it's a lot slower. I didn't account for that."

"Plus, I'm sick of staying in shitty motels."

"You know what? Anytime you wanna get out and walk, just let me know."

She rolled her eyes at him. "Whatever."

He hated when she got all cranky, and he hated it even more when he didn't have the backbone to give it right back to her. This time, he'd stood his ground. With a girl like Stephanie, that's what it took sometimes. Otherwise, she'd bend you around her finger like a piece of baling wire.

A few miles down the road, she caught his eye and stuck her tongue out at him, all playful. He ignored her.

"Oh, Mr. Tough Guy," she said. She swung sideways, her back

against the passenger door, her long, tan legs draped over into his lap. She began to work her foot along his zipper. "Let's see how tough you really are."

Later, after he pulled back onto the road, she said, "What if they come looking for us?"

"Who?"

"The cops. Who else?"

"I told you they won't."

"How do you know for sure?"

"They won't have any reason to look for you. Not too hard, anyway. Me, there's nothing to connect me to him, really."

Lucas was just trying to put Stephanie at ease. They'd look for him, all right. The question was, would they be able to find him? The Corvette, too, would be a problem. He'd known that from the start. That's why he'd decided to sell it—and Miami was probably the best place to do it. Find a chop shop and unload the damn thing. Far enough away from home that the cops wouldn't be watching for it.

6

"IF YOU DON'T mind, Mr. Pritchard, just start from the beginning," Bobby Garza said. Marlin noticed that the sheriff was looking tired this morning. Garza had a sweet little three-year-old boy, but the kid was currently battling the stomach flu. It had probably been a long night at the Garza household. Garza was a good-looking guy with thick black hair, but today he looked nothing short of rumpled.

Pritchard was a pear-shaped middle-aged man with sandy hair and glasses. He had arrived at nine o'clock, as promised, and he was now seated at the small table in the conference room at the sheriff 's office, Garza to his right, John Marlin to his left. Marlin had already given Garza the high points the night before, but they both wanted to hear the full story.

Pritchard took a sip of coffee, then began his tale. "Like I mentioned, I'm president of the Rotary Club in Blanco. Every year, we raffle off a vehicle—usually something high-end, like a Hummer, a BMW, something like that. This year, it's a Corvette. Anyway, it's all for charity. What happens is, every member of our chapter sells tickets, and there's even a prize for the person who sells the most. Just a trophy, though. Nothing extravagant. It's a friendly competition, you know, to show who has the most spirit. That kind of thing. Is this too much detail?"

Garza said, "No, that's fine."

"Okay, see, Vance is the treasurer, and that means he took care of buying the car from the dealership in Austin. They're really good to us as far as a discount and everything. Actually, Vance hadn't bought the car just yet. He had an arrangement where we'd pay the dealer later from the proceeds. That's the way it always works, so we don't have to shell out a big chunk of cash before we sell the tickets. They let us sign some papers and get the car early so we can show it around and get people excited about the whole thing."

Marlin remembered an article about the raffle in the *Blanco County Record* a few weeks ago. "When's the giveaway?" he asked.

"Two weeks from Saturday."

"When did tickets go on sale?"

"About two months ago. They're a hundred dollars apiece. It takes a while to sell tickets that expensive."

Marlin nodded for Pritchard to proceed.

"So the situation is, we've got all these members out there selling tickets, and about once a week or so, most of them meet up with Vance and give him all the money they have on hand. Either they swing by his house or do it at our weekly meeting. Most of them don't want to hold on to a bunch of cash. Makes 'em nervous."

"The ticket sales are all in cash?" Garza asked.

"No, it's mostly checks, but some people pay with cash. Maybe a third."

"Hundred bucks a pop?" Marlin asked.

"Yep."

"How many tickets do you sell?" Garza asked.

"It varies from raffle to raffle, but obviously we like to sell enough to make it worthwhile. We have to cover the cost of the car, and then everything after that goes straight to one of the charities we support. This year, it's the food bank. Minus our expenses, of course. Anyway, for the Corvette, we figured we had to sell somewhere around seven hundred tickets to cover the cost of the car and come away with a decent donation."

Marlin was surprised. "You manage to sell that many tickets right here in Blanco County?"

Pritchard smiled. "No, not just here. We have members from around Dripping Springs, too, and even a few in south Austin. So we sell the tickets all over central Texas. Last year we sold about eight hundred."

Marlin whistled. That was a cool eighty grand.

Garza said, "So what you're saying is, in addition to the Corvette, Vance Scofield had a fairly large sum of cash in his possession."

"That's pretty much it."

"Why doesn't he put it in a bank account?" Marlin asked.

"He told me there was no sense in putting it in the bank for just ten weeks. He said he had a safe."

"Any way of knowing exactly how much cash he had on hand?"

"Vance kept all the records, but I'd guess somewhere between twenty and thirty thousand."

Marlin glanced at the clock on the wall out of nervous habit. He had called Phil Colby the night before and told him about the call from Pritchard. Colby had said he would join the deputies out at the river this morning and help with the search for Scofield. Apparently, there had been no progress yet or Marlin would have heard. At first light this morning, Marlin had driven out to Scofield's place to have a look around for himself.

"Tell us about last night, when you went over there," Marlin said. "You're saying the Corvette was inside that metal pole barn on the east side of Mr. Scofield's house?"

Pritchard nodded. "Exactly. When I heard the news about Vance, well, I just figured I'd better check on the car. Make sure everything was okay. But it was gone, and that had me worried. So I called."

"How long had the car been there?"

"About eight weeks. Like I said, we'd take it out and drive it around on occasion, especially when we were selling tickets at large events. We drove it to the rodeo in Austin last month and sold tickets in the parking lot." Pritchard removed a photograph from his jacket pocket and slid it to the center of the table for both men to see. "You asked me to bring a picture," he said. "This is the only one I had."

Marlin bent closer to study the photo, which showed a young brunette woman leaning against the front fender of a red Corvette. She was dressed in boots and tight jeans, with a halter top and a cowboy hat. It could have been a shot from a cheesy auto-parts calendar. The woman was well endowed up top. "Who's the girl?"

Pritchard had a boys-will-be-boys grin on his face. "Her name's Jenny. See, a car like that draws people like flies—but especially when you have a good-looking girl selling the tickets. Like at an auto show. Hot car, hot babe." He shrugged. "Sex sells. What can I say? I think she does a little modeling."

"Friend of yours?" Garza asked.

"No, Vance rounded her up somewhere. He and I drove the car to the rodeo in March, and she met us there. I think she works part-time for some kind of company that specializes in that sort of thing. If you can believe it, there's actually a pretty big market for ticket sellers like her. If you've ever been to a hunting show or a wild-game dinner, any kind of event where they have an auction or raffle, you'll see a bunch of girls just like her. When a beautiful girl walks up to a guy, suddenly he's willing to spend a little more cash."

"Can we keep this?" Garza asked, tapping the photograph.

"Yeah, sure."

"Do you know Jenny's last name?" Marlin asked.

"I think it was something like Gilmer or Geller. You need to talk to her?"

"We might," Garza said. "At this point, we need to talk to anybody who might have seen Mr. Scofield recently. This Jenny—did she and Scofield know each other pretty well?"

"I think they went out a few times. Vance dated a lot of girls. I say 'girls' because most of them were a lot younger than he was."

"Anyone he saw regularly?"

Pritchard smiled. "Vance never really limited himself to one woman. He was, pardon my language, but what a lot of guys would call a 'pussy hound.' Didn't matter if they were young, old, beautiful, or not pretty at all. If there was a woman he thought he could score with, well, Vance would be all over her. Especially if he'd had a few drinks."

Garza stood to refill his coffee cup. "So you said Scofield was the only one with keys to the Vette?"

"That's right."

"And you can't think of anyplace else where the car might be? Maybe he parked it in another location."

"No, that's the only place we kept it. It wouldn't be anywhere else without me knowing."

"Are you thinking it might've been stolen?" Garza asked.

Pritchard looked down at the table. "Uh, well . . . no. I don't know."

Garza sat down and leaned back in his chair. "Mr. Pritchard, I get the feeling there's something you want to tell us about Vance Scofield. Something you're reluctant to say."

Pritchard hesitated and spread his hands. "There is, but it's all just conjecture on my part. I want to make that clear."

"And?"

"Vance's a friend of mine, and I feel bad saying this, but I think he might've been using drugs."

Senator Dylan Herzog had just returned from his weekly manicure, and now he was looking down on the parking lot two stories below. He couldn't stop himself from glancing out there on occasion, watching as people parked their cars and made their way inside. Of course, most of the visitors weren't coming to see him—there were several other professionals who officed in the small building in central Austin—but one person *was* coming to see him, and that person was to arrive at nine-thirty, according to Chuck Hamm. A man named Buford Rhodes. This guy Rhodes, Hamm said, would be able to fix this horrible mess.

Herzog noticed a shiny new Suburban pulling up outside. A man stepped out wearing an expensive suit, carrying a briefcase. The man certainly didn't appear to be the type who could "kick ass and take names," to use Hamm's crass expression. Couldn't possibly be Rhodes.

Herzog's chin lowered to his chest, and his eyes began to droop. He'd hardly slept at all the previous two nights, the worry keeping him up till all hours. Even his wife was concerned about him. If only she knew.

Another vehicle pulled into the lot, parking in the handicapped spot just below Herzog's window. A vintage Cadillac convertible, canary yellow, with the top down and two men inside. The driver was wearing a Stetson. He stepped out, lean and tall, with a braid of long hair hanging down his back. His suit was a god-awful baby blue, covered with silver studs, like something straight from the Grand Ol' Opry. Porter Waggoner stuff. The passenger was shorter, dressed in dirty jeans, sneakers, and what appeared to be a bowling shirt.

The driver dropped a cigar stub on the pavement and ground it out with his heel.

Please, Lord, Herzog thought, *don't let these be the guys. Don't let my future depend on these two clowns.*

Two minutes later, Susan buzzed.

"What makes you say that?" Bobby Garza asked.

David Pritchard pondered the question. "Just, I don't know . . . there were times when he seemed like he was gonna bounce off the walls. Just all this energy, like he couldn't sit still." Pritchard paused for a moment. "See, back in the eighties, my sister used a lot of speed—about one step away from being addicted, I think. I recognize the signs."

"Anything else?"

"Well, I know he partied hard. We were on the same softball team, and we'd always have a few beers after the game. But Vance, well, he was always drinking way too much. Sometimes on the weekends, if I called too early—and I'm talking ten A.M.—you could just hear it in his voice. Sounded like hell. Still half wasted from the night before. He'd tell me stories about clubbing in Austin. Acted like a college kid. *Sounded* like a college kid."

"But you never saw him use drugs."

"No."

"Never saw any drugs in his house."

"No."

"You and him are good friends?"

"Well, friends, anyway. We're not real close. But I know him fairly well."

Garza took a deep breath. "Mr. Pritchard, let me make sure we're clear on what you're saying. Scofield leads kind of a wild life, he chases a lot of women, maybe uses speed. So you're wondering if Scofield might've taken off in the car, maybe he's off partying somewhere?"

Pritchard frowned. "I hate to say it, but yeah, that's the first thing I thought of—Vance doing something wild like that. But I guess you're also thinking in terms of robbery. Either way, I sure would like to know if the money from the raffle is still in his house. I don't mean to be cold about Vance's situation, whatever trouble he might've gotten into, but all that cash . . ."

"We're gonna check on it," Garza said, but Marlin knew they were both thinking the same thing. *If there was a robbery that turned into a murder, where is Scofield's body?*

Garza looked at Marlin, seeing if he had any more questions. Marlin shook his head.

"One other thing I think I should share," Pritchard said. "I've gotta be kind of vague about this because of attorney-client privilege, so forgive me—but Vance had . . . well . . . he wasn't very responsible when it came to his finances."

"Money problems?"

Pritchard nodded slightly.

"How bad?"

"Bad enough."

"To the point of filing bankruptcy, something like that?"

Pritchard hesitated. "I really don't feel comfortable going into that much detail."

"All right, then, Mr. Pritchard. Anything else?"

"That's about it."

"Thanks for coming in. You've been a big help."

"I'd appreciate it if you'd keep me updated. It won't be much of a raffle without a car."

After Pritchard left, Garza and Marlin sat back down. The sheriff blew out a long sigh. "I'm gonna be pissed off if we're wasting our time while Scofield's out chasing skirts."

Marlin had to grin. He and Garza had worked together and been friends long enough that they could be blunt with each other. Garza, after eight years as a deputy, had been the sheriff of Blanco County for nearly three years now—arguably the best man ever to hold the job. He had earned the respect of every law-enforcement officer in the county, Marlin included. The sheriff commonly involved Marlin in all types of investigations, from homicides to burglaries to drug-related crimes. It was funny: When working those types of cases, Marlin found that people were often surprised to learn that game wardens were in fact *real* police officers, commissioned with the power to enforce any state law, not just hunting and fishing regulations.

"What do you think?" Garza continued. "Maybe he's off on a bender?"

Marlin had to figure it was a possibility, because he'd run into similar situations—emergency calls that didn't turn out to be emergencies at all. The previous summer, a drowning had been reported on the Blanco River. A boy, fourteen years old. The search began, with divers and the whole bit, and it turned out the kid had decided to swim across the river and walk home. He had been angry at his friends and wanted to put a scare into them. But this case had something different.

"Still doesn't explain the vehicle in the river," Marlin said. "Unless he wants us to think something happened to him." He had seen that scenario, too—a man faking his own death. It happened with alarming frequency around the country. Some desperado, usually facing felony charges, would decide it was the best option and try to stage the most convincing scene he could. But they were nearly always sloppy, and you could spot the fix from halfway across the county.

"Guy'd be a real dumb-ass, wouldn't he? Taking off in the Corvette? And wanting us to think he'd drowned?"

"Maybe he thought *we'd* think the car was stolen."

Garza drummed his fingers on the table. "I guess Scofield could be off somewhere in the Vette, and somebody else borrowed or stole his SUV. Maybe they ended up in the river but climbed out and made it home okay."

"Or whoever was driving it might not even know the SUV's in the water. Remember the high water last fall? Rodney Bauer drove his wife's car partway into the water, then decided not to chance it?"

"Yeah, what was the deal on that?"

"Plugs got wet and the car died. He just left it there, figuring he'd come back for it later. But the water rose even higher and the car ended up downstream about forty yards."

Garza shook his head. "I don't know. You think that happened here?"

"No, my money's on door number one. Scofield drowned."

"And the Corvette?"

"Sitting somewhere else, maybe at a friend's house. And Pritchard just doesn't know it."

Garza rose from his chair. "I've already got an APB on Scofield and a BOLO on the Corvette. I'm gonna get a warrant for his house, but that means I'll have to pull my deputies off the river."

"We don't have a lot of choices."

"We're already stretched thin as it is, between this case and the Lucas thing."

"Anything new there?"

"Get this. Nicole found out that Lucas didn't have a phone. He'd disconnected it. So no recent phone records. Also, we talked to his landlord—this old guy up in Waco. He didn't say much, but he told us that Lucas had been paying his rent for the last few months in money orders. He's always used checks before that."

Marlin could decipher what that meant. Lucas paid with money orders because he didn't want to deposit quantities of cash into his checking account. Money that he had made by selling drugs.

"The state fire marshal sent a team down, and they're overhauling the place today," Garza said. "Then we'll know for sure." Garza rapped his knuckles on the desk, hoping, Marlin knew, for some good luck. Nobody wanted Lucas's body to be found in the rubble. "What's your plan?" Garza asked.

"Back to the river, I guess."

"Gonna keep looking, huh?"

"For now."

"Sounds like you got yourself in a shitpot of trouble," Buford said, seated, looking around the room. Damn nice office. Mahogany desk. Matching bookshelves. Oil paintings on the wall. The hot secretary from outside was fetching coffee. Hell of a deal, this public service gig.

The senator—Herzog—didn't appear to like Buford's way of phrasing things. Kind of got this prissy look on his face. "That's one way of putting it," he said. "And you're supposed to help me out of it . . . somehow?"

The guy was looking Buford and Little Joe over, like a man who had just discovered a cockroach in his chili. Buford had seen that look before, people thinking he was a rube. He could handle it, though, as long as Herzog didn't maintain an attitude. Hell, Buford had been known to play it up a little, Columbo-style. Let people think he was a yokel. Nobody keeps an eye on a yokel.

Uncle Chuck—or "Mr. Hamm," as Buford had called him in front of the senator—had given Buford the lowdown, but he wanted to run it by Herzog, make sure he had the story straight. Make sure Herzog wasn't candy-coating some of the details. "What I hear is, you got a nasty phone call. Guy mailed you some pitchers, and now he wants something in exchange. I got it right so far?"

The senator started to say something, but apparently thought better of it and simply nodded instead. He came across as fidgety, like he had better things to do.

"And these pitchers are what you'd call embarrassing. You and a woman."

"That's the gist. I already told Hamm all of this. In detail."

Buford looked at him. "Bear with me. No sense in rushing through it." He flipped through his notes. "You got no idea who it mighta been who called, how long they been watching you, nothing like that." He looked up. "You mind letting me have those photos?"

Herzog immediately shook his head, Buford seeing the impatience in the man. "Out of the question," Herzog said, almost like he was ready to call the whole thing off. "That's just ridiculous, anyway. What reason could you possibly have for needing them?"

He was still talking down to Buford, and it was starting to piss him off.

Buford smiled at him. "See, them photos can tell me things, maybe point me in the right direction."

Herzog snorted. "Yeah, right. If you think I'm—"

"For example," Buford said, cutting him off, "were they taken from up close or with a zoom lens? A zoom lens tells me the guy knows something about photography. He'll have equipment lying around somewhere when I find him. Same thing with a date stamp. Could tell me what kind of camera it is, even the model.

What's on the back of the photos? Anything on there from a processor? Because if there is, that's something else to worry about. Means it's been out of the man's hands and there might be somebody else with copies now. Maybe some curious kid down at the one-hour shop made copies for his secret stash, loose ends we'd have to run down. The envelope, too, with the cancellation mark. Tells me where he mailed it from. Did he buy stamps at the counter? Maybe someone at the post office can help us out, for a price. Might even get a look at some video, if they've got cameras. That's why I want to see the photos, Senator. Not for my own personal jollies, but to keep your dick out of a sling."

Little Joe let loose with a mean little giggle, and Buford could see the look in Herzog's eyes changing as he revised his opinion of the both of them. Surprise. Maybe things are not what they seem.

"You gotta realize," Buford said, "I'm gonna see 'em eventually anyway, right? I can't get the negatives from this guy without seeing what they are, can I?"

After a pause, Herzog dug into a desk drawer and came out with a manila envelope. "Please look at these later. I don't want to see them again. And for God's sake, don't lose them."

Buford tucked the envelope into his jacket. "I understand your caller ID didn't work out so well."

"If it did, I wouldn't need you, would I?"

The man was still a tad feisty. Pissed off because of Buford's little speech. Buford wanted to turn Little Joe loose, let him bitch-slap the man right across his capped teeth.

Instead he said, "That's 'cause we're dealing with a clever boy. What he did was, before he dialed your number, he dialed a code that blocks out caller ID."

Herzog didn't looked particularly impressed, but he did ask, "How do you know that?"

Buford grinned and retrieved some papers from his other coat pocket. "Trade secret." He was tired of trying to impress this asshole. It had all been fairly simple anyway. He'd made a few calls, dangled the right amount of money in front of the right person, and just like that—phone records.

Buford said, "The call came in at ten-oh-seven. That sound about right?"

"Yes, that is correct." The senator sounded like he was testifying in front of some damn committee.

"Then answer me this," Buford said, glancing up from the papers. "You know a man in Blanco County by the name of Phil Colby?"

Herzog didn't answer, because right then the good-looking gal came in with the coffee.

7

BUFORD WASN'T MUCH for gadgets, but a few years back he'd forced himself to learn how to operate a computer. He knew, in his line of work, it was a necessary evil. A person can find out all kinds of great shit on the computer. Most of it's just right there in front of you, free for the taking. Tax rolls. Phone directories. Marriage and divorce records. Hell, even criminal records for a small fee. Poke around long enough, you can dig up dirt on just about anybody.

Probably even a man named Phil Colby.

Herzog had said the name sounded familiar but wasn't able to place it. Not much help. So what Buford and Little Joe did, before they left Herzog's office, they asked the secretary where the nearest quick-print shop was. A place where they could use a computer. She sent them down Lamar.

Heading south, the top down, Buford was checking addresses,

knowing they were getting close, while Little Joe opened the manila envelope. He gave a low whistle as he thumbed through the photographs. "Aw, man, you ain't gonna believe this," he said. Then he started laughing, excited as hell. "It's her! Damn, take a look!"

"Who?" Buford said, trying to sneak a peek without hitting some asshole on a bicycle.

"The secretary!" Little Joe held one of the photographs out at arm's length, studying it. "And check out this getup she's wearing. My oh my."

But Buford saw the sign for the quick-copy and had to hit the brakes and pull in quick, someone honking behind him, Buford flipping the bird.

Buford whipped it into a parking spot, killed the engine, and made a *gimme* motion with his hand. Little Joe passed the pictures over, and Buford took a look. "Lord have mercy. Last time I saw leather stretched that tight, Troy Aikman was throwing it for a touchdown. And check out ol' Herzog."

"One fucked-up mess, ain't he?"

"I'd say his mama didn't give him enough loving."

"His choice of women, though, I'd vote for the man."

Five minutes later, they were inside the quick-print shop, Buford working a PC, Little Joe watching over his shoulder. Buford went straight to Google and typed in *phil colby blanco county.*

He found a lot more than he was expecting.

One o'clock sharp, steering with one hand, Lucille crushed out her cigarette, then swigged the last of her beer and tossed the empty in the backseat. Chewed some gum real quick to cover her breath. Time to earn some money.

The pet this time was a German shepherd and the customer was an old lady, so Lucille figured it would be a cinch. The older folks were so trusting it was almost ridiculous. Lucille remembered a line she'd heard somewhere: *The most important thing is sincerity, so if you can fake that, you've got it made.* And you know something? Whoever said that was exactly right.

The woman's name was Gladys Smith, and when Lucille shook her hand, it felt like a small suede bag filled with dry sticks. Gladys's home was a tidy little cottage that smelled like cinnamon and liniment, maybe a touch of Lysol.

"That's my husband, Jerry," Gladys said softly, gesturing toward a white-haired geezer being swallowed up by an easy chair in front of the television. *Jeopardy!* was playing, and the volume was plenty loud. Lucille noticed a clear oxygen tube snaking down from the man's nostrils to the floor, then trailing down a hallway, probably to a generator in the bedroom. She was guessing emphysema, maybe COPD. She'd seen plenty of those cases. Tough deal.

"Hello, Mr. Smith," Lucille called out, working hard to be friendly. It didn't always come easy.

The old guy didn't so much as budge.

"He doesn't hear so well anymore," Gladys said, smiling behind her glasses, so sweet and lovely Lucille nearly had to retch. As the saying goes, if you looked up the word "grandmother" in the dictionary, you'd find this woman's picture. Probably had a slew of grandkids who visited her every weekend, and she'd bake cookies special for the occasion.

But over in the corner of the living room was Lucille's reason for being here: There lay the dog, sacked out on a large pillow, eyes half open, watching her. Its tail thumped a few times slowly, but it made no effort to get up.

"Oh, isn't he a sweetie," Lucille said. "May I?"

"By all means," Gladys said.

Lucille knelt and began to stroke the dog's head.

"We've had him for four years, since he was a puppy," Gladys said, clasping her hands in front of her chest. "He's our baby."

"He's wonderful. Full of life, I can tell." *Don't push it,* Lucille thought to herself. The dog was kicking its hind leg slowly as Lucille rubbed its belly, but that was about the extent of Duke's liveliness. *Christ, I'll cut my own wrists if this mutt gets a boner.*

"Where are my manners?" Gladys asked. "Would you like something to drink?"

That was exactly what Lucille was hoping for. "That'd be nice."

"I could make some coffee . . ."

Lucille smiled. Making coffee would take time. "Excellent," she said. Then she turned her gaze back to the dog. "I'll just stay here and keep him company."

"Cream or sugar?"

"Both, please."

"I'll be right back," Gladys said, and retreated into the kitchen.

Lucille gave the shepherd one last pat on the head, then rose and nonchalantly inspected the living room. The photos on the wall were her first stop. There were plenty of shots of people, and Lucille assumed these were family members—kids, the grandkids (as expected), siblings probably, and cousins. Lucille wasn't interested in those. She focused on the shots that featured the dog. Like that one, right there, showing Jerry fishing from a dock, the dog by his side. *Oh, could this be more perfect?* There was a date stamp in the corner of the photo. The picture was taken in the spring, four years ago.

Another shot showed the shepherd, still a puppy, and an aging Labrador retriever lolling in their doghouses, apparently in the backyard of the Smith home. *Bingo.* The shepherd was named Duke and the retriever was Shasta, according to the gaily painted names on the doghouses. Where was Shasta now? The answer was obvious. Doggie heaven.

This was going to be a cakewalk.

Other photos showed Duke and Gladys in front of a sign: PEDERNALES FALLS STATE PARK . . . Jerry, Gladys, and Duke on a boat . . . Duke and Jerry sitting in a bed of springtime bluebonnets. The most recent shot was from two years ago. Lucille figured that was about the time ol' Jerry's health began to decline. Before that, they had apparently been a fairly active couple. She could use that knowledge. Boy, could she use that.

She could hear the clatter of dishes in the kitchen, cups being placed on saucers. She still had time.

Lucille noticed a leash hanging on a hook by the back door. She lifted it and rattled the clasp gently at the dog. Duke raised his head with a look of anticipation on his face. Lucille replaced the leash, and Duke's head went back down on the pillow. *Okay,* Lucille thought, *so Duke and Gladys still go on walks occasionally, something the dog looks forward to.* That was also good to know.

She picked up a few more clues around the room, and by the time Gladys returned with the coffee, Lucille was more than prepared.

"Here we go," Gladys called merrily, carrying a tray.

"Smells wonderful," Lucille replied, wishing it was beer instead.

They sat at a small oak dining table next to a bay window, and Lucille could see a bird feeder hanging in a nearby tree. *I bet Duke chases squirrels away from the feeder,* she thought. Something else she could mention.

Gladys blew on her coffee, then said, "You know, I feel a little silly about this, to be honest." She smiled sheepishly. "I've never used a pet psychic before."

Lucille nodded, just as understanding as can be. "Most people haven't. There are doubters out there, and I can understand that. But I can promise you this: You won't have any doubt at all by the time I leave." Followed by a big, warm smile to put Gladys at ease.

"Have you been doing this long?"

"All my life," Lucille said, because that's what they all wanted to hear. "When I was a little girl, I noticed I had this . . . gift. I could—well, I could understand what my cocker spaniel was thinking. That's the only way to describe it. Now, I don't mean I could simply tell when he wanted to go outside or when he was hungry. It was more than that."

Lucille placed her hands together, prayerlike, in front of her face. Time to play it up. "I could connect with him on an emotional level. He could express things to me, like the fact that he was lonely all by himself when we went to church . . . or he would tell me—I know this sounds a little crazy—but one time he told me his stomach didn't feel good. The vet said it wasn't his stomach, but I insisted it was, so my mother asked for X-rays. It turned out the poor thing had swallowed a golf ball. Can you imagine that?"

"That's . . . that's amazing." Gladys stared at her with rapt attention, and Lucille knew the hook was set.

Lucille shrugged her shoulders. "I decided, if I have this ability, I might as well share it."

Gladys placed her coffee on the table and chose her words carefully. "When I saw your note posted at the grocery store, I thought, well, this woman might be just what we need. See, we realize we're both getting older . . . and we have to think about the future. If something happened to us . . ."

"You want to know where Duke would like to live."

Gladys's mouth fell open. "I don't remember telling you his name."

"No, no you didn't," Lucille said. She turned her gaze to Duke, who was now licking himself contentedly. "He shared it with me earlier."

Gladys had tears in her eyes now. "Why . . . I've never seen anything like it."

"Sometimes I don't understand it myself," Lucille said, patting Gladys's hand. "Shall we get started?"

"Oh yes . . . please."

"There is one thing we need to take care of beforehand," Lucille said softly, acting mildly embarrassed, such a distasteful topic. "My regular fee is two hundred dollars."

"Why, of course," Gladys said, scurrying out of her chair to grab her purse.

"I prefer cash if you have it," Lucille called after her.

Marlin officially called off the search at sundown. He'd been straight up with the rescue squad and the other volunteers, telling them the situation with Scofield and the Corvette, letting them know there might not be a body in the river after all. It nagged at him, though, knowing Scofield's SUV couldn't have ended up in the water by itself.

Thirty minutes after dark, he met with Bobby Garza, Bill Tatum, Ernie Turpin, and Nicole Brooks in the conference room at the sheriff's office in Johnson City.

When he walked into the room, all the deputies looking up,

Marlin got the sense they'd learned something. He was right.

Garza, with a pained smile on his face, said, "John, I wanted to keep you posted. Ernie and Nicole searched Scofield's house this afternoon, and I don't think you're gonna like this. Wait—first things first. Nothing on the river today?"

Marlin shook his head. "The water's down about three feet from yesterday, so I used the boat for a while. But no, nothing."

Garza shook his head, clearly frustrated. "That's what I expected. So here's the deal. There was no sign of robbery or burglary at Scofield's house. But we did learn that he was seeing a gal named Stephanie Waring—a local girl who works at a nursery in Dripping Springs. Plants, not kids. Anyway, here's the kicker. We called her mother, her boss, her friends—and surprise, nobody knows where *she* is either. Her boss said she left a message on his voicemail saying she had to quit. Didn't give a reason."

Marlin pulled a chair out and sat. "Let's hear the story."

Brooks said, "We found this on his fridge." She slid a color photograph across the table. Marlin found himself looking at a shot similar to the photo David Pritchard had provided of the woman named Jenny. Here, a young blonde woman in a bikini top, jeans, and boots was posing in front of the same Corvette. Written across the bottom of the photo in felt-tip pen: *Love you! Steph.*

"I recognized her right off," Turpin said. "Wrote her up for shoplifting at the Save-Mart a couple years ago. It was a big deal, because it was her third time, which meant it was a felony. The manager wouldn't budge."

"She was also the prom queen during her senior year," Brooks added, "but judging from the way you're studying that picture, I guess that's not so hard to believe."

She raised an eyebrow at him, and Marlin rolled his eyes. He had noticed that Brooks had a dry sense of humor, and he liked it. In fact, there had been occasions, when she first joined the department, when he found himself smiling at her more readily than he should, sometimes inventing excuses to meet with her. It didn't take him long to realize he had a schoolboy crush on her. The kind that makes your palms damp and ties your tongue in knots.

He said, "I was just thinking I knew her from someplace, that's all."

"We found some other cards and notes," Brooks continued. "Nothing important, but enough to make it clear they were dating." Now she held up a sheaf of papers. "Plus, when we dumped Scofield's phone, there were plenty of calls between the two of them. The last one was on Sunday morning, about eleven hours before the rain started. We called every number on the list from the last month, plus every number in this little gem." She held up a little black book—Scofield's personal phone directory. "Stephanie Waring is the only person he's talked to recently who we haven't been able to reach. I left a voicemail. But Scofield was definitely a player, or he used to be. Dated tons of women, although it looks like he slowed down in the last couple of years. Lots of the numbers were disconnected, and some of the women had gotten married or moved away. By the way, there was also a call to Scofield from Phil Colby on Saturday."

Marlin raised his eyebrows. *Why on earth would Phil call Vance Scofield?* "And?"

"Phil said that Scofield was starting to build a high fence, so he called and told him to make sure the fencing crew stays off his property." Brooks frowned. "He said he was just harassing the guy. Something to do with a lawsuit."

Marlin thought that sounded like something Phil might do.

Now Ernie Turpin spoke again. "We also found a bunch of vials in various places around the house. Most of 'em empty, but some of them filled with meth. Totaled about three grams.

"Then there's this," Turpin added, opening a manila folder, placing several documents on the table. "According to these, Scofield was several months behind on his car payment and his mortgage, and he owed . . . let's see . . . forty-seven grand in credit card bills. A big chunk of that went to Lone Star Fencing."

"Jack Chambers," Marlin said. "The high fence."

Garza made a noise of frustration and said, "All of this supports everything David Pritchard told us. Young girls, drug and money problems, et cetera."

"And then there was the one thing we couldn't find," Turpin

added. "A safe. Pritchard said Scofield had a safe, right?"

Marlin said, "Maybe it's at his office."

"He works from home," Turpin said. "No, all we can figure is that it was a pretty small safe. Something portable."

Nobody had anything to add, so Brooks switched gears.

"There were a lot of tire tracks in and out of there," she said. "Most were washed out pretty bad from the rain, but there were a couple of decent patches, so we went ahead and casted them. Might give us a clue if the Corvette was driven recently."

"Okay," Marlin said slowly, "where does this all leave us?" He had the feeling the group had reached a conclusion before he came in.

Garza said, "We've been bouncing all kinds of theories around, but I don't think we're in danger of figuring it out in the next few minutes. Bottom line is, I think the chances are slim we're gonna find Vance Scofield in the river. Let me ask you something, John. What does your gut tell you? What are the odds Scofield's still out there—or Stephanie Waring, for that matter—if one of them was in the SUV?"

"That's a tough one. If there *is* a body, yeah, I'd normally expect it to be found by now. But it could be miles downstream."

"You think it is?"

"I just don't know. All I'd be doing is guessing."

Garza laughed. "That's what we're all doing at this point."

Bill Tatum, silent until this point, said, "Let's all remember, we're dealing with a druggie. Who knows what went on? I can picture a scene where Scofield is high as a kite and says, 'Screw it, my life is a shambles, I might as well take off on a big ol' road trip.'"

Marlin said, "Maybe so, but I'm still having trouble with the Explorer in the river. I mean, it had to get there somehow."

Tatum said, "Maybe he put it there himself, thinking it would keep everybody off his back for a while. Hell, maybe it's his idea of a practical joke."

"But if the river was already high, how does he get the Corvette across?"

Tatum opened his mouth, then closed it.

Garza said, "Guys, we might be making this too complicated. It could've been some kids on that side of the river going for a joy ride. You gotta drive right through Mucho Loco to get to Scofield's ranch, and you know there are plenty of punks around there who might pull that sort of thing. This is all guesswork anyway. We're working in the dark, really, until we can find Scofield. Or Stephanie."

With the mention of the girl's name, Marlin picked up her photo again, wondering. Something so familiar. Then he had it, like suddenly remembering a hard-to-place tune. He hadn't recognized her at first, because the one time he had met her, she had barely been a teenager. "Y'all aren't gonna believe this," he said. He looked up at Garza and the deputies. "Do you realize it was Stephanie Waring's stepfather who died in the flood five years ago?"

Judging from the startled looks on the faces around him, Marlin knew they hadn't made that connection.

"You're kidding. The guy that ended up in Lake Travis?" Garza asked.

"Yeah, that's him. Doyle Metzger. In fact, his truck went in at the same crossing as Scofield's SUV."

"Oh, come on," Bill Tatum said. "What are the odds of that? We're being played."

"If I remember right," Marlin said, "the Metzgers lived over in Mucho Loco."

"And now Stephanie Waring is missing," Tatum said. "Hell of a lot of coincidences here."

"See, you're just a natural part of the team," Garza said to Marlin, smiling. It was a running joke between the two of them. Garza, on several occasions, had tried to persuade Marlin to join the sheriff's department. But the way Marlin saw it, as a game warden, he had the best of both worlds.

Marlin shrugged at Garza. "Lucky."

"Well, let's keep after it. I think we need to have a face-to-face with Stephanie's mother."

8

RED WAS IN the Friendly Bar with Billy Don, drinking a cold one, thinking about what Jack Chambers had said that morning.

When it got right down to it, Red didn't really know where his three-year-old marriage to Loretta stood. Were they still married? He hadn't heard from her since the day she left, and he hadn't ever received any legal papers saying it was over. But then again, was their marriage even really legal? He thought so, and he still had the marriage license tucked away somewhere. Yeah, okay, Loretta had apparently married Billy Don before she married Red—without a divorce in between, if you wanted to get all technical. But did that mean the touching ceremony he had shared with Loretta, performed by the best dadgum Elvis impersonator in all of Las Vegas, wasn't legit? If that was the case, he'd just as soon go home and burn the secondhand leisure suit he'd bought for the occasion, because he'd never get married again. He just couldn't stand the heartbreak.

Back then, he'd been so happy that he'd finally found a woman who liked all the same things he liked—pro wrestling, pork rinds, welding, and all kinds of other neat shit. He should've known it was too good to last.

Sylvia, the bartender, came over to ask if they wanted another round. Red nodded that yeah, they did. Sylvia was wearing a low-cut top today, but Red was too preoccupied to even comment.

Loretta was a prize, and he knew that. No, she wasn't good-looking in the traditional sense. That skin condition of hers was a little distracting, and so was the lazy eye. But she had a sturdy, reliable look about her, like the kind of woman you might find working at a diner in a coal-mining town. Or behind the counter at a bait shop.

So the question was, what would Red do if it was true, that Loretta was actually back in town? There was Billy Don to consider. The big man had feelings, too, Red knew that much. He'd even seen a few tears leak from Billy Don's eyes during a rerun of *The Waltons* just last week. And now that Billy Don was Red's best friend, there was loyalty and all that bullshit to think about. Plus, he sure didn't want another brawl on his hands, like the one they'd had the first time they'd met. It happened when Billy Don tracked Loretta down at Red's trailer. They were both laying claim to her, one thing led to another, and the next thing Red knew, they were going at it like two yard dogs fighting over a dead squirrel. That's when tires squealed and Loretta took off in Billy Don's car, never to be seen again. The memories made Red choke up a little, and that Ray Price song in the background wasn't helping.

"What're you thinking about?" Billy Don asked.

"Truck needs a tune-up," Red said.

To Marlin, the words "prom queen" brought to mind visions of a beautiful girl from a nice middle-class family. And yes, Nicole Brooks was right, Stephanie Waring had the first part covered. But as they approached the Metzger residence, it became apparent that the home where Stephanie had been raised didn't quite deliver on the second part of that equation.

Riding in the backseat of Bobby Garza's cruiser, behind Bill Tatum in the passenger seat, Marlin saw that Stephanie's mother—Rita Sue Metzger—lived in an aging mobile home surrounded by brush that needed to be cleared. The front lawn, mostly weeds and native grasses, was bathed by a pair of floodlights bolted above the front door. To the side of the house was a rusting metal shed, with an equally unsightly truck parked in front of it.

There were three steps up to a covered plywood porch that groaned under the weight of the three men as they knocked on the door. On the porch was a large freezer, and on top of the freezer, a basket of wet laundry that, judging from the smell, had soured. An empty clothesline stretched from an eyebolt in a porch post to an oak tree in the yard. Next to the freezer was a tattered recliner, a small-block engine resting on some newspaper, half a dozen milk crates filled with mason jars, several cans of paint, and other assorted junk.

Then there was the lady of the house. Marlin, having met her before, was prepared for the sight of Rita Sue Metzger. But apparently Bobby Garza was not, because the sheriff actually moved back about a half step when Rita Sue opened the door. She was easily six feet tall and well over two hundred pounds—but she wasn't specifically fat, merely big-boned and thick all over. When Marlin had met her five years ago, she had been a large and imposing woman, but she had bulked up even more since then. Rita Sue was wearing thick-lensed eyeglasses, slippers, and a smudged blue housecoat, and she held a trembling Chihuahua in her arms.

"Oh, y'all come on in," Rita Sue said, swinging the door open as if they were next-door neighbors coming over for dinner. "I got some coffee going, if y'all want any."

The three men stepped inside, wiping their feet on a mat, but the multicolored shag carpeting had seen plenty of muddy boots in its time. The house smelled of dog urine and milk that had turned.

"Ma'am, I'm Sheriff Bobby Garza, this is Sergeant Bill Tatum, and I believe you've met John Marlin."

Rita Sue gave Marlin a long squint. "You're the game warden, right? The one that fished Doyle out?"

"Yes, ma'am."

She nodded. "Yeah, that was you. Been a long time, but I 'member it." She plopped the Chihuahua onto the floor, and it instantly bounded onto a nearby easy chair, then sat eyeing the men suspiciously.

If Marlin were to estimate Rita Sue's age, he'd put it in the early sixties, meaning Stephanie had come along fairly late. Marlin seemed to remember that Stephanie had two or three brothers, all much older, who had driven in from various parts of Texas to help in the search for Doyle Metzger five years ago.

Rita Sue bustled her way into the kitchen without asking who wanted what, then came back a minute later with a tray holding four cups of black coffee. The men thanked her, didn't ask for cream or sugar, and had a seat on a stained sectional sofa.

Rita Sue lowered her massive rear end into the easy chair, the Chihuahua scrambling to get out of the way, and said, "I sure hope Stephanie ain't giving y'all any trouble. Lord knows she's good at it."

"No, ma'am," Garza said. "It's just that we really need to verify her whereabouts." He outlined all that had unfolded, beginning with the discovery of Vance Scofield's SUV. When Garza was finished—after making it clear that it was possible that Stephanie had either drowned or run off with a drug-using financially bankrupt older man—Rita Sue hardly seemed fazed.

Her first question was "Who's this Scofield fella?"

"You don't know him?"

"Heard about him yesterday in the news, but Stephanie never said nothing about him."

"Like I said, we're under the impression they've been dating."

Rita Sue frowned, running a massive hand over the dog's tiny head. Marlin noticed a can of Copenhagen on the TV stand next to the easy chair, and he realized that Rita Sue had a boyfriend.

He figured there was somebody out there for everyone. She said, "Could be. Of course, my Stephanie, looking the way she does, she always has a lot of boys after her. Kinda hard to keep track of 'em."

"She, uh, dated a lot of men?" Garza asked.

"Always did, even during high school. But she's living away from home now, so I don't hear much about it. Have you checked her duplex? Them ones off Lady Bird Lane in Johnson City?"

"Yes, ma'am, a deputy stopped by and left a note. We were wondering—could you let us in to have a look around her place?"

"I sure enough would if I had a key." She shook her head. "I hate to see y'all going to all this trouble. Steph is liable to be anywhere. Maybe off on a camping trip, or down at the beach this time of year."

Marlin said, "She'd just take off like that? Without telling you?"

Rita Sue chuckled, and Marlin could see dark strands of wayward snuff between her front teeth. No boyfriend after all. "Oh, heavens, yes," she said. "That girl's a handful, I'm tellin' ya. Got fired from her last job 'cause she took off for Vegas, no word to nobody."

"Do you know who she went with?" Garza asked.

"To Vegas?"

"Yes, ma'am."

"I believe it was a girlfriend from work. I hadn't ever met the gal, so I cain't remember the name."

Marlin asked, "Was Stephanie friends with Lucas Burnette?" He'd been thinking about Lucas a lot lately. Another mystery, the third day now with no sign of the kid whatsoever. To Marlin, the odds seemed slim that Lucas and Vance Scofield could vanish from sparsely populated Blanco County just hours apart without the cases being somehow tied together. The deputies had already checked for a connection between the two men—after all, Lucas might've been running a speed lab, and Scofield looked to be a user—but they hadn't found anything. No phone calls from Scofield to Lucas. No friends or relatives saying they knew one another. Marlin was hoping Stephanie would be the link between Lucas and Scofield.

But Rita Sue seemed surprised by the question. "The boy from the feed store?"

"Yes, ma'am."

"I imagine they know each other from school. He was a year ahead of Steph, I believe."

"But they didn't see each other on a social basis?"

"Uh-uh. He's a sweet boy, though. Always carries my chicken feed out for me. A shame to hear about that fire. I sure hope he's all right."

Garza said, "We've left voicemails for Stephanie. Do you know if she carries her cell phone?"

"You know how those things are. Half the time you cain't reach nobody, or you cain't hear each other talking. Pieces of junk, if you ask me."

"But does she carry it most of the time?"

"Far as I know. Most of them kids do, right? You see 'em all over the place gabbing on them. Driving. In the malls. Plain rude sometimes."

Marlin could see that this interview was getting them nowhere. He wondered if Garza would explore the fact that Scofield had disappeared in the same manner as Rita Sue's husband. But the sheriff simply asked a few more questions. *When was the last time you talked to Stephanie? Who are her closest friends? Can you name anyone she was dating recently?* Nothing useful came from any of it.

Ernie Turpin and Nicole Brooks had stayed behind at the office to take care of a few things, including calling David Pritchard. Brooks got him on the phone and asked if he knew Stephanie Waring.

"Yeah, she's another one of the car models. I met her at the fairgrounds in April. The chili cook-off. We were selling tickets there. Well, she and Vance were."

"What can you tell me about her?"

"Like, in general terms?"

"Sure."

"Very pretty girl. Kinda wild, I think. Kept asking me to buy her a beer."

"Did you?"

"No, she's underage."

"You said Vance Scofield was there?"

"Yeah, he drove her over in the Corvette. I just stopped by to see how things were going. A friend of mine was in the chili contest. Got second place."

"Do you know if Vance and Stephanie were dating?"

Pritchard laughed. "Like I told the sheriff, Vance did like to date them kind of young. But to answer your question, I don't know for sure. I guess you should ask her."

"We would, but we're having some trouble tracking her down."

"Oh. *Oh.* Okay, I see why you're asking. You're thinking Vance and Stephanie might be together."

"It crossed our minds. Or that Stephanie might be in possession of the Corvette."

"I don't think so. At least not alone. Stephanie couldn't drive a stick."

"The Corvette is—"

"Yeah, one of those six-speed models. I remember Vance asking if she wanted to drive it around the parking lot, sort of stir up some interest, but she couldn't handle the stick shift."

Buford liked the look of the Best Western motel in Johnson City. Big enough, with enough vehicles in the parking lot that they could keep a low profile. They were in the room now, queen beds, Buford leaning back against the headboard, boots off, sipping bourbon from one of those sorry foam cups you find wrapped in plastic next to the sink. At least the ice machine worked.

Little Joe was sunk into a chair over by the air conditioner, drinking straight from the bottle. Buford knew the quart would be half gone before Joe's eyelids would begin to sag. The little guy was the most wired-up man Buford had ever met, not counting druggies.

Boy couldn't hardly ever sit still. Always tapping a toe, drumming on the dashboard, something. Feisty as hell. Prone to violence.

Buford had met Joe a couple years ago in the city lockup in Fort Worth, them sharing a cell overnight.

"What'd they get you for?" Joe had asked him right from the get-go, sitting on one of the bunks, jiggling a leg.

"Stopped me for speeding and tossed my car. Bullshit search, but they found a gun."

"All *right*." Joe grinned, apparently liking what he heard. "Me, it's assault. I was selling dogs to this Korean guy with a restaurant. I went out to see him and—"

"Whoa. Back up a sec." Buford had been leaning against the wall, lighting a smoke, not paying much attention, but *that* caught his ear.

"What?"

"Selling dogs?"

"Yeah, just strays I'd round up. I'd take 'em to his house." Joe said it like it was no big deal. Like delivering pizzas.

"You're saying this guy served dog meat in his restaurant?"

Joe frowned. "Hell, I don't know what he done with 'em. Maybe he just liked dogs."

"How many'd you sell him?"

"Couple dozen. Twenty bucks apiece." Joe paused, waiting to see if Buford had more questions. Buford didn't. "Anyways," Joe said, "I took him this pointer mix, and he said it was too small. Seeing as how he was paying by the dog and not the pound, he wanted big ones only. That's what he'd told me earlier, but I figgered this one was big enough."

Buford was smiling, not able to help himself. He wasn't much for strangers, but he already liked this guy. Not putting on an act, just telling a story.

Joe went on, saying, "We had some words, then I finally grabbed that little slant by the hair and smacked him a good 'un. His wife called it in. Deputies show up and all that crap. Wouldn't have been a problem, 'cept I was on parole for shooting homeless guys with a paintball gun."

Buford shook his head, thinking, *What is this guy made of?*

"Man paid me to do it," Joe explained. "Bums was hanging around outside his office at night, getting wasted, pissing all over the place. Somebody finally broke in, so the guy'd had enough. I didn't want to lay hands on those nasty bastards, so I figgered I'd holler at 'em and run 'em off with the paintball gun. The thing was, I figgered the cops couldn't get me on assault for something like that. Not touching them or nothing. Stupid me."

They'd both posted bail the next day, and Little Joe had asked for a ride.

"Where to?" Buford asked.

"Wherever you're going."

Joe turned out to be a pretty good little assistant, running details down for Buford, spelling him on stakeouts. Buford got used to having the extra set of ears and eyes real quick, so they had worked up a loose employment agreement. Buford decided, since he was the one with contacts and experience, they'd split the dollars three to one. Joe didn't have a problem with it. It had worked out real nice so far.

Joe was holding the bottle with one hand, thumbing nonstop through the channels with the other. "You got a plan yet?"

"Working on it."

"Which way's Colby's ranch?"

"Down 281, right on Miller Creek Loop. About ten minutes to get there."

9

"KINDA CHILLY THIS morning," Phil Colby said.

"Yep," Marlin replied. "Don't you worry. It'll warm up quick."

"No doubt. So what's the plan?"

It was minutes after sunrise, and they were parked side by side near the low-water crossing into the Mucho Loco subdivision. Just the two of them, no more volunteers.

"I'll cross to the other side, then we'll just walk the banks downstream. Let's keep an eye on each other, and just holler if you see anything."

Colby nodded and pulled his truck onto a grassy area beside the road. Marlin drove slowly across the bridge; the water was low enough now that it barely reached his hubcaps.

He couldn't shake the feeling that he was wasting his time, but he couldn't give up the search yet with so many unanswered questions. Suppose Scofield had been driving the Corvette and Stephanie

Waring had been following, maybe an hour later, in the SUV? But what if the water had risen too high by then and she had been swept away? Scofield might've waited for her at some meeting place and, when she didn't show, figured she had changed her mind. He'd think, *Well, she didn't want to run away with me after all.* Then he'd hit the road alone.

Who the hell knows?

Any number of scenarios were plausible, and several of them ended with a body in the river. That's why Marlin had to keep looking.

Ernie and Nicole were starting from scratch, speaking to the same people they had already interviewed, hoping to learn where Scofield might have gone. But last night, after talking to Rita Sue Metzger, Bobby Garza had warned Marlin that he couldn't commit much manpower to the investigation. "We've got two possible scenarios," Garza had said. "Somebody drowned in Scofield's vehicle, in which case there's not a lot we can do at this point. Or Scofield took off in the Vette, with or without Stephanie Waring, and there's not a lot we can do there either, except wait and see. Until we can find out *why* the SUV ended up in the river, we don't even know that a crime has been committed."

"What about the stolen Corvette?" Marlin had asked.

"I talked to a guy at the dealership, and they don't want to report it as stolen yet. They want to wait and see if Scofield turns up with it. That means all we've got on it is a BOLO."

So Marlin parked his truck on the far side of the river and began to trudge along the soggy banks. Colby matched his pace on the other side, roughly eighty yards away. Marlin couldn't remember the last time he'd seen the river this ugly, with all kinds of trash and debris snagged in trees and brush along the banks. It was slow going, stepping through mud that tried to suck his boots off, crossing over, under, or through barbwire fences, stopping to inspect items that offered promise, anything that might reveal who had been in Scofield's vehicle.

After covering less than three miles in two hours, Marlin was getting discouraged. Then he heard a shout from across the river.

He looked up and saw that Colby was pointing downstream.

A buzzard was drifting lazily above the water.

Then Marlin saw another . . . and another. Two hundred yards downriver, five or six of the scavengers circled, with a dozen more perched in the upper branches of a sycamore tree. Marlin knew from experience, the larger the carcass, the more buzzards that showed up to feast.

He lifted his binoculars but couldn't see what had attracted the birds' interest. He continued his hike.

Sitting in a Denny's in Miami, Lucas had to decide how he was going to approach this whole car business. He needed to dump the Corvette, but he had to be careful how he went about it. You don't just walk right up to somebody and say, "Hey, you wanna buy a stolen car? I'll make you a hell of a deal." They needed the money, though. He didn't have much left, less than a thousand bucks.

Stephanie was having waffles, but she'd eaten just a few bites. She seemed depressed. Or maybe just tired. They hadn't spoken much this morning.

"So, my hair looks okay?" Lucas was no longer a blonde. His hair, according to the package, was now "chestnut brown," and his goatee was coming in quickly. Stephanie had refused to do anything to her appearance.

"Looks fine," she said.

"You all right?"

She nodded and yawned. "Just wanna get there."

They'd covered less than three hundred miles yesterday, mostly because Stephanie had started bitching about riding in the car. She'd wanted to take a break. They could've been in Key West by now, but he didn't bring that up. He managed a smile. "We'll sell the car, then we won't have to worry about nothing." Nothing except money, a place to stay, and a phony ID for him, maybe for her. "It's gonna be great, Steph, I promise." How many times had he told her that in the last three days?

Stephanie picked at her waffles, then stopped. "If we sell the car, how we gonna get to Key West?"

He knew that question would come up, and he'd been trying to think of an answer. There were a couple of possibilities. "I was thinking maybe a bus."

Her face scrunched up. "A bus? We gotta ride a fuckin' bus?"

For the first time, Lucas was starting to get seriously angry. He leaned forward and said, "In case you don't remember, you came along on your own. Nobody forced you."

She laughed sarcastically. "I must've been really drunk."

"Oh, come on, Stephanie. Vance treated you like shit. He wasn't ever gonna marry you, you know that. And the scumbag was *cheating* on you. You don't deserve that kind of crap."

"Yeah, but *I* was cheating on *him,* too. With you." She said it like an accusation. Like it was his fault.

"That was different. That was only 'cause you already knew what he was doing." Lucas knew it sounded lame.

She shook her head and sat in silence.

Lucas could hear dishes clanking back in the kitchen, the sound of a microwave. An old man a few tables away was griping about his eggs to the waitress.

"Man, I bet Vance is royally pissed," Stephanie said.

Lucas had no idea at all how to respond to that.

"Especially since you were working together," she said. "Now he'll have to find someone else."

"He'll be okay." He hated himself for lying.

"And you were making good money. Now what? We're gonna run out of cash sooner or later. Can't use our credit cards, can't write checks."

Lucas knew Stephanie was wavering, ready to change her mind and scrap the whole plan. He just had to get her to Key West before her spirits sank completely. He dug into his pocket and came out with two small tablets, which he placed on the table.

She saw the Ecstasy and her eyes lit up. She even smiled a little.

He said, "I was kind of saving these for a celebration. For when we got there. But I figure we're close enough."

* * *

It was a dead cow, bloated and ripe and stinking in the sun on Marlin's side of the river. He could smell it from fifty yards away.

Here, the river shot straight and true for a good half mile, and Marlin shook his head in frustration. How many more miles was it to Lake Travis? Maybe twenty-five? He couldn't possibly comb the entire length of the Pedernales.

And if the body *had* reached the lake, the odds were really stacked against him. Then he'd have to rely on pure chance, on an observant boater noticing something odd floating in the water, or a fisherman stumbling across a gruesome discovery on the shore.

He looked across the river at Colby, who raised his arms, his body language asking, *What now?*

Marlin pointed back the way they had come. Back to the trucks. It was time to come at this from a different angle, the one that assumed nobody had been in Scofield's SUV after all. Maybe Bobby Garza's intuition was right.

Buford drove slowly past the entrance to Phil Colby's place, the Circle S Ranch. Just doing a little reconnaissance, getting a good look-see. He couldn't spot a house anywhere back there off the road, but he didn't expect to. Place was big, and the house was likely smack in the middle, maybe a mile or two inside the ranch. Could be a challenge.

The radio was playing a Derailers tune, those boys smooth as silk with that mix of Bakersfield, back-to-basics honky-tonk, and a little swing thrown in. But Little Joe was singing along, off key, tone-deaf for sure.

"I figure we'll try this the easy way first," Buford said, working a cigar in his mouth. "Get inside the house and have a look around. Maybe we'll get lucky."

"Works for me."

Buford found a gravel driveway and turned the big Caddy around, cruising past the ranch entrance again.

The tricky part was, how could they get onto the ranch without causing a stir?

"We could say we're deer hunters," Joe said, as if Buford had asked the question out loud. "We already know he leases the place out."

Joe was onto something. The Internet search had revealed all kinds of things about Phil Colby. For one thing, the boy had caused a big ruckus in the hunting community. Colby hated high fences and had sued a man over it. The more Buford had read, the more he was certain they had found their man. Now they just needed to find the negatives.

"Thanks for your help," Marlin said, sitting on the tailgate of his Dodge, uneasy about what he was about to say next. Colby was next to him, sipping from a plastic bottle of Gatorade. It was nearly noon now, the temperature in the upper seventies. A beautiful day, with high cirrus clouds rippling the sky as if a stone had been tossed into still water.

"No prob," Colby said, wiping his mouth with a sleeve. "Sorry we didn't turn anything up."

Marlin started talking before he decided to delay it yet again. "Hey, listen. You remember Max Thayer?"

"Yeah, sure. That warden down in San Antonio. We met up with him at the Spurs game last year."

"Uh-huh. Well, he's retiring."

"Oh, yeah?"

"Yeah, and moving down to Corpus."

"Good for him. He seemed like a really nice guy."

"He is." Marlin paused for just a moment, all raw nerves now, then simply blurted it out. "They're looking for someone to transfer into his place. I'm thinking about putting in for it."

Colby stopped with the bottle halfway to his mouth, his eyes locked on Marlin's. "You gotta be shittin' me."

"Nope. It'd be a promotion to captain. More pay. I'd be in charge of seven counties."

Colby shook his head, staring at Marlin as if he'd just announced that he liked accordion music. "But San Antonio? Living in a big city like that?"

"Not San Antonio. I could live anywhere I wanted in that region, out where it's quiet."

"But what—" A look of realization spread across his face. "This is about the wedding, isn't it?" He laughed.

"No, I've been thinking about this for a long time."

"It was the wedding," Colby repeated. "It brought on some kind of midlife crap, and now, well, now you're fixing to do something really stupid."

"Thanks for your support."

"Man, you don't need my support, you need a shrink. Picking up and moving ain't gonna help."

"I'm burned out, Phil. I need to make a change."

Colby stared at the river.

"My parents are long gone," Marlin said. "I don't have a family. There's nothing keeping me here."

It was the wrong choice of words, and he could immediately see the hurt in Colby's eyes.

"I didn't mean it that way," Marlin said.

Colby shook his head again and drained the last of the Gatorade. He tossed the empty bottle into the bed of Marlin's truck. "Yeah, whatever. I personally think you're insane." He reached for the keys in his front pocket.

"I've been here all my life," Marlin said. "Maybe it's time for me to try something new."

"Yeah, like Prozac," Colby said, then turned for his truck. "I'll catch you later, John. I've got work to do."

Bubba Parker was a mere five minutes away from finishing a transmission job, but he stopped what he was doing because it was seven minutes before twelve. Without exception, he broke for lunch at seven till twelve every day. If there was one thing in

Bubba's life that didn't vary, that was it. Seven minutes gave him just enough time to wash up and get ready.

Today, as always, he wiped the bulk of the grease and oil off his hands with a red shop rag, then went to the restroom sink and scrubbed off the rest. He made his way to his small office in the back of the shop, closed the door, and lowered the blinds in the two large windows facing the hydraulic lifts.

The four employees of Bubba's Foreign and Domestic Auto Repair knew better than to disturb the owner during the next sixty minutes. As far as they knew, Bubba was in there taking his daily nap, and he was as grouchy as a hungry coyote if you bothered him. In fact, Bubba had once fired a guy for knocking on the door during lunch hour, wanting to get Bubba's input on an engine rebuild. Of course, Bubba had rehired the guy the next day, but still, he had made his point. Nobody dared intrude.

In the corner of Bubba's office was a tiny refrigerator, and from it Bubba removed his sack lunch and a Mountain Dew. He sat behind his desk, then opened the top drawer and took out a small set of headphones, which he plugged into the thirteen-inch color TV resting on his desktop.

At precisely twelve o'clock, he turned the TV on.

And there she was, in all her glory.

A goddess among mortals.

The most intriguing and captivating woman on the planet.

Erica Kane.

Boy, was she beautiful, and what an exciting life she'd led! Actress. Model. Discotheque owner. Author. And she'd done it all from the remote little town of Pine Valley.

Yeah, sure, Erica had her problems. She'd been married, what, nine times now? Or was it ten? Let's see, there was Jeff, Phil, Tom, Adam (twice), Travis (also twice), and Dimitri (again, twice). She been engaged a bunch of times, too, sometimes to men who were worthy of her, other times to total sleazeballs. But Erica stood fast and continued to search for her one true love. Erica had had her share of legal troubles, too. She'd been suspected of murdering her boyfriend Kent, which caused her, naturally, to go on the run disguised as a nun, but in the end it was proven that the death was accidental. Later, she went on trial for the attempted murder of her husband Dimitri, but she managed to slip out of that one, too, as well as another trial for the murder of Frankie, the lesbian lover of Erica's daughter Bianca. Then there was that whole nightmare when Erica delivered Maria's baby inside a remote cabin, then attempted to rush the newborn to the hospital but had a horrible wreck along the way. The baby was presumed dead, washed away in the river, but Erica later discovered that it had been found by some deranged lady living in the woods. So Erica did what many women would do in a similar situation; she claimed it as her own, of course. But the cops figured it out and she had to give the baby back. It was all very awkward.

Over the years, Erica had survived rape, a mental breakdown, an abortion, an attempted rape, several miscarriages, addiction to painkillers, emergency cardiac surgery, and the burning of her house by an arsonist. She'd been shot, she'd been stabbed, she'd been kidnapped—and yet, her spirit was still strong and proud. What an amazing woman!

For years, Bubba had been infatuated with Erica.

Enamored.

Totally in awe.

Mesmerized.

That's why he was utterly unprepared when his soon-to-be ex-wife burst through his office door and screamed, "Bubba, what the hell is this?"

She was holding a shoebox, and her face was as contorted and angry as the time she'd found a bra in Bubba's gun case.

Bubba could see a couple of his mechanics looming in the background, outside the office, watching the drama unfold.

He quickly turned the TV off, removed the headphones, and sat up straight in his chair.

"Jesus, Donnelle, you scared the snot out of me. What are—"

"Don't pull no bullshit on me, Bubba. I know it was you, and I want you to know my lawyer is gonna hear all about it. Then we'll see how funny it is."

"What in the world are you—"

"We may be getting divorced, but I never thought you'd sink this low."

"Donnelle, really, if you'd just tell me—"

"Damn it, Bubba!" Her face was so red it was practically glowing. "One more little stunt like this and I'm calling the sheriff's department. And I mean it!"

She tossed the shoebox onto Bubba's desk and stormed out of the office, slamming the door as she went.

Bubba had to sit there for a moment and collect himself, thinking, *What in the hell just happened?* Finally, he slid the shoebox over to his side of the desk, and he could see that someone had written *For Donnelle* in black ink on the lid.

He'd never seen the damn box before in his life.

He opened it.

Inside was a battery-operated vibrator. Ten inches long. Anatomically correct.

Right then, Erica Kane was the last thing on Bubba's mind.

10

PHIL COLBY WAS in his barn, unloading hay from a gooseneck trailer, when he heard a vehicle coming up the road toward the house. He stepped outside and saw an old Cadillac convertible approaching the fork in the road. It paused, then steered to the right, coming toward the barn.

The driver parked and killed the engine, and two men stepped out, dressed like they'd just raided a yard sale.

"Howdy," the driver said. He was tall and slender, smoking a cigar, wearing a hideous baby blue suit covered with silver studs. "You Phil Colby?"

Just then, the other man, shorter, wearing a bowling shirt, bent over and threw up.

The tall one said, "Damn, Bill, you might oughta get back in the car." He looked at Colby. "He ain't been feeling too good. Stomach problem."

The shorter one, Bill, groaned and eased himself back into the Cadillac.

The tall one stepped up. "I'm George Jones."

Colby smiled.

"Yep," Jones said. "Just like the singer."

Colby removed his leather gloves and shook Jones's hand. "I'm Phil Colby. Can I help you with something?"

Jones smiled. "Sorry to barge in, but a man in town told us you had some good hunting out here. We're from Houston, in the area on bidness, and we figured we'd check out a few leases while we was here. Don't mean to intrude."

Phil Colby looked past Jones to the Cadillac. "Your buddy all right? Can I get him some water or something?"

Bill, in the car, waved a hand, saying he was okay.

"He just needs to let it pass, is all," Jones said. "Something in his breakfast, I think."

"Where'd y'all eat?"

"Some Meskin joint in Austin. He won't be eating *migas* again for a while, that's for sure." Jones turned and studied the horizon. "Sure is a pretty place you got here. Lots of deer?"

"We've got a few."

Jones laughed. "I imagine so. I must've seen a hundred on the roadsides early this morning. Hell, that's more'n I'll see in a lifetime over 'round Houston. You lease by the day or by the season?"

"Season."

"You got any openings for this fall?"

"I might have a couple. Don't know yet who's staying on and who isn't."

"You mind me asking how many acres you got?"

"Just over four thousand. I've got the place divided into two pastures, a dozen guns on each pasture."

"How much per gun?"

"Fifteen hundred. That includes hogs, turkeys, and exotics."

"That sounds real good," Jones said, nodding.

The man seemed like a colorful character. Colby figured Jones would fit right in with the bunch that hunted the ranch.

Jones said, "I noticed you got it low-fenced."

"I got no use at all for high fences," Colby said. "If you're looking for that kind of hunting—"

Jones held up a hand. "No, sir, not at all. I wouldn't hunt behind one of them fences myself. Damn things are gonna ruin the sport of hunting."

Colby was liking this guy more and more. "I tell you what, if you want to leave your name and number, I could call you when I know for sure."

"I'll do that," Jones said, nodding again. "Sure would like to lock down a place for the season."

"I hear you."

Now Jones had a hopeful look on his face. "You got another hand working, Mr. Colby? Because what I was hoping—I know you're busy and all—but I was hoping we might be able to take a look around the place this morning. Well, me, anyway. I don't think Bill's quite up to it."

The man's ready to plunk down some money, Colby thought. "No, it's just me." He glanced back at the trailer loaded with hay.

Jones said, "You know, I could help you unload them bales real quick if it'd free up your schedule some. Don't mind at all."

Marlin found Bobby Garza and Bill Tatum drinking coffee in the break room at the sheriff's department. Marlin poured a cup of his own and pulled up a chair.

"Damn, John, you look like you've been chasing pigs," Tatum said.

Marlin's khaki pants were speckled with mud up to his knees. His hiking boots were thoroughly caked.

"Phil and I went back to the river," he said. "Hiked for four hours, all we found was a dead Hereford. Anything from Nicole and Ernie?"

Garza shook his head. "They've done all they can do. We've talked to everybody two or three times now. If Scofield wanted to take a sudden vacation in a car that had been signed over to him, there's not much we can do about it. You know, as a point of fact, no law's been broken so far."

"What about the missing money?" Marlin asked.

Garza shrugged. "Maybe he stuck it in a bank, in spite of what Pritchard said. Now, I'm not saying he didn't steal the car and the money—he probably did—but until he turns up, our options are limited. Even then, with the car legally in his possession, he's on pretty solid ground. Now, if he sold it or wrecked it or blew all the money, then he's looking at some trouble. But even that might have to be worked out in a civil suit."

"What about Stephanie Waring?"

"Hell, who knows? Maybe she's with Scofield, maybe she's not. I'd love to get into her duplex, but we'd need a warrant. No probable cause at this point."

Marlin hated facing these facts, but he knew Garza was right.

"Y'all want to grab some lunch?" Tatum asked.

Marlin nodded, but asked, "Anything new on Lucas?"

Garza said, "You haven't heard yet?"

Marlin had been too consumed by the search for Scofield to keep up with the details on that case, especially since he wasn't directly involved.

Tatum said, "Good news and bad news. The guys from the fire marshal's office overhauled the place yesterday. What we know for sure is that nobody was in the house."

Marlin felt a surge of relief. He knew that a typical house fire, contrary to popular belief, doesn't generate enough heat to completely consume a human body. It's not even close. A wooden structure such as a house or barn burns at well under a thousand degrees. Cremating a body takes close to three thousand degrees, and even then there are bone fragments that remain.

"What's the bad news?" he asked.

"Two things, really. First, it was arson for sure," Tatum said. "They brought one of their dogs along. You ever seen one of them work?"

"No, but I heard they've got one over in Austin."

Darrell Bridges, one of the dispatchers, stuck his head in the room. "Bobby, Rita Sue Metzger is on the line for you. Says you'll want to talk to her."

Garza stood. "This could be interesting. I'll be right back."

Tatum continued. "See, they train the dog to sit when it detects an accelerant. It'll just plop down right there as soon as it smells gas or kerosene or whatever." Tatum smiled. "They brought this black Lab out, hell of a dog, and she was sitting down about every five feet. Whoever did it, man, they just soaked the place with gas. Okay, so later, when they overhauled it, they found the source. Somebody stuck a coffee can full of gas on the electric stove, then turned on the burner and hauled ass. Gave 'em a few minutes to clear out before the place went up. Kind of a crude timing mechanism."

"And the rest of the bad news?" Marlin thought he already knew what it was.

"Meth lab in the back bedroom, just like we thought. Some of the equipment was melted—mostly lines and hoses—but there was enough hardware left over to figure out what was going on. Lucas was using a propane tank, and that's what exploded. And I don't know if I ever told you, but the night the place went up, Ernie found about a hundred empty packages of allergy medicine in the trashcan by the curb. None of us had a clue what the hell that meant, but those fire guys knew right off the bat. See, you can use ephedrine or pseudoephedrine to make speed. It's one of the raw ingredients."

Garza came back into the room, carrying a notepad, not as excited as Marlin had hoped he would be. "Rita Sue said Stephanie left a message on her answering machine about an hour ago. Apparently, Stephanie decided to take a trip to Colorado with a friend."

"But it wasn't Vance Scofield?" Tatum asked.

"If only it were that tidy, but no." Garza glanced down at his notes. "Stephanie didn't give a name, but she said this friend went to visit some of *her* cousins, and Stephanie decided to tag along."

Marlin said. "Does Rita Sue know whether Stephanie was calling on her cell phone?"

"No," Garza said, "but Nicole called that number again this

morning with no answer. Left another message. She'll keep calling. If Stephanie's gotten those messages, I would've expected her to call back by now. Maybe she didn't take her phone with her."

"Does Rita Sue have caller ID?"

"No, I asked her that."

Something else popped into Marlin's mind. "Did y'all ever talk to that girl named Jenny? The one Pritchard told us about?"

"Haven't tracked her down yet," Garza said. "Judging by Scofield's phone records, the two of them hadn't spoken anytime recently. And we couldn't find a number for her anywhere in Scofield's house. We figured if they ever were an item, it was a while ago."

Something wasn't right about all of this, but Marlin couldn't nail it down. A man doesn't simply disappear without somebody knowing something about it. If Scofield hadn't drowned—if he had simply left town with a bunch of cash and a car that wasn't his—he would've left some kind of trail to follow, even a faint one.

"You mind if I give it a shot?" Marlin asked. "Finding Jenny?"

Garza said, "Hell, I wish you would."

"I really appreciate this," Buford said, bouncing along in the passenger seat of Phil Colby's truck, figuring Little Joe was inside the house by now. "I know you got better things to do."

Colby waved him off. "Not a problem. Sorry your friend's feeling bad."

"Aw, he'll be all right. Might be a long ride back to Houston, though."

Buford turned to admire the little lever-action carbine in the gun rack behind Colby's truck seat.

"For snakes," Colby said.

Buford nodded.

"What line of work are y'all in?" Colby asked.

Buford told it straight. "Collections. But I'm trying to get out of that and into the entertainment industry. I manage a few bands. Thinking about starting a record label."

"Country music?"

"Yeah, mostly. Rockabilly, swing, that kind of thing."

Colby checked him out and smiled. "I thought it might be something like that."

"Yeah? Why's that?"

"Well, the way you're dressed."

Buford could feel himself getting hot. Muscles tightening up. "What, you don't like it?"

"No, it's kinda cool. Retro, I guess."

All right, then. This old boy was okay. It even made Buford feel a little guilty for pulling a fast one on him. "How long've you owned this place?"

"It's been in my family for more than a hundred years."

Buford had been raised on the flat, dusty plains of West Texas, where your morning shit was liable to dry up and blow away by lunchtime. Compared to that, the Hill Country was paradise. Rolling hills covered with live oak and cedar, elm and hickory, some madrone trees here and there. Steep ravines dotted with sotol plants and yucca. Seemed like there was water everywhere—springs and creeks and rivers. Buford figured maybe he could own a ranch like this someday, if things went his way. Get a few head of cattle. Stock a big tank with catfish and bass. Kick back and just enjoy life. But first he had to take care of business.

As soon as they drove out of sight, Little Joe stepped from the Cadillac, went straight to the front door of the house, and walked right in. Dumb-ass had left it unlocked.

The place was big, with polished concrete floors and lots of raw cedar beams and posts throughout. There wouldn't be enough time to search the entire house, so Joe did what Buford had told him—he quickly found the master bedroom, the most common hiding spot for valuables. He looked in the closet, under the mattress, beneath the bed, in the chest of drawers. Everywhere. Nothing. They knew it was a long shot that he'd get lucky enough to stumble across the photographs, but if he didn't, he was hoping to discover a safe or a strongbox—something they could come back and break into later.

He checked his watch. Ten minutes had gone by. Not to worry yet, because Buford had figured out a way to warn him.

Joe went down the hallway, through the living room, and into the den on the other side of the house. Colby's office, from the looks of it. Nice and neat, which would make things easier. He sorted through the desk drawers and quickly found a bank pouch, the kind that zips across the top. No photographs inside, but about six hundred dollars in cash. Damn! Buford had told him not to steal anything at all, but it was sure as hell tempting. He tucked it back into the drawer untouched and resumed his search.

He turned to a massive glass gun cabinet next to the fireplace. Joe was impressed. Colby had a nice collection, ranging from Rugers to Remingtons to Sakos. Mostly hunting rifles, but a couple of shotguns in there, too. Pistols hung on pegs on the side walls of the cabinet. Probably twenty grand worth of hardware in there. Joe would have to remember that. Who knew when he might get a chance to come back later? At the bottom of the case, beneath the guns, was a drawer. Joe opened it but found nothing in there except ammo, cleaning supplies, reloading equipment, and that kind of crap.

He checked his watch. Twenty minutes had gone by.

Where, where, where? Where would Colby hide the damn negatives? Christ, there were a million possibilities. The attic, the garage, the barn. Hell, if the man had any brains at all, he'd have them tucked into a safe-deposit box at a bank. Shit, Joe had forgotten to check the bank statements to see if Colby had a safe-deposit box. He went back over to the desk and dug into the second drawer again. In a manila envelope, there was a year's worth of statements, the most recent one right on top. It looked like Colby had two business accounts—checking and savings—for the Circle S Ranch, but these were bare bones. No overdraft protection, no line of credit, nothing like that, and no safe-deposit box as far as Joe could tell. He looked for other statements, maybe from another bank. Zilch. He remembered seeing a key ring in the shallow drawer in the middle, so he pulled it out and took a look. Ten or twelve keys on there, but none that looked like a bank key.

Christ, now thirty minutes had passed. Obviously Buford was having pretty good luck keeping Colby occupied, but it made Joe a little nervous. He raced to the front door again and peeked out. No sign of Colby's truck. He stepped out the front door for a look at the barn, a hundred yards away. No truck there, either. Just Buford's Caddy.

He darted back inside and went to search the other bedrooms.

"That's pretty much all of it," Phil Colby said.

"That was quick. We've covered the whole place already?"

"All except for one little pasture in the northeast corner."

Buford knew he shouldn't get too pushy. Man might get suspicious. Besides, Joe had been inside the house for forty-five minutes. If he hadn't found the photos by now, a few extra minutes wouldn't help.

They'd seen plenty of deer, all right. Dozens of them, bouncing away in the tall grasses, tails like surrender flags. Does and fawns everywhere. Bucks with growing antlers. Along the way, Buford had to remind himself to act excited, to ask questions that a hunter might ask.

"You ever have any problem with trespassers?" he asked now. "Poachers?"

"Naw, not really. No more'n anyplace else."

"Could we stop for a sec? I've gotta take a leak."

"Oh, yeah, sure."

Colby brought the truck to a halt, and Buford stepped out. He'd recognized a few landmarks and knew they were within a half mile of Colby's house. He relieved himself, and now it was time to give Little Joe the signal.

He pulled his cell phone from his jacket. "You mind if I make a call real quick? Kinda hard to hear when we're driving."

"Go right ahead."

Joe didn't have a cell phone, so Buford would call Colby's home phone and let it ring one time. That was the warning. When Joe heard it, he knew to get the hell out, no matter what he was doing.

Buford flipped his cell phone open.

He saw that the battery was dead.

Oh, son of a bitch.

Phil Colby dropped the truck into gear.

Buford was getting good and pissed at himself. Damn stupid mistake to make. Like a friggin' amateur. Sure, he'd known it might come to a point where they'd have to get right in Colby's face, probably put the hurt on him. He didn't want to just blunder into it, though. He wanted to plan this shit out right, do it on his own terms, because something told him it would take more than a good push to turn this guy. Colby seemed friendly enough, but you could tell he had backbone. Buford had dealt with enough men that he'd learned how to size them up pretty good. This man would be a fighter, Buford had no doubt. Built solid as hell, too, muscles hard from ranch work. Strong, scarred hands.

He could see Colby's barn coming up now, the house back behind it.

"When are y'all heading back to Houston?" Colby asked.

"This afternoon."

"I can mail you a copy of the lease if something opens up."

"That'd be just fine. I'll fill it out and drop a check in the mail."

Buford reached into the pocket of his jacket and wrapped his hand around the little snub-nosed .38. A throwaway. Something he'd bought from a guy after a gun show. No forms to fill out, no names exchanged.

They were getting close. No sign of Little Joe popping his head up in the car window.

Buford was starting to get a bad feeling.

Getting close now, the barn blocking out the house behind it.

He used his thumb to take the gun off safety.

He'd already decided that if this went south, it might be best to take Colby away from the ranch. Maybe even drive him all the way back to Buford's place outside Fort Worth, where he could work on him real good. Wasn't but a four-hour drive.

Why was he feeling so damn nervous? Was it that steely look Colby sometimes had in his eyes? The one that said he was a lot more dangerous than the scum Buford usually dealt with? Sure as hell had something to do with it.

Colby pulled up next to the Caddy and parked.

Still no Joe showing.

"Where's your buddy?" Colby asked.

Buford tried to look puzzled. He had a feeble idea. "I guess he mighta went to use your bathroom or something."

That turned Colby's head, and Buford could tell the man didn't like the idea of a stranger in his home. Even in Texas, the land of hospitality, and even with Joe's "sickness" as an excuse, entering Colby's house uninvited would really be pushing it. Might even make Colby realize it was all a setup.

Buford said, "Ordinarily he wouldn't do something like that, but he was feeling pretty sorry. I hope you won't take any offense."

Colby didn't say a word, just stepped from his truck and peered into the Cadillac, front seat and back. He shook his head, starting to look peeved.

Buford pulled the .38 from his jacket and climbed out of the truck, keeping the gun low where Colby couldn't see it. He had two choices: Take Colby now. Or walk with him to the house and see how bad the situation was. Colby would likely catch Joe rooting through a desk drawer or rummaging through a closet, and then all hell would break loose.

No, it was better to go ahead and get it over with. Do it now.

Colby started walking toward the house.

Buford came around the truck, his revolver leveled.

He was about to call out to the man. Better yet, fire a round down by his feet. Start out real strong with a tough old boy like Colby. That's the way to do it.

His finger tightened on the trigger.

Then Buford heard a retching sound coming from the barn.

Colby turned quickly, but Buford managed to slide the gun back into his pocket.

Little Joe came staggering out of the barn, covered with hay, looking exactly like he'd been taking a nap. "Damn car was like an oven," Joe said. "Mr. Colby, you suppose I could bother you for some ice water?"

11

LUCAS WASN'T SURE he'd ever seen an actual Cuban before, not face-to-face, but he was pretty sure the guy behind the desk wasn't a Mexican. Lucas had heard a lot about all the Cubans down here, so he assumed that's what the man was. Something about the tone of his skin seemed different than the Mexicans back home.

Then again, it might've been due to the fact that Lucas was flying on Ecstasy and his senses were a tad short-circuited at the moment. *Unwise to attempt to sell a stolen car when blitzed on hallucinogenics?* Probably. But right now it seemed kind of funny. Lucas couldn't quit smiling.

The name tag on the man's shirt said ENRIQUE. And since the small, run-down shop had a sign out front that said ENRIQUE'S PAINT & BODY, Lucas quickly deduced that he'd found the owner. Pretty good luck, right off the bat. Two other men, both short and dark-skinned, were eating lunch at a coffee table farther back in the room. They were watching Lucas and eating something with their hands.

"Help you?" Enrique asked.

The Corvette was parked in the side lot at a convenience store two blocks away, Stephanie waiting inside. With the doors locked. It was that kind of neighborhood.

"Yeah, uh, I was wondering . . . do you ever buy any cars here?" Lucas was trying his best to be smooth, but he wasn't sure it was working out all that well.

Enrique leaned back in his chair and studied Lucas for thirty minutes. Or it might've been three seconds. "What kine of car?" he finally said.

That was promising. If Enrique wasn't a buyer, why would he even bother asking? "It's, uh, a Corvette."

"Wha' year?"

Good question, Lucas thought. It was this year's model, right? He couldn't get his thoughts straight. "Nearly brand-new. Two thousand miles on the odometer."

"Why do you sell it?"

Another good question. And now Lucas had to do a tap dance around the facts. He didn't want to come right out and say it was stolen, just in case Enrique ran a legit shop. So he had a line all prepared. "I don't have the title," he said, and let it hang there in the air. Surely Enrique would understand what that meant. *I don't have the title because I don't own the car.*

"Brand-new Corvette," Enrique said. "But no title?" The other two men stopped eating and seemed to be studying Lucas with a newfound respect. "Where is this car?"

"Right around the corner," Lucas said.

"Okay, you bring it in and we—"

"Uh-uh. We make the deal right now."

Enrique frowned, as if Lucas had just spit on the floor.

"The car is perfect," Lucas said. "No scratches, no dents, never been wrecked. Just like the showroom. You can see it before you buy it, but we make the deal first." Lucas didn't want to park the

Corvette in front of the shop and then have Enrique pull some sort of stunt.

Enrique pondered Lucas's proposition for a minute or two. "Do you have the keys?" he asked.

Lucas knew what that question really meant: *Is the steering column broken? Was the car damaged when it was stolen?*

Lucas pulled the keys from his pocket and dangled them from one finger.

Enrique held out a palm, and Lucas tossed them over. Enrique grinned. Then he pulled a small yellow booklet from his desk drawer and thumbed through it. Half a minute later, he said, "If this car is in perfeck shape, I give you five thousand dollars in cash."

Five thousand dollars? Christ, the car was worth ten times that much. Yeah, it was stolen, but even without the title it had to be worth more than that.

Enrique must have seen the look of uncertainty on Lucas's face, because he nodded toward the telephone on his desk and said, "You know, you must be careful in a car like that. Someone might call the police on you. You never know."

Suddenly Lucas realized how stupid he had been to hand over the keys. He'd set himself up to be screwed, and there wasn't a damn thing he could do about it. It was the Ecstasy. He knew he wouldn't have made such a dumb mistake if he had been straight.

He also knew he wouldn't have had the balls to push back, as he did now. "I'm gonna need some new wheels," he said. "Something decent to drive, on top of the five grand."

Enrique rubbed the little goatee on his chin, then looked back at his buddies. All three of them laughed in unison, shaking their heads at this gringo who wanted so much. Enrique turned back around, saying, "Okay, my frien', we have a deal."

Back on the fencing job, Red waited until lunchtime, when they were all sitting in the shade, before he brought it up. He timed it right, too. When Billy Don struggled to his feet to get another quart of cold Dr Pepper from the truck, that left just Red, Jack Chambers, and Jorge sitting there—and Jorge couldn't hardly speak the king's English anyway. So Red said, "How'd she look?"

Jack, with his mouth full of bologna, said, "Who?"

"Loretta." Red tried to make it sound casual. "The other night."

"Oh, you know, the same, I guess."

"Still lookin' good, then."

Jack stopped chewing for a second. "Hey, different strokes."

Red wondered what that was supposed to mean. Well, it didn't matter. Not everyone agreed on what made a woman pretty. It reminded him of something his daddy used to say. *Beauty is only skin deep, son, but ugly goes clean to the bone.*

"You talk to her?" Red asked.

"Naw, just saw her across the room is all."

"She with anybody?"

"Didn't appear to be."

"Just sitting there, huh. Drinking a beer?"

"Yeah, and smoking."

"Boy, that sounds like Loretta." A stupid thing to say, really. It sounded like most of the women Red had ever met who hung out in bars. What else were they going to do? Drink and smoke, maybe shoot some pool. Except Loretta didn't play much pool on account of one arm being shorter than the other. Plus, she always had to squint that lazy eye shut and it gave her a headache.

Billy Don was coming back now, chugging his soft drink, so Red decided he'd asked enough questions. Didn't learn anything useful at all. Then Red remembered a question he should've asked. *What was Loretta smoking, a cigarette or a cigar?* It'd be a dead sure tip-off if the woman Jack had seen was smoking a cigar, because that was what Loretta preferred. Swisher Sweets. In fact, as far as Red was concerned, the smell of a good stogie was as intoxicating as the finest perfume.

Lucas was driving a twelve-year-old Honda Civic not much nicer than his ratty Toyota back home. One hundred and ninety thousand miles on the odometer. The dash was cracked, the seats were torn, and the whole car smelled like mildew. But it felt solid. The engine purred, the clutch was smooth, and there wasn't any smoke from the exhaust. Even the inspection sticker was up to date.

Enrique was in the passenger seat, an envelope thick with cash in his hand. Lucas had counted the money back at the body shop, and he'd been keeping an eye on the envelope ever since. He wasn't falling for any damn switcheroo.

He pulled into the side lot at the convenience store and parked between the Corvette and a Dumpster. Stephanie looked over, and she was already making a face about the car he was driving. Christ, was he going to catch heat about the Honda?

Without a word, Enrique got out and walked around the Corvette, studying it. Meanwhile, Stephanie exited the Corvette and came over to the Honda with her small suitcase in hand. She still had a grimace on her face. Lucas noticed that she had her cell phone in her hand. "Damn, Stephanie, you're not using that, are you?"

Enrique stepped up next to the driver's window and held out the envelope. Lucas took it and looked inside. The cash was there. He stepped out, popped the Corvette's trunk, removed his suitcase, then handed the keys to Enrique for the second time. The Cuban slipped inside the sports car, fired it up, and backed out. He squealed the tires as he left the lot.

Lucas got back into the Honda. Stephanie was still holding her phone.

"Stephanie!" Lucas snapped. "Tell me you didn't call anyone."

She shook her head and started to cry. Lucas was starting to wonder if she was having a bad trip on the Ecstasy.

"No," she said. "They called me. I just checked my voicemail."

"Who called you? Who?"

She was actually trembling. "The cops from Blanco. They called three times."

Lucas's heart sank. More than anything, he had wanted to keep Stephanie out of all this. The cops weren't supposed to figure out where she was or what she was doing. Then again, maybe they hadn't. Lucas tried to remain calm. "What did they say?"

"Nothing. They just said I was supposed to call them."

Lucas grabbed the phone from her hand, getting angry now. "You weren't supposed to bring this, remember? You can't make any calls because they can track where we are. Remember?"

Stephanie nodded, tears running down her cheeks.

Lucas leaned out his window and threw the phone into the Dumpster.

John Marlin was a state employee, but his office was located in the county building that housed the sheriff's department. After lunch, he closed his office door and was preparing to make some calls when Darrell, the dispatcher, put Howell Rogers through.

"How the hell are ya, Howell?" Marlin asked. Rogers was one of the old-time game wardens, in his midsixties and still as tough as an old boot. He'd been nailing poachers in Burnet County, just north of Blanco County, since Marlin was a boy. Rogers had been friends with Marlin's father, who had also been a game warden.

"Doing great, Johnny. I hear you're keeping busy."

"As always." Marlin quickly brought him up to speed on the Scofield investigation.

"I might have something for you on that," Rogers said. "It may be nothing, but I figured I'd share it."

Marlin's ears perked up. Howell had provided critical information in plenty of cases in the past. "What's up?"

"It took me a while to place that name, Scofield, but this morning I sorted it out. Remember when I gave you a hand in January?"

"Yeah, sure."

Near the end of the last deer season, there had been a particularly high number of poaching calls in Blanco County—more than Marlin could handle alone. Rogers had responded to several of them at Marlin's request. A common courtesy among game wardens.

"Well, if you recall, one of those calls was to a ranch out on Yeager Creek Road. I get there, and the landowner—man named Chuck Hamm—you know him?"

"I've been to his place a couple of times. Never any problems out there."

"Runs that Wallhangers Club."

"Right."

"Anyway, I get there and Hamm is hopping mad, saying this guy Scofield was out there with another guy—man named Pritchard?"

"Yeah, that's Scofield's lawyer."

"What the problem was, Pritchard had shot one of Hamm's best bucks. So I separate the men and get the story. Apparently, Pritchard had done some legal work for the club through Scofield or something, so Hamm was gonna let him do a little hunting. But Pritchard was supposed to take an eight-point or smaller." Rogers was starting to chuckle. "Turns out he wasn't a hunter and didn't know what the hell he was doing. He ended up shooting a fourteen-pointer, and damn was it a fine buck. I'm talking massive. Hamm was furious. Started hollering that Pritchard was Scofield's guest, so Scofield owed him twenty thousand dollars. Scofield was getting just as mad, saying it was an honest mistake. They went back and forth for a while like that."

"What'd Pritchard say?"

"He more or less stayed out of it. Just looked embarrassed as hell."

"So how'd it end up?"

"Hell, you know, the money issue—that was up to them to figure out, not me. But I didn't want to see these two hotheads shoot each other, so I stuck around until they cooled off. Last thing I knew, they agreed to work it out themselves. But, like you were just saying, if Scofield took off because of money troubles, I guess this fits right in, huh?"

"Yeah. Yeah, it does."

Marlin thanked Howell for the information and hung up. Then he thumbed through the yellow pages in the Austin phone book. He flipped to the heading MODELING AGENCIES, deciding it was as good a place to start as any. There were fewer than a dozen listings, so he chose a number at random and dialed it.

A woman who sounded about fifteen years old answered

the phone. Marlin explained who he was trying to locate.

"I think you might want to try one of the other agencies," the woman said with a mild laugh. "We don't offer that sort of service here."

He thanked her, then tried a second number. Again, it was answered by a young woman, but this time it was a recording:

Hi there. Thanks for calling Touch of Class. For discreet and pleasurable lingerie modeling in the comfort of your own home or hotel room, please leave a message at the tone. I'll return your call as soon as possible.

Marlin smiled and told the machine to have a nice day.

Okay, so some of these "agencies" offered services beyond what one might consider traditional modeling. That explained why the first woman had giggled. Judging by the names of the companies, Marlin realized he could delete five of them.

He tried two more numbers and found that they had been disconnected.

Finally, at a place called Image Makers, a man named Bob answered the phone. Again, Marlin identified himself and explained the situation.

"Can't help you," Bob said, "but you might want to call some party planners instead. That's more up their alley."

Marlin thanked Bob and returned to the phone book, looking under the heading PARTY PLANNING. There were more than a hundred listings, so Marlin chose a company that specialized in "Las Vegas style events." It just felt right, considering the way some of the casino employees in Vegas dressed. Young attractive women in revealing outfits.

Marlin had his patter down to a routine now, so he quickly told the woman who answered what he was trying to find out.

"There's a man named Sid Smith who specializes in that sort of thing," she said. "If you'll hang on I'll find his number."

Thirty seconds later, Marlin was dialing again, and when Sid answered ("Yo, this is Sid"), it sounded like a cell phone connection.

Sid had the flat, distorted inflections of a Texas native trying to sound like a player from the West Coast.

Marlin, on autopilot now, told Sid he was looking for a woman named Jenny Geller or Gilmer.

"I know a Jenny Geiger. She does some work for me now and then."

Marlin's ears perked up. Was it the same woman? "Did you ever send her to work for a man named Vance Scofield?"

"Name doesn't ring a bell, chief."

"The job was selling tickets for a Rotary Club raffle."

Sid laughed. "Not one of my jobs, that's for sure. I only deal in high-end appearances, minimum fee of a thousand bucks a girl. Mostly for the black-tie crowd. Benefits, fund-raisers, that kind of thing."

Marlin heard a car horn. He could picture Sid driving a sports car in downtown Austin, wearing pointy-toed boots and one of those trendy silk shirts buttoned all the way up to the neckline. Marlin said, "But Jenny could've arranged it on her own, right? Or through another agency?"

"Yeah, I guess, if she's lowered her standards."

"Is Jenny Geiger in her early twenties?" Marlin asked. "Nice-looking, maybe five-ten?"

Sid snorted. "They're all tall and good-looking."

There was a beep on the phone line. Darrell was attempting to come through on the intercom.

"Brunette?" Marlin asked.

"Yeah."

"Blue eyes?"

"I don't know, maybe," Sid said. "Big jugs?"

"Well, yeah."

"Sounds like the same Jenny. You want her number?"

According to Sid, Jenny Geiger lived in an apartment on the south side of Austin. She was attending Austin Community College, studying marketing, paying her way through as a cocktail waitress, income that she supplemented by occasionally working for Sid.

Marlin dialed the number and got an answering machine:

Hi, it's Jenny. I'm gone until Saturday, but leave a message and I'll get back to you. Have a great day!

As Marlin was listening to the recording, Darrell knocked and poked his head into Marlin's office. There was a beep on the woman's machine. Marlin waved the dispatcher in and said, "Hi, Miss Geiger, my name is John Marlin, and I'm the game warden in Blanco County. If you could give me a—"

He stopped in midsentence. Darrell had just slid a note onto Marlin's desk: *Body found in the Pedernales.*

Marlin hung up without finishing the voicemail.

12

HE TOOK HIS truck north on Highway 281, Nicole Brooks riding along beside him. When Marlin had told Garza and Tatum the news, Garza had said, "Take Brooks with you. I want to see how she handles herself."

Now, in the truck, Nicole's first words were "Got stuck with the new kid on the block, huh?"

Marlin looked over at her. "Makes no difference to me. I imagine you saw plenty in Mason County." He realized how silly that sounded. Mason County was as quiet and relatively crime-free as Blanco County. She didn't seem to notice.

They drove in silence through the tiny town of Round Mountain, then, just south of Marble Falls, he swung the truck southeast on Highway 71.

"How long have you been in Blanco County?" Nicole asked.

"All my life."

Marlin cracked a window. Only April, and already it was damn warm outside. Humid, too. "How about you?" he asked.

"Six weeks," she said, sounding puzzled.

"No, I mean, where're you from?"

"Born in Seguin, but I've lived all over the state. I was with the department in Mason County for seven years. Before that, my first job was up in Amarillo for five years."

Twelve years on the job, Marlin thought.

"I'm thirty-five," Nicole said, "if that's what you're wondering."

"No, I wasn't trying—"

"Let me ask you something, and please don't take this the wrong way. Did I do something to piss you off?"

The question caught Marlin off guard. "What? Not at all. Why would you ask that?"

She seemed to consider her words carefully. "When I first got here, for a week or two, we seemed to have a pretty good rapport. Joking around and stuff. But since then—it's like you've been avoiding me." She laughed. "Or maybe I'm just being paranoid."

He could feel her looking at him, but he kept his eyes on the road. She was damn sharp. "I think that's probably it," he said. The alternative was telling her the complete truth. That he had been very attracted to her right from the start. That he had been considering asking her out, until that day in the Super S, when he had stopped to pick up a few groceries. That's when he had seen Nicole and Ernie Turpin shopping together. Ernie—young, single, and handsome—had already made his move.

"So I haven't done anything to get us off on the wrong foot?" she asked.

"Absolutely not."

A mile went by slowly.

"Okay, that makes me feel better," Nicole said.

Another mile, and then she said, "Heard you went to Dallas."

"Yeah, last weekend."

"You have a special friend up there?" She was using the same tone she had used when he'd been holding Stephanie Waring's photograph. Teasing him.

"Well . . . no. Kind of. Long story, but I was up there for a wedding."

Nicole gave him an appraising look but didn't respond.

Ten minutes later, now in western Travis County, Marlin turned left on FM 2322, the road to Pace Bend Park (known to longtime locals as Paleface Park) on Lake Travis.

There was a quiet little community out here called Briarcliff, with an eclectic variety of homes nestled in cedars and live oaks, some of the houses widely spaced along a ragtag nine-hole golf course once owned by Willie Nelson. Marlin seemed to remember that Willie still owned a recording studio out here somewhere. Or maybe he sold it. Hard to keep track, considering Willie's troubles with the IRS back in the nineties.

Three miles later, near the entrance into Briarcliff, Marlin went left on Old Ferry Road, which paralleled several miles of the Pedernales as it made a few more abrupt twists before it reached the lake.

Down in this quiet rural area—that's where the body was found. Stuck under a fishing dock, according to Mike Werner, one of four game wardens in densely populated Travis County. Marlin had known Werner since their days together at the academy.

Marlin matched a mailbox to the address he was given and turned down a winding dirt driveway. He followed it for two hundred yards and came to a rustic stone cabin sitting on a bluff above the river. No deputies' cruisers or other county vehicles on site yet, just a small sedan, probably the homeowner's.

Marlin and Nicole stepped from his truck and made their way to the back of the house, where they could see down to the river. Below, two figures were on the riverbank, standing beside a body on a tarp. A Parks and Wildlife boat was tied to a small dock.

Marlin led the way down the heavily treed slope on a rugged switchback path where the dirt was packed hard and worn smooth, dry as a bone, even after the rain earlier in the week. Mike Werner saw them coming and met them at the foot of the path. Werner was a slender man with a rambunctious sense of humor, but today he looked stone-faced.

"Thanks for coming, John," he said, extending his hand. He introduced himself to Nicole. "I'm pretty sure it's your man," he said to both of them. "Judging by the height, weight, age, all that. No other missing-persons reports in the area, so . . ."

The landowner, a paunchy, bespectacled man in his fifties, appeared at Werner's elbow. He was pale. "Are you all done with me for now?" he asked. "I'd just as soon go back up to the house."

"That's fine, Mr. Ritts," Werner responded. "Thanks for calling it in. There'll be some deputies here soon, some detectives, too, and someone from the medical examiner's office. They'll have some questions."

Ritts nodded and headed up the hill.

As the men walked toward the corpse, Marlin saw that Ritts had covered the head with a towel. The rest of the body—stripped of clothes by the violent floodwaters—was heavily scratched and abraded, coated with a thin layer of mud. Werner said, "Mr. Ritts pulled him out of the water. I haven't touched him. No signs of trauma that I could see, beyond what the river did to him."

Werner bent and removed the towel that was covering the head. Marlin found himself staring at the face he was having trouble remembering just a few days ago. He'd seen pictures since then, though, and even with the bloating and the beginnings of decomposition, it was clearly Vance Scofield.

Driving the Honda, with Stephanie sleeping again, Lucas was able to calm down and think a little more clearly. Now that the damn Ecstasy had cleared out of his system.

It made perfect sense that the cops would try to contact Stephanie. No matter where they thought she went or what she was supposedly doing, they'd want to talk to her. After all, she dated Vance. They'd be able to find that out pretty quickly. So that's probably all it was—they wanted to question her. She probably wasn't a suspect at all.

But what would happen when she didn't come home? What would they think then? Would they think she did it?

All of this mess for a scumbag like Vance.

Lucas remembered a conversation he'd had with Vance late one night, the only time he'd really ever talked with the guy one on one. He and Stephanie had partied with Vance in Austin, and afterward they'd crashed at his place. Well, Stephanie had crashed, but Lucas and Vance had stayed up until sunrise drinking.

"I'm thinking about staying with Stephanie for a little while," Lucas had said, testing the waters. "Until I can find a cheaper place to live. Place I'm living at now, the rent's too high."

"Yeah, really?" Vance answered. "That's cool." Then his eyes narrowed. "You're not banging her, are you?"

Before Lucas could say, *Hey, we're just good friends,* Vance let out this big laugh, letting Lucas know he was only kidding. "Just fucking with you, dude," he said.

Har de har har.

At the time, it made Lucas want to punch Vance in the face.

Now it just made him feel queasy.

13

IT WAS ABOUT eight o'clock that night when she came into the bar, and for a second, Red thought his knees were going to buckle. He got a funny feeling in his belly and he had to lean on his pool stick for support.

She was just as pretty as he remembered—hair the color of smoked sausage, wearing an oversized Dallas Cowboys T-shirt, stirrup pants, plenty of makeup to cover the fine dark hairs that grew along her jawline. She was a sight for drunk eyes.

Then she passed right by the pool table, looking for a place to sit.

That's when Red realized it wasn't Loretta at all. The gal looked almost exactly like his wife or ex-wife or whatever she was, but it simply was not her.

About then, Billy Don slammed the eight ball into the corner pocket and looked up to gloat, but Red couldn't take his eyes off the woman, now seated at the bar.

Billy Don saw who he was looking at and said, "Hey, Red."

Red said, "Yeah, I know."

Billy Don stood next to him. Red glanced over and saw a look of total disappointment on the big man's face. "Ain't her, is it?" Billy Don asked.

"Nope."

"Looks like her, though."

"Sure enough does."

This woman had a different way of sitting. Loretta was always hunched over, like the world had beaten her down. This new gal sat up straight, with her chin out, like she could handle anything that came her way.

"Just as purty," Billy Don said softly.

"You think?"

"Don't you?"

Just then, the woman looked up from her beer and scanned the smoky room. Her eyes came to rest on Red and Billy Don, and she gave them a knowing smile, the kind that said, *Yeah, I've met a million guys just like y'all.* Then she looked away and lit a cigarette.

"Damn sure is," Red said.

Billy Don broke the moment, digging into his pocket, coming out with some quarters. He held them out to Red. "Loser racks."

Red should've known what Billy Don was up to. He should've remembered that the loser pays, too, and that Billy Don wouldn't normally part with that money any more than he'd part with a bucket of fried chicken.

But Red wasn't thinking clearly. He took the coins and bent down to insert them into the little slots. He pushed the tray in and the balls came tumbling down into the trough at the end of the pool table. When Red stood up, he realized his mistake.

Billy Don was already across the room, leaning against the bar, talking to the gal who looked just like Loretta.

* * *

Lucille saw the two scruffy pool players checking her out, and she knew they'd be heading her way shortly. Sure enough, less than a minute later, she heard a voice at her elbow.

"Howdy. My name's Billy Don."

She turned to look, and Lord, the man was as big as an outhouse. The smell, to be honest, came pretty close, too. She gave him a cool nod, hoping he'd take the hint and leave her alone.

But he didn't.

"Buy you a drink?" he asked. "What you got there, a beer?"

A real rocket scientist.

"It don't look like vodka, does it?" she said.

Billy Don laughed and sat on the stool to Lucille's left. "No, ma'am, it don't. Hey, Sylvia," he called to the bartender, "can we get a couple beers?"

Now the other pool player—the smaller one—showed up, nestling in to Lucille's right. "This big ol' boy bothering you, miss? 'Cause if he is, I'll make some calls and get his parole revoked."

"He's just funnin' with you," Billy Don said. "You been skipping your AA meetings, Red?"

"That's hilarious, Billy Don, but I'm afraid your medication ain't doing its job."

"Speaking of medication," Billy Don said, "how's that Viagra working out?"

"Whyn't you call your mama and ask her?"

"I think I'd have to call your mama too for a full report."

Lucille didn't know if this was some stupid routine the two had worked out, thinking it was cute, or if they really were this annoying.

Sylvia slid two large mugs of beer onto the bar, and Billy Don removed his wallet, which was chained to his belt. But the smaller one beat him to it, plunking a twenty down. "One for me, too, Sylvia. And keep the change, darlin'." He returned his attention to Lucille. "Now where were we?"

"You was telling us how you can't get it up too good," said Billy Don.

"Only when the wind blows," said Red.

"Speaking of blowing—"

Lucille held her hands up and said, "If y'all keep it up, I'm gonna have to smack you both. Honestly, you're giving me a headache. Now, if you wanna drink some beer, sit down and do it quietly. But if you're gonna keep this bullshit up, do me a favor and take it outside."

There was a pause, then the big one said, "I think I'm in love."

"I saw her first," replied the smaller one. He leaned in and said, "I'm Red O'Brien. Who might you be?"

When Marlin got home, he called some of the volunteers from the Blanco County Search and Rescue Team to let them know Scofield had been found. Then he called David Pritchard, figuring the Rotarian had probably already heard anyway. News crews had shown up at the scene just minutes after the Travis County homicide detectives, shooting footage from boats on the Pedernales River. Bill Tatum had sent Ernie Turpin to inform Scofield's father hours earlier, so Marlin felt comfortable relaying the facts to Pritchard. The homicide team had examined the scene and the body carefully, and the unofficial conclusion, pending the Travis County medical examiner's report, was that it had been an accident.

"Christ, what a waste," Pritchard said. "I guess he drowned then?"

"Looks that way, but I can't say for sure at this point. Not until the autopsy."

"Now I feel kind of stupid," Pritchard said. "Implying that he might've taken off in the car. The drugs and all that."

"No, you did the right thing," Marlin said. "Don't doubt yourself for a second."

Pritchard sighed. "I can't figure how Vance got himself into trouble like that. He's lived along that river long enough to know how dangerous it is."

Not if he was as high as a kite, Marlin thought. Marlin figured the autopsy would show that Scofield had drowned, but it would b everal days before toxicology reports revealed whether he had een doped up at the time. "People make mistakes," he said. "The vater can be hard to judge, especially at night." In Marlin's experince, it was the people who crossed through high water on a regular asis who most often got swept away. They became comfortable aking risks until they took a fatal one.

Pritchard said, "I don't mean to be a complete jerk asking this ight now, but any clue about the Corvette?"

That was the one thing that still bothered Marlin. How had he Corvette disappeared? He supposed it was still possible that cofield had moved it to another location and Pritchard simply lidn't know it.

But it also nagged at him that Stephanie Waring happened o leave town at the same time the car went missing. Then again, ccording to Nicole, Stephanie couldn't drive a stick shift. "We alked to the dealership," Marlin said, "and now we're listing it as tolen."

"Aw, crap," Pritchard muttered. "That's really gonna screw up ur ticket sales."

Marlin started to say good-bye, but instead he said, "Hey, tell ne about this little hunting expedition out at Chuck Hamm's lace."

Pritchard groaned. "Boy, was that a mess. I shot the wrong leer, I guess, and Chuck was really mad about it."

"Mad at you?"

"At Vance. He was sitting in the blind with me and was suposed to tell me which deer to shoot. He pointed one out, but I uess I screwed up and shot the wrong one. I tried to tell Chuck it vas my fault, but he kept blaming Vance. Weird, huh?"

Marlin didn't find it unusual at all. When an experienced unter guides a beginner, most ranch owners place the responsiility for the hunt squarely on the guide's shoulders. "How did you nd up hunting out there?"

"Vance got sued because of this high fence he wanted to build.)h, wait—look who I'm talking to. You probably know all about he lawsuit."

"Yeah, I'm familiar with it."

"Okay, so you know that the suit could've set a precedent against high fences."

"Yeah."

"Well, Vance talked to some of the board members of his hunting club—I guess they figured it was an important case—and they all decided to pitch in. They also gave me a free hunt on each of their ranches, not that I really cared about hunting." Pritchard let out a rueful laugh. "In fact, out at Chuck's ranch, that was the first time I ever hunted. It was also the last. I don't want to get involved with that kind of fiasco again."

It took several hours and multiple tequila shots to get the woman named Lucille to warm up a little, but she finally came around. In fact, Red noticed, once they got her to talking, they couldn't hardly get her to shut up. She'd told them where she was from originally (Dallas) and how many times she'd been married (three). She said she was a home health aide (which was something like a nurse, as far as Red could tell, except she worked at people's homes instead of at a hospital). She told them what kind of car she drove (a rusty Cutlass Ciera with a bad transmission), why she liked unfiltered cigarettes better than filtered (that extra little kick), and how to cut up an onion without crying (wear swimmer's goggles).

Later, they'd moved to a table in the back, and now they were all laughing, singing along to the jukebox whenever an old George Jones or Johnny Cash song came on, having a good time in general. That's why Red, with a belly full of beer, finally spoke up and said what was on his mind.

"You know, Lucy . . . you mind if I call you Lucy?"

The woman made a funny little twirling gesture with her cigarette and said, "Whatever boats your float." Red could tell she was as drunk as he was.

"You know," he said, "you might could tell that me and Billy Don had our eyes on you earlier. Back when you first came in. D'you see us starin' at ya?"

She nodded. "Hard to miss. You boys ain't too subtle."

"Yeah, well, we wasn't meaning to be impolite or nothin'," Red said. "See, you're purty and all, but the truth is, that ain't the only reason we was looking at ya. The facts is, you look almost zackly like my ex-wife. Billy Don's ex-wife, too, which is the same woman. Long story. Anyway, you might be a touch classier than her, but other than that, y'all could be sisters."

Lucy finally fell quiet, and now she gave Red a long poker stare.

"In fact," Red said, "if I remember right, she was from Dallas, too. Right, Billy Don?"

Billy Don nodded in agreement.

Lucy took a long drag off her cigarette, then said, "This wife of y'all's . . . her name Loretta?"

Red could feel his eyes popping wide. "Jesus. How on earth did you—"

"She *is* my sister," Lucy said, grimacing, picking a piece of tobacco off her tongue.

Red was starting to sober up fast.

"Seriously?" he asked.

"Ever since when?" Billy Don asked.

Red shook his head. "What kinda question is that? Since they was born, for Chrissakes."

Lucy said, "Actually, Loretta was born a couple years after me, so Billy Don is sorta right. She's been my sister since I was two."

Billy Don was looking smug, and Red tried to ignore it. "Well, where the hell is she?" he asked.

"Got me," Lucy said. "Last I heard from Daddy, she was up in Abilene but wasn't planning on staying." She took a big drink of beer. "We ain't close."

Red didn't hear any sadness in her voice at all, and it made him feel bad.

"There was one thing she told me a few years back that might make y'all feel better," she said. "Wait, let me tell you something about Loretta." She drained the rest of her beer, and Red and Billy Don simultaneously signaled to Sylvia for another round. "She kinda made a habit of getting married. I know that's the pot calling the kettle black, seeing as how I've been married three times. But Loretta . . . well, it was her way of getting by. She'd find some halfway decent guy with a little bit of money, stick with him until the excitement wore off, then get a divorce. She'd usually walk away with a pretty good sack of money. Then she'd just burn through it till the next guy came along."

Red wasn't sure how to take that news. Loretta sure hadn't married him or Billy Don for their money, because neither of them had any. "How many times was she married?" he asked.

Lucy shrugged. "Who the hell knows? I lost count."

Sylvia arrived with three more beers. Red saw from the clock on the wall that it was nearly midnight. Working the fence line tomorrow was going to be hell with a hangover.

"But what I was saying," Lucy continued. "Last time I talked to her was three or four years back. What she told me was, she'd finally found someone she really loved."

"I married her four years ago," Billy Don said.

"I married her three and a half years ago," Red said.

"That's what I'm getting at," Lucy said. "I don't remember if she mentioned a name, but I figure it was one of y'all."

Red let that sink in, and then he began to wonder why he wasn't feeling more heartbroke, hearing news like that. He knew from sad songs and Hallmark cards that he should be filled with regret, longing for things that might have been and all that crap. But he wasn't. And he figured it was because he was having a hard time taking his eyes off Loretta's sister.

Thirty minutes before last call, Lucy said something else that surprised Red. She was slurring pretty good by then, and Billy Don was all but passed out. "You know," she said, "since we're gettin' to be such good friends and all, let me tell you a little secret." She leaned in over the table, Red to her left, Billy Don on her right. Red could tell that Lucy was about to deliver some big nugget of wisdom, like maybe a foolproof way to steal gas from the convenience store.

"I don't make all of my money as a home health aide," she giggled. "In fact, I've got a couple other things that bring in a lot more money."

This woman was looking better all the time.

Billy Don belched softly and his chin settled on his chest, his eyes closed.

Red said, "Let's hear 'em."

Lucy looked him in the eye for a long time. "This is all just 'tween you and me, right?"

"Absolutely."

She lit a fresh smoke and rambled on for ten minutes solid—and the things she told Red were enough to make him realize he was in the company of a master con artist.

For starters, Lucy had been operating as a pet psychic for the past six months or so. *A pet psychic.* "Can you believe that?" she asked. "Can you believe people are that gullible?"

Red said hell no, he couldn't believe it, and he decided not to mention that he'd run up a pretty good phone bill calling a late-night TV psychic last month. Madame Crustacean or something like that. Truth was, he could see how an authentic psychic could maybe figure out human-type affairs and all, but talking to poodles and parakeets? He shook his head, like it was all totally ridiculous. Lucy said her clients wanted to *believe* she could communicate with their animals. That's what made it so easy, she said. The clients were believers to begin with, which is why they called her.

But there was more. Lucy's second husband—this was about fifteen years ago—had been an accomplished scam artist. He'd wheedle his way into an old geezer's home, get into the attic, then proceed to find "evidence" of termites or a leaky roof or whatever was on the menu that month. Then he'd take a down payment, fill out an official-looking work order (bogus, of course), then vanish in the wind:

"The problem with that," Lucy said, "is that you've gotta move around all the time. People know you're cheating 'em, so sooner or later someone's gonna look hard enough to find you.

We must've lived in a dozen towns in five years. Gets old real quick. No, the way I see it, there are only two ways to go. One, you come up with a scam where the people don't know they're being duped. Like the pet psychic thing. Or two, you pull it off so that they never know who you are anyway. Never even see your face."

Red was having trouble following all of this. "How do you do that?"

Lucy laughed. "All kinds of ways. Let me tell you about an old classic. You start with a list of about a hundred people. They gotta be rich folks, with plenty of extra cash to spare, so maybe you focus on a hoity-toity little neighborhood on the right side of town. Then you send them all an anonymous letter about a football team, like maybe the Cowboys. Okay, in half the letters you say that the Cowboys are gonna win on Sunday. In the other half, you say the 'Boys are gonna lose. You follow me?"

"I think so."

"So then, after the game, half of the people think you're pretty smart, right? You predicted the outcome of a pro game. So you send those people another letter, but you split 'em in half again, same as the first time. Half the letters say Dallas will win, half say they'll lose."

Red was starting to catch on.

Lucy said, "And you keep doing that every week, splitting it each time, only sending letters to the people who received the right prediction the week before. Pretty soon, they think you're about as slick as frozen snot. By the time you get down to just one guy left on the list, hell, you've already told him what's gonna happen in six different games. He's watching his mailbox each week, just dying to see what's gonna happen next. That's when you make your move."

Red couldn't help it, he was grinning wide. Lucy was about as clever as a girl could get. "Then you ask 'em for money," he said.

"Damn right, you do. I always say five thousand bucks if they wanna know what's gonna happen in the game that week. Most of 'em think it's a pretty small price to pay for information like that. They start thinking about flying to Vegas and placing a big ol' bet."

"So you've done it?" Red couldn't imagine having the guts to pull something like that off.

"Yep."

"They go for it?"

"Some of them do. Not a lot, but enough. Plus, you gotta be real careful how you go about picking up the money. Just in case they report you. Feds would nail you big time for that."

It was all so simple . . . and so smart. Red wasn't sure if he should be disgusted or thoroughly impressed. In his state of inebriation, he went for the latter.

She told him about some other neat tricks, too, like how to swindle a cashier out of extra change, or how to convince a widow that her late husband ordered a bunch of encyclopedias right before he died. "You look in the obituaries," she said, "and go from there."

Red was starting to realize how much money a person could make if he—or in this case, she—tried hard enough.

Sylvia hollered out last call, and Red was starting to wonder if he'd get a chance to see Lucy again. He was trying to work up the nerve to ask for her phone number, but it turned out *she* wanted to see *him* again—real soon.

"I'm working on something right now," she said. "One of my patients—an old guy who's not doing so good—he's got a ton of money and nobody to leave it to. Doesn't even have a will, at least not one that's valid anymore. And I figure, hey, why should it all go to the state, right? I mean, what right does the government have to it?"

That made sense to Red.

"So I'm working on a way to get some of it for myself," she said. Then she added slowly, "But the thing is, I need some help. I need someone like you to work this thing with me."

She gave him that look again—the long stare, almost as if she was questioning his manhood.

Red glanced at Billy Don, who was snoring like a hooker after a long night. He looked back at Lucy, who was watching him patiently. "Who *is* this old guy?" he asked, wondering what in the hell he was getting himself into.

Lucy downed the rest of her beer, stubbed out her cigarette, and said, "His name's Scofield. Vance Scofield. Senior."

14

LUCAS WOKE EARLY in the motel room because he still had a lot to figure out. Like fake IDs. That was number one on the list. He was trying to decide whether he should try to get a phony set here in Miami, where he had a better chance of finding someone who could supply that sort of thing, or go ahead and make the four-hour drive to Key West. The island was infamous for sheltering all types of refugees—those who were running from the law, and those who simply wanted to leave the past behind. There, he could take his time, live on the cash they had, until he was able to make some connections. Get in with the right group of people, ask a few questions, and don't rush anything. He figured he was less likely to get caught that way. So that's what he decided. Maybe make one more stop in Miami to buy some clothes and other supplies, then hit the road.

Stephanie was breathing softly next to him, still fast asleep. The clock read 7:14.

She'd calmed down last night, and once again seemed happy about this adventure they were on. He'd told her the only reason the cops were looking for her was to question her. To ask her if she had any idea what had happened to Vance.

He thought there was a pretty good chance he was right.

Buford and Little Joe woke early in the motel room because they still had a lot to figure out. Like getting Colby to talk.

"I don't see what the big deal is," Joe said from the other bed. "We just go back to his place, stick a gun in his mouth, and tell him what we want. Do it real fucking easy that way. You always say the best plans are the simple ones."

"Yeah, but it could get messy real quick," Buford said. He'd already followed that line of thought out to the end. He'd lain awake last night pondering all sorts of possibilities, and nothing had panned out. "What if he's got the negatives stashed away in a safe-deposit box?"

"What if he does?"

"Think about it. Once he gets into that bank, he's safe again. He figures we're not gonna blow him away inside a bank, right? So all of a sudden, he's back in charge. Plus, he woulda seen our faces, and that ain't no good."

"He's already seen our faces."

"No, I mean seeing our faces and knowing we're the bad guys."

"Whatsisname, the doctor the other day, he saw our faces."

"That was different."

"How was it different?"

Buford didn't have the patience for this.

Joe said, "I'm just trying to learn something, is all."

"Winsted knew he was in the wrong. Man owed us money, no way around it. Plus, he couldn't go to the cops, not without a lot of bad publicity. Thing like that wouldn't look good for a man in his position. But it's more than that. It's more about the *type* of person we're dealing with."

Joe had a vacant expression on his face, and Buford knew he wasn't following the logic.

So Buford said, "This guy Colby, he isn't like the others at all. The way he's going about it all—the things he's saying to Herzog, the things he's doing—he's more like you and me. He's a cat, not a mouse."

Joe nodded, and Buford wondered if he really understood. "What we gonna do, then?" Joe asked.

"Hell, Joe, that's what we're trying to figure out."

Buford had the color TV tuned to CMT, watching videos with the volume turned all the way down. Brad Paisley was on there right now, singing his head off without making a sound. Buford handled a few guys like that—talented as hell, and they could write the shit out of a song, but so far, they couldn't get that one lucky break. Or, to be precise, Buford couldn't get it for them. Nashville was an incestuous little town, and if you were an outsider, you didn't have much chance at all. There were times, sitting across the table from some label exec, he wanted to reach across and grab the guy by the hair. Start whacking his head on the table until he got that smug goddamn look off his face. Wouldn't work, though. Even if he did it for real, all it would get him was arrested. He had to play by their rules, even if it meant being excluded forever.

Joe said, "Sounds like we need something besides just whacking him upside the head. Or maybe shooting him in the foot."

Buford reached to the nightstand and grabbed a cigar. He lit up and said, "Yeah, something a little more clever than that. We can't go at him head-on."

They sat in silence for fifteen minutes. Buford was at a loss. Every idea he had ultimately involved beating Colby until he cooperated. Violence, pure and simple. The kind of stuff Buford was good at. But this required a smarter approach.

Then Joe surprised Buford by spitting out a damn good idea. Simple as hell, but good.

* * *

Marlin called Garza from home first thing Thursday morning, checking in.

"Getting back to your regular routine?" Garza asked.

"Pretty much. Unless you need an extra hand with Lucas."

"That's the problem," Garza said. "There's nothing we *can* do—not until we find him."

"Then I'll be out all morning," Marlin said. "If you hear anything from Austin, catch me on the radio, will ya? I'd like to hear what the autopsy says."

"Will do. It could be this afternoon, but I'm guessing tomorrow's more likely."

Marlin hung up and walked outside to his truck, content to be returning to his normal duties. He drove the quiet back roads of the county and stopped at several hunting camps. The weather was crisp and beautiful, the temperature in the low seventies, big white clouds hanging in the sky like balls of cotton. The toms were strutting, and several of the hunters had had some luck. All the birds had been properly tagged.

At lunchtime, he drove back into Johnson City and stopped at a pay phone. The dispatchers and some of the deputies were always after him to get a cell phone, but he hated the damn things. He dialed a number, and Phil Colby answered on the fourth ring.

"Wanna get some lunch?" Marlin asked.

"Who the hell is this?"

"Funny."

"Well, I'll be. Is this John Marlin? I thought maybe you'd already moved to San Antone."

"You crack you up," Marlin said, but he was glad that Colby was in a good enough mood to be a smart-ass. "You wanna get some lunch or not?"

"Wish I could, but I've gotta run some culls up to Lampasas later this afternoon."

"Need some help loading up?"

"Naw, I already got 'em penned. I'll be back late tonight. I'll catch you later this week, all right?"

* * *

By early afternoon, Red couldn't stand it anymore and he went behind a cedar tree to throw up. His sweat smelled like stale beer, and his head felt like someone was inside with a pickax trying to get out. Jesus, he couldn't remember the last time he'd been this hung over. The fact that he was operating a bone-rattling hydraulic T-post driver didn't help matters much. He'd heard about prison work that was easier than this crap.

Normally they used a tractor-mounted post driver—a big son of a bitch delivering more than seventy thousand pounds of force with each blow. But they were working in a ravine, down low in some rough country where the tractor couldn't go. They were having to do it all by hand.

Good thing Jack Chambers had made a run into town, so he couldn't complain if the unofficial captain of the work crew called a little break. Red took a seat on the ground in the shade. Billy Don dropped down beside him. Jorge, the wetback, shook his head at them and kept working.

"God Almighty," Billy Don said, rubbing his temples, "if I could work up the strength, I'd shoot myself."

Red didn't reply. All he could think about was his soft, comfortable bed, and the fact that they'd be finished with this job before sundown. He was going to sleep for about three days when he got home. He'd drink a gallon of water, curl up, and wait for the demons to quit howling.

Despite the way he was feeling—pounding skull, trembling hands, and bowels that were churning with a liquid ferocity—Red couldn't help but smile on occasion.

Lucille.

Even the name alone was enough to lift his spirits. There was something special about her, and any moron—including him—could spot it from a mile away.

"So . . . you gonna call her or what?" Billy Don asked, grinning. The look on Red's face must've given him away.

They hadn't discussed her yet. Red had been putting it off. He wasn't sure how Billy Don would react. "She's a handful, ain't she?" he said.

"Shee-yit," Billy Don said. "She's just like Loretta, only more so."

Red didn't see how Lucille could be more like Loretta than Loretta was, but now was not the time for an argument. So he said, "Well, speaking of Lucy, there's something we need to talk about."

"Hell, she likes you better'n me, Red. I can see that. Y'all have your fun."

"I appreciate that, Billy Don, but that's not what I'm talking about. It's something more important." Red removed his baseball cap and used it as a fan, trying to generate a small breeze to fight the humidity. "See, Lucy's got a little problem. Something to do with one of her patients. And I came up with a way to help her out of it. Turn it from a challenge into an opportunity. A real money-maker. But she needs our help."

Actually, Lucy had said she needed *Red's* help, but Red had made it clear last night that he wasn't getting involved without his partner. She'd said, yeah, sure, that's fine. So she and Red had figured out a doozy together, and now all Red had to do was get Billy Don on board. Which wasn't always easy.

The big man eyed Red with suspicion. "What now?"

"Now see," Red said, "how come you're always so negative about everything? I haven't hardly opened my mouth yet, and you're already looking for problems that ain't there. How come you can't give me a little credit now and then? I mean, I know some of my ideas don't always work out, but some of them are pretty damn good. Least you could do is say thank you ever' once in a while."

Red could tell that Billy Don was about to deliver some kind of smart-ass answer, but he must've changed his mind. He simply said, "All right, then, let's hear it."

"That's more like it," Red said, forgetting his hangover for a second, getting excited about the possibilities. "Before I get into all the little details, let me ask you something: How would you feel about impersonating a plumber?"

15

BUFORD WAS HAVING second thoughts. Hell, he was having third thoughts by this point. Was this the best plan they could come up with? Something about it didn't feel right.

"I feel like a horse's ass," he muttered, with Little Joe lying right beside him. "What kind of clothes are these for a man, anyway?"

"You don't like camo?" Joe asked.

Buford didn't answer. He thought he heard the drone of an engine in the distance.

"Camo's kinda cool," Joe added. "College kids are wearing it all over the place nowadays. I'm gonna keep mine."

Buford checked his watch. Not yet four o'clock. They still had plenty of daylight. He looked through the rifle scope one more time. Rock steady and clear as a bell. He could almost read the note they'd taped to the front door. But the rifle itself? It was one of

Colby's, so if it wasn't sighted in—accurate as hell at two hundred yards—that was Colby's own fault. They'd stolen it from the man's gun safe just an hour ago. Joe got a kick out of smashing the glass, wanting to grab a bunch of other weapons, but Buford just wanted to get in, get one decent firearm, and get out. Buford prided himself on being prepared for all sorts of shit, but in this case, he hadn't foreseen the need for a high-powered rifle. He hadn't brought one, but now they had a good one. A Sako .270. Made in Finland, of all places. Buford couldn't imagine what they needed a long-range rifle for in Finland, except maybe target practice on baby seals.

Joe started to say something else, but Buford held up his hand. Yeah, now he could hear it. Definitely an engine. Getting closer.

"It's gonna work, smooth as a baby's ass," Joe whispered. "Just you wait and see. Hell of a lot better'n a paintball gun."

Phil Colby ran a typical cow-calf operation, with a hundred and fifty brood cows, all Black Angus. Seven bulls got the job done breeding his herd in the spring, and the cows dropped their calves the following winter. Colby would sell the calves the next fall, well after they'd been weaned, wormed, vaccinated, and branded.

Today, he was auctioning some of his older cows, culls that were unlikely to produce in the future. Late last year, he'd debated wintering them, wanting to avoid unnecessary expenses. But he'd had an intuition that prices would be up in the spring, and he'd been right.

Colby had six head in a small pen, ready to load. He worked them through the crowding alley, then through the loading chute and up into the livestock trailer. Everything went smoothly, and just before four o'clock, he was ready to hit the road for Lampasas. Tomorrow's auction began at sunrise, and check-in for the livestock ended tonight at seven.

He dropped his truck into gear and drove back to the ranch house, wanting to change into a fresh shirt and grab a cold drink for the ride.

He parked out front and hopped from the truck, and as he walked toward the front door he spotted a note taped to the small inset window.

But when he got closer, he was confused by what the note said.

BACK OFF!

That's all. No signature, no explanation, nothing.

What the hell is this all about?

He didn't recognize the handwriting. Who would have left this? Someone playing a weird joke?

He pulled the note from the glass, and he was reaching for the doorknob when the window exploded, shards of glass flying everywhere, followed a millisecond later by the roar of a high-powered rifle.

Colby's entire body flinched, and as he scrambled inside the house to safety, he was acutely aware that a bullet had just missed his head by inches.

Blackie climbed into the Dumpster at ten minutes past four, because he knew that the nice clerk—Blackie didn't remember his name—came on duty at four. The other guy, the one with the earlier shift, he was a hard case, and he chased Blackie away as soon as he saw him. But not the nice one. He was more of a live-and-let-live sort. Even gave Blackie a few bucks one time, asking him not to spend it on booze.

Blackie nearly always found some decent stuff in the Dumpster. Stale bread. Half-eaten doughnuts. Maybe part of a burrito or a slice of pizza. Sometimes he even found things that didn't come from the store. People dumped their own personal garbage into the Dumpster. Everyday trash usually, but sometimes tattered clothing or old books. Junk like that. Things that could just as easily go to a charity, where they'd do some good.

Today he hit paydirt. With just a little digging, Blackie found a box of old magazines. *People. Time. Popular Mechanics.* Blackie leaned out of the Dumpster and dropped the box into his shopping cart. Yessir, he'd take those back to his tent. Give him something to do with his time. Or maybe trade them for cigarettes.

Next, he rooted around under some cardboard boxes and came up with a gallon jug of Gatorade, still half full with the orange-flavored stuff. He took a long swig, and boy did it taste good, even though it was kind of warm. He replaced the cap and gently dropped the bottle into the cart, next to the magazine box.

Then he found something else, and for a second he didn't know what it was. He'd never actually held one in his hand before. Just a small, black, rectangular object. Hard plastic, rounded corners. Then he realized it was designed to unfold, so he unfolded it. Well, hot damn. It was a phone, that's what it was. One of those portable jobs. He remembered they were calling them cell phones nowadays. He saw people using these things all the time. Like when Blackie stood at an intersection, holding a sign, asking for spare change, a lot of the drivers sat there, waiting on the light, yakking on their phones. Eyes straight ahead, a good reason to act like they didn't even see Blackie. Too damn busy and important talking on their phones.

The thing was all lit up now, ever since Blackie opened it. Almost like it was asking him to dial it. But there was nobody to call. Blackie's brother back in Indianapolis, if he was still alive, wouldn't want to hear from him. What had it been, nineteen years? There was nobody else, either. Everybody Blackie ran around with, well, they damn sure didn't have phones.

Blackie decided he'd trade it, too. Then something else occurred to him. Whoever owned this phone was probably looking for it. They were bound to call their own number eventually. And they'd probably offer a pretty good reward to get it back.

"Hell of a shot," Joe muttered, both of them still hunkered down between some cedar trees.

"It did the job," Buford replied, satisfied with himself.

Originally, Joe had asked if he could do the shooting, but Buford had decided against it. He figured Joe might've ended up shooting Colby in the leg or something on purpose, just out of pure spite.

Now the plan was to watch the house for a while. If Colby tried to leave, or if he showed his face in a window, Buford would lob another round at him. Get the man good and freaked out. Let him know they weren't fucking around.

The house had a few large, well-trimmed live oaks around it, but no cedar or other brush to block the view. Behind the house, the ground sloped upward to a ridgeline, which could be seen easily over the rooftop. So even if Colby made a run out the back door, they could spot him. Besides, Buford figured, if Colby was scared enough to bolt, that would mean their plan had worked.

Next, they'd just call him up and tell him exactly what they wanted.

"You gonna take out his truck before we leave?" Joe asked.

"That's what I said."

"An engine shot?" Joe was getting excited. "Blast one right through the block?"

Colby slammed the door behind him and went straight to the nearest phone.

The line was dead.

He ran to his den and immediately saw more broken glass. His gun cabinet was a wreck. He reached through the empty doorframe and grabbed a Winchester .30-06. From the lower cabinet he grabbed a box of ammo and a pair of 20x60 binoculars.

Staying low, he made his way to the master bedroom. Here he would have a good view out the front of the house. Chances were, whoever had fired the shot was on the edge of the brush line a couple hundred yards away.

He lowered himself to the floor and crept to the window, where he raised the miniblind about six inches—just enough that he'd be able to stick the barrel out the window and still see through the rifle scope. He was lucky; the window itself was already open.

He raised the binoculars and began to scan the trees in the distance. The problem was, there were any number of places where the shooter could be hiding. And if he was wearing camo, or standing in the shadows, Colby would have very little chance of spotting him. Unless he moved. Same thing was true in deer hunting. When a deer's instincts told it to hold still, it could blend in with the scenery so well a hunter might walk within ten feet of it. But when the deer decided to make a run for it, that's when it seemed to suddenly materialize out of thin air.

So Colby continuously swept the binoculars back and forth, looking for the motion that would be the dead giveaway.

He waited, but nothing moved. So he waited some more. After twenty long minutes, Colby finally decided that the shooter had taken off.

Then another shot rang out.

"You hit the tire," Joe said, sounding disappointed. "Did you mean to hit the tire? I thought you was gonna hit the engine."

"This is better," Buford replied. "We'll know for sure he's out of commission." He worked the bolt on the Sako and chambered another round. It was one fine-shooting piece of iron. Accurate as hell. *Take out two tires,* he thought. *Then it'll take more than a spare to get him back on the road.*

He swung the scope onto the back tire, held it steady, and squeezed the trigger.

Boom!

The tire flattened on the ground, easy as pie.

Buford chambered another one, more out of habit than anything else. He figured he'd done enough damage. He was turning toward Joe, about to tell him it was time to vamoose, when he heard Colby's first shot.

He'd never know for certain, but he was pretty damn sure he heard the whine of the bullet passing about an inch from his left ear. He thought he felt a slight puff of air.

Then another shot came. And another.

Things got kind of loose and disorganized after that. Buford was crawling backward on his belly, Joe chattering something at him, wanting to charge the house, Buford saying hell no, and then they finally managed to pull back behind a massive line of brush and hightail it.

Colby was still firing. Buford knew there was no way the man could see them now, but he could feel his butthole tighten with every round.

"Jesus Christ!" Joe shrieked, giggling, sprinting through the trees, apparently amused by the idea he might die of acute lead poisoning at any second. "He keeps it up, he's gonna melt his damn barrel."

"Just go!" Buford hollered.

Trailing behind Joe, Buford saw a dark red stain—small, but growing—on the backside of his shirt.

16

"MAMA, I CAN'T find my frosted blue eye shadow!"

Donnelle Parker was in a tizzy. Here she was, going on her first real date since Bubba moved out, and already she was running late. This fellow was a catch, too. Clayton Bassett. He owned his own backhoe.

"For heaven's sake, Donnelle, take it easy," her mother said, bustling down the hallway, her thighs swishing back and forth in rayon pants. Thank goodness Mama had been willing to give up her weekly Bunko night and babysit Britney. She poked her head into the bathroom. "I ain't never seen you so worked up."

"But I can't find my eye shadow!"

"Well, where did you leave it last?"

"If I knew that, I wouldn't have a problem, would I?"

"Don't you sass me, young lady."

"I'm sorry, Mama, but will you just help me look? If I can't find it I'm gonna have to pick out a whole new outfit. It's all color coordinated."

"Why in tarnation are you wearing blue, anyway? It's wrong for your complexion."

"Mama! My eye shadow!"

"Okay, simmer down. Where do you keep your makeup?"

"Right here in this drawer."

Her mother rummaged through various eyeliners, blushes, and mascaras and magically came out with the eye shadow. "Go easy on it, that's all I'm saying," she said, then retreated to the living room.

Donnelle spent several minutes getting her face just so, then she hurried to her bedroom to dress. The short black skirt tonight, with the periwinkle V-neck blouse. And the open-toed pumps with the two-inch heels. She'd knock him dead. But first, her undergarments. She had something spicy picked out. It wasn't as if she was planning on going all the way on the first date, but then, well, you never knew. Damn, it had been *so* long.

She went to her dresser, opened the top drawer, and realized something was missing. Dadgummit, not now. Clayton would be here any minute. She slipped her bathrobe on and raced to the living room.

"Honeybunch, have you been getting into Mommy's underwear again?"

Donnelle's five-year-old daughter was sitting cross-legged in front of the TV, watching a strange cartoon that, Donnelle worried, might warp the precious baby's mind before she even had a chance to enroll in school and do some learning.

"Uh-uh," Britney said, but her eyes never left the set. Just like her dad, a TV addict. And the stuff she was watching was no better than what he used to watch. The only difference—Britney was eating a bowl of applesauce whereas Bubba used to eat candied peanuts.

"Sweetie, if you did, just tell Mommy so—"

"I said no!"

Donnelle took a deep breath. Her mother was watching the

whole spectacle, shaking her head. They'd had some serious debates over the whole discipline issue.

"I wish you wouldn't use that tone of voice, honey," Donnelle said. "Haven't we talked about that?"

No reply.

"Mommy doesn't like it when you yell like that."

Still no reply.

Donnelle worried at times that she was too lax with Britney, especially since Bubba moved out. Her daughter was going through a stage—Donnelle expected her to sprout horns and a tail any day now—and she wondered if the pending divorce was the cause of it. Like the episode with the panties last week. Britney had gotten angry because her mother wouldn't let her stay up late, so she had flushed a pair of Donnelle's red bikinis down the toilet. Clogged the pipes and made a big mess.

"What's missing now?" her mother asked.

"Pair of leopard-print panties."

That earned her nothing but a cocked eyebrow.

"Now don't you start, Mama. I haven't got time for it."

She turned her attention back to Britney. "Sugar, I know you like to dress up like a big girl, but you need to stay out of Mommy's things, okay?"

Like talking to a brick wall. Or Bubba. Donnelle had read some magazines, and she knew that little girls tended to "assert their independence" more when they had an audience. That's why Britney was ignoring her. Because she was showing off for her grandma.

"If you want to be treated like a big girl," Donnelle said, "you need to act like one. Now tell me where you put—"

That's when Britney dug her spoon deep into the applesauce and flung it at Donnelle. A thick gooey wad caught her right in the cheek, ruining her makeup.

Britney giggled and began to roll on the floor.

Mama said, "I'd give her a good swat for that, if I was you."

The doorbell rang.

Donnelle wanted to cry.

She never did find her panties.

* * *

John Marlin returned to the sheriff's department in the early evening, ready to take care of a few things in his office and then head home.

As soon as he stepped through the glass door, Darrell said, "Phil Colby was just here. Somebody took some shots at him."

Marlin stopped in his tracks. "Do what?"

"Yeah, he came riding up on an ATV. Busted in here hollering about someone shooting up his house and his truck. Said he fired back and thinks he hit somebody. He found blood."

"But Colby's okay?"

"Madder'n hell, but yeah."

"Why didn't you radio me?" Marlin snapped.

"I was about to."

"Where is everybody now?"

"They all just left."

"Where to?"

"Back to Colby's place."

Darrell kept talking, coming around the counter, but Marlin didn't hear much of it as he busted through the doors and hopped back into his truck.

They were back in the motel room now, and Little Joe said for the tenth time, "I never even felt it. Never felt the damn thing."

"That's how it works sometimes," Buford said, though he didn't have any firsthand knowledge of that himself.

Joe was tough, he'd proven that much. When he'd pulled his shirt off in the Caddy, they'd both seen a small hole low on his gut, on the right side, about six inches over from his belly button. A couple more inches and the bullet would've missed entirely. Of course, a couple more inches upward, through the lung or the liver, and Joe'd be lying dead on Colby's ranch.

The exit wound wasn't quite so tidy—ragged, ugly, about the size of a quarter—and it had Buford concerned.

"Think I need a doctor?" Joe asked, a hint of worry in his voice.

"It's not bleeding much," Buford pointed out. *Yeah, but it could be bleeding bad inside,* he thought. "Let's just wait and see." He'd never say it out loud, but Buford couldn't take Joe to a hospital. Not with a gunshot wound. That kind of thing meant an automatic call to the cops.

"Let's just get a bandage on it," Buford said, trying to sound upbeat. "Looks like it went clean through without hitting anything major. Day or two and you'll be good as new."

Joe didn't look so sure.

When Marlin arrived at Colby's place, just before sundown, he wondered if he'd find a scene reminiscent of the OK Corral. But all he saw was Nicole Brooks, alone, stringing yellow crime-scene tape around Phil's truck and the empty trailer behind it. The other deputies and Colby were nowhere to be seen.

Brooks gestured west, toward the brush line and the orange-bottomed clouds on the horizon. "He's showing Ernie and Bill where he found the blood. A rifle, too, laying in the cedars. But it probably won't do much good, since Colby says it's one of his own."

"Where's Garza?"

"He went home earlier today. His kid's still pretty sick, and I think he was pretty out of it, too."

Marlin nodded. "Any idea what happened?"

She wrapped the tape around a small oak tree, then tied it fast. "Guess we don't really need tape out here," she said, "but maybe it'll keep the cattle away." She smiled at Marlin, and he tried to smile back, feeling a bit awkward about it.

Brooks continued, "Colby says he loaded some cows around four o'clock, then stopped at the house before leaving town. He found a note taped to his front door. We've got it bagged, but I can tell you what it says: 'Back off.' "

"Back off?"

"Yep. That's all. And darn the luck, whoever left it forgot to sign his name. So Colby's standing at the door, wondering what the note means, when a shot takes out the glass window in the door. He ducks inside and grabs a rifle of his own."

"Why didn't he call it in?" Marlin asked. He hoped there was a good reason, because he could too easily picture Phil trying to handle the situation himself.

"Says the phone wasn't working, and it wasn't, because somebody had opened the box on the side of the house and unplugged the line. So Colby sets up in the bedroom, watching out the window. After about twenty minutes, the shooter takes out his tires. Colby's watching, and he sees movement out in the trees, so he returns fire. Says he shot something like fourteen times. He had to reload in between."

Fourteen times?

"I don't blame him," Marlin said.

Brooks had a noncommittal expression on her face. "No. No, I don't, either. Then he waited another hour, hoping somebody might've heard all the shots and called it in. Guess nobody did. So he starts holding up a baseball hat in front of the window, seeing if the guy'll take a shot at it. Keeps doing that off and on at different windows, and finally decides the guy's gone. Waits another thirty minutes, just to be safe, then goes outside and has a look around."

"But the shooter's long gone."

"Looks that way."

"What about the rifle he found? You said it was one of his?"

"Yeah, someone busted into his gun case. The front door was unlocked. Used Colby's own weapon to shoot at him. At least, that's what it looks like."

"Tell me he didn't touch it."

"Nope, left it where it was."

The sun had dropped well below the horizon now, and darkness was setting in. Marlin thought he saw a flashlight through the trees. He decided to wait for Colby and the deputies to return, rather than walking out to them, because he didn't want to compromise the scene they were working. He faced Brooks. "You need any help with anything?"

"I was about to see if I could round up one of these slugs," she said, nodding toward the two flat tires. "Then we're gonna dust his house. You mind starting on the telephone box? See if they might've left some prints?"

"Not at all. I'll get after it." He turned to retrieve his evidence kit from his truck, but stopped after a few steps. He faced Brooks again. "Listen, about our conversation yesterday—"

"My overactive imagination," Brooks said. "I shouldn't have even said anything."

He nodded. "I just don't want you to have the wrong idea."

She gave him a quizzical look. "Yeah, okay."

They both heard footsteps approaching. Phil Colby, alone. Even in the twilight, Marlin could tell from the set of his best friend's jaw that Colby still hadn't completely calmed down.

"You believe this shit?" Colby asked, looking at Marlin. "You've heard the whole story?"

"The basics, yeah. You okay?"

"Yeah, I'm fine. Goddamn lucky is what I am."

Marlin looked back at Brooks, just a dim figure in the dark now, but she had removed her flashlight and was crawling under Colby's truck to look for lead.

"I found two drops of blood, John," Colby said. "Not much, but they're looking for more. Whoever it was, I hit him."

"This is crazy," Colby said. He'd been oddly quiet so far. He was holding a flashlight while Marlin dusted the telephone box on the side of the house. The area surrounding the box was cedar planking, and the rough texture of the wood wouldn't hold any collectible prints.

"You get a look at the guy?" Marlin asked.

"Not really. Jesus. All I saw was a guy in camo running through the brush." Colby was too agitated to stand still, and he was doing a poor job holding the light steady. "It's one of those high-fencers, that's my guess."

Marlin didn't respond. He wasn't having any luck finding prints. He hadn't expected to.

Colby said, "What's the name of that hunting club Scofield belonged to? The Wallhangers or some crap like that? None of those guys like me, that's for sure."

Marlin still didn't reply.

"But shooting at me—that's completely out of line, don't you think?"

"Of course it is. But we don't know who it was yet."

"I feel like driving my truck through every high fence in the county. Just tear the shit out of them."

Marlin shook his head. "You gotta remember, Phil, they have a right to build those fences. You keep harassing them about it and you won't do anything but get yourself in trouble. You lost the court case, remember?"

"Hell yes, I remember," Colby said, raising his voice. "You don't have to remind me. But this . . . I can't even tell you how pissed I am. That first shot missed me by inches."

Marlin finished with the telephone box, finding nothing.

"You're not saying much," Colby muttered.

Marlin took a breath, his cheeks getting hot. "I'm working the case, Phil. Just take it easy and let us do our jobs."

He walked around the house toward his truck, leaving Colby standing in the dark.

An hour later, things had changed dramatically, and Marlin was confused. He was sitting in his truck, simply waiting, when Bobby Garza arrived. The sheriff parked his car and climbed into the passenger side of the truck.

"You feeling all right?" Marlin asked.

"A little rough around the edges, but I'll be okay."

"How's your boy?"

"I think he's about over it. Where is everybody?"

"In the house, looking for prints."

"Colby?"

"Still talking to Bill. Going through the whole story again, I think. I'm not real sure, to be honest, because when I started to go inside, Bill said it might be better if I waited out here for you." It was that one small request by the senior deputy that had set off alarm bells for Marlin. Something critical had happened, but he didn't know what. He was being left out of the loop. He tried to gauge the sheriff's expression, but it was difficult in the dim light. "What's going on, Bobby?"

Garza took too long to answer. "I called Bill on his cell phone and told him you probably shouldn't work the case. Colby is your best friend."

"Yeah? How does that impact on this? We're not investigating Phil, we're looking for—"

"He's a suspect, John. At the moment, anyway."

"A suspect in *what?*" Somehow Marlin knew what was coming.

"Travis County just called me thirty minutes ago. Vance Scofield didn't die in the flood. He was dead before he went in the water."

17

BUFORD WAS SLEEPING hard when his cell phone rang. He sat up, fumbling for the phone on the nightstand, answering before it went to voicemail. "Yeah?"

"What in the hell are you doing?" a voice growled on the other end.

Here we go, he thought.

"Uncle Chuck. Damn. What time is it?"

"Six-thirty in the morning, son. Rise and shine and answer one fucking question for me: Have you put a name to this blackmailer yet?"

"Yes, sir," Buford said proudly. "That part was easy. Guy's name is—"

"Phil Colby."

"Well, yeah."

"Why didn't you tell me that?"

"You know him?"

"Hell yeah, I know him. He sued a guy I know about a high fence. Real pain in the balls."

"How was I supposed to know you knew him?"

Uncle Chuck didn't answer, and Buford knew he'd made his point.

"Besides," Buford said, "what difference would it have made? I still gotta go after the guy, right?"

"Damn right you gotta go after him, but I don't want another supreme fuckup like you got into last night. I heard all about it."

Buford had figured word would get around. Blanco County was a small place, tongues wagging every morning at the coffee shop. And with Uncle Chuck knowing who Phil Colby was, it must have been pretty easy to figure out what the shooting was all about.

"Just puttin' a scare into him," Buford said, glancing over at Joe. Still sleeping. Something smelled bad. The room was stuffy and hot.

"Don't sound like it worked all that good," Hamm said. "I hear he came after you loaded for bear. I'm thinking y'all mighta underestimated this guy. Word is, deputies found some blood. We got a problem?"

"Nothing to worry about. I got it all under control."

The old man snorted. "I think you better run the whole mess past me. If this thing's getting out of hand—"

"No, sir, it ain't. It's all part of the plan." And Buford explained what had happened so far. He told him how they had posed as hunters two days ago, and Little Joe had searched Colby's house. Then he told him about yesterday—how they had started with reconnaissance in the morning, cruising Miller Creek Loop, looking for a place to stash the car. They'd pulled into an overgrown driveway and found a neglected hunting cabin way back in the trees. Later, in the afternoon, they parked behind the cabin and hiked onto Colby's place, then they got into position and simply waited. Everything had gone smoothly—until Colby fired back.

Buford could hear Uncle Chuck let out a small groan of impatience. "So you're thinking—what?—he'll freak out and turn the photos over?"

"That pretty much sums it up." Looking back on the plan now, Buford knew it made him and Little Joe sound like rank amateurs. Emphasis on the word "rank." Damn, something smelled bad.

Uncle Chuck took a long pause. "I'd say you boys screwed the pooch on this one."

"Maybe, maybe not. I'll work something out. I always do." Buford kept it short and to the point, not wanting to get into a discussion with his bullheaded uncle. He looked over at Joe again and saw that the bandage around his partner's lower torso was soaked through with blood. Not a good sign.

"He'll be ready for you now," his uncle said. "He knows we know who he is."

"Let me deal with it." Buford didn't want the old man nosing into all the specifics.

"Well, keep me in the loop."

Little Joe's color was way off.

"You hear me?"

"I hear you," Buford said. "Just give it a little time."

Buford stood up in the small space between the two beds, looking down on Joe now. He pulled the covers back, and the smell got worse. The kind of odor that comes from bowels letting loose.

"Here's what you oughta do . . ." Uncle Chuck said, but Buford folded the phone, ending the call.

He placed a hand against Joe's cheek. *Aw, Christ.* Stone cold.

Red woke up Friday morning feeling like a new man, with a hardy resolve to quit drinking completely. Then he decided, heck, there was no reason to go overboard, so he made a silent vow to cut back a whole bunch. Or if nothing else, he was going to keep a bottle of aspirin handy on his nightstand. Right about then, before Red could even shower, Lucy showed up fifteen minutes early. She was carrying a bag filled with all the fixings for Bloody Marys.

"I kinda figured you didn't have any horseradish," she said, lining up all the ingredients on Red's kitchen countertop. She'd marched right into the trailer, Red following behind in a T-shirt and a pair of dirty denim shorts.

"You figured right," he said, watching her work, running a hand through his matted hair, trying to make himself presentable.

Lucy was looking as good today as she had on Wednesday night, wearing black sweatpants and a shirt with a picture of Jeff Gordon on it. Red judged her to be about five-seven, going about one-fifty. Perfect. He liked a woman he could hold on to.

She opened a cabinet and found two plastic cups with the Austin Wranglers logo on them. She peered into the cups and made a face, then shrugged and placed them on the counter.

"We'll need three of those," Red said.

She glanced over her shoulder. "Billy Don's here already? I only saw one truck outside."

"He ain't got a vehicle."

"You're shitting me. How'd he get here?"

"Well, uh, he kinda lives here. He's still sleeping."

She stopped what she was doing and turned around, grinning. "Aw, ain't that cute. Two precious boys setting up house together."

She giggled, so Red glared at her, and that only made it worse. She went back to mixing up each concoction: a healthy dose of vodka, a splash of tomato juice, a blob of Tabasco and Worcestershire, followed by the horseradish, some salt, and a blast of pepper. Then she jammed a stalk of celery into each drink and handed one to Red. He couldn't remember ever holding a beverage so exotic. He tasted it, and the vodka brought tears to his eyes.

Lucy moved in close and quietly said, "You and Billy Don live here together, but you've got your own bedroom, right?"

Red nodded, feeling a sneeze coming on from the pepper.

"That's good," she said, strutting her way into the living room, speaking over her shoulder. "You never can tell when you might need a little privacy."

Red's eyes got wide.

* * *

The first thing Buford had done was panic. He'd gathered up his gear, wiped down every surface that might hold one of his prints, and hauled ass, leaving Little Joe right where he'd died. Sure, Buford would be letting Uncle Chuck down—giving up on the job like that—but some things are more important. Like staying the hell out of prison.

He'd been fifty miles up Highway 281 when he realized something. Little Joe had signed for the motel room, not Buford. Buford hadn't even set foot in the office. There was nothing to connect Buford to Joe on this. There were no prints on Colby's rifle, no prints in Colby's house. In short, no reason to run. *Hell, boy,* he'd told himself, *just calm down and think things through.*

So he turned around and drove back to Johnson City. This time, though, instead of parking right in front of the room, he parked around back. Didn't need some busybody describing the car later.

Inside the room, he stripped off all his clothes—to keep them clean—and dragged Joe to the bathroom. Then he flopped the stiffening corpse into the tub.

Buford got dressed again and poked his head out the door for a look-see. Lucky thing was, the ice machine was right around the corner. He grabbed the trashcan, which was much bigger than the ice bucket, and got to work. It took a dozen trips, but twenty minutes later, Joe was buried under a foot of cubes.

Next, Buford called the front office, changing his voice a tad without sounding obvious about it. "I want to book my room for three more days . . . That's right, till Monday . . . Just use that credit card I gave you when I checked in . . . Okay, thanks. Oh, one more thing. Let's put a hold on the maid service . . . Yeah, no service at all. I'll take care of it myself . . . No, I won't even need fresh towels. No service at all . . . Yeah, thanks."

Buford hung up and remembered to wipe off the handset. No prints anywhere, because he might not be back. He'd told them three days, but that was just a cushion.

Hell, he might be ready to leave in three hours. Because he was going back to see Phil Colby again.

And this time, he wasn't fucking around.

* * *

Phil Colby and Bobby Garza entered the interview room at ten o'clock, and Marlin was watching from behind the one-way glass. He could tell from Colby's body language that he was tense, maybe a little angry, and the questions hadn't even begun yet. In fact, Colby had no idea what was in store.

Marlin hadn't talked to him since the night before, when Garza had revealed the findings of Scofield's autopsy. There were several times, lying awake in the middle of the night, when Marlin had wanted to call Colby and talk it through, but he decided it was best to keep out of it for now, as Garza had asked. Another thought had occurred to Marlin at about four in the morning. There was another person who needed to be looked at closely. A man who had become very angry at Scofield because of a dead white-tailed buck.

"Thanks for coming in," Garza said as he and Colby took seats around the small round table. "You sure you don't want coffee?"

"Thanks, but let's just get to it," Colby replied. "Like I said last night, I'm not sure what else I can tell you."

"No, you've done great so far, Phil. We appreciate your patience. You get your truck fixed?"

"It's over at the shop right now getting new tires."

"Good. Man's gotta have his wheels. I guess you didn't have two spares on hand, huh?"

To Marlin, Garza seemed to be stalling. Why the interest in Colby's truck?

"Even the one spare I had was flat," Colby said.

"Listen," said Garza, "I know we've gone over this, but I want you to think hard and see if you can come up with any reason somebody might've fired those shots. Any recent run-ins with anybody?" Garza smiled. "You been chasing somebody's wife?"

"Yeah, you know me, a regular Casanova. But for the record, no."

Now the door to the interview room opened and Bill Tatum entered, carrying a manila envelope. He sat next to Garza without saying a word. He looked at the sheriff and nodded once.

Garza continued, "Actually, Phil, the other thing I wanted to talk about is Vance Scofield."

Colby nodded. "If he hadn't drowned, I would've figured he was the one who shot at me. Could be one of his high-fence buddies, though. Is that what y'all are thinking?"

By now, Marlin could feel his face flushing with guilt. Last night, Garza hadn't told Colby how Scofield had died, and he had asked Marlin to remain silent about it, too, until Garza held a news conference later this morning. So Marlin had had no choice. Now he had to sit back and watch Colby get ambushed.

Bill Tatum quietly said, "That could be a possibility, Phil, but let's put the shooting aside for a minute. What I need to tell you is, Scofield didn't drown, he was the victim of a homicide."

Colby looked from Tatum to Garza and back again. "He was murdered?"

Tatum nodded. Garza didn't speak.

"How was he killed?"

"Well," Garza said, "we're gonna keep that to ourselves for the time being."

His skull was cracked, Marlin remembered Garza saying. *Subdural hematoma. The kind of injury that has a lot of anger behind it. Not a drowning, according to the ME. No water in the lungs.* That's why, at that very minute, Ernie Turpin was returning to Vance Scofield's house, securing the place in preparation for a more exhaustive search.

"I'm not seeing what this has to do with me," Colby said. "Am I a suspect or something?" Colby was smiling, but he was starting to stiffen up.

Garza drummed a pencil on the table, and Marlin was familiar enough with the sheriff's mannerisms to know he was searching for the right words. "Considering the bad blood between the two of y'all, we're just trying to get a better picture of the situation. All we're doing right now is trying to rule various people out. That includes you, because you and Scofield had a history."

Colby leaned forward. "So I *am* a suspect? Oh, come on, Bobby. You've gotta be kidding. You know me better than that."

"Yeah, I do, Phil. But you almost got into a fistfight with the man a few months back. So I've gotta ask you some questions. If I didn't, I wouldn't be doing my job. It's just routine."

Colby now had an expression that Marlin knew all too well. A pained smile that signaled a flaring temper. His voice was getting more belligerent with each statement. "This is ridiculous. You're wasting your time."

"Just bear with us, Phil. Will you answer a few questions?"

"Hell yeah, I'll answer them. Why wouldn't I?"

"Okay, then, just settle down and let's get through this. For starters, tell us why you called Vance Scofield last Saturday."

Colby leaned his head back in exasperation. "I already told your deputy. The fencing crew was working my property line, so I called Vance and told him they'd better stay off my land. It was just a harassment call, I admit it. Besides, he's got a couple of poachers working on that crew."

Marlin noticed that Colby referred to Scofield in the present tense, which was a good thing.

"What did Scofield say?"

"He told me to fuck off and hung up."

"Those were his words?"

"Yes, exactly. He said, 'Fuck off,' and hung up on me."

"What did you do?"

"What do you mean, what did I do?"

"Right after the call, what did you do?"

"I didn't do anything. Like I said, I just wanted to get under his skin, and I figured, with a response like that, it must've worked."

"You didn't decide to drive over to his place, maybe settle this thing once and for all?"

"Hell no."

"Have you ever been to his ranch?"

"No."

"Does anybody else ever drive your truck?" Garza asked.

"Nobody drives it but me."

"So your truck was in your possession and nobody else's last Saturday?"

Marlin was starting to sweat. Garza had something, there was no doubt about it.

"Well, yeah. I was working cattle all day."

Now Bill Tatum opened the manila folder. He removed several photographs and placed them on the table in front of Colby.

Marlin's heart sank as he realized what was in the photos. *Oh, Jesus. There's no way.*

"These are shots of one of the tire tracks we found at Scofield's place," Tatum said. "Last night I compared them to the tires on your truck. They were close enough that we're gonna send the tires to the DPS lab in Austin for a closer look."

Colby leaned forward in disbelief. "You're gonna take the tires off my truck?"

"Actually, we'll have to take the whole truck, plus the two flat tires." Tatum slid a document in front of Colby. Marlin couldn't recall the sheriff and the senior deputy ever looking so grim as they served a warrant.

There was a long pause, and Marlin waited for Colby to provide a reasonable explanation. He wanted his friend to defend himself, to spit out some logical reason why the photographs couldn't possibly be accurate.

But all Colby said was "Am I under arrest?"

"No, you're not," Garza said.

"Then I'm done answering questions," Colby said, rising from his chair. "If you want anything more from me, call my lawyer."

18

AFTER PHIL COLBY left the interview room, Marlin entered and sat in the same chair his friend had been using. Bobby Garza was stone-faced. Bill Tatum wouldn't meet Marlin's eyes. None of them spoke for several minutes, until Marlin finally said, "I wish y'all would've warned me about all that."

Garza said, "We didn't even know for sure if we had anything. We wanted to see what Phil would say."

"But still—"

"Hey, we don't like this any more than you do, John. We're his friends, too. Maybe not as close as you are, but friends just the same."

Tatum murmured something similar.

Marlin said, "I'm surprised you didn't get a warrant for his house, too."

Garza and Tatum exchanged glances.

"Let me guess," Marlin said. "You *did* try to get a warrant for his house."

"Yes, we did," Tatum replied. "Judge Hilton said we didn't have enough."

Marlin didn't know what to think. "I'm having a tough time following your line of thinking, to be honest," he said. "I mean, why did you compare those tracks to his tires to begin with?"

Tatum softly said, "It had to be checked. We had things pointing at Colby—his problems with Scofield, the phone call he made. When Bobby called and said Scofield was murdered, I knew we'd have to take a look at Phil. If nothing else, to rule him out, like Bobby said."

Marlin found himself looking for a mental foothold that would allow him to make sense of everything. Surely, the answer was somewhere in the details, the one piece of information that would clear Phil Colby and reveal what had really happened. But it wouldn't come. "What about the shooting last night? How does that come into play?"

Garza said, "That happened before we even knew Scofield was murdered. Colby might be right—just one of Scofield's buddies keeping the high-fence feud going."

Marlin figured that made as much sense as anything else. "So are you looking at other people for this, or just Colby? Have you talked to this guy Chuck Hamm? I told you what Howell Rogers said."

Garza said, "At this point, we're looking at everything. Reinterviewing everybody, for starters. We'll talk to Hamm and the rest of those guys again if we need to, but, well, it just doesn't look likely, John."

"From what Howell said, Hamm was angry as hell."

"Yeah, but that was months ago, and why would he all of a sudden decide to do something about it? Besides, I don't think Scofield's been in touch with anybody in that hunting club since then. There weren't any phone calls in his records."

"Let me talk to Hamm."

"Pardon?"

"I want to talk to Hamm."

Garza and Tatum exchanged a glance. "You're jumping the gun. We haven't been through Scofield's house top to bottom yet, but that's our next step. Let's wait and see what we find. I've got Henry coming in."

Henry Jameson was a young and very talented forensics technician who worked for five counties in the central Texas area. The Blanco County budget alone couldn't handle the expense, so Garza had worked a deal with several neighboring counties, pooling resources, giving them all access to Jameson's services.

Tatum calmly said, "John, if Hamm was involved, which is a stretch, he had plenty of time to plan it out. This type of murder—someone whacking Scofield over the head—that suggests . . . spontaneity."

Marlin could understand that assumption. Murderers who plan in advance rarely kill through blunt-force trauma. They use guns or knives, or in some cases poison. They rarely use clubs, bats, or other crude weapons unless it's a heat-of-the-moment killing. But Marlin also knew that that line of thinking continued to point the finger at Phil Colby. It would be easy to envision: Colby gets enraged by Scofield's "Fuck you," he goes to Scofield's house, they get into a fight, Colby finds a handy two-by-four . . .

"But what about the Corvette?" he asked. "Can't we assume, just for the sake of argument, that whoever killed Scofield also stole the car?" His point was that it was robbery, not animosity, that fueled the murderer. That motive would seem to eliminate Colby. Of course, it probably eliminated Chuck Hamm, too.

Garza said, "It's a possibility, if Scofield didn't park the Vette somewhere else. Hell, he could've stashed the money somewhere else, too. That's why we're gonna tear that place apart. Trust me, if there's something to be found, we'll find it."

Marlin said, "What about Stephanie Waring?"

Garza spread his hands in a gesture of helplessness. "We're still calling her. Until we can track her down, we just don't know."

"Can we search her place? Maybe figure out exactly where she is?"

"We still don't have probable cause. We can't get a warrant just because we want to talk to her."

"Okay, then at least let me try to find her," Marlin said. "I know you don't want me on this case, but what can that hurt? Let me talk to Chuck Hamm and let me try to find the girl."

Garza glanced at Tatum, who didn't say a word.

Marlin continued. "Damn, Bobby, you've obviously got your hands full. Gotta search Phil's truck, take another look at Scofield's place."

"I've already talked to the night shift. Brought in some reserve deputies to cover the regular patrol. Everyone's working overtime."

"And they'll need every minute of it," Marlin said, not far from pleading. If push came to shove, Marlin could make his own call and work the case anyway. Anything having to do with Scofield was tied in to his original case, and he knew, technically, he was free to pursue it. But the sheriff is the highest-ranking law enforcement officer in any Texas county, so Marlin wanted Garza's blessing before he forged ahead.

Garza gave Marlin a stern look. "Let us know if you get anywhere."

"What'll you have?" the bartender asked, setting a napkin down. Lucas had no idea what time the bars had opened that morning in Key West, but Duval Street was buzzing and the drinks were flowing by the time he got there. They'd decided it would be best if Stephanie stayed back at the motel—the cheapest place in town and still a small fortune, but it had cable TV, even Internet access, and that would keep her occupied until he got back. Hopefully, by then, he'd have things all set up.

"Beer," Lucas said.

"Bottle or draft?"

"Whatever's cheaper."

While the bartender grabbed a glass and poured from the tap, Lucas looked around the bar: already crowded and it wasn't even lunchtime yet. Nothing but a bunch of sunburned tourists wearing baseball caps and gaudy T-shirts, eating nachos and Buffalo wings. The place wasn't anything like he thought it would be. From what he'd read, he'd pictured a place dark and quiet, where artists brooded and writers tried to spark their creative juices. Instead, there was peppy music piped in from recessed speakers and neon-colored parrots dangling from the rafters. Some guy was setting up equipment on a small stage.

"Three dollars." The bartender's name was Mike, according to a name tag on his shirt. He wasn't much older than Lucas.

Lucas handed him four singles, the extra being a tip for not asking to see ID. He was about to ask Mike an important question when he heard a woman say, "Oh, Rob, it's fabulous!"

A loud male voice responded, "Was I right or was I right?"

"You were right!"

Then Lucas's elbow was jostled as a man wedged himself onto the barstool to his right.

"Sorry about that, pal."

Lucas turned and saw a middle-aged man with a broad, smiling face, a salt-and-pepper beard, and a gut the size of a beach ball. The woman, who was still oohing and aahing about the bar's decor, had a similar build, short hair, and a masculine jaw.

"No problem," Lucas muttered, returning his attention to his beer. Shitty luck. Now he'd have to wait for them to leave before he could talk to the bartender.

"How's the beer in this place?" the man asked, and Lucas couldn't imagine a more idiotic question. Worse, the man had a funny accent.

"It's, uh, cold."

Lucas hadn't meant to be funny, but the man let out a hearty chuckle. Then he stuck out his hand and said, "I'm Rob Norris."

Lucas reluctantly shook hands and said, "Luke."

Rob Norris ordered two beers, then jerked a thumb to his right. "Luke, this here's my wife, Fiona."

Fiona leaned forward, looking past Rob, and said, "We're from Wisconsin," making it sound like an explanation for something.

Lucas nodded and turned back to the bar.

"Where are you from?" Fiona asked, refusing to let the conversation end.

"Texas," he said, without offering anything more.

"Oh, really!" Fiona replied. "That's funny because—"

"My parents are in Texas right now!" Rob said.

Fiona shook her head. "Traveling in an RV. Can you imagine?"

"We talked to them this morning."

"They said it's hot down there."

"And the people drive like maniacs!"

Lucas gave them a weak smile.

"Have you been to the gift shop next door yet?" Fiona asked, her eyes glowing with excitement.

"It's the first place we went!" Rob added.

"Look at this key chain!" Fiona demanded. "Only five dollars!" Now she was emptying all kinds of crap from a paper bag. "We got a paperweight and a cigarette lighter—"

"Of course, we don't smoke," Rob interjected.

"And a snow globe and golf balls—"

"Don't play golf, either."

"But the deals were just too good to pass up!" Fiona gushed.

"Great prices," Rob agreed.

"I'm doing all my Christmas shopping," Fiona whispered. "Right here in Key West. Can you imagine?"

"We'll probably ship everything home."

"It's worth it, though."

"But I don't think your mother is going to like the shot glass, honey. She doesn't drink."

"I know, Rob. That's the joke!"

Now they both chortled, their bellies jiggling under their shirts.

"The beach towels were pretty, but they were too big to carry around all day," Fiona confided.

"We'll buy them later," Rob said. "Right before we leave."

They both smiled at Lucas, expecting him to add something to the banter.

"Smart plan," Lucas said.

Fiona nodded, and as she opened her mouth again, Lucas felt an overwhelming urge to run from the bar screaming. But right then a smooth voice over an amplifier said, "Hello, folks, we're the Sea Breezes." Three men were onstage, preparing to play. "Thanks for joining us today. We'll be playing until happy hour, but judging from all the empties on the tables, I'd say most of you are plenty happy already."

A few people whooped, and someone raised a beer mug in salute.

"Do we have any Jimmy Buffett fans here?" the cheesy guy with the microphone asked, and of course most of the customers applauded with enthusiasm, including Rob and Fiona. So the Sea Breezes launched into a nearly unrecognizable version of "Margaritaville."

Thank God, Lucas thought. *Finally these two bumpkins will shut up.*

"It's our ten-year anniversary!" Rob shouted over the synthesized sounds of a steel drum.

"We're here to celebrate!" Fiona proclaimed.

"I grew my beard just for the trip," Rob said, rubbing his furry jaw.

"On account of Ernest Hemingway used to live here," Fiona hollered.

"They have a look-alike contest in July," Rob pointed out. "Maybe I'll come back and try to win it."

Sorry, dude, Lucas thought. *Your wife looks more like Hemingway than you do.*

"First prize is two plane tickets!" Fiona screeched.

"Not bad for sitting on your butt all day drinking beer!" Rob said.

It went on like that for several more minutes until the band finished the first number and proceeded to butcher the opening chords of "Open Arms" by Journey.

The couple suddenly went quiet, and Lucas couldn't help but risk a glance at them. Fiona was beseeching Rob with her eyes. "Oh, Rob. It's our song," she said.

To Lucas's amazement, the couple stood and began to dance—even though there wasn't a dance floor. They held each other close and began to weave slowly among the tables, as graceful as two bull elephants, banging into tables, knocking over one customer's piña colada in a top-heavy souvenir glass. Some patrons cheered; others yelled for them to take it outside.

Lucas recognized his opportunity, and he waved at Mike, the bartender.

"Ready for another?"

"Yeah, sure."

Mike brought a second draft, and Lucas dropped a ten onto the bar, saying, "Keep the change."

"Hey, thanks, buddy. I appreciate it."

"Listen," Lucas said, "I lost my driver's license."

The bartender waved him off. "Don't worry about it. You look twenty-one."

"No, what I'm saying is, I need to get another one. I'm looking for a place to get another ID. Can you help me out?" Lucas had practiced the wording to get it just right, to make his point without flat-out saying he was looking for false identification. But Mike was confused. And now another customer was calling from down the bar, so Mike held up a finger in a give-me-a-minute gesture and scooted away.

By the time Mike had come back, so had Rob and Fiona. Mike said to Lucas, "So what's the deal? You need a new ID?"

Rob and Fiona were cooing at each other, not paying attention to Lucas, so he quietly said, "You know where I can get one?"

Mike said, "You mean, like, a real ID?"

Now Rob was swiveling around, taking a drink from his beer, and Lucas was getting nervous about the whole situation. You don't just let complete strangers know you're looking for phony papers. "Yeah," Lucas said, abandoning the plan. "You know where I'd go to replace my driver's license?"

Mike shook his head. "Sorry, man. I just moved here three months ago.

"You lost your ID?" Rob asked.

"I lost my ID once," Fiona said. "A real hassle."

"Took months to straighten it all out," Rob groaned.

"But I ended up with a better picture!" Fiona said cheerily.

Colby no longer had possession of his truck, so Marlin drove south on Avenue F and spotted him walking past the parking lot at the electric cooperative. He pulled up next to him and said, "Want a ride?"

Colby glared at him. "You were watching all that shit, weren't you?"

Marlin shrugged. "I had no idea what was going to happen."

Colby looked at him with suspicion.

"Really," Marlin said.

Colby shook his head.

"Garza doesn't want me working the case," Marlin said. "I probably shouldn't even be talking to you." A truck pulled up from behind, and Marlin waved him around. "Look, just climb in, will you?"

After a few seconds, Colby opened the door and settled into the passenger seat. Marlin hit the gas and headed toward Miller Creek Loop.

The crisp spring air whipped through the open windows of the truck as both men rode in silence.

Colby finally said, "Those guys are so far off base it's not even funny."

"I know, Phil. I know. But they've gotta check everything out."

"Total bullshit."

"Give it time."

"Time? It's a waste of goddamn time."

Another mile went by.

"The best thing you can do is answer their questions," Marlin said.

"Not a fucking chance." Colby hadn't cooled down, not even a little.

"Right or wrong," Marlin said, "when a suspect asks for a lawyer, well, it looks like . . ."

Colby snapped his head around. "Like what? Like I'm guilty?"

"That's what gets into some people's heads."

"Into your head?"

"Nope."

Colby ran both hands over his scalp in frustration. "Oh, man, this is such an amazing crock of shit. Yeah, so I didn't like Scofield. The man was an asshole, and plenty of people hated his guts. Why did they zero in on me?"

Marlin kept his voice low and measured, hoping to bring some calm to the conversation. "The incident at the courthouse. That doesn't look good for you."

"That was months ago."

Marlin followed the twisting road past a ranch called Selah, where a man with a vision had single-handedly redefined modern habitat-restoration techniques. Selah was five thousand acres of thriving grasslands and wooded canyons, an ecosystem as healthy as any in the state. On most days, the drive along this narrow, pitted blacktop instilled in Marlin an overwhelming sense of serenity. Not today.

"The tire tracks, too," he said. "That's a problem."

"I get my tires at Save-Mart in Marble Falls," Colby said. "Just like half the people in this county."

"Yeah, I know, and you didn't even mention that back there."

"Are you defending them?"

Marlin could feel a small pool of anger welling in his gut. "I don't have to defend them, Phil. They're cops, and they're doing their jobs. End of story."

Marlin slowed and steered through the gate to the Circle S Ranch, just as he had done a thousand times before.

"Doing their jobs like a couple of Nazis," Colby muttered.

"Goddamn, just take it easy," Marlin snapped, and immediately regretted it.

"Yeah, okay," Colby said, full of sarcasm. "I'll just take it easy until I wind up in Huntsville. How's that? I'll just take it easy and let these local pinheads screw up the rest of my life."

Marlin clamped his jaw tight and said nothing. Neither man

spoke as Marlin followed the rugged caliche road to the front of Colby's house.

"Go ahead and ask me," Colby said.

"Ask you what?"

"Oh, come on. You know you want to ask. Was I over at Scofield's house? Are those my tire tracks they found?"

Marlin came to a stop and put the truck in park. "Phil, I—"

"Just ask!"

Marlin couldn't contain himself any longer. "Okay, tell me, then, if it's so damn important to you. Were you over there or not?"

It was as if someone flicked a switch that controlled the emotion in Colby's face. The anger drained out immediately, replaced by an expression of such profound disappointment that Marlin felt himself cringe.

Colby stepped out of the truck without another word.

"Hey!" Marlin called after him. "Hey, Phil!"

Colby said something without turning. Marlin couldn't be sure, but it sounded like "Have fun in San Antone."

19

"HEY, LUKE!"

Lucas turned and saw Rob and Fiona trundling after him as he walked down Duval Street. When they caught him, they were both short of breath.

"We couldn't just let you leave," Rob huffed.

"Not without an ID," Fiona gasped. "How are you going to write checks? How are you going to use credit cards?"

"We wondered if you might need a few bucks."

"To help you get home."

"That way your vacation won't be spoiled."

They both had such honest and open faces, and their gesture was so kind, Lucas felt guilty for being short with them in the bar.

"Guys, that is really nice," Lucas said. "But I'll be okay."

"Are you sure?"

"Absolutely positive?"

"You could call it a loan."

"Yeah, pay us back if you want."

"Or not. It doesn't matter."

Lucas was starting to like this annoying couple. They reminded him of people back home, where strangers could become friends in a matter of minutes.

"Really, I appreciate it, but I'm all set."

"Well, if you change your mind," Rob said, "we're staying at the Happy Clam."

"Nice little place," Fiona chimed in, "but nothing too fancy."

"Clean sheets."

"Plenty of hot water."

"Just give us a call."

"Or come see us."

"Where are you staying, Luke?"

"Someplace close?"

Lucas waved vaguely to the east and said he'd forgotten the name of the motel. Then he thanked them again and continued on his way.

"Hey, Luke!" Rob called out again.

Lucas turned. Now they were back to being pests. Maybe he should take their money.

"Smile!" Rob called. He was holding a small camera, and he snapped a picture of Lucas.

"For our scrapbook!" Fiona said.

Lucas gave them one last wave and quickly lost himself in the crowd.

Colby closed the front door behind him and waited until he heard Marlin drive away. He knew he shouldn't have made that last remark, but he couldn't help himself. He'd never been that angry before in his life.

He plopped into a living room chair and sat without moving for fifteen minutes, taking deep breaths, letting his mind settle down.

A cold beer. That's what he needed. Maybe several.

He stood and made his way to the darkened kitchen. He turned on the lights, and he heard a voice say, "I think you and me need to have a long talk."

Colby turned and saw a man sitting at the table. Baby blue suit. Stetson. The man who had presented himself as an interested hunter had a bottle of beer in his left hand. His right hand covered a revolver that rested on the tabletop.

"Mr. Jones," Colby said, "come on in and make yourself at home. Oh, wait, you already have."

Jones—which was obviously not his real name unless the guy was a total moron—raised the gun and pointed it at Colby. "Have a seat, Phil."

"I prefer to stand. Sitting is hell on my hemorrhoids."

Jones gave a slight smile, but there was steel in his voice. "Have a fucking seat. Now." Colby moved toward the table, and Jones said, "Uh-uh. Not at the table. Right there, on the floor."

Colby quickly pondered his options. There were knives in the drawers, but what good was a knife against a .38? And speaking of guns, Colby kicked himself for not carrying one himself. He was licensed to do just that, but he had figured they might not like him bringing it to the sheriff's office. For the moment, that left two possibilities: Run like hell and hope this guy was a poor shot. Or sit down. He sat.

"Very good," Jones said, nodding. "A wise man makes wise choices, Phil, and I think you just made a good one. Trust me."

Colby couldn't help but let out a small snort at that.

Jones ignored it. "I'm gonna tell you how this is gonna go, Phil, and I want to be absolutely clear on it just so there's no confusion. So here's the deal. I'm fixing to ask you a question, and you're immediately gonna answer me. No lies, no bullshit, and no reason for me to put a slug in your forehead. 'Cause believe me, I'm prepared to do that. In fact, it really don't make much difference to me either way. The only thing on the plus side is, I get paid more if you give me what I want. You follow me?"

"Sounds fairly straightforward to me," Colby said, thinking, *What the hell does this guy want?*

"Good, then," Jones said. "We have an understanding. But I should tell you—I'm not gonna ask twice. You get one answer, and one answer only. We clear?"

Colby rubbed a finger on the linoleum floor. "Look at all this waxy buildup. I'm not much of a housekeeper, to be honest."

Jones pulled the hammer back on the .38. "Are . . . we . . . clear?"

Colby shrugged. "Yeah, sure, we're clear."

"Okay, then. Here we go. The big question. Where are the negatives?"

Colby hadn't known what to expect. Maybe a question about Vance Scofield, because, after all, who the hell was this guy? Some lunatic Scofield's buddies had sent? Some nutcase who, like the deputies, thought Colby was a killer? But what was this about negatives?

Colby tried to appear appropriately meek and submissive as he held up a finger. "Uh . . . I'm not sure I understand. Did you say negatives?"

Jones's face was a vivid red. He extended his arm, and now the barrel of the gun was less than five feet from Colby's head, "I'm warning you. Not another fucking word unless you're telling me where they are."

So Colby didn't say anything.

Jones stared at him. Colby stared back. Ten seconds went by. Then twenty. Colby could hear the clock on the wall ticking.

Jones shifted his weight, the old wooden chair squeaking beneath him. "Well?"

Colby held up his arms in a gesture of helplessness.

"Talk, goddamn it!" Jones screamed, his arm visibly shaking.

"Okay," Colby said in the most soothing voice he could muster. "Okay, but help me out a little. What're we talking about here? Prom photos? Graduation? What?"

Jones squeezed and the gun in his hand roared.

"You ready to hear the plan?" Red asked.

He and Billy Don and Lucy were sitting at the small dinette in

Red's kitchen, swilling back their fourth round of Bloody Marys. Red had been holding off on telling Billy Don all the specifics, because the big man was liable to be a problem, but now, with Lucy here, she and Red could sell the plan to Billy Don together. It would be a big help, mostly because Lucy was so much more persuasive than Red was. When words came out of her mouth, they sounded like individual nuggets of unvarnished wisdom and truth. She even made the dishonest part of it sound all right.

Billy Don nodded.

"Okay," Lucy said, "here's the deal. Like I said, this old guy Scofield is one of my clients. I go to see him three times a week to give him his shots, make sure he's taking his medication, that sort of thing. He's kinda deaf, confused half the time, so he's a shut-in."

"Shut in what?" Billy Don asked.

"That means he don't leave the house. His health ain't good enough."

"What's he got?"

"All kinds of great shit. He's rich."

"No, I mean what's he sick with?"

"Does it really matter? He's just old, okay? And besides, we're not really stealing from him. We're stealing from his son."

"The dead one?"

"That's the only one he has."

"But I don't—"

"Just let me explain everything first, okay? Then you can ask all your questions."

Lucy was getting impatient, and Red could understand. "Yeah, let's just let her lay it all out, Billy Don. It'll all make sense."

Billy Don mumbled for Lucy to go ahead.

"So the son, Vance—he comes over to the house several times a week. Maybe more, because all I have to go by is the times he showed up when I was there myself. At first, I thought he was just being a good son and all that, coming to see his dad. But then I started noticing that Vance would only stick around for a few minutes each time, and he'd always go into one of the back bedrooms before he left. He'd just duck in there, close the door, and be back out a couple minutes later. Well, there's a big walk-in closet in that room, and you wanna guess what's in that closet?"

The question was directed at Billy Don, so Red didn't say anything. He already knew what the answer was.

"Dirty magazines?" Billy Don asked, grinning. "That's what I keep in my closet."

"That's a good guess," Lucy answered. Red could tell she was just being nice so Billy Don would get on board. "But no, what he's got in there is a safe."

"A safe? Like a . . . safe?"

"Yeah. It's about yea high, maybe three feet square. Heavy as hell."

"What's in it?"

"Well, hell, ain't no way to know for sure. But I think we can safely assume it's something valuable. Probably money."

"Cash money?"

"I'm betting so. Let me ask you something. Have you heard about that Rotary Club raffle? They're giving away that Corvette?"

"Yeah, I think so. Shoulda been a truck, you ask me."

"You're probably right. Anyway, I come to learn that Vance was the treasurer for all that. He was in charge of all the money from the ticket sales." She laughed. "He even tried to sell me a ticket one time. Like I was gonna go for that sucker bet."

"So you're thinking he was keeping all the money in the safe."

"That's what I'm thinking."

Billy Don pulled a stalk of celery out of his Bloody Mary and started munching on it, apparently thinking things through. Then he said the one thing Red was afraid he was going to say. "I'm not sure I like it. It's stealing from charity. They give that money to poor kids and such."

It was the same thing Red had said to Lucy on Wednesday night at the bar. But then she had explained everything to him, and in a weird kind of way, it had all made perfect sense.

"Yeah," Lucy said to Billy Don, "but they got an insurance policy against theft and that sort of thing. All of them raffles do. A policy issued by the U.S. government."

Billy Don looked confused. "I didn't know the guv'mint handled stuff like that. You sure?"

"Damn right they do. It's the law. Just like bank deposits. Fully insured."

Red hadn't known that fact himself until Lucy had informed him of it.

"I don't know," Billy Don said. "It still don't seem right."

Billy Don wasn't coming around as quickly as Red had hoped, but he knew Lucy wasn't done yet.

She said, "You ever take a close look at one of your paychecks, Billy Don?"

"Not really."

"Well, if you did, you'd see that the IRS takes a big whopping chunk out of it every time. Income taxes, Social Security, Medicare—it's all lopped right off the top. They take way more than their fair share, and you and me don't hardly wind up with anything to show for it, do we?"

"Naw, I guess we don't."

"Then you got your property taxes, just like Red pays on this fine mobile home, and that's where some of your rent goes. Those property taxes includes school taxes, and you ain't even got any kids, do ya?"

"Don't think so."

"Then why the hell you got to pay school taxes?"

Billy Don scratched his scalp with the stalk of celery, then took another bite. "That's a damn good question."

"There's county taxes, too, which pays for the roads and such, and that don't seem fair because you ain't got a car, neither. And if you *did* have a car, they'd slap a tax on you just for driving the damn thing."

Billy Don looked at Red for confirmation. Red nodded. "I get a bill every year. Plus, they make me get it inspected."

"And of course there's a fee for that," Lucy said. "And don't forget sales tax. Every time one private individual buys something in a store owned by another private individual, the government sticks its nose in and charges you for it. Does that seem right?"

"Dadgum, no it don't. Those greedy sumbitches. It ain't really their affair."

"Hell no, it ain't. They tax you coming and they tax you going. Every damn day of your life, including the day you die, there's a tax for it. They take your hard-earned money away from you, and there's never been anything you can do about it. Until now. The money in that safe is rightfully yours, Billy Don. We're not taking it away from the charities, because they got insurance. We're taking it away from the government, and hell, they practically owe it to you. It's a rebate on all the money they been conning you out of all these years."

Billy Don smacked his fist on the tabletop. "I want my damn money back!"

"Okay, then! That's what we're gonna do. We're gonna take it back!"

"But how we gonna get the money out of the safe?"

Lucy held up a finger. "One thing at a time. First, we've gotta get the safe out of the house."

They explained the plan in more detail to Billy Don, and the first question he asked was "We're supposed to be plumbers, huh?" He smiled. "We gotta wear pants that show our butt cracks?"

"Just wear what you always wear," Lucy said. "It ain't like they got a standard uniform."

Red said, "When are we gonna do it?"

"I figure this afternoon. Might as well get after it. The bedroom where the safe is—it has its own bathroom. I already told the old man I thought there was a problem with the toilet in there. Yesterday I told him I'd see about getting somebody in to look at it."

They discussed a few more odds and ends, Lucy coaching them on how to behave, what to say, things like that. To Red, it almost felt like they were getting ready for a school play.

"Speaking of toilets," Billy Don said. He rose from his chair and steered himself down the hallway to the bathroom. A moment later, Red could clearly hear a stream of urine hitting the water in the toilet.

"Damn, Billy Don, shut the door! We got a lady present."

Billy Don grunted in reply, and Red heard the door close.

Now the trailer was quiet. Almost too quiet. It was the first time Red and Lucy had been alone since she'd asked him if he had his own bedroom. *You never can tell when you might need a little privacy.* Probably just talk, he figured, but he noticed that she was staring at him now, and it was making him nervous. He looked down at his drink, then back up, and she had a strange look in her eye.

"This celery sure is crunchy," he said.

She didn't say anything.

He took a small bite. "I wonder what makes it so dang crunchy."

She was still staring.

"Tasty stuff," he said.

She lifted an eyebrow.

He couldn't stand it anymore. "What're you looking at me like that for?"

There was a pause. "I'm just wondering."

"Wondering what?"

"Whether you're ready for this or not. You think you can pull it off?"

"Hell yeah, I'm ready," Red said. "Just acting like a plumber, is all. No problem."

Lucille leaned in close, and a wicked smile broke across her lips. "I got an idea. Instead of playing plumber, how about playing doctor?" she whispered.

It wasn't just talk!

"Well, I, uh . . ." Red wanted to come up with something witty, but suddenly his tongue was as thick as fresh cement.

"How about we send Billy Don to the store for something . . ." Lucy said.

"Uh-huh?"

"Then we can go back into your bedroom . . ."

"Yeah?"

"And you can give me a complete examination."

Red managed to blurt out something in reply, but he wasn't even sure what he said. There was a frog the size of a Suburban in his throat.

The next thing he knew, Lucy's hand was on his thigh. Then it crept higher, and she laughed. "See there, Doctor. I've already found a place to hang your stethoscope."

"Billy Don!" Red hollered, his voice cracking all over the place. "We need more tomato juice!"

20

BACK AT THE sheriff's department, Marlin decided to put his conversation with Phil Colby out of his mind. Just not think about it at all. Not now, when there was work to do.

He started by trying a shot in the dark. He closed the door to his office and dialed Stephanie Waring's cell phone number. His heart jumped when it was answered. Sounded like an elderly male. There was lots of static on the line.

"This is John Marlin. Who am I speaking to, please?"

"This is Blackie. Is this your phone?" The old guy sounded half in the bag.

"Pardon me?"

"I said, is this your phone?"

"Uh, I'm not sure what you mean, but I'm trying to reach Stephanie Waring. Is she there?"

"Don't know no Tiffany."

"No, it's Stephanie."

The man didn't reply.

"Sir," Marlin said, "do you know Stephanie Waring?"

"Don't know no Tiffany."

Whoever this man was, he sounded like he was heavily medicated. Or needed to be. "Sir, please tell me where I'm calling."

Marlin heard nothing but traffic noise in the background. "Sir, where am I calling?"

"Hold on a dang minute." Several seconds passed. "Down on Holtz Boulevard. Near the shelter."

"No, I mean what city?"

The man answered, and it sounded like he said, "Miami."

"Miami, Florida?" Marlin asked.

Nothing.

"Sir? Did you find that phone somewhere?"

But the line was dead, or the man had hung up.

Marlin dialed the number again. No answer—just an automated message stating that the customer's voice mailbox was full. He tried two more times with the same result.

Florida? Had he misdialed? Had to have been a wrong number.

Okay, great. Now what?

The deputies had already interviewed all of Stephanie's friends, family members, and coworkers, and Marlin wasn't sure what else he could do to find her. He flipped back through his notes, checking everything he and the deputies had done so far.

There was a light knock on the door.

"Yeah?"

Nicole Brooks stuck her head in. "How's it going, John?"

"Hey, Nicole, come on in."

"Actually, I was just leaving for Scofield's, but I wanted to come by and say . . . well, sorry, I guess."

"For what?"

"This thing with Phil Colby. I know the two of you are tight, so I figured this must be driving you crazy."

He started to shrug it off, to say it was no big deal and it would all work itself out—but there was something about her demeanor, the look of sincerity on her face, that made him want to be sincere right back. "Yeah, it is," he said. "Right up the wall." He added a half-hearted smile just to let her know he wasn't going completely nuts.

She glanced down the hallway behind her, then back at him. "Listen, I have to get a move on, but do you want to get together and talk about it tonight? Maybe over a beer or something?"

Marlin wondered, *Am I misreading this, or is she asking me out?*

"Yeah, sure, that'd be great," he said. *No, she's just showing professional courtesy,* he thought. *Wants to keep me updated on the case.*

"How about I meet you back here at seven?"

"Okay, good. I'll see you then."

She started to close the door, but Marlin said, "Hey, Nicole, I don't see anything in my notes about Stephanie Waring's phone records. Somebody pulled those, right?"

"Actually, no. We were about to, but her mother called and said she was in Colorado. At that point, it dropped lower on the to-do list—especially since we didn't know yet that Scofield was a homicide. You still working on her?"

"I'd sure like to talk to her."

"Yeah, we all would."

He looked at his computer. "Just like a regular affidavit, right?"

"You've never pulled phone records?"

He smiled. "Yeah, but it's been maybe fifteen years. Memory's a little rusty."

"Her home phone or a wireless account?"

"Just the wireless for now."

"You know which carrier?"

"Yeah, it's on her voicemail."

"Okay, then your best bet would be to fax the subpoena to the carrier." She stepped into his office and gestured toward his computer. "We've got a list of all the carriers and their fax numbers on the server. Want me to show you?"

"That'd be great."

She came around his desk and leaned across in front of him to operate the mouse. A few clicks later, she had the list on his screen. "I'll save this document onto your desktop."

Marlin kept his eyes forward, but he could smell her perfume just a light scent, and maybe the soap she had used earlier tha morning.

"As far as the affidavit," she said, "you just need to show cause fo the records being important to an ongoing case, and so on." She wa clicking into areas of the network Marlin had never accessed before "I'm going to pull one of my affidavits so you can use it as a tem plate. Just change a few names and details and you'll be good to go."

As Brooks navigated the system, she used her free hand to tuc a stray lock of auburn hair back into place. Marlin could feel a warn glow—maybe real, maybe imagined—coming off her body.

"There," she said. "You're all set." She came around to the fron of his desk.

"I'll let you know if I get anywhere," Marlin said. "I really ap preciate it."

"Hey, no problem. Ask them to put a rush on it. Sometime that helps." Again, she started to close the door but paused. "Se you at seven?"

"Yeah. See you then."

"I'd like to report a possible fugitive," a man said.

"Yes, a *possible* fugitive," a woman's voice added. "But I hop we're mistaken."

"He seems like a nice guy," the man said. "But something's a lit tle hinky."

"Unfortunately, my husband is rarely wrong."

Sergeant Damon Watley glanced up from the paperwork on hi desk. The Key West Police Department didn't get too many walk in visitors, and those they did get were usually locals. Not thes two. They had come straight from Mallory Square or Duva Street. Out-of-towners all the way. Sunburned, overweigh tourists in loud clothing. Watley grabbed a pen. "Name?"

"Luke," the man said. "I don't know his last name."

"He never did give it," said the woman. "But we never asked."

"I'm not even sure about the 'Luke' part. Might be fake."

"But he *looked* like a Luke, if that helps."

"I don't think it does, Fiona."

"I'm just trying to be useful, Rob."

"No," Sergeant Watley said. "I mean *your* name."

"Oh," said the man.

The woman laughed. "We thought—"

"You meant *his* name."

"That's funny!"

"We're the Norrises."

"We're from Wisconsin," the woman said, making it sound like an explanation.

"I'm Rob."

"I'm Fiona."

"Been here all week."

"And it's such a lovely town. Absolutely lovely!"

"First rate. And I have to say, it looks like you guys are doing a great job. I should know. I'm involved in law enforcement myself."

"The streets feel so safe."

"We expected more of a criminal element, to be blunt."

"But all we've seen is tourists!"

Sergeant Watley held up his hands in an attempt to get the couple to quit talking. Surprisingly, it worked. "Why don't you start from the beginning?"

"Okay," Rob said. "We were in a bar on Duval Street this morning. About ten o'clock."

"We don't usually drink that early," Fiona stressed, "but we're on vacation!"

"And I overheard this guy Luke talking to the bartender. He asked where he could get a new driver's license."

"I didn't hear that part."

"He wanted to know where he could get a new one. But he wasn't from Florida."

"He told us he was from Texas."

"And that makes you wonder—"

"Why would he try to get a new driver's license—"

"If he isn't even from this state?"

"Isn't that peculiar?"

"It seemed suspicious to me, so I asked him some question He was very evasive."

"I hope we're mistaken. For his sake."

"Except we'd hate to waste your time."

"We snapped his photo!" Fiona Norris held up a digital camera

"Even better, I've got his fingerprints." Rob Norris held up plastic bag, inside of which was a glass beer mug.

Sergeant Watley scratched his head. "You're a cop?"

"Uh, well, no."

"You said you were in law enforcement."

"Well, in a way," said Rob. "I'm the president of our Neighbor hood Watch program."

"And he does a really good job!" Fiona proclaimed.

"I do have an eye for it," Rob confessed.

"It's like an intuition."

"More of a sixth sense."

"Our neighbors love him!"

"I can just look at a guy—"

"And tell if he's up to no good!"

"Like this guy here," Rob said, tapping the camera.

"He was so sweet," said Fiona.

"But I saw right through it."

"Rob says he's on the run."

Rob nodded solemnly. "No doubt about it."

"Kind of sad, really."

"Unless he's, like, a murderer."

"Or a rapist!" Fiona shuddered.

"You should contact Texas."

"See if they've got—"

"Okay! Okay!" Sergeant Watley said loudly. "We'll look into it *Just to shut both of you up.*

* * *

"You just shot my stove," Colby said. "That was an antique. It was my great-grandmother's."

The man had hardly even flinched, and Buford had to give him credit for that. This was the second bullet he'd sent sailing past Colby's skull, and Colby hadn't even broken a sweat.

"Next one goes in your head," Buford said, but he knew he was losing credibility. That was the problem—he kept saying he was going to shoot Colby, but he couldn't actually do it. Not if he wanted to find the negatives. There were other things he could do, though. Plenty of them. "Mister," he said, "you want my advice, you'll just give me the negatives and be done with it."

Colby remained silent.

"Ain't worth the trouble," Buford said.

Nothing.

"You think this high-fence shit is worth dying for?"

Buford must've said the right thing, because the look on Colby's face changed. Now he was shaking his head, like he'd figured something out. "You know something? You're absolutely right. This whole thing has gotten out of hand."

Now we're getting somewhere, Buford thought.

"So I'll do it," Colby continued. "I'll give you the negatives. But we got one small problem."

"Yeah, what?"

"They're in a safe-deposit box down at the bank. It closes early on Fridays. We can't get in it till Monday."

It was bad news, meaning this was going to take a lot longer than he had hoped. But Buford was prepared for it. He had a backup plan. He pulled the roll of duct tape out from his jacket pocket. "On your stomach. Arms behind your back. We're going for a little ride."

Marlin had just sent a fax when Darrell put a call through.

"Uh, John Marlin?" a woman's voice asked.

"Yes, ma'am."

"Yeah, I think you called me earlier this week. My name's Jenny Geiger."

For a moment the name didn't register. Then it clicked. "Oh, right, thanks for calling me back. I left half a message on your machine. Sorry about that."

"That's okay, I tracked you down. I was out of town. Just walked in the door."

"Miss Geiger, you're a friend of Vance Scofield's, right?"

A pause. "Well, sort of. I haven't seen him in a while."

"How long has it been?"

"Probably two months or so."

"From what I understand, you and Vance dated?"

"Uh, yeah. Briefly."

Jenny Geiger did not sound comfortable.

"Have you seen the news lately?"

"Yeah, about Vance. I already heard. I figured that's why you were calling."

"Are you aware that it was a homicide?" Marlin knew Bobby Garza's news conference had ended thirty minutes ago.

"Yeah, I heard it on the radio coming home from the airport. Some of my friends called me earlier this week when it first happened, but they were saying he drowned. What happened?"

"That's what we're working on," Marlin said. "Let me ask you something, Miss Geiger. Do you know of any reason somebody would want to harm Vance? Anyone angry with him—that sort of thing?"

"Not that I know of. Like I said, we only went out a few times."

Marlin tried the same questions, but in different words. Sometimes that technique elicited different responses. "Did he ever mention any arguments with anybody, or talk about anybody that didn't like him?"

"Not really, no."

"Not really?"

"No, he didn't."

"Did you ever meet any of his friends?"

"He was in the Rotary Club. I met a couple of those guys when I was selling tickets for the raffle."

"That's how you met Vance? Selling the tickets?"

"Right."

"Did he ever mention anyplace else where he might've parked the Corvette?"

"He kept it in his barn. That's all I know."

Marlin switched gears. "Where did you and Vance usually go when you went out?"

"Just clubs in Austin."

"The Warehouse District?"

"Sometimes."

"Did y'all ever meet up with anybody down there?"

"Nope."

"He ever get into any trouble at any of the clubs?"

"What kind of trouble?"

"Maybe exchange words with somebody. Get into a confrontation."

"Not that I ever saw."

"Did he seem to know many people at the clubs?"

"Well, maybe a couple, but he'd just say hi and that was it."

"You catch any names?"

"None that I remember."

"How about phone calls? Did you ever hear him get angry with anybody?"

"No, I—" The line clicked. "Can you hold on just a second?"

Before Marlin could answer, she switched to the incoming call. Just as well. So far, she wasn't offering much. In fact, she seemed reluctant to speak, and Marlin thought he knew why. After a good minute and a half, she finally came back on the line.

"I'm sorry about that. It was my mother, long distance. Checking up on me."

"No problem. I won't keep you much longer. The thing is, Miss Geiger, we're having a really tough time finding out much about Vance—his friends, who he hung out with, that sort of thing. But one thing we do know is that he was into drugs, at least to some degree. I just want to make it clear that whatever you tell me as far as the drugs are concerned, it won't get you into trouble. We're working a homicide, and that's our main focus right now."

When she spoke again, there was genuine irritation in her voice. "You think *I* use drugs?"

It had certainly occurred to him. Birds of a feather. "No, ma'am, I didn't say that. But some people are hesitant to mention that kind of thing when they're talking about their friends. What I'm asking is that you be straight up with me and tell me anything you think might be useful. It would be a big help."

Marlin could feel the tension over the phone line, and he wondered if she would answer. Then she said, "I am not a drug user. I want to make that clear."

"I understand."

"The truth is, it was the drugs that made me quit seeing Vance. I mean, he was an okay guy and everything. He liked to have a lot of fun, and we always went to nice places. But after a couple of dates, I could see that he was a pretty heavy user."

"What did he use?"

"Speed, mostly. He talked about Ecstasy a couple of times, but speed is all I ever saw."

"Did he offer it to you?"

"Yes, but I never did any."

"Where did he get it, do you know?"

Then she threw him for a loop. She finally gave him something he could use. Something huge.

"No idea," she said quietly. "I think he might've been dealing it."

Marlin wanted to shout at her, to tell her that that little bit of news was extremely important. Why hadn't she told him earlier? But he didn't want to scare her off, so he kept his voice low-key. "Why do you think that?"

"One time, he was on his cell phone, and I thought I heard him saying something about twenty grams. When he hung up, I asked who he'd been talking to. He said it was his partner. So I said, 'Your partner in what?' He just laughed and said, 'You don't want to know.' All mysterious, like it was real cool or something."

Marlin's heart was thrumming. This could be the lead they'd been needing for the past five days. The only problem was, he didn't like where it pointed. One name leapt to mind as a potential partner of Vance's. "Did Vance ever mention a man named Lucas Burnette?" he asked.

She didn't answer right away. "You know, that does sound kind of familiar. Maybe."

Maybe. Not good enough.

"Do you remember when that was?" Marlin asked. "The phone call to his partner?"

"It would've been the last time I went out with him. The idea that he was dealing . . . that was enough for me."

"Do you remember the exact date?" Marlin could check the phone records that had already been pulled. Find out who Scofield had been talking to.

"I don't know. Sometime in March."

Again, not good enough. "Miss Geiger, do you keep a diary or a date book or something like that? I really need to know the date."

"I'm sorry, I don't."

A dead end. There was no way—yet—to identify the "partner." So he said, "If you think of a way to figure out that date, please give me a call. It's very important."

"Yeah, no problem."

The line was quiet for a moment. She was lingering, not as eager to hang up as he thought she would be.

"Is there something else I need to know?" Marlin asked.

He heard her take a big breath. "This is really gross, but I guess I better tell you. When Vance and I quit seeing each other, it wasn't a big deal, really. He was a little upset, but nothing major. I told him flat out that the drugs bothered me, and he bitched about it, then let it go. But then, the next day, I came out of my apartment and . . . well . . . I think he masturbated onto my front door."

Marlin found himself at a loss for words. He knew Scofield was a drug user and a womanizer, but he hadn't expected this. "He . . . uh . . ."

"Yep."

"You found—"

"There was . . . a mess. And I sure couldn't think of anyone else who would've done it."

21

EVEN BEFORE THE news conference, Chuck Hamm had heard the rumors: Phil Colby was the number-one suspect in the murder of Vance Scofield. It was almost too good to be true.

Hamm knew firsthand that Vance was a lowlife scum who had had all the ethics of a rutting pig. He'd been a womanizer, a thief, and a liar—so the cops should have had a suspect list a mile long. Jealous husbands. Jilted girlfriends. Maybe even fellow drug users, if Hamm's suspicions in that area were correct. But the cops were focusing on Colby. It was enough to make Hamm giggle like a tipsy sorority girl. Finally things would be set right. Colby—the man who had filed a nuisance lawsuit against high fences, and who was now blackmailing Senator Herzog—would get what was coming to him for being such a major pain in the ass.

But it also made Hamm nervous. The cops were sniffing around Colby . . . and what would happen if they found the negatives before Buford did? Buford had said he had searched Colby's place, but how well?

Apparently, Hamm wasn't the only one rattled by these recent events, because his phone rang late in the morning. It was Senator Dylan Herzog, with traffic in the background, calling from a pay phone. "I understand your friend Vance Scofield was murdered," Herzog said with urgency. "This is a horrifying development." Hamm was disgusted at the fear he heard in the man's voice.

"Yeah, yeah, I heard," Hamm said impatiently. "But why does that have your panties in a knot?"

No answer for a moment, and then: "You know, Chuck, there are times when I wish you would speak to me with a little more respect. After all, I *am* a Texas state senator."

"Yeah, well, some people would say that's not something to brag about. Now what can I do for you?"

After another moment of icy silence, Herzog said, "I have concerns that these two things—the recent phone call I received and the death of Scofield—are somehow related."

Hamm's first instinct was to calm the senator down, to tell him that Vance Scofield probably had all sorts of enemies. Then it occurred to him that the more people who suspected Phil Colby, the better. "Now why in the hell would you think that?" Hamm asked, leading the senator along. Herzog always responded better if he thought he was doing his own thinking.

His reply was snippy. "Well, if you insist on being obtuse, I'll spell it out for you. Colby is obviously a bit . . . unstable. I realize you didn't hear him on the phone, but believe me, he came across as vindictive and hateful. I find it entirely plausible that his animosity could manifest itself this way."

"Wanna talk English?"

"Okay, how's this? I think he might've killed Vance Scofield, and he did it because he hates high fences. He did it because he wants to send a message—to me, to you, and to all of your buddies. Blackmail isn't enough."

Hamm was impressed. Herzog had come up with that theory

without even knowing that Colby was already a suspect. "I think you nailed it on the nose," he said.

"You do?"

"Damn right. Word is, the cops have already talked to him."

"Oh my God. Are they holding him?"

"Nope."

"You think I'm in danger?"

"I'd say anything's a possibility."

"Good Lord."

"Senator, let me bring you up to speed on Colby. Per your instructions, we've been telling you things strictly on a need-to-know basis. And now, there are a few things you truly need to know."

"I'm listening."

"When my nephew first mentioned Colby's name, did you recognize it?"

"It seemed somewhat familiar."

"That's because Colby filed a lawsuit against one of his neighbors, trying to block the construction of a high fence."

"Okay, now I remember it. Happened last fall."

"Exactly. But do you remember who Colby's neighbor was?"

"No, I do not."

Hamm paused for drama. "Vance Scofield."

"Jesus," Herzog whispered.

"Damn right."

"He's a lunatic."

"Possibly."

"He might come after us all."

"I wouldn't put it past him. You have a bodyguard?"

Herzog sounded haughty. "I've never felt as if I needed one. Besides, I'm thinking it might be wise if I asked for police protection."

Oops. Maybe Hamm had pushed this a little too far. "I wouldn't do that, Dylan."

"And why not?"

"You pull the cops in, ain't they gonna ask why?"

"What do you mean?"

"They're gonna ask why you're feeling threatened. You'll have to tell them the whole story—that you're being blackmailed by Colby, and now, considering what happened to Scofield, you're worried about your own safety." *And,* Hamm thought, *you'll tell them all about our little arrangement.* Hamm had no doubt he and Buford would wind up in the same jail cell, considering his nephew's bumbling tactics recently.

"But the very fact that Colby is blackmailing me shows how venomous he is," Herzog said. "It shows a pattern of aggression in his campaign against high fences."

"But wouldn't they ask what he's got on you?"

"I could remain vague."

"And what happens if a deputy finds those photos?"

"I . . . I tell him that they were created on a computer, and I could keep his mouth shut by offering certain . . . rewards."

Yeah, Hamm thought. *A cushy law-enforcement position at the state level.* There was only one catch. "But this isn't just about blackmail, it's about murder. They'll want to use those photos as evidence in Colby's trial. Can't you just picture those shots plastered all over Court TV? You sure you want to go that route?"

"But . . . it's my duty to come forward." Herzog sounded a lot less sure of himself.

"Relax. They'll nail him without even knowing about your little problem."

"You think so?"

"Yeah, I do. No, the best thing for us to do is to find the negatives first. Then you can tell the cops whatever you'd like. Paint the story any way you want it."

Herzog was silent. Then: "I could say yes, he was blackmailing me, but the photos were doctored. As long as they don't have the negatives, they'd never know."

"There you go. Sounds like a plan." Hamm was amazed at how rapidly the senator was willing to abandon the truth.

"But we *have* to find those negatives."

"We will."

Neither man spoke for a moment. "You think he did it?" Herzog finally asked. "Colby killed Scofield?"

"Sure looks that way," Hamm replied.

The man calling himself George Jones had stashed his Cadillac inside of Phil's barn, and Phil cussed himself for failing to notice earlier that the door was closed. He usually left it open.

"Where's your partner?" Phil asked.

"Huh?"

"Bill. The little guy with the bad stomach."

A look of pure malice crossed George's face. "Shut your damn mouth and get in."

George opened the door, and Phil slid into the passenger seat, his arms bound tightly behind his back. "This is a nice ride," Phil said. "Buy the right clothes and you could be a hell of a pimp."

George climbed into the driver's seat without answering.

Up at Miller Creek Loop, Colby expected him to take a right, toward Highway 281, but George turned left. Could be that George was taking the back roads to Johnson City, or maybe he wanted to hook up with Highway 290 and go west.

But they had only gone three hundred yards when George slowed the car and pulled into an overgrown driveway. Wade Morgan's ninety acres. The old man hadn't set foot in his hunting cabin for more than three seasons. Colby rousted partying teenagers off the land every now and then, occasionally a few poachers, but other than that, the property was virtually abandoned.

"I wanna make something clear right from the start," Phil said as they bounced along the rutted road. "I never put out on the first date."

When Marlin got to Vance Scofield's ranch house, half a dozen vehicles were parked outside. One was a livestock trailer, owned by one of the night deputies, and it was already half filled with cardboard boxes.

There are two types of search warrants in Texas. One allows officers to enter a dwelling and search for a specific item or items alleged to be evidence related to a particular crime. The other, known as an "evidentiary search warrant," allows the police to load up virtually anything they might want to sift through later—bank statements and other financial records, personal letters, computers, firearms, even furniture, if necessary. Apparently, that was the type of warrant Garza had secured on Scofield's house.

There was a subtle nuance involved here that lifted Marlin's spirits about Phil Colby's situation. Because it was the second time the deputies had entered the premises—and they had relinquished control of the house in the meantime—the evidentiary search warrant had required the approval of a district judge, not a local justice of the peace. Getting a district judge to sign off takes more time and effort. What it meant was, Garza was serious about digging deeper. He wasn't pointing his finger at Phil and letting it go at that.

As Marlin neared the front door, Ernie Turpin was coming out, wheeling a dolly piled high with more boxes.

Marlin held the door for him. "Garza around?"

Turpin's forehead was beaded with sweat. "He had to run back to the office for something."

"How about Tatum?"

"In the back."

When Marlin found Bill Tatum—in a small, stuffy office, cleaning out a desk—he had a tough time deciphering the expression on the senior deputy's face. Was he angry at Marlin's presence? The two of them had always gotten along well, but they hadn't spoken since Phil's interview that morning. "Just couldn't stay away, could you?" Tatum said, but with a smile tugging at the corners of his mouth. Before Marlin could reply, Tatum held up his hands in a just-kidding gesture.

"I talked to Jenny Geiger," Marlin said. "The girl from the photograph."

Tatum stopped what he was doing. "Yeah? When?"

"Ten minutes ago."

"And?"

Marlin ran through the entire conversation, hoping Tatum would appear as excited about the possibilities as Marlin was. But his expression didn't change until Marlin got to the end. "Somebody jacked off on her door?"

"That's what she said." Marlin switched to the part of the phone call that interested him the most. "If Scofield was dealing, that opens up a whole new angle. Maybe a drug deal gone bad. Who knows what kind of scum he was dealing with."

Tatum drank from a liter-sized plastic bottle of water on the desk. "I got more of these in my cruiser."

Marlin shook his head.

Tatum chugged down the remainder of the bottle, then wiped his mouth. "If drugs were involved, we'll find names, numbers . . . something. Nothing like that has leapt out at us yet."

Marlin didn't want to be the one to say it, but he did anyway. "Maybe he was hooked up with Lucas."

Tatum let that sink in. They'd all considered it before, based on the fact that the two men had disappeared at the same time, but Tatum appeared doubtful. "We have absolutely nothing that says they even knew each other." He screwed the cap back onto his empty water bottle. "Come on outside with me."

They walked outside to Tatum's cruiser. The trunk was open, with an ice chest inside, and Tatum grabbed another liter of water. He held it toward Marlin. "You sure?"

"No thanks."

Tatum opened the bottle and drained half of it. "Hot in there."

Marlin studied the surrounding countryside—rolling hills thick with cedars, live oaks, persimmon, and mountain laurel, with waist-high native grasses filling the gaps in between. Beautiful, but the scorching summer to come would turn the bluestem as brittle as uncooked spaghetti.

Tatum cleared his throat. "Listen, I want to be clear about something. I do *not* think Phil Colby has it in him to kill Vance Scofield. Not deliberately, anyway."

Marlin waited. He didn't like that last sentence.

"On the other hand," Tatum continued, "the lab in Austin is going over Phil's truck right now. They're not done, but so far, they're saying the tires look like a match."

Marlin didn't like that sentence, either, but he wasn't discouraged. Matching tires to a particular set of tracks—like linking hairs to a specific person—was still an imprecise science. There was plenty of room for error. "So what this Geiger woman said . . . you think I'm grasping at straws?" he asked, unable to keep a small amount of challenge out of his voice.

"I didn't say that."

"All I'm doing is checking other angles."

"I can appreciate that, John, but I just want to know why Phil was over there. If something happened, he needs to be up front with us. Whatever the case, I really think you should prepare yourself for . . . well, for anything. And I'm saying that as a friend of yours—which I've always considered myself to be—and not a cop."

Anger had been building in Marlin's gut, but he didn't want to take it out on Tatum. He turned to lean against Tatum's vehicle, and he saw Nicole Brooks approaching, carrying a large brown box, much like the ones Ernie Turpin had carted out earlier. But as she neared, Marlin spotted commercial printing on the side, along with a logo that had been drilled into his brain through countless magazine ads and television commercials. A surge ran through him as unexpected as touching a live wire.

Marlin said, "Scofield must've had a hell of a sinus condition."

Tatum looked at him, puzzled. Then he, too, spotted Brooks. The box in her hands was a wholesale lot of over-the-counter allergy medicine. She reached inside and came out with one of the individual retail packages.

"Pseudoephedrine," she said. "The same brand we found at Lucas's house. We got four more boxes just like this in the garage."

"I'll be damned," Tatum said.

Marlin could hear a vehicle coming up Scofield's long caliche driveway. "Thank you, Nicole."

She gave him a wink.

Whoever was driving the vehicle was going heavy on the gas. The car came through an opening in the trees, and Marlin saw that it was Bobby Garza's cruiser.

The sheriff pulled in behind Marlin's truck and quickly climbed out, carrying a single piece of paper. "I just got this by e-mail from a sergeant in Florida," he said, frustration in his voice. He slapped a laser-printed photo down on the hood of a cruiser. "Tell me that ain't Lucas Burnette."

22

LUCAS HAD SEEN plenty of cops in the past six days. Small-town Barney Fifes keeping a watchful eye on their domains. Highway patrolmen cruising the interstates. County deputies looking stern as they ran radar on state highways. But none of them had made Lucas particularly nervous. He had realized early on that—even on lesser-traveled roads—he was virtually anonymous, just one car among thousands, like one ant in a swarming mound. His sense of confidence had come from the fact that they wouldn't pull him over as long as he didn't give them a reason to do so. Sure, maybe they had been looking for the Corvette back when he was still driving it, but there were a lot more Corvettes on the road than one might think. And now that he was driving a plain-vanilla hatchback, well, the odds were astronomically in his favor.

Why, then, as he pulled into the motel parking lot, did his gut tighten up when he spotted a black-and-white parked at the motel across the street? The cruiser was empty, parked in front of the office. This struck him as odd. If the motel manager had called in a complaint, it would almost certainly be against a guest. And if a guest was causing trouble, wouldn't the cop park in front of that guest's room?

Lucas decided that he was being way too jumpy, that his nerves were shot from the failed mission at the bar on Duval Street. That didn't stop him from pulling into the parking lot of his own motel, climbing out, and poking his head around a corner to get a clear view across the street.

He lit a cigarette—so any other guest who came along would peg him as a smoker staying in a nonsmoking room—and he waited.

This is silly, he thought. *I'm nearly two thousand miles from home. Nobody is looking for me here.*

He absentmindedly ran a hand through his brown hair, wondering if the color change, along with the goatee, was enough to disguise his looks. Maybe he should've bought some cheap glasses at a drugstore. He took a drag and could feel the nicotine rush, the pulse pounding in his temple.

He was halfway through his smoke when the cop exited the office carrying a sheet of paper. Or maybe it was a stack of sheets, it was hard to tell.

Now Lucas wondered: *Am I being paranoid? Or is this cop handing out flyers at motels?*

Seconds later, he had an answer. Or, at least, all the answer he needed.

The cop got into his cruiser, swung from the lot, and came directly across the street to Lucas's motel. He parked at the office. He climbed out, still carrying a stack of papers, and went inside.

Oh, no. Not now. Not after all he'd been through.

Lucas sprinted to his room, swiped the key card, and threw the door open. Stephanie was sitting on the foot of the bed, a keyboard in her lap, staring at the TV screen.

"We've gotta go!" he yelled. "The cops are out front!"

Stephanie didn't budge, but Lucas hardly noticed. He grabbed the two suitcases. They'd take what was in them. Everything else would be left behind. They'd have to start all over, in some other town, probably in another state. Everything they had wanted—or maybe it was only what Lucas had wanted—had evaporated in a matter of seconds.

Stephanie still hadn't made a move. "Come on, Steph! What are you waiting for? Let's go!"

He saw that she was crying—maybe homesick, or maybe just one of her moods.

"Steph," he said quietly, trying to keep the panic out of his voice. "Seriously, we've gotta get out of here. I know I said they wouldn't find us, but they did."

She finally turned his way, and he was shocked by the look of pure hatred on her beautiful face. "What the hell happened on Sunday, Lucas?"

Her tone stopped him cold. He set the suitcases down, then turned and closed the door. "What are you talking about?"

She gave the tiniest shake of her head.

"Steph? Steph, talk to me. What's going on?"

"I'm talking about Vance!" she screamed. She threw the keyboard at him, but it reached the end of its cord, stopped in midair, and clattered harmlessly to the floor.

What the hell is going on?

Stephanie pointed at the television. "Did you think I'd never find out?"

Lucas turned to the screen. Stephanie had been surfing the Internet. She had logged on to the Web site for the *Blanco County Record*. Right there, at the top of the page, next to a photo of Vance, was the headline:

DROWNING NOW LABELED HOMICIDE

Stephanie was sobbing. "Why, Lucas? Why the fuck did you have to do that!"

There was a knock at the door, and Lucas realized it would all come to an end now. Actually, it was just the beginning of a new stage, one that was certain to be a nightmare. There was so much to explain, and he knew that nobody would believe what had really happened. Not the cops. And not Stephanie, now that she knew he'd deceived her.

"Steph, I can explain." His words sounded so feeble and inadequate. "I swear to God—I didn't do it."

She looked at him, and Lucas was heartbroken to see that there was fear in her eyes. She had her knees drawn to her chest, gently rocking, as pitiful as a lost child.

There was a second knock, firmer this time, and Lucas realized he had no more fight left in him.

"I love you, Stephanie."

She didn't respond.

Lucas turned and opened the door. Standing there was a cleaning woman. "Make up your room?"

When Red came out of the bedroom, it was several hours later than he had expected. Of course, most of that time had been spent sleeping off the vodka, but as for that other part—doing right by Lucy—he figured he'd done a pretty good job. They'd had the radio on, and Red had made it through a George Strait song and most of a Faith Hill. In hindsight, it might've been that image of Faith bouncing around in his head that had put him over the edge. But he hadn't heard any complaints from Lucy, and he took that as a good sign. She'd even commented on the blanket he'd bought down in Nuevo Laredo. Orange and white, with a ten-point buck staring you in the face. One hundred percent acrylic, and fuzzy as a newborn chick. In the twenty years he'd owned that blanket, she was the first lady who'd ever liked it. That right there said something about her good taste.

Red found Billy Don in the living room, parked on the couch, watching some old John Wayne war movie. Red eased himself into the recliner, not saying much, playing it cool, but when he cut his eyes to the side, he saw Billy Don grinning at him.

"Where's Lucy?" the big man asked.

"Still sleeping," Red replied, fighting to keep the smile off his face, but his cheeks wouldn't cooperate.

"You ol' dog." Billy Don tossed an empty beer can at him. "Tomato juice, my ass."

Red was about to bust with pride. But there was something else there. Something he was afraid to acknowledge, because he might scare it away, or somehow jinx it. It had been a damn long time since he had felt this way, the last time being when he had bought his Remington Model 700 at the pawnshop in Austin. The excitement rippled through him like the kick from a good slug of tequila.

Red was pretty sure he was in love.

There. Now he had at least admitted it to himself. It wasn't something he was ready to blurt out to Lucy quite yet, and he and Billy Don sure didn't discuss that sort of thing. So, for now, it'd be his own little secret. Which wouldn't be a problem, because Billy Don was already distracted by some kind of commotion on the screen. Bunch of bombs going off and stuff.

When things had quieted down, Billy Don said, "Hey, Red, why did they call it the longest day?"

"Do what?" Red hadn't been paying much attention. His thoughts were still on Lucy, and he was wondering if she expected him to return to the bedroom for an encore.

"The invasion at Normandy," Billy Don said, nodding at the TV.

Red mulled it over. "Because they timed it with the summer whaddayacallit . . . the solstice. Longest day of the year. Sun don't set till, like, nine o'clock. Gave 'em plenty of time to kick some ass."

Billy Don looked at him with uncertainty, then seemed to accept the explanation and returned his eyes to the screen.

When a commercial came on, Billy Don had another question. "What time we going after the safe?"

"This afternoon. Lucy says she normally drops by the old man's place at around four."

That project seemed so unimportant to Red now. What was money when you had love? Who needed to pay the bills when you could share a bed with a gal like Lucy? He'd just as soon hole up in the bedroom and not come out for a week or two. Hell, he'd be making it all the way through the Country Top 40 by then. Song after song, he and Lucy exploring each other like a couple of kids with—

Billy Don cut into Red's thoughts by saying, "I'm still feeling kinda funny about the whole thing."

Red could understand that. He had a few doubts himself, when he thought too long about it. But he said, "You heard how Lucy explained it. The taxes and all that. Don't you want your money back?"

Billy Don grunted, which could've been taken as either a yes or a no. "What about the old man?" he asked. "Won't he notice the safe's gone?"

"See, that's the perfect part of this," Red replied. "Lucy says the old man is getting a little nutty in his old age. She says she mentioned the safe to him one day, and he had no idea what she was talking about. Looked at her like she was crazy. What that means is, he don't even know it's there. Besides, even if he said something to somebody, they'd think he was confused."

Yep, it was perfect, all right. Which made Red wonder all the more why he felt like they were crossing some line he shouldn't cross. He considered himself a fairly moral person overall. Sure, he'd kill a deer out of season now and then, do a little spotlighting at night, and maybe even cross a few property lines to get a shot at a wild pig, but he never could see why that was such a big deal. Those wild animals belonged to everybody. And what's the difference between shooting a buck from your truck instead of a deer blind? He wished someone would explain that to him sometime—somebody other than a judge.

On the other hand, carting off a strongbox full of money? Well, Red figured the ethics involved were a lot more hazy. He had a hard time making it right in his head, no matter what Lucy said.

A few minutes later, the movie came back on, and Billy Don said, "The Duke would never do nothing like this."

* * *

Rita Sue Metzger's truck was parked in front of her house, so Marlin pulled in behind it.

Just minutes earlier, back at Scofield's house, the discussion had moved at a rapid clip as the team weighed their latest break.

Marlin, holding the photo: "Where'd it come from?"

Garza: "Tourist took it in Key West. They're already canvassing the motels."

Marlin, shaking his head: "Florida? Okay, check this out. I called Stephanie's cell phone an hour ago. Some old guy answered, and I thought I had the wrong number. He said he was in *Miami*. Didn't know who Stephanie was—but he asked me if it was my phone, like he didn't know whose phone he had."

Garza: "Rita Sue said Lucas and Stephanie didn't hang around together. They were just schoolmates."

Marlin: "Looks like she might've been wrong."

Garza clapped his hands once, excited. "Okay, we've got a possible link between Lucas and Scofield, and now a possible link between Lucas and Stephanie Waring."

Nobody had to point out the possibilities. The allergy medicine tied Lucas to Scofield. The Florida information tied Lucas to Stephanie—possibly together, on the run. It didn't look good for either of them.

Tatum: "Let's get her phone records."

Marlin: "I'm already on it. Faxed the subpoena about an hour ago."

Garza: "Have you talked to Chuck Hamm?"

"Well, no, not with this—"

"Yeah, put that aside for now. Can you talk to Rita Sue again? See if she's heard anything more. Woman's nutty enough, she might not let us know if Stephanie calls again."

"How about a warrant for Stephanie's duplex? We still short on probable cause?"

"Yeah, and I don't want anything booted on appeal. We can't jump the gun here. We have to prove that Stephanie and Lucas were more than passing acquaintances. For all we know, Stephanie left her phone over at Scofield's place, and maybe Lucas grabbed it later. Maybe he's the one who took it to Florida. Let's wait for the phone records and see what we can dig up from that."

"Sorry to bother you again," he said when Rita Sue answered the door wearing the same blue housecoat.

She waved her hand at him in a don't-be-silly manner. "Come on in. You want some coffee?"

Marlin stepped inside, the Chihuahua sniffing at his ankles. "No, ma'am, but thank you."

"I could make a fresh pot."

"Really, I'm fine. I just had a couple of quick questions."

Rita Sue motioned for Marlin to sit, and she planted herself in the easy chair again, the dog hopping into her lap. The TV was tuned to a talk show, a man apparently revealing to his wife that he was a closet cross-dresser. Rita Sue reached for the remote and reluctantly turned the set off.

"Y'all heard from Stephanie yet?" Rita Sue asked, before Marlin could ask the same question.

"No, ma'am. We were wondering if you had."

"Lord, no. Far be it from that girl to remember her mama. 'Bout knocked my socks off to get a call from her in the first place."

"If she does call—"

"I'll let you know."

"Don't just let us know. You need to have her call the sheriff's department, and tell her it's extremely important. She needs to call us immediately."

"Oh, I will. I saw on the news where y'all found that man's body. If Stephanie knew him, I can see where you'd need to talk to her. They saying he was killed?"

"Yes, ma'am."

She studied him over her glasses. "Now, y'all don't think Steph had somethin' to do with it?"

"No, not at all. But she might have some information that could really help us out."

"What sort of information?"

"His friends, business partners, that sort of thing."

"Steph might be able to help?"

"That's exactly right. That's why it's so urgent."

Rita Sue had an odd twinkle in her eye. "This is sort of exciting, really. Like something out of *Murder, She Wrote.*"

Marlin handed her his business card. "This has the number for the sheriff 's department on it."

"Yeah, you gave me one last time, remember?" From the pocket of her housecoat she produced one of Marlin's cards and one of Bobby Garza's. She waved a scolding finger at him. "I'm not as batty as you think I am."

23

MOST PEOPLE WOULD have called the structure on Wade Morgan's property a hunting cabin, but considering its present condition, "shack" would have been a more accurate description. Plumbing that no longer worked. Rough pine flooring that sagged under each footstep. No electricity. Rodent droppings everywhere, bugs skittering for cover.

The furnishings were spartan. In one room, a crude plank table encircled by four chairs, a bookshelf filled with rat-gnawed hunting magazines, a plaid sofa devoid of cushions, and a cheap gun cabinet (empty, just as Colby had expected it to be). In the other room, two sets of metal-framed bunk beds with flimsy foam pads. Mounted on one wall was a row of kitchen cabinets. Beneath the cabinets, two sawhorses supported a drooping half-sheet of plywood, on top of which sat a rusty propane stove.

"I'd be pissed at my travel agent if I were you," Colby

said. "This couldn't possibly be the room you reserved."

George responded by shoving Colby roughly into one of the chairs. The duct tape appeared again, and soon Colby's arms and legs were securely wrapped to the wooden frame. His arms were still behind his back, and he wasn't looking forward to the discomfort to come.

George sank low into the sofa, his knees even with his shoulders. "Everything's a big joke to you, huh?"

Colby decided it was time to make a play. "Yeah, and you know what the funniest thing is? I'm supposed to have dinner with a friend of mine tonight."

"So what?"

"When I don't show, he's gonna wonder where I am."

"He'll think you forgot."

"Maybe. But then he'll call me again tomorrow. After that, he'll probably come by my house to see what's going on. Because we're best friends. Grew up together. Like brothers."

That seemed to lodge a good-sized thorn into old George's brain. "You're a lying sack of shit," he said, but without much conviction.

Colby ignored him. "Then he'll start asking around town. 'Anybody seen Phil?' He'll call some of my other friends, my family. And they'll all start to wonder: Just where in the hell did Phil go? And the cops? Boy, they'll really want to figure it out. Wanna know why?"

George didn't answer.

"I'll tell you why," Colby continued. "You might've heard about that guy they found in the river. Vance Scofield? Well, it turns out poor Vance didn't drown, somebody killed him. And the weird part is, somehow the cops got it in their heads that I did it. That's right. Little ol' me. So they're gonna be *real* interested when it looks like I left town all of a sudden."

"Bullshit."

"People are gonna be talking about it all over the county. 'Did you hear about Phil Colby? He's on the run from the law!' It'll be big excitement for these parts. A genuine fugitive. Cops'll put out an APB, get word to the highway patrol, send out flyers with my picture on it. And it's all gonna happen because of missing one dinner with a friend."

George was glaring at him hard now, trying to read his face. Colby gave him time to chew on it all. After a minute, Colby said, "Then—and this is the capper—I'm supposed to waltz right into the bank on Monday morning, like nothing happened, and get into my safe-deposit box? We try that, the cops'll be there before I even get my key into the slot. And *that—that* is funny."

George rose from the couch and towered over Colby, his jaw clenched. Colby was prepared for it, but he still felt the sting when George backhanded him across the face.

They were back on the road again, driving north, and Stephanie didn't know if she was riding with a murderer or not.

This is what she knew for certain about last Sunday:

It started with a phone conversation that morning. She called Vance's number—and a woman answered.

"Is Vance there?" Stephanie asked, not jumping to conclusions just yet. Wanted to make sure she had dialed correctly before she got royally pissed. Again.

"He can't come to the phone right now." The woman sounded sluggish, like she was lying in bed.

"Who is this?" Now Stephanie was starting to feel the heat of anger creeping up her neck.

"Who the hell is *this?*"

"Just get Vance on the phone."

"Can't. He's in the shower."

"Well, get him out."

Stephanie could hear the woman sucking on a cigarette. "Let me guess. You're his girlfriend."

"None of your damn business!"

"Hey, don't take it out on me, sugar. He told me he didn't have one."

Stephanie slammed the phone down and smashed the heel of

her hand against the wall hard enough to break the plaster. Christ, what was she thinking? She'd talked about marrying that asshole!

When Lucas came home for lunch that day, he sensed that something was wrong. She told him what had happened, and by the time she was done, she was bawling, making an idiot of herself over a jerk who made promises he never kept.

Lucas had heard it all before, and he usually responded with all sorts of empathy, and then a single question: "How long're you gonna let him treat you like this, Steph?"

But not this time. Instead, he rubbed both hands over his face and let out a groan of anger. Then he turned for the front door.

"Where are you going?"

"Gonna go talk to that son of a bitch."

Stephanie couldn't count how many times in that next hour she wanted to pick up the phone. She wasn't even sure which one of them she wanted to call—Vance or Lucas. The truth was, she loved Vance, in spite of all his faults. Besides, over time, couldn't he fix those faults? Can't people change if they want to bad enough? If not, why do we have rehab clinics and Alcoholics Anonymous and makeover TV shows? Sometimes people *can* better themselves, she was sure of it. She held out hope for Vance, and for *them* as a couple.

But then there was Lucas. Such a sweet guy, and he made her laugh all the time. It wasn't but the second or third time they'd hung out together that she started to suspect he was in love with her. Unlike a lot of other guys, he wasn't all over her, pressuring her, asking for things she wasn't ready to give. He *understood* her, and God, when had that ever happened before? They were quickly best friends, and then it became more than that one night when they'd both had too much to drink.

She counted it as a one-time slip, but then it happened again. And again. It made her feel guilty, but Lucas was giving her things Vance was too selfish to offer. When Lucas had suggested moving in with her, she was firm: *If you do, we're just going to be friends,* she insisted. *No more than that.*

Because she didn't love him. She just didn't feel that way. She asked herself why sometimes—pondered it for hours, in fact—and finally decided there was only one answer: You can't force yourself to love someone, no matter how perfect for you they might be. And then it dawned on her that Vance might've reached the same conclusion.

When Lucas finally got back to their duplex, more than an hour later, the anger—or something else—had drawn all the blood out of his face. "He wasn't home," he said, shaking his head. "Either that, or he wouldn't answer the door."

Fine. As far as she was concerned, Vance could stay holed up in his house until hell froze over. Stephanie decided to get drunk. Numb the pain, and say good-bye to Vance once and for all. Who needs that asshole, right?

She pulled out the blender and whipped up a wicked batch of margaritas, Lucas egging her on. After the second pitcher, they switched to kamikazes. That was when Lucas said, "Wanna get back at him?"

At that point—hammered and still mad as a hornet—Stephanie said, "You got something in mind?"

A grin flashed across Lucas's lips, and for an instant he looked positively evil. "Let's steal the Corvette."

She remembered thinking that was an excellent idea.

Now, riding in the Honda, she realized how stupid this whole trip had been. She turned to Lucas, who was glancing in the rearview mirror every thirty seconds. "Vance was good to you, you know?"

"Yeah, only because he was getting something out of it, too."

"But you were making good money."

"I know it, Steph, but how much fun do you think it is to clean fucking houses?"

Stephanie could understand that attitude. She wouldn't like that particular job herself. When Vance had a home that he was about to put up for sale, it usually needed a good cleaning from top to bottom, sometimes some minor repairs, some lawn care. Vance had been offering that work to Lucas, strictly cash, off the books, and Stephanie thought it was a nice thing for Vance to do.

It made her mad that Lucas couldn't see how generous it was.

"You said you could explain what happened on Sunday," she said. "I'd sure as hell like to hear it."

As a reserve deputy, Homer Griggs didn't get much in the way of pay, but he enjoyed the job just the same. Felt good to carry a badge and a gun. Hell of a lot more exciting than selling funeral arrangements, which is what he did full-time.

Yes sir, this job had its moments. Arrested a naked lady at a biker party one time. Halfway to the station, she kicked one of the rear windows out with her bare feet. Another time, he pulled a water moccasin out of an old lady's toilet during a drought. And there was the drunk guy who tried to parachute off the water tower—may he rest in peace. Homer had even got shot once. It was a BB gun, but he didn't always share that part of the story.

He didn't expect this current call to be nearly as eventful. A woman named Donnelle Parker had called to say her ex-husband had been harassing her. Wanted a deputy to come out and talk about it. Didn't want to explain it over the phone. Truth was, it was a letdown. While the full-time deputies got to conduct a genuine murder investigation, Homer had to stick his nose into a domestic dispute. Ex-husband wasn't even on the premises, so there wasn't likely to be much action. That's the way it went sometimes.

So Homer loaded himself into his private vehicle, stuck the cherry on the roof—just to look official and everything—and drove to the address on the western edge of Johnson City.

Before Homer even had it parked in the driveway, here came the woman of the house, meeting him outside. She was cute as a button—big old mop of blonde hair teased up on her head, itsy-bitsy white shorts, and Homer's favorite, a pink tube top. Holding a cigarette in her right hand. Homer couldn't help but notice the long pink fingernails. Pink bracelet, too. *Woman knows how to accessorize,* he thought. Homer's wife was big on accessorizing. Every time she came home from the Save-Mart, she had a new bag of doodads to pin, clasp, dangle, or wear somewhere on her body.

Homer figured he was lucky that the Chinamen made jewelry s cheap.

Anyway, this gal Donnelle, she launched right into it, tellin him how she'd sent her daughter over to her grandma's house s the poor little thing wouldn't hear all this nasty stuff about he daddy. Told Homer all about it. Late-night phone calls with noth ing but breathing on the other end. Then a vibrator showed up i a shoebox on her doorstep. Homer felt his cheeks get warm whe she explained what a vibrator was. After the vibrator, somebod raided her panty drawer. And now the big prick—Donnelle choice of words, not Homer's—had gone too far. Waaay too fa Donnelle said a couple of times.

When she showed Homer what she was talking about, he ha to agree. It was plumb disgusting, that's what it was.

After leaving Rita Sue Metzger's house, Marlin stopped at a pa phone and dialed Phil Colby's number. Maybe he was still angr and if so, fine. But Marlin wanted to let him know, in gener terms, that things were looking better by the minute. He couldn share the specific developments with him, but he could certainl drop a hint that—for all intents and purposes—Colby was n longer the chief suspect. Marlin's rationalizing didn't matter any way, because Colby didn't answer. Probably sitting right by th phone, screening his calls.

Marlin had just climbed back into his truck when Darrell, th dispatcher, radioed and said he had received a fax. Stephanie War ing's cell phone company had already responded to his subpoena Marlin had expected to hear something on Monday, or even late in the week, so this was a lucky break.

He turned his truck around and drove back to the sheriff's of fice. Darrell had the thin document waiting at the front desk, an Marlin quickly retreated with it to his office. It consisted of tw pages: a complete record of Stephanie Waring's incoming and out going calls for the preceding thirty days. He focused on the last si days.

Since Sunday, there had been several incoming calls, including those from the deputies. But none of them had lasted longer than one minute, meaning, Marlin assumed, that they had all been routed into voicemail.

On the other hand, there had been no outgoing calls at all. Next step, Marlin would call all of the incoming numbers to see if anyone could verify Stephanie's whereabouts.

Marlin was reaching for the phone when he noticed a small note on the fax cover sheet:

Mr. Marlin, perhaps you'd be interested in one of our phone plans. Did you know that you can have two phones, with two different phone numbers, on one calling plan? —*N. L.*

What the hell? This guy was too much, trying to sell a wireless service when—

And then Marlin understood what N. L. was saying. It was a subtle message: *Stephanie Waring had two phones on one account.* Of course, Marlin hadn't asked for the records on the second phone because he hadn't even known it existed. But N. L., the person responding to the subpoena, couldn't legally share information that hadn't been requested. So he—or she—had found a clever, though dubious, way to tip Marlin off. Marlin sure wasn't going to complain.

He scanned the entire thirty days' worth of records, and he found more than a dozen incoming calls from a phone number that differed from Stephanie Waring's by a single digit.

He dialed it and immediately heard a voicemail greeting:

Hey, it's Lucas. Can't take your call, so leave a message.

When Marlin entered the small, crowded conference room, it appeared that Garza and his deputies were just finishing up. They'd been pulling boxes from the left side of the room, sorting through them, then moving those boxes to the right. There was a small stack of paperwork on the table—items of interest that had been pulled from Scofield's belongings—but it didn't look like much. The atmosphere in the room was bordering on bleak.

"Y'all want to take a break for a minute and let me make your day?" Marlin asked.

24

THEY'D BEEN SITTING silently for more than an hour when George finally broke down and asked, "Who's this friend of yours?"

Colby played it coy. "Who?"

"This friend you're supposed to be having dinner with."

Colby had been preparing for that very question. "Wade Marlin," he said calmly.

The question was, would George recognize that last name? If he was from around here, he most likely would. Colby was betting George was not a local.

"Marlin?" George asked, and Colby held his breath. "Like the fish?"

"Or the rifle," Colby replied.

George stared at him for a good ten seconds before saying, "Okay, here's how we're gonna work it." He slipped a cell phone from his pocket. "You're gonna make up an excuse. And the whole time, I'm gonna have this"—he hefted his revolver—"pointed at the back of your head. Any bullshit at all and you're a dead man. We clear on that?"

Colby nodded.

"You get cute," George said, "and I'll kill you first. Then I'll find out where your friend lives and kill him, too."

Colby nodded again.

"What's his number?"

Colby gave it to him.

George dialed, and Colby prayed that Marlin hadn't suddenly decided to change the greeting that had been on his answering machine for years, the one that simply said, "This is Marlin. Leave a message."

After a few seconds, George seemed satisfied. He held the phone to Colby's mouth.

"How do I look?" Billy Don asked, tugging upward on the tool belt around his waist. Red was wearing one, too. *Do plumbers even wear tool belts?* he wondered. Red couldn't remember for sure, and if he didn't know, he seriously doubted the old man would know, either.

"The pliers, the screwdriver, the wrenches—that's all fine," Red said. "But you gotta lose the hammer."

"Why for?"

"When was the last time you fixed a leak with a hammer, Billy Don?"

Billy Don pondered the question, then said, "Good point." He slipped the hammer from its loop and laid it on the cable-spool coffee table.

"Okay, one last thing," Red said. "Try not to use my name. But if you do, call me Bart or Clem or something like that. Don't use my real name. I don't think this'll be risky at all, but ain't no reason to take chances."

"What'll you call me?"

"Hell, I'll just make something up. Now, you ready? Lucy said we should show up around four-thirty. Get in and get out."

"Where's the dolly?"

"Already in the truck."

In the small town of Marathon, Florida, Lucas pulled into a parking lot of a restaurant and killed the engine. He noticed that Stephanie was pressed against the passenger-side door—nearly *cowering*—and she still had that same combination of anger and fear on her face.

Sunday morning. That's when this shitstorm had begun. And now he had to explain it all. Somehow.

He'd been wondering for days what he was going to say if he ever had to describe what happened. Should he tell the truth, which was almost impossible to believe? Or should he tell a bunch of lies? He'd been thinking that he wouldn't have to make up his mind unless he got caught. And even then, he could've just kept his mouth shut. The cops can't force you to talk.

But Stephanie—

She deserved some sort of explanation. The question was, what sort of explanation should he give? The truth . . . or something else? He had to make a decision.

Lucas took a deep breath and said, "I went over to Vance's that morning, and yeah, I was angry as hell. He'd been jerking you around for so long, Steph . . . I just wanted to get in his face, you know? Let him know that you were tired of his bullshit. *So was I.* You may not realize this, but everything he did—or didn't do—affected me, too." Lucas shook his head. "I've been waiting around like a moron, hoping you'd see what kind of scumbag he really is, and then you'd finally cut him loose. I dreamed about that day—when Vance would be out of the way, and you and me could finally have our shot. It always made me mad that he had a girl like you . . . and he kept acting like such an asshole. I'm a good guy, Steph. I would never treat you like that. I *love* you. I was hoping you'd eventually see that. Maybe you'd even feel the same way."

He looked to her for acknowledgment—maybe she'd been thinking these same things all along—but she wouldn't make eye contact. All she said was "I want to know what happened."

The traffic filed past on Highway 1, and Lucas was jealous of all those people leading normal, uncomplicated lives. If only he could go back one week and change the way things had happened.

"When I got there," he said, "I didn't see any cars except his. The woman you talked to on the phone was gone. So I bang on the front door, but he doesn't answer. The door's unlocked, so I go in and start calling his name. I figure maybe he saw me pull up, so he's acting like he isn't home. He knows I'm pissed off and he's trying to avoid the whole scene. So I go from room to room, but I can't find him. The TV's on in the living room, his Explorer's out front—he's gotta be somewhere, right? So I go back to my car and start honking the horn. I wait five or ten minutes, just in case he's out on the ranch somewhere, but he doesn't show. Then I decide to check the barn."

Lucas could feel his palms getting damp. He found himself checking the rearview mirror again, the paranoia kicking in, expecting to see a group of burly, well-armed cops closing in behind him. There was nothing back there except parked cars.

He was reluctant to say the next few words. Even if Stephanie believed him—and he wasn't so sure she would—it was a big step to take. He knew the cops could use her testimony against him, and the girl he loved could wind up sending him to Death Row. But he didn't have a choice.

"He was down there, Steph. Laying in the grass just outside the door. At first—well, I couldn't tell what was wrong with him. There wasn't any blood or nothing. He looked like he was sleeping. I was thinking maybe he had a heart attack or something like that. So I squat down beside him and start feeling for a pulse, and I could feel one. I put my head against his chest, and I could barely feel his heart beating. So then I'm freaking out, you know, wondering what I should do next. I started to go back to the house and call nine-one-one, but then I realized it would be quicker if I just took him to the hospital myself."

Stephanie was eyeing him now, and he thought he could see disbelief on her face. Had he made the right choice?

"So I drove my car down to the barn," Lucas said, wanting her to see it exactly the way he was describing it. "When I went to pick him up—I felt a big lump on the back of his head. There was just a tiny cut, and barely any blood at all. The thing is, it was all grass where he was laying—no rocks—so I knew he hadn't just tripped and banged his head. Somebody had done that to him . . . and it scared me, Steph." He could remember the fear, too, like a winter freeze burrowing into his bones, setting up shop deep beneath his heart. "I put him in my car, and by the time I'd reached the road, he was nearly gray. I stopped and felt for a heartbeat again—on his wrist, his neck, and his chest—and I couldn't feel it this time. I put my hand up to his mouth to see if he was breathing . . . and he wasn't. I'm sorry, Steph, I truly am. But he was dead, and now I had him in my car. I didn't know what to do or where to go."

Lucas was trembling now, just as he had been six days ago. He *really* didn't want to tell Stephanie what had happened next.

"What'd you do with him, Lucas?" Stephanie asked. Her voice was so full of bitterness and pain, Lucas barely recognized it.

He hesitated. "You gotta understand, I knew how it was gonna look, Stephanie. If I went to the cops—"

"But that's what you should've done!"

He rubbed one hand across his forehead, trying to massage the pain that was blooming behind his eyes. "I know. I know. But I didn't think anyone would believe me. Think of the position I was in. I had all the reason in the world to want this guy dead, and all of sudden I've got his body in my car? How does that look? Jesus Christ, even you, Stephanie. The first thing you thought was that I had killed him. You're my best friend, but you figured I'd done it. So what chance did I have with a bunch of cops?"

But there was no softness in her eyes, only tears. "You haven't answered my question," she said. "What did you do with him?"

Lucas could see no way around it. It was obvious he hadn't put Vance's body in the river. He had to tell her who did. "I took him to your mother's house."

Her head swung around. "You did what?"

"I didn't know where else to go. I knew Rita Sue would help me figure it out. She's smart that way, you know? I thought she might be able to help me explain it all in a way that made sense."

Lucas could imagine the thoughts that were running through Stephanie's head. He was asking her to believe that her own mother had had a part in all of this.

Stephanie didn't say anything, so Lucas continued. "But the worst thing was, I could see the doubt in her eyes. Just like you, she thought I had done it. She didn't come right out and say so, but I could tell that's what she thought. I told her exactly what had happened, just like I'm telling you, but she didn't believe me. She said the same thing—that I never should've touched the body, because now I had Vance's blood and hair in my car. Threads and stuff from his clothes, too. The cops can find all that and use it as evidence. So I asked her what I should do. And you know what she told me, Stephanie?"

No reply at all. Stephanie was staring out the front windshield now, looking like she was in shock.

"She told me I should get out of town. She said the cops would nail me for it, whether I'd done it or not, so I should just take off."

They sat in silence for a good half minute, the car getting hot in the Florida sun. Lucas was so tired. He wanted to find a long pier and drive the car right off the end of it. Sink into the water and forget everything. Then the last six days could vanish. It wouldn't matter what anybody thought—whether they believed he was a killer or not. It seemed like a much easier path than the road in front of him.

"My old car wouldn't have gotten us anywhere," he said. "And the Corvette . . . was just sitting there. I figured the cops would think someone killed him when they were stealing the car. *Everybody* knew about that car. Lots of people might've thought about stealing it. Maybe it was stupid, but I thought it might throw them off course a little. Buy me some time."

Judging from the cop at the motel, it hadn't worked. None of it had worked. Lucas had hoped that Stephanie would run away to

Key West with him—for just a week or so, he'd first told her—and then agree to stay down there with him forever. They could find a little home, get a couple of decent jobs, and forget about everything that happened in Blanco County. What a complete fool he had been.

"So how did his body end up in the river?" Stephanie asked quietly. Her tone of voice suggested that everything Lucas had told her was a gigantic fairy tale.

"I don't know," he said. "I guess your mom . . ."

Again, she looked at him, and her eyes were on fire. "You're saying my mother did that?"

Lucas nodded. "I guess so. I don't know how else it could've happened. She did it for us, Stephanie. She wanted us to be together. She hated Vance."

It was the wrong thing to say. Before Lucas could stop her, Stephanie sprang from the car and slammed the door behind her. "You're a fucking liar!" she screamed through the open window.

He couldn't blame her for feeling that way.

And when she walked straight to a pay phone and dialed three numbers, he couldn't blame her for that, either.

Lucas started the car.

25

WHEN MARLIN FINISHED telling Garza and the deputies what he'd learned, the sheriff cussed Lucas Burnette under his breath.

"I still need to confirm that those two phone numbers are actually on the same calling plan," Marlin said. "But since the two numbers only differ by one digit . . ."

"In any case, Stephanie knew Lucas damn well, despite what Rita Sue thought. How many calls were there from Stephanie's phone to Lucas's?"

Marlin scanned through the phone records in his hand. "In the last month, a couple dozen. Plus, I looked back at Scofield's records, and he made plenty of calls to this other number, too. He was calling Lucas. It didn't raise any red flags because it was listed as Stephanie's phone, and we never noticed that it was actually a different number."

Nobody commented for several moments. The implications spoke for themselves.

Finally, Garza said, "Okay, folks, I'm gonna spell a few things out and see if anybody can poke holes in it. There's a real good chance that Vance Scofield and Lucas Burnette were in the methamphetamine business together. They were making the stuff at Lucas's house, but they kept some of the supplies, namely allergy medicine, in Scofield's garage. If they kept any kind of written records—customers, transactions, et cetera—we can assume those went up in the fire. Speaking of the fire, we know it was arson, and we know it was torched right around the time Vance was killed. Since we don't have a solid time of death, we can't be sure of the timing between those two events. Vance might've been killed before or after the house burned, but my guess is before. My guess is that Lucas and Scofield had some kind of argument, it got out of hand, and Lucas killed him. Then Lucas tried to cover it up by dumping the body in the river. But he was nervous, because he knew we'd eventually make a connection between the two of them. He didn't want us finding the lab in his house, so he burned it down."

"Then he took off in the Corvette," Marlin added. "Probably with Stephanie Waring."

Garza nodded slowly. "Yeah, probably. Maybe she's with him, maybe she's not. Maybe she knows what happened, maybe she doesn't. All we know is that her cell phone—the original one, anyway—appears to be in Miami, and Lucas was spotted in Key West this morning. Until we can get Lucas's story, I'd say he's our number-one suspect. Let's finish with these boxes, then knock off till tomorrow morning. I know y'all have been working hard, and there's not much more we can do until Lucas trips himself up. When he does, maybe we can finally get this fiasco sorted out."

As the deputies went back to work, Garza followed Marlin out of the conference room. The sheriff ran a hand through the graying hair at his temple. "Regarding Colby . . . if you want to let him know what's happening in a vague sort of way, I don't have a problem with that."

Marlin was about to reply when Darrell bustled into the hallway. "Sheriff, you've got a call from Florida. Stephanie Waring just turned herself in."

The old man lived in a nice house on a quiet street, and Red could see Lucy coming out the front door before he even got his truck backed into the driveway. "It's perfect!" Lucy said through the driver's window. "He's asleep!"

Billy Don grabbed the dolly from the bed of the truck, then they followed Lucy inside, where they saw a white-haired geezer wearing a bathrobe, sitting in an easy chair in front of a television. His chin was nearly touching his chest, and he was snoring loudly. The TV was tuned to the same war movie Billy Don had been watching back at the trailer.

"This way," Lucy whispered, and proceeded down a carpeted hallway. She led them into a darkened bedroom, but there was no bed, just a large wooden desk with a computer resting on it. Next to the desk, a matching file cabinet was covered with dust.

"In the closet," Lucy said in a quiet voice, and all this hush-hush bullshit was starting to make Red nervous. He'd never known a plumber who was this damn quiet. Most of them went banging around like they were being paid by the decibel.

All three of them stepped into the large walk-in closet, and for a couple of seconds, they stared in reverence at the bulky object against the far wall.

The safe.

Lucy's description hadn't done it justice. Sure, it was just like she'd said—maybe three feet square, as sturdy as a brick shithouse. But there was more to it than that. To Red, the safe seemed to actually glow with mystery. It seemed to stare back at him, smug and cocky, as if daring Red to bust the door open and find the magical prize inside. Suddenly, without Red even realizing it, his misgivings about the project vanished into the muggy, mothball-scented air. Yes, the safe had secrets, and Red wanted to know those secrets real bad.

"Think you can move that thing?" Red said to Billy Don. Red meant it as a challenge—something to motivate the big man, like betting him he couldn't eat a ten-pound ham.

Billy Don responded by stepping over to the safe and running the fingertips of one hand along the top of the iron box, like a game-show model stroking the fender of a brand-new Dodge. Then he squatted down low, with his massive legs spread, and flattened his palms against the side of the safe, up high. With a soft grunt, Billy Don began to push. There was no doubt it was a tremendous effort. Billy Don's arms began to tremble with the strain, and his joints were making noises like a bowl of breakfast cereal.

But one side of the safe came right off the floor.

Red decided they shouldn't bother with a practice lift. He snapped into motion, saying, "Hold it right there, Billy Don. Let me get the dolly under it."

It was all going smoothly, and Red was thinking they'd be long gone in a matter of minutes. They had the safe on the dolly, and Lucy had slipped down the hallway to check on the old man—to make sure he was still asleep. That's when the problem popped up.

Billy Don, wheeling the safe toward the closet door, said, "Sumbitch won't fit."

"What do ya mean it won't fit?"

"It won't fuckin' fit, Red, that's what I mean." Beads of sweat had emerged on Billy Don's forehead.

"How tight?"

"An inch on either side."

Red refused to panic. Someone had gotten the safe in here, so they'd just have to take it out the same way. "We're gonna have to remove the door," he said.

"Remove the door?" Lucy said. She was outside the closet, in front of Billy Don.

"Won't fit through," Red said. "All we gotta do is take the pins outta the hinges. Door'll come off and give us a couple more inches."

"What about the door over here?" Lucy said. "The one into the bedroom. Ain't we gonna have to remove that one, too?"

"Shit," Red said.

"Didn't nobody measure this damn thing?" Billy Don asked.

"And don't forget the front door," Lucy said.

"Double shit," Red said.

"It'd be a hell of a lot easier to remove those pins if we had a hammer," Billy Don muttered, glaring at Red. "And I left mine at home."

Red used a flathead screwdriver, tapping it as quietly as possible with a crescent wrench. Each pin groaned slightly as it was removed, but it didn't take long to have the closet door off the hinges.

Billy Don rolled the safe through the opening—with a half inch of clearance on either side—and Red quickly put the door back into place.

They repeated the process with the bedroom door, and twenty-three minutes after they had entered the house, they were trundling the dolly down the hallway toward the front door.

"He's still sleeping," Lucy said, coming back from another quick check.

"We're leaving wheel marks," Red pointed out.

"I'll vacuum those up later," Lucy said. "You sure you wanna take the front door off the hinges? I think I've got a better way."

Red knew what Lucy was thinking.

The old man was watching TV in a small living area. There was a sofa on one side and an entertainment center against the opposite wall. Just past the sofa, at an angle to the TV, was the old man's easy chair.

Behind the easy chair was a sliding glass door.

"We'll never get it past him," Red whispered. "Ain't enough room." Billy Don was waiting in the hallway with the safe.

"There will be if we move him back some," Lucy replied.

She may be a woman, Red thought, *but she's got balls the size of coconuts.* "What if he wakes up?"

"He won't."

"Yeah, but if he does, he'll—"

"He won't," Lucy said again, sounding downright certain. "He had a little snack earlier, and there was something in it to help him sleep."

"You gave him drugs?" Red asked.

Lucy shrugged. "The same shit he takes every night. It's no big deal."

Red had to wonder about that. What right did she have to give the old man something he hadn't asked for?

Lucy leaned and spoke right into his ear. "Let's just get this done so we can get back to your bedroom and celebrate."

Now that Red thought about it, it all made sense. So what if the old guy got a little extra shuteye? Hell, he could probably use it. He looked at Lucy. "You sure he won't wake up?"

"Let's give it a little test." She clapped her hands, and Red nearly jumped out of his Wranglers.

The old man was still snoozing away.

Billy Don poked his curious head around the corner. Red motioned him over and explained the plan to him.

"You serious?" Billy Don asked.

"Damn right. Let's do it and get outta here."

Billy Don retreated down the hallway and returned a minute later with the dolly. Red positioned himself behind the easy chair. Lucy nodded at him with a smile on her face.

Red began to tip the chair over backward.

The old man's slippered feet came off the floor and dangled in the air like baby booties from a rearview mirror.

For the first time that day, everything went according to plan.

Two minutes later—with all three of them lifting—they managed to get the safe into the bed of the truck.

* * *

"You didn't plan this very well, did you?" Phil Colby asked.

His arms and legs were throbbing from being bound. He was thirsty as hell. And then there was the heat. The forecast earlier that morning had called for the low nineties, but it was hotter inside the cabin, even this late in the day. George had stripped off his jacket, rolled up his sleeves, and kicked off his boots. He'd even removed his Stetson. But that wasn't enough. He was fanning himself with a hunting magazine, and his hair clung to his head in damp strips.

"I could say the same thing about you," George replied. "Yeah, you got your photos of Herzog, but after that, your little act fell to shit. And, Jesus—how stupid were you to call from your own phone?"

Herzog? Colby recognized that name from somewhere. He bounced it around in his brain but couldn't come up with anything. He wanted more. "What does Herzog have to say about all this?" he asked. "He know what kind of trouble you're going to?"

George ignored him.

"You get a chance to see those photos yourself?" Colby asked. "I was pretty proud of them." He was taking a risk, talking about photos he had never even heard of, much less seen.

For the first time, Colby thought he saw a glimmer of a smile on George's face. "Yeah, they were pretty good," George said. "How'd you find out he was banging that gal?"

What gal? Colby wondered. "Just got lucky," he said. "Pieced it together and went from there."

That seemed to satisfy George. "Pretty slick," he said, smiling, showing crooked teeth. "You sure rattled Herzog's cage, I'll give you that much. Especially with this being an election year."

Colby immediately felt sick to his stomach. *It was Dylan Herzog, the senator.* Someone was blackmailing the chairman of the Natural Resources Committee, and this goon thought it was Colby. But it all made sense. Herzog was known to cater to the whims of the high-fencers, and Colby had become their worst enemy. Anyone looking to hurt the high-fencers would realize that the senator was a perfect target. But what did Vance Scofield have to do with it? Maybe nothing at all. Maybe the murder of Scofield was completely unrelated.

For the first time, Colby realized what kind of jam he was in. It was one thing when he thought the high-fencers were trying to put a scare into him. It was something completely different to know that the political future of a high-powered senator—a man who had openly voiced aspirations to the governorship, and who was rumored to have his eyes set on the White House—was depending on George to make sure Colby and the damning photographs weren't a problem. Would George—psychopath that he was—be content merely to retrieve the negatives? And what would he do when Colby came clean and revealed that he didn't really know anything about the photographs at all, that the only reason he'd said he did was because George had a nasty habit of shooting at him? One thing was certain: Colby had to *do* something. He couldn't just sit there, trussed up, and wait for Monday.

"You know," Colby said, "I'm gonna have to use the bathroom pretty soon."

George said, "Well, I guess you're in a hell of a spot, then, ain't ya?"

"Yeah, I guess I am, but you're not thinking things through, George. When we go into the bank on Monday morning, how's it gonna look if I go in there smelling like an outhouse? Hell, we're both gonna be ripe enough as it is, just from the heat. Don't you think we'll need to clean up at some point? Fresh clothes, maybe a shower? Otherwise, people are gonna know something's up. Besides, if you keep me taped up like this much longer, I doubt I'll even be able to use my arms. Right now, I can't even feel my fingers."

The way George stared at him, Colby knew he was thinking it over.

"I've got all kinds of chains and rope in my barn," Colby added. "You could fix it where it's a lot easier to turn me loose for bathroom breaks and that sort of thing. Maybe you could grab us some food when you're over there. Towels, water, maybe some other stuff. Sure would make things nicer, don't you think? As it is, I don't think you even brought anything to drink, did you? How're we gonna make it till Monday morning without something cold to drink?"

The way George glared at him, Colby was wondering if his ulterior motives were obvious. "Think you're pretty smart, don't you?" George said. "But I been thinking the same thing all along. Any fool would know I wasn't planning on going three days without food and water."

"That's what I figured. That you had it all worked out in your head."

"Damn right I do. Sure as hell don't need any help from you. I was just waiting for the right time, is all. Maybe after dark."

Colby nodded. "Makes sense to me."

"Don't get a smart mouth."

"No, I wasn't."

"Nothing I can't stand more than a smart mouth."

Rita Sue Metzger was watching a CMT biography of Dolly Parton—Lord, how did that woman tote those things around for all these years without ruining her back?—when her phone rang. She considered not answering it, but she had a peculiar feeling about this call, and she was right.

"Mama?" a small voice said on the other end.

"Stephie, is that you? Where in the world are you, hon?"

"Florida."

Rita Sue could hear the sounds of traffic in the background. "With Lucas?" she asked.

"Not anymore."

That wasn't what Rita Sue wanted to hear. If the two of them had split up, that could only mean that something had gone wrong.

"Mama, I called the cops. They're coming for me," Stephanie wailed. "I have to tell them—I think Lucas killed Vance."

Rita Sue sat up straight in her easy chair. "Is that what he said?"

"No, but I think . . . I think he's lying."

"What did he tell you?" Panic was welling up in Rita Sue's chest. Everything was coming unraveled.

"That he went to Vance's and found him by the barn. He said he was alive at first, but he died later, in Lucas's car."

Rita Sue's heart went out to her daughter. The poor girl had fallen for Vance Scofield early on, after just a few dates. And later, when he'd revealed himself to be a dyed-in-the-wool son of a bitch, Stephanie still couldn't see it. She couldn't see that Lucas—an honorable young man who was getting his life together—was a much better choice. Rita Sue and Lucas had had long talks about the situation, and she had done her best to steer Stephanie in the right direction. Now Rita Sue wondered if she'd screwed Stephanie's life up for good. Lucas's, too. Maybe she'd given him bad advice. Maybe the cops would've believed him.

Rita Sue was ashamed of herself, especially when Stephanie said, "Mama, he said he came to see you. He said that you must've put Vance's body in the water. Is that true?"

Rita Sue didn't know what to say. So many of her intentions had started out good—and then gone straight to hell. Nothing had worked out the way she had intended.

"Mama?"

"Steph, baby, I only wanted what was best for you. That's all I ever wanted."

Stephanie was crying uncontrollably now. "So you did it? You put Vance in the river?"

Before Rita Sue could answer, she heard other voices, followed by Stephanie's anguished cries. Rita Sue's heart was breaking. She could hear the phone being jostled, and then she heard a stern voice on the line: "This is Lieutenant Klante with the Florida State Police. Who am I speaking to?"

Rita Sue stroked her Chihuahua's tiny head. There weren't any choices left. She had to set things right. She had to throw herself on the fire. "My name is Rita Sue Metzger," she said. "I killed a man named Vance Scofield. I did it for my baby."

26

MARLIN DROVE SOUTH on Highway 281.

Deputy Nicole Brooks lived in the southern tip of Blanco County in an area known as Twin Sisters—named for a pair of prominent hills that could be seen for miles around.

Marlin shook his head and loosened his grip on the steering wheel. He was nervous. He had been ever since Brooks had stopped him in the hall and asked if he still wanted to grab a beer.

"Is my house okay?" she'd asked.

"Yeah, sure."

"Give me ten minutes, then come on down."

This was after Garza had promised to keep them all up to date on Stephanie Waring. As it had turned out, the Florida State Police hadn't even picked her up yet. She'd dialed 911 from a pay phone, and the dispatcher had told her to stay put until a trooper arrived. When and if Garza learned anything important, he'd relay it to Marlin and the deputies. "Y'all just clear out for a couple hours," the sheriff had said. "Go take a nap or something."

Now Marlin hung a left on Loma Ranch Road and thought about what he was going to say to Nicole. No doubt about it, he had to be straight with her, tell her why he'd been acting as he had. Then she could laugh in his face and send him on his way.

He found her mailbox, pulled in, and saw her cruiser sitting in the gravel driveway that ran to her small, well-kept house. He'd been here once before, about a month ago, when some people from the sheriff 's office had gathered for an impromptu barbecue. As he remembered, he'd spoken exactly seven words to her: "Hi, Nicole. Nice place you have here." Later, he'd slipped out without even saying good-bye. She'd been talking to Ernie Turpin at the time, laughing with him, touching his elbow, and the juvenile pangs of jealousy Marlin had felt convinced him it would be best just to leave.

He parked his truck, and when he knocked on the door, Brooks answered wearing a pair of jeans and a dark green top. She didn't have any shoes on. Her auburn hair was down, and Marlin immediately knew he'd made a huge mistake. She was ridiculously beautiful, and he was afraid he wouldn't even be able to speak.

"Come on in," she said, stepping aside. "I've got beer, Cokes, or iced tea.

"A cold beer would be great."

"Take a load off," she said, gesturing toward the living room. "I'll be right back."

"You mind if I make a phone call real quick?"

"Yeah, sure. There's a phone on the end table." She disappeared through a swinging door into the kitchen.

Marlin sank into the leather sofa and dialed the cordless phone. He'd already figured out what he would say: "I can't go into details right now, Phil, but I don't think you have anything to worry about. I'll be able to explain more later. Oh, and sorry if I was an ass earlier today."

But Colby didn't answer. It was nearly seven o'clock, and there was still plenty of light this time of year. He might still be out working the ranch.

Brooks reappeared with two frosted mugs of beer and handed one to Marlin. "I hope you like light beer."

"Yeah, sure. Thank you."

He decided to get right to it. "Nicole, not to beat a dead horse, but I wanted to talk to you about the conversation we had in my truck."

She frowned. "I thought we'd cleared that up."

"Well, yeah, maybe. But there's something more I wanted to say. About the way I've been acting."

She had taken a seat in the matching leather chair, and now she placed her mug on the end table. "I didn't mean to open up a can of worms. You don't need to tell me—"

"No, really, I want to explain. It's been bothering me. All this time, you were thinking I didn't like you or something, when . . ." He felt like such a klutz. "Well, the opposite is true." He searched for the right words to polish off his humiliation. "I think you're great."

I think you're great? What kind of lame proclamation was that? Now she'd be flustered and uncomfortable, and they'd exchange some stilted small talk to make the moment go away, and then Marlin would leave, and afterward, the atmosphere between them would be riddled with a clumsy and false friendliness.

He finally brought his eyes to hers.

The surprising thing was, there was a slight grin on her face. "You didn't have to say that, you know? I consider myself a fairly bright girl. I sort of pieced it together already."

Marlin felt something loosen in his torso, some bit of tension uncoiling. "You did?"

"Yeah, I'm real clever that way. Might even make a good cop."

He laughed in spite of himself. Then he remembered the other problem. "The thing is . . . I don't want to get into the middle of anything here."

"Oh, right." She picked up her mug and took a sip. "Wait. I'm not sure I follow you." She was staring at him intensely.

"What about Ernie?"

"Ernie? What about him?"

"A couple of days before your picnic, I saw the two of you shopping together."

"Yeah?"

"Well, if you and Ernie have something going on—"

He was interrupted by laughter. Nicole was giggling so hard, she spilled her beer. Marlin sat there, totally confused. He could feel his face turning red.

"Oh my God," she finally said, "you didn't know. That's why you acted that way in the grocery store."

Marlin felt like the butt of a joke, and he didn't understand why. "Know what?"

"This is too funny."

"Nicole. Know what?"

"Ernie," she said, "is my cousin."

"Your cousin?"

"Yeah, I thought everybody knew."

"I must've missed that somehow."

"I guess so."

"I feel kind of stupid."

"No, don't."

"Excuse me while I crawl under the couch."

"Better not. I haven't vacuumed under there lately."

Marlin chuckled. *Her cousin.*

Brooks smiled. "Listen, I've got an idea. Why don't we go to lunch sometime next week? That'll give me another chance to tease you about all this, and then I promise to ease up."

"That sounds good."

"Or dinner. Either way."

"So you' re—everything I told you—the way I feel—"

"I don't have a problem with it."

The anxiety was gone. Marlin felt good. Hell, he felt incredible.

Of course, the phone rang and ruined the moment.

Brooks answered, and her demeanor instantly changed. "Yes, sir . . . Yeah, I can, in about twenty minutes." She looked at Marlin, and her eyes were wide with surprise. "You've got to be kidding . . . But how—yeah, I understand. No problem. I'll see you shortly."

She hung up, shaking her head in amazement. "That was Bobby. Florida troopers picked up Stephanie. But are you ready for this? Rita Sue Metzger just confessed to killing Vance Scofield."

An hour after sundown, Red was ready to call the owner of the company who built the goddamned safe and threaten to cut his nuts off.

They'd tried drilling it, and the steel-tipped bit had done nothing more than scratch the finish. Billy Don had worked it over with a crowbar, trying to pry the door open, and the crowbar had ended up as straight as a flagpole. Next, Red had taken a jackhammer after the hinges, but all he'd managed to do was drop the damn thing on his foot. He suspected his pinkie toe was broken.

"Ain't this a bitch?" Lucy said, standing to the side, drinking a tallboy.

Red saw disappointment in her eyes, and it pained him. "We'll get in there, darlin', just you wait and see." But the truth was, he was running out of ideas. Short of dropping the safe off a high-rise in Austin, he didn't know how they'd crack the bastard open.

Red sat on top of the safe to take a breather. He glanced at Lucy and winked, but she just stared at him in the dim glow of the porch light.

"What about the seven mag?" Billy Don asked.

That idea hadn't even occurred to Red. "That's what I was thinking," he said.

"What's a seven mag?" Lucy asked.

"Biggest damn deer rifle I got. Thing would stop a chargin' rhino, even better than taking away his credit cards."

Red was hoping for a smile—he was just trying to lighten things up a bit—but all Lucy said was "Well, go get the damn thing then. What are we waiting for?"

He didn't like this side of her. Snippy. Impatient. Nothing like the gal he'd had in his bedroom earlier in the day. "Be right back."

Red went inside the trailer, removed the rifle from a case underneath his bed, and grabbed a single shell from his dresser drawer.

Back outside, he slid the round into the chamber. "Now, we're only gonna be able to do this once. If it sounds like a shooting gallery over here, someone's liable to call the game warden, and we damn sure don't want that."

Lucy pitched a cigarette butt into the weeds. "Let's do it."

Red knelt down and studied the safe. In the center of the door was a handle shaped like a four-legged starfish. Right smack in the middle of the handle, that's where he would aim. Maybe break something loose inside, shake up the tumblers or whatever the hell was in there.

He backed up about twenty yards and laid down on the ground, facing the safe head-on. Then he remembered a video he'd seen on one of those cop shows. A guy was trying to break into a convenience store, and he threw a brick directly at the front window. The brick bounced off and hit him right in the face. So Red scooted over about five yards, giving the shot a slight angle. "Y'all stand behind me," he said. "Safer that way. Billy Don, point the flashlight at the handle so I can see what the hell I'm doing."

When they were in position and Billy Don had the light shining on the handle, Red dialed his rifle scope down to the lowest power and squinted through the lens. The handle filled the crosshairs.

"Y'all ready?" he asked.

"Get on with it," Lucy replied.

Red took a breath, held it, and squeezed the trigger.

The rifle roared, followed by a loud *thunk!* and the whining sound of a ricochet.

Lucy raced forward and examined the damage. Red stayed on the ground, waiting to hear the results. He'd be a hero now, and Lucy would thank him accordingly. In all kinds of interesting ways.

"Not a damn thing," she muttered. "Not even a dent." She turned around. "There's not even a goddamn dent!"

Red didn't care for her tone. "Well, Jesus, it was your idea to steal the safe—but did you have any ideas about how we was gonna actually open it up? It don't appear that you did."

She shook her head and stomped up the steps into the trailer.

Meanwhile, Billy Don had wandered over to Red's truck and was fingering a dime-sized hole in the tailgate. "Lookee here, Red. You bagged yourself a Ford."

Nicole Brooks was in the interview room, in uniform again, her hair back in its familiar braid. Marlin watched her through the one-way glass, along with Bill Tatum and Ernie Turpin. She appeared comfortable and collected as she positioned the microphone and inserted a cassette into the recorder. Rita Sue Metzger was directly across from her, Bobby Garza to her left.

Garza had asked Brooks to lead the interview—a tremendous responsibility and a hell of a vote of confidence. The sheriff had speculated that Rita Sue might be more comfortable speaking to a woman. There didn't appear to be much that could calm Rita Sue's nerves at the moment, though. Her eyes darted around the room. She kept clearing her throat, and she was petting her Chihuahua's head so furiously that Marlin thought she might accidentally rub the little dog bald. It was a nice touch by Bobby—allowing her to bring the dog along.

"Mrs. Metzger," Brooks said, "I'm going to ask you about the statement you made to Lieutenant Klante, the officer you spoke to in Florida. Would you please repeat it for me and Sheriff Garza?"

Rita Sue stopped stroking the dog for a moment, and rubbed her hands together nervously. "Ain't I supposed to have a lawyer?"

Marlin noticed that Garza opened his mouth as if to speak, but he let Brooks address it.

"As I mentioned earlier when I informed you of your rights," she said, "we can certainly provide an attorney for you if that's what you want. But there's really no need for one. We're just trying to get to the truth. If you're ready to tell us what happened, we're ready to listen. There's no reason to get anyone else involved."

Rita Sue nodded, but Marlin wondered how much she really understood. Did she fully realize that she didn't have to answer any questions? Did she know that her statement to Klante could easily be brushed aside by any competent criminal attorney? Many defendants did more damage to themselves by opening their mouths than all of the other evidence combined.

For a long moment, nobody spoke. The dog whined, and Rita Sue went back to petting it. Then she simply blurted it out: "I killed Vance Scofield."

Marlin realized that until then he had been holding his breath. Now he let it out slowly. Phil Colby was, without question, officially in the clear.

"Could you tell us when and where this happened?" Brooks asked casually.

"At his house on Sunday morning."

"Inside or outside?"

Rita Sue bowed her head, looking down at the dog. "Outside."

"How did this come to pass?"

"Pardon?"

"What happened exactly? What led up to the incident?"

Again, there was a long pause. Garza shifted in his chair but didn't say anything. Brooks waited with an expression of empathy on her face. Finally, Rita Sue spoke again. "Vance Scofield was dating my daughter. I'm sorry I had to lie to y'all about that—saying I hadn't heard of him. I hadn't ever met him, but I did know that Stephanie had been seeing him for several months. But the problem was, he treated her something terrible. Always running around on her with other women. They talked about getting married, but he never did anything about it. No ring or nothing. Took advantage of her, that's what he done. I told Lucas—" She stopped talking abruptly, and her hand went to her mouth.

"Mrs. Metzger," Brooks said, "we know that Stephanie and Lucas were in Florida together. Stephanie has already told the Florida police that they had a romantic relationship. She also told them everything that Lucas told her. About finding Vance. I understand completely if you're fond of Lucas—we all like him—but it will be best if you tell me everything. In fact, it will be the best thing for him if you just tell the truth."

"Lucas didn't do nothing," Rita Sue quickly insisted. "I don't want him getting in trouble for what I done."

"I can respect that."

"He found the body and brung it to my house, but that's it. I told him to run."

"Okay."

I like that boy."

"I know you do."

"I kept telling Stephanie he was the one she oughta go with, not that Vance, but she wouldn't listen."

Brooks was leaning forward, making good eye contact, showing as much polish in her approach as a twenty-year homicide detective. "What I need to know, Rita Sue, is what happened. What happened between you and Vance?"

The dog appeared to be napping in Rita Sue's lap. "I stuck him in the freezer on my porch. Later, when the rains come, I put him in his truck and rolled it into the river. It's dangerous, you know—driving through water like that."

Next to Marlin, Tatum quietly said, "She's ashamed of herself. Doesn't want to tell how it happened."

But in the interview room, Brooks wasn't showing any frustration. "That's what we thought," she said. "But now that we know for sure, it clears up a lot of questions. I appreciate you telling me. I'm wondering—how did Vance behave when you got to his place on Sunday morning? What did he say?"

Marlin recognized that Brooks was altering her strategy, asking peripheral questions instead of directly addressing the moment of violence.

"He'd had another girl there," Rita Sue said. "Musta picked her up the night before. Stephanie called and told me about it, and that's what got me so mad. I hated to see my baby so sad. So I went over there to talk to him about it."

It was the most important bit of information Rita Sue had shared so far. If she truly had gone to Scofield's to talk, rather than to kill, she was looking at a lesser charge. Everyone, in both rooms, waited for Rita Sue to continue. She was simply shaking her head, staring at the tabletop.

Brooks prodded her, speaking softly. "What happened when you got there?"

Rita Sue raised her head. "You sure I ain't supposed to have a lawyer?"

"As I've said, you are entitled to one, but at this point, I don't think—"

"I wanna go ahead and get a lawyer. I think it'd be best if I had a lawyer."

Brooks sat back. Garza reached forward and turned off the tape recorder.

Then Rita Sue asked the most heartbreaking question Marlin had ever heard: "They gonna let me take my dog with me to prison?"

27

MARLIN GOT HOME at around midnight, dead on his feet but feeling pretty good, considering. Henry Jameson, the forensic technician, would check Rita Sue's freezer in the morning to confirm that portion of her story. By then, they'd have a full account of the Florida cops' interrogation of Stephanie Waring. It should clear up a lot of things, including what role she had played in all of the events.

Marlin had called Phil Colby again an hour earlier, but he still wasn't answering, and Marlin was starting to worry. After all, somebody had fired a shot at Colby—or *near* him, anyway—just yesterday. Marlin picked up the phone to try again but noticed the message light blinking on his answering machine. He hit the button.

Hey, Wade, it's Phil. Listen, I can't make it over to your place for dinner tonight. Got stuck down here at the auction in Uvalde. But hey, I'll call you and we'll get together soon. Talk to you later.

Marlin played the message a second time, thoroughly confused. Who was Wade? Colby must have meant to dial someone else. And how did Colby get to Uvalde without his truck? Had he ridden with someone else?

Odd, but at least Colby was okay.

Marlin shut the lights off and went to bed, planning to sleep as late as possible the next morning. Seven, maybe even seven-thirty.

Red was a big fan of late-night cable TV and cheap beer by the twelve-pack, a combination that gave him a whopper of an idea just after midnight. They were watching highlights from a tractor pull in Arkansas when it hit him. "That's it!" he shouted, pointing at the screen. "We'll use my truck! Just like that!"

"What're you babbling about?" Billy Don asked.

Lucy was stretched out on the couch, a beer between her legs. She had shown no inclination whatsoever to retire to Red's bedroom, and Red knew it was because she was thinking about that damn safe. He wouldn't get any more loving until he found a way in. And now he had it.

"We'll jerk the sumbitch open!" he said, rising unsteadily from the recliner, scooting out the door, not caring if anyone followed or not. He'd do this alone if he had to, and come out looking like a genius.

He went straight to the shed behind the trailer, and when he came out carrying a fifty-foot length of chain, Billy Don and Lucy were sitting on the front steps. The safe was still hunkered at one corner of the house under a floodlight. It wasn't like anyone was going to walk off with it.

"You sure about this, Red?" Billy Don called.

Red ignored him. He was too focused. They were about sixty seconds away from getting their hands on some serious cash!

"Hell, let him give it a try," Lucy said. "Neither of y'all have had any other brilliant ideas."

Red staggered over to the safe and wrapped one end of the chain around the handle, securing it with a padlock. Then he climbed into his truck and backed it up to within three feet of the safe. Next, he wrapped the loose end of the chain around his trailer hitch. He snapped a second padlock into place, and now he was ready for action.

He went to his truck door, but changed his mind and walked over to the porch steps. "How 'bout a kiss for good luck?"

"I ain't in the mood," Billy Don said.

Red shot him a scowl, then looked at Lucy.

She rolled her eyes, then leaned down and gave him a quick peck on the lips. It wasn't much, but Red figured it would do for now. He went back to the truck and got in.

There were two ways he could go about this. Option number one: He could pull forward slowly and take the slack out of the chain, then just continue to pull. But he decided all that would do is tump the safe over and he'd end up dragging it through the weeds.

So he went with option number two. He gunned it, and he gunned it hard. He mashed the gas to the floor, popped the clutch, and took off down the driveway like a scalded dog.

It was a quarter second later, just as the truck reached the thirty-foot mark, when the realities of practical physics dawned on him. *If that door comes loose,* he thought, *it's gonna be flying like a goose on steroids.*

He suddenly had a sick feeling in his stomach.

And he ducked just in time.

He felt a tremendous *thump!* from the rear of the truck, followed by an ear-splitting crash, and the rear window exploded into thousands of tiny shards, which rained down on him.

Red sat up straight and immediately stomped the brakes, bringing the old Ford to a halt just before it hit a cedar tree. *Hell's bells, I've done it!* he thought. The door of the safe had come right through his rear window, but who cared! He could buy a whole new truck!

He climbed out of the truck and screamed, "Did y'all see that? I mean, did y'all *see* that!"

But something was wrong. Lucy and Billy Don weren't running

up to him, clapping him on the back, congratulating him on his clever idea. In fact, Lucy had risen from the porch steps and was going back inside the trailer.

Billy Don was walking down the driveway, shaking his head. "Didn't work," he said, handing Red a beer. "Chain broke."

"I'm serious, man," Colby said. "If you don't cut me loose soon, I'm gonna lose my arms. I can't feel a damn thing. And I'm about to piss my pants."

After a long moment, George rose to his feet in the darkness, walked over to Colby's chair, and tested the duct tape with his skinny fingers. "I'm going over to your place. You try to get loose, I'm gonna know when I get back."

"I'm not going anywhere."

"Damn right you're not."

28

MORNING CAME SLOWLY, with the light seeping through the dirty windows of Wade Morgan's hunting shack.

Phil Colby wasn't bound with duct tape anymore. Now he was lying on his back, arms spread, with a chain leading from each wrist to a heavy-duty eyebolt screwed into the plank floor on either side of him, five feet away. Not ideal, but a hell of a lot more comfortable than the chair. The feeling in his hands was back. He'd been allowed to take a leak when George had returned from the house with the supplies. Colby had even managed to sleep for an hour or two just before sunrise. George, on the other hand, had slept hard the entire night, snoring regularly while Colby tried to figure a way loose from the chains. Or closer to the empty gun cabinet. If he could talk George into unchaining one arm, Colby would have more maneuverability. He might have a chance.

* * *

Red woke up, hung over again, at eight-forty on the couch. Not because Lucy wouldn't let him sleep with her (although he had noticed with despair that she had come to bed fully clothed), but because she was a flailer—the kind of gal who throws her arms and legs around at night, like some kind of puppet with a brain injury. At two o'clock, she nailed him with a solid jab to the ribs. At three-fifteen, she rattled his teeth with an elbow to the jaw. At four-twenty, when she brought a knee squarely into his family jewels, he'd had enough. He grabbed a spare pillow and camped out in the living room.

Now he heard the sound of the TV and opened his eyes. Billy Don was in the recliner, eating a bowl of Froot Loops, watching cartoons. Some moron shaped like a sponge was dancing around on the screen.

Billy Don noticed that Red was awake. "Had me a big idea this morning," he said, smacking away, multicolored bits of chewed slop in his teeth. "Huge idea. An idea so big, I'm surprised I had room for it in my brain."

Red knew what Billy Don wanted—for Red to ask what the idea was. So he didn't. No sir, he wasn't in the mood for any more stupid schemes. He'd fucked up his truck, his woman was acting uppity, and they weren't any closer to getting hold of the cash in the safe.

After five minutes, Billy Don relented. "All right, then, I'll tell ya. Remember what you got out in your tackle box? From when we went fishing a couple years ago?"

Red sat bolt upright.

"Okay, folks, I appreciate all of you coming in," Bobby Garza said.

Nine o'clock Saturday morning in the conference room. All the deputies on the case were there, in street clothes, and Marlin felt a pleasant tingle when Nicole nodded a casual good morning to him, with a nice smile behind it.

"I just got off the phone with Florida," Garza continued. "I want to run through a few things, then you can get back to your day off." He looked down at some notes on the table. "Here's a surprise you'll all enjoy. According to Stephanie Waring, Lucas Burnette was no longer living in his rent house in Blanco. He was living with her. But when we talked to the landlord last week, Lucas was still paying the rent."

"So he'd still have a place for the meth lab," Bill Tatum interjected.

"Apparently so," Garza said. "Anyway, Stephanie had been dating Scofield, which we already knew, and we learned yesterday that she had also been seeing Lucas. They kept it hush-hush, she says, because she had a felony on her record and, according to the terms of Lucas's parole, he wasn't supposed to keep company with known criminals. His parole officer would never have allowed them to live together.

"Now, here's how it all unfolded. There are some holes here, but I think we can patch them up with the facts we have. Last Sunday morning, Stephanie calls Scofield and a woman answers. We all know what kind of woman-chaser Scofield was, and so did Stephanie, so she got angry and called Rita Sue, who tried to calm her down. Later, when Lucas came home, Stephanie told him about it, too. Lucas also got angry, and he went over to have a word with Scofield. According to what Lucas told Stephanie, Scofield was already injured and nearly dead when Lucas got there. This was about an hour after Stephanie talked to her mom, which gave Rita Sue plenty of time to whack Scofield over the head. So, as I was saying, Lucas found Scofield and put him in his car."

"Lucas's car or Scofield's?" Bill Tatum asked.

"Lucas's car. That old Toyota of his. But Scofield died before Lucas could even get out of the driveway. Lucas panicked and went to see Rita Sue. An odd place to go for advice—I think we'd all agree on that—but that's what he says he did. I can just imagine what Rita Sue was thinking when Lucas showed up with the body in her driveway. In any case, Rita Sue convinced Lucas that we'd pin it on him and that he'd better get out of town."

"So he stole the Corvette," Ernie Turpin said.

"Not yet. First, he went back to Stephanie's place—their place—and the two of them commenced to get very intoxicated. Stephanie, at this point, still doesn't know that Scofield is dead. Later that afternoon, Lucas offers up a way for Stephanie to get a little revenge for the way Scofield had been treating her."

"Steal the Corvette," Turpin said again.

"Exactly. Stephanie agreed, so Lucas left and came back a while later with the car."

"So where's Lucas's car?" Marlin asked. It was one of the unanswered questions that had bothered him all along.

Garza grinned. "I had a hunch about that. I went over to Rita Sue's house this morning with a warrant for the freezer. Henry is working on it in his lab right now. While I was there, I had a peek inside the big metal shed on her property. Didn't open the door or anything like that, mind you, because that wouldn't have been legal. But Rita Sue, or maybe Lucas, had taped newspaper over the window, and one of the corners was sagging down—enough that I could see Lucas's car sitting in there. I'll get a warrant for the shed today."

"Where's the Corvette now?" Brooks asked.

"I'm glad you asked," Garza said, "and we can thank our brothers—and sisters—in Miami for their quick work on this. Lucas sold it to a chop shop. Stephanie was able to tell them where it was, and Miami raided it this morning. Found the Vette, still untouched, in the back garage. David Pritchard will be thrilled to hear that, because now his precious raffle can proceed as planned. I've got a few forms for him to sign so he can get the car back."

"I'll get them to him," Brooks volunteered.

"Great. At least we'll have one happy customer."

"So how is Lucas getting around?" Marlin asked. "How did they get to Key West?"

"An old Honda. It was part of the deal at the chop shop. The Florida troopers have the plate number, but Lucas had a pretty good head start. Stephanie told them all of this last night, but he still had a couple of hours to get moving. Could be just about anywhere in Florida by now, or even Georgia or Alabama."

Garza dropped his notes onto the table. "Other questions?"

"Did Stephanie say anything about the meth lab?" Tatum asked. "Were Lucas and Scofield working together? Did Lucas cop to torching the house?"

"We haven't even delved into that area yet," Garza replied. "I asked the Florida troopers to take a statement on the murder, that's all. We'll do a full interview when we get her back here."

"When will that be?"

"The charges they're holding her on are ours, not theirs, so we can get her anytime we want. I'll need a couple of you to fly down and get her, maybe as early as tomorrow morning. Let me get the paperwork in order and I'll let you know."

Bill Tatum stopped Marlin in the hall and said, "We'll get Colby's truck back to him this afternoon. Will you tell him that if you see him?"

"Yeah, no problem."

"I'll drive it out there myself. I feel like I should talk to him . . ."

Marlin nodded.

He knew exactly how the senior deputy felt, so he told a quick story about a poaching incident several years back. Marlin had questioned a local who, according to a witness, had shot a trophy buck across a neighbor's fence. Marlin went to the suspect's house, found blood in the bed of his truck, and proceeded to rake the guy over the coals. The suspect was adamant that he had shot a wild hog on his own property. Marlin asked where it was now. The man said he had given it to his cousin, who had just left for home—in Amarillo. How convenient. So Marlin collected blood samples from the truck and from the neighbor's oat field. He sent them to the department's forensic lab in San Marcos—and was later surprised to learn that the man had indeed shot a hog. "Mistakes happen sometimes," Marlin told Tatum. "Not much you can do about it."

"Yeah, I guess," Tatum replied, and turned to leave.

Marlin called after him. "You might want to call first. Last I heard, Phil was at a cattle auction in Uvalde."

"Uvalde?" Now Tatum was frowning. "They don't have an auction down there."

Marlin wondered, *Didn't Phil say Uvalde?* It was one of those moments when, in hindsight, something should have clicked. Warning bells and flashing lights should've gone off in Marlin's head: *Absolutely nothing about Phil's message makes any sense!* But right then, a reserve deputy named Homer Griggs appeared in the hallway with a man named Bubba Parker. *Speak of the devil,* Marlin thought. Bubba was the man who had been cleared by the lab a few years ago. Marlin nodded to Bubba as he filed past with a somber expression on his face.

Red woke Lucy up and asked her a question.

"It's dynamite, that's what I think it is," Lucy replied, immediately sitting up in bed. Something in her voice had changed, and Red liked what he heard. She was grinning at him, too, like a teacher at her best pupil. He could see the respect in her eyes. Red could feel it: The old Lucy was back.

"Damn right," Red replied, cradling the stick in his gloved hand. No telling how old the dynamite was. Three years, at least, because that's when it had come into Red's possession.

"Where the hell did you get it?"

"Broke into a trailer where they was building a road," Red said truthfully. "Had to sneak past two armed security guards," he lied.

"Oh, this is great," she said, without that sarcastic tone she'd been using the night before. "I *knew* you'd come up with something. Clever guy like you, I never lost faith."

"Only thing is, we gotta figure out where to set it off."

"What do you mean?"

"Well, I figger we can't do it here. Neighbors'd get all uptight and probably call it in. We gotta go somewhere insulated. I got an idea, though."

Lucy patted one hand on the mattress. "So do I. Why don't you come back to bed for a few minutes and we'll figure out how we're gonna do it."

Marlin had told Bill Tatum the poaching story because it was something that had always stuck in his mind. Over the years, that incident and others like it had taught him a valuable lesson: Don't believe it until you can prove it.

Blood in the bed of a truck? Might be from a pig, just like the man said. The same thing with a matching set of tire tracks. Unless you saw the truck driving through the mud yourself, you'd better find something else to back it up with.

Witnesses, too, had to be carefully scrutinized. They were prone to exaggeration, embellishment, or distortion of the facts—occasionally on purpose, but usually on accident. A blue truck becomes a green truck. A hunter in camo turns out to be a man in overalls. They'll swear he's six-two when he's really five-nine. Blond hair? Nope, it's brown.

And suspects? Well, that was always a real crapshoot. Sometimes the person who was nervous and fidgety was being honest, while the one who was lying to your face came across as the most trustworthy person you'd met all day.

So, for Marlin, it always boiled down to that one simple statement: Don't believe it until you can prove it. The problem was, it didn't always matter what you believed or what you thought you could prove. Sometimes the facts were incredibly misleading, and the truth was more elusive than a deer in a cedar break. Marlin had learned that the hard way a couple of times in his career. And he was about to experience a harsh reminder.

He was in the break room, filling a thermos with coffee, preparing to make the rounds through the county, when Homer Griggs came in. Homer was a decent guy and a fairly competent deputy, though he was a bit overeager at times.

Marlin was curious, so he asked, "Hey, Homer, what's going on with Bubba?"

Homer was pulling two soft drinks out of the refrigerator. "Aw, he's been giving his ex-wife a hard time."

"Oh, yeah?" Marlin found that surprising. Bubba had come across as a gentle, quiet man, even when Marlin had been in his face, demanding the truth.

"Doing some pretty weird stuff, too," Homer said, cocking an eyebrow.

Marlin asked the question Homer wanted him to ask. "Like what?"

Homer stepped in closer and lowered his voice. "Left one of them dildos on her front porch."

All Marlin could think was *Bubba? Bubba did that?* He didn't seem the type to behave that way.

"Been stealing some of her panties, too," Homer continued. "But here's where it really gets gross." Homer glanced over his shoulder to make sure they still had the break room to themselves. "Just the other night, he . . . well, he played with himself outside her house, and he left evidence of that fact on her front door."

For a good five seconds, Marlin was too stunned to respond.

Homer appeared pleased with himself for eliciting that sort of reaction.

Finally, Marlin asked, "When did this happen?"

"Lessee, it was Thursday night, because she called it in on Friday morning. But Bubba was fishing all day, so I'm just now talking to him."

Homer continued to rattle on, but Marlin wasn't listening. He didn't have room for it in his head. He was too busy processing what he'd just learned—and the conclusion he came to was this: Vance Scofield had allegedly done the same thing outside of Jenny Geiger's apartment. But Vance was long dead, so he couldn't have been the one outside this other woman's house on Thursday night. Assuming the same man was responsible for both incidents, that meant Vance Scofield was responsible for neither. Somebody else had done it. Somebody had been harassing a woman that Vance Scofield was dating.

Why would a man do that? Marlin wondered. Jealousy? Anger? Some kind of sexual psychosis he would never understand?

"You mind if I talk to Bubba?" Marlin asked. Homer said something in reply, but Marlin didn't hear that, either. He went straight into the interview room and closed the door behind him. Bubba Parker was seated at the table, and he looked at Marlin with confusion, no doubt wondering why the deputy had gone out and the game warden had come in.

Marlin took a deep breath and tried to slow himself down. This was too important to rush. He pulled out a chair and sat down. "You been doing all right, Bubba?"

"Been better. I don't know what the hell's going on."

Marlin nodded sympathetically. "Homer just told me what's been happening over at your ex-wife's place," he said, "and I want to see if I can help figure it out. You okay with that?"

"Heck yeah."

"All right, then. Do you know if your ex-wife—"

"She's not my ex yet. Her name's Donnelle."

"Right, Donnelle—do you know if she locks the house up when she's gone?"

"Every time."

"You have any idea who else might've been inside her house lately?" The Thursday night incident had happened outside, but the panties had been taken from *inside* the house.

"I know she's started dating again," Bubba said. "But I don't know who."

Marlin realized he might have to call Donnelle to get more information, but he had a few more questions. "Y'all still talk to each other, right?"

"I talk, she usually yells."

Marlin smiled for him. "Has she mentioned any repairmen coming over lately? Deliverymen? Anything like that?"

"Nope."

Marlin was getting discouraged. "Can you think of anyone else who would have reason to be in her home?"

"No, like I said, just the guy she's been seeing. Oh, and her lawyer."

"Her lawyer?"

"Yeah, for the divorce. He's been over to the house a couple of times."

A buzz went through Marlin's brain as he finally figured it out. He knew what the answer would be, but he asked the question anyway. "Who's Donnelle's lawyer, Bubba?"

"Guy named David Pritchard."

He knew he was unraveling. The pressure was too great. There was a word for it that the cops used about serial killers. De-something. Deconstructing?

He had woken up that morning with a strange compulsion to shave every hair off of his body. He'd been fighting it, but his willpower was weak. Besides, nobody would ever know. Nobody ever touched his body but him. He wouldn't shave his head, of course, because people would wonder about that. But he could do all of the other parts. Legs. Chest. Groin. If he shaved his arms, he'd have to wear long-sleeved shirts. He was okay with that.

29

ONE STEP AT A TIME, he said to himself. *Don't jump to conclusions.* Marlin walked to the dispatcher's cubicle in the back of the main room. "Darrell, I need you to run this guy through TCIC."

"When do you need it?"

"Can you do it now?"

Marlin returned to his office and waited. He picked up the phone to buzz Tatum but slipped it back into its cradle. This case had taken so many left turns, he wanted to see what he had first.

Three minutes later Darrell dropped a single page on Marlin's desk.

"Son of a bitch," Marlin said. He could feel the pace of his heart quickening. David Pritchard had one felony on his record. *Stalking.* The charge was nine years old, out of Beaumont. The complainant was a woman named Cheryl Moreland. Marlin gave Darrell the woman's date of birth and driver's license number;

thirty seconds later he had her married name—Cheryl Cooper—along with her current address and phone number.

When Marlin dialed, a man answered.

"Cheryl Cooper, please."

"She's not here right now. Can I take a message?"

Marlin identified himself and asked, "Is this her husband?"

"Yeah, it is. Uh, what's this about?"

"Mr. Cooper, I need to talk to your wife about a man named David Pritchard."

Marlin could've gotten frostbite from the silence that followed. Then: "What has that sicko done now?"

Marlin found Bill Tatum in his office.

"Has Nicole left already?"

Tatum glanced up, saw Marlin's face, and said, "Are you okay?"

"Where is she, Bill?"

"She left about fifteen minutes ago."

"To Pritchard's house?"

"Yeah, on her way home."

"We've gotta get her on the radio."

"She's driving her personal car. No radio."

"Call her cell phone."

"John, what's going on?"

"Bill, please, just call her cell phone."

Tatum dialed the phone and let it ring. "No answer. You know how bad the coverage is down there. Now what—"

"Come with me. I'll explain on the way."

Red strutted into the living room feeling like the biggest, baddest buck of the woods. He'd made it through a Merle Haggard, a Pam Tillis, and most of a Kevin Fowler song. Getting better every time.

Billy Don was sitting in the recliner. "I guess her mood's changed a little, huh?"

Red struck a pose and gestured at the length of his body with one hand. "Can you blame her?"

"Shee-yit."

"She's had a taste of Red O'Brien, my boy, and now she's got the fever."

"I'm gonna puke."

"Poor woman cain't get enough."

Billy Don tapped his wristwatch. "I can understand why. Ain't like you're setting any records in there."

"Funny man."

"I can hear both of y'all," Lucy called from the bedroom.

Billy Don giggled and covered his mouth with his hand.

Red plopped down on the couch. "Okay, remember that big ranch out on Sandy Road? I figure it'll do the trick. People from Austin own it, so they ain't hardly ever there."

"How we gonna do it?"

"We'll just blow the sumbitch open, grab what's inside, and haul ass."

"Just leave the safe there?"

"Yeah, why not? We won't need it for nothing. Nobody will know where it come from."

"Sounds kinda risky."

"Hell, Billy Don, we'll be in and out in five minutes."

"You're the expert on that."

Marlin wheeled onto Highway 281 and had the speedometer past ninety, lights flashing, before he started talking. First he told Tatum about the incident at Donnelle Parker's house on Thursday night and pointed out that David Pritchard was Parker's divorce attorney, thereby having access to her home. Then he said, "Pritchard was convicted of stalking a woman in Beaumont nine years ago. I spoke to the woman's husband, who was her boyfriend at the time. Guy's name is Craig Cooper. Cooper said he and Pritchard were good friends for several years, but Pritchard acted sort of odd at times. In Cooper's words, Pritchard 'fixated' on the women Cooper dated."

"Fixated how?"

"All kinds of ways. Sometimes he'd just call them on the phone repeatedly, or he'd send little notes in the mail. He sent one girl some flowers. Whenever Cooper would ask Pritchard about any of these things, he'd say he was just trying to be friendly."

"Maybe that was the truth."

"Hold on. Another time, one of the girls Cooper was seeing threw a party, and Pritchard was there. It was an outdoor party, around the pool. Cooper says his girlfriend's panties disappeared from the changing room, but she figured she'd lost them somehow. A few days later, Cooper was at Pritchard's apartment and he saw the panties on Cooper's nightstand."

"What'd he do?"

"He asked Pritchard about it, and Pritchard said he'd had a girl over the night before and she must've left them. But Cooper said these were some kind of panties the girl had bought in France. The odds against that same brand showing up at Pritchard's place . . ."

"This is just weird."

"Tell me about it."

"What happened with Cooper's wife?"

"Cooper said that when they first started dating, he warned her that Pritchard was a little strange at times but he was harmless. Sure enough, Pritchard started pulling all his old tricks—calling her when Cooper was out of town, showing up at her doorstep at weird hours. Cheryl didn't like Pritchard at all and wanted nothing to do with him, so Cooper started trying to distance himself from Pritchard. Pritchard got pissed off about it and started leaving some really angry and obscene messages on Cheryl's answering machine. All kinds of threats on there. She saved them all."

"Smart girl."

"There's more. Cooper decided to go over to Pritchard's place and have a talk with him about all this mess. He gets there and Pritchard starts apologizing and saying it won't happen again. Cooper says that's fine, but he figures it's best if they go their separate ways. Pritchard goes into the bedroom, comes out with a gun, and shoots Cooper in the gut."

"Jesus."

"Nicked his spine, and he had to go through ten months of rehab before he could walk again."

"Did Pritchard get charged?"

"Yeah, but Pritchard claimed Cooper was threatening him, so he shot him in self-defense. Nobody could prove otherwise, so the DA dropped the charges."

"But they nailed him for stalking?"

"Yeah, with those tapes, and plenty of witnesses to his bizarre behavior."

"So you're thinking Vance Scofield basically took the place of Craig Cooper."

"That's exactly what I'm thinking."

"And Rita Sue? Is she lying just to keep Lucas out of trouble?"

"I think so. I'm betting the story Lucas told Stephanie is exactly what happened. But it was Pritchard, not Rita Sue, who killed Scofield."

"But how does Donnelle Parker fit into it? Did she know Scofield?"

"I have no idea. Maybe they went out. Or maybe, with Scofield dead, Pritchard is just picking women at random now."

A mile whipped past outside the window.

"Think Nicole's in trouble?" Tatum asked.

Marlin thought it over. "I really doubt it, but I want to be sure."

Nicole Brooks knocked on David Pritchard's door at 9:43 A.M. When he answered, he was wearing a bathrobe. His feet were bare.

"Mr. Pritchard?"

"Yes?"

"I'm Deputy Nicole Brooks. We talked on the phone the other day."

"Yeah, right."

"Sorry to bother you this morning—"

"You're, uh—you're not in uniform."

She was wearing jeans, a green blouse, and tennis shoes. "Well, it's my day off. But we just had a meeting at the sheriff's office, and I have some news about the car. The Corvette."

"The Corvette?"

Nicole wondered, *Did this guy just wake up? He seems out of it.*

"Yes, sir, we found it. May I come in? I have a couple of forms I need you to sign. So you can get the car back."

"Yeah, sure."

He swung the door wide, and Nicole walked into his living room. He closed the door behind her. "I guess I should offer you something to drink. Isn't that what most people do?"

"No, that's okay. This won't take long."

He was staring at her now, and she found it somehow unsettling. Something in his eyes . . .

"You don't want coffee? I could make some."

"No, thanks."

He gestured toward a brown leather couch, and she sat. He lowered himself into an upholstered chair next to an end table.

"Okay, here's the good news," she said. "The Corvette has been recovered and it has not been damaged. Only problem is, it's in Miami. Stephanie Waring turned herself in yesterday, and she has admitted that she and Lucas Burnette stole it."

He looked at her as if he didn't quite comprehend.

"Mr. Pritchard?"

"Yes?"

"Are you okay?"

"Yes, I'm fine. Why would you ask me that?"

Something wasn't right. "If now isn't a good time to talk—"

"No, it's fine. Don't go yet."

"Are you sure?"

"I'm positive. It's just that I take medication, and sometimes it leaves me a little . . . foggy."

"You sure you're taking the proper dose?" Even from eight feet away, Nicole could see that his pupils were dilated. Maybe he had overmedicated. But that didn't explain the staring—or what he said next.

"You have beautiful red hair. Auburn, really. Is it natural, or do you dye it?"

Okay, now she was starting to get the creeps. "Mr. Pritchard, I believe we'd better talk at another time."

Slowly and deliberately, he reached over to the end table and picked up a gold-plated letter opener. Nicole suddenly realized how vulnerable she was without her .38 strapped to her hip.

Pritchard now had a twisted grimace on his face. "You're a very pretty woman, do you know that? I bet you do."

In the summer of 1976, a fifteen-year-old boy helped a forty-six-year-old man build a porch. The man paid the boy three dollars an hour, which, back then, was a fair rate. The boy would've done it for free, because it gave him something to do, but the man always slipped him some money at the end of each day.

"Working in this dang heat," the man would say, "you deserve more'n that."

The boy's job was hauling long, heavy pieces of treated pine from a trailer, then measuring and marking each board to the correct length. The man did all the cutting with a circular saw. They both drove nails with a framing hammer, and the boy's arms were soon as hard as a chunk of central Texas limestone.

They'd break at noon for lunch each day, and the man would drink beer and tell all kinds of stories about the history of Blanco County. Tales about shootouts in the hills. Moonshiners dodging the law. Cedar choppers who opened the country up for grazing and turned the soil into decent ranchland. "Most of this was told to me by my daddy, see," the man would say. "He was the sheriff in the twenties and thirties. Boy like you should know this stuff."

Before they'd get back to it, the boy would usually cross the road and jump into Miller Creek to cool off and prepare himself for the hot afternoon. One day, when the temperature reached 108, the man declared that it was too damn hot to work. "Come inside and cool off," he said. "You ain't seen the inside of the cabin yet, have you?"

So they went inside, and the boy marveled at what the man had built by himself the previous summer. The interior walls were lap-and-gap cedar. The floor was six-inch pine planks, stained a dark brown. Metal-framed bunk beds were stacked in two corners. "That's for when my brother comes hunting with his boys," the man said, pointing to the beds. "We get a couple of nice deer every year."

On this particular day, the man had had quite a few beers, and he said, "Wanna know a secret?"

The boy nodded.

"Okay, lookee here." The man crossed the room and knelt, pointing to a plank that ran parallel to the wall. "See this here nail?" The boy saw that the nail wasn't fully seated into the board; it stuck out about a half inch. The man pulled on it, and the plank swung upward, as if it were hinged on one end. "Come have a look."

The boy knelt beside the man and looked into the hole in the floor. He expected to see the floor joists, and beneath those the crawl space under the cabin—but he didn't. The man had built a long, skinny box beneath that plank, and inside that box was a rifle resting on a strip of carpet.

"That's my old Krag thirty-forty," the man said. "Only rifle I ever owned. Hell, only one I need. It'll knock a deer down right quick at two hundred yards."

The boy was puzzled. Right next to the hole in the floor was a perfectly good gun cabinet.

The man explained. "Kids been breaking into this place. They done stole a few things, but nothing important. That gun cabinet's just to fool 'em. They see it empty and figure there ain't no guns around. Now I don't have to tote my rifle from the house every time I hunt."

The man smiled, and the boy couldn't help but smile with him.

Phil Colby remembered it like it was yesterday.

Chained to the floor, his head no more than two feet from the wall, he wondered if there was still a surprise beneath that plank.

* * *

Marlin turned left on Loma Ranch Road, following the same path he had followed the evening before. "How do you want to handle it?"

Tatum said, "Let's be cool for now. Just make sure Nicole's okay, then we'll do some more checking up on Pritchard. We'll try to pull prints off the shoebox Donnelle Parker found on her doorstep."

"And DNA off the semen on the door."

"Definitely. We gotta prove this guy is still a sicko."

Marlin shook his head. "It never even dawned on me."

"Hell, it didn't dawn on any of us. We had no reason to look at him."

Nicole stood, and so did Pritchard, much more quickly than she anticipated. He pointed the letter opener at her like a dagger. "Sit back down."

She remained standing. "Do you realize what a world of shit you're getting yourself into?"

"Sit back down!"

As far as Nicole was concerned, David Pritchard had just leapt to the number-one position on the list of suspects, regardless of Rita Sue's confession. The man was clearly unstable enough to resort to violence.

She eased herself back onto the edge of the sofa cushion, her weight forward, ready to spring to her feet if she had to move suddenly. He had her boxed in; she'd have to get past him to get to the front door.

He made no move toward her. He simply stood in place, his eyes roaming the length of her body. "What kind of panties are you wearing?"

Oh, no.

"Something pretty, but not too wild, I'm guessing. Not a thong. Maybe silk, with a little bit of lace. Am I right?"

How do I respond to something like that? she wondered. Deflect the question? Change the subject? Put him on the defensive? So she said, "Why did you kill Vance Scofield?"

His expression clouded over.

Red went outside and vacuumed most of the glass out of his truck. Then they loaded the safe in the bed.

Lucy said, "We oughta call and make sure they ain't home."

"Yeah, I think she's right," Billy Don added.

"That's fine," Red said. "But even if they was there, the house is a long ways from the road, like maybe a mile. We could do it on the front part of the property and be gone before they even knew what was going on."

Lucy didn't appear too keen on that idea. "Let's not screw this thing up now. I don't wanna take no chances. We've all worked too hard."

So they went back inside, where Red recited the number out of the phone book and Lucy dialed. A few seconds passed and Red thought they were home free—but then he could tell from Lucy's expression that someone had answered. "Why the hell ain't you people in Austin?" she asked, then hung up. "That won't work."

"All right," Red said. "Okay. Let me think of someplace else."

Her intuition told her to keep pressing, so Nicole said, "You did it, right?"

Pritchard seemed to be having some sort of internal struggle. He was gazing at the wall, fidgeting, bouncing the fist that held the letter opener off of his thigh.

But he nodded. "I called him Sunday morning. There was a woman there that shouldn't have been there. Vance was a crummy partner, and an even worse friend."

Partner? Partner in what?

Pritchard continued, "He was a liar, in case you didn't know that. He was supposed to be sharing the profits with me, but he never did. He was horrible with money."

She sensed that she was about to learn it all. The murder. The drug lab. Everything. "Profits from what?"

He didn't answer.

"The profits from what? Selling speed?"

Still no response.

"When did you put Vance in the river?"

His eyes came back to her. "I didn't. I have no idea how he got there."

"You didn't put him in the river?"

He smiled. "Stalling. You're a clever girl, but I haven't forgotten. I want to add your panties to my collection."

30

"I GOTTA GO to the bathroom again," Phil Colby said.

George Jones was in his usual spot, on the couch, eating a can of beans cold. "You're worse than a woman. Gotta pee every ten minutes."

"It's been more like three hours."

"I ain't lettin' you outside again. I'll turn one arm loose and you can piss out the window."

"Hey, whatever. As long as I can go."

George finished his beans first, rattling the spoon around the bottom to get every last one. Colby's mouth was watering. "You gonna share any of that stuff?"

Piled on one of the bunk beds was an assortment of canned goods George had brought back from Colby's house the night before.

"Wasn't planning on it."

"You know, proper nutrition is the cornerstone of good health."

George tossed the empty can into one corner of the room. "What the hell are you talking about?"

"Just making conversation."

"Well, stop it. I don't need to hear any of your weird fucking comments."

"You gonna let me piss or what?"

George rose from the couch and produced a ring of keys from his pants pocket. He bent down and popped the lock that secured one of the chains to one of the eyebolts in the floor. Colby could now stand, and he had a loose five-foot length of chain attached to one arm. It would make a hell of a weapon—except George was wise enough to remain out of reach.

Colby turned and faced the window. He was standing on the hinged plank, and it moved slightly under his feet. As he relieved himself, Colby casually glanced downward. There were no new nails in the hinged end of the plank, which meant that Wade Morgan had never sealed up his secret hiding spot.

But was the rifle still in there? Even if it was, Colby couldn't possibly bend down, raise the plank, and remove the rifle before George stopped him.

Colby zipped up and said, "There's no reason you gotta chain both arms. I damn sure can't get away. It'd be a lot easier for you that way. Wouldn't have to unlock me every time I need to take a leak."

George eyeballed him for a moment, and Colby did his best to appear as unthreatening and docile as possible.

George held up the handgun he'd been carrying all along. "See this?"

"Yeah. You won't get any problem from me. I just want to give you those negatives on Monday and be done with it."

"All right, then." George stretched out on the couch and began reading a magazine.

* * *

"What kinds of things did Vance lie about?"

"Uh-uh. Don't try to change the subject."

"No, I'm really interested. I want to know why you did what you did. Sounds like you had a good reason."

Pritchard squinted at her, skeptical. "You don't care. Women like you don't care."

Nicole could see that this guy was a total nutcase. "That's not always true. You can't just generalize like that. It's not fair."

"Don't talk to me about unfair. Vance treated all his woman like shit, and they still couldn't get enough of him. But take me, a regular nice guy, and they don't want anything to do with me. *That's* not fair."

"What did he lie about? Give me an example."

"You don't think he lied?"

"No, I believe you. I just want to know what he lied about."

"I'll tell you, and then you'll take off your jeans."

She snuck a glance at the front door. Not far, but he'd be right behind her if she made a break for it. Maybe she needed to do just the opposite. Instead of being defensive, go on the offense. "I'm not doing anything," she said, "as long as you're holding that letter opener."

He pointed it at her. "Without this, you wouldn't even be listening to me. It's the only way women like you ever listen to a guy like me—if I *make* you listen."

"You're generalizing again, David."

He nodded at her. "Using my first name. I know what you're doing."

"Tell me what Vance lied about."

"Then you'll take off your jeans?"

"If you'll put the opener down. It makes me nervous." It was important that he believe her.

He nodded. "Okay, here's one. There was a woman I was interested in. Vance knew her. She wasn't . . . she wasn't as pretty as you. But I'm not a handsome man, and I know that. My choices are limited. Besides, this woman had something beyond looks. She was . . . special. I thought maybe she'd go out with me. Vance said he'd set me up. But he ended up sleeping with her himself. Just to piss me off."

"He shouldn't have done that," she said. He was talking about Jenny Geiger. Pritchard had harassed her because he was jealous—because he was as sick and twisted as they come. "Is that why you did what you did outside her apartment?"

For the first time, he laughed. "You think I'm talking about Jenny?"

"Aren't you?"

"Don't be ridiculous. Her name was Lucille."

Colby hadn't made any headway by being a smart-ass, so he decided to change his approach: Make friends with the guy.

"You married?" he asked.

"Fuck, am I married? Hell no, I'm not married."

"Neither am I."

George continued reading his magazine.

"I was almost married once," Colby said. "I was engaged when I was twenty-four. Didn't work out."

George glared at him. "I look like I give a shit?"

Colby shrugged. "Just passing the time."

"Who's Lucille?" Nicole asked, trying to buy time.

Pritchard shook his head. "I don't want to talk about her. We're drifting off the subject again." He held up the letter opener—displaying it for her—then set it back on the end table. He grinned at her, and it was the ugliest thing Nicole had ever seen.

She wondered if she could handle him. He was pudgy, not very big. But he was demented. An absolute psycho. He'd be stronger because of his sickness.

He opened his mouth. "Okay, you said that if I—"

That's when she rushed straight at him.

* * *

"This girl I was engaged to," Colby said, laughing, as if he were recalling some sweet memory. "She had a twenty-year-old sister, and man was she hot. Blonde, with this killer body. A little bit of a slut, too. She was always coming on to me, walking around in nothing but a long T-shirt."

Colby could tell that George wasn't reading anymore. He was listening.

"So one day," Colby said, "about two months before the wedding, I had to stop by her house to pick up some of the invitations. She was wearing this miniskirt, and I'm telling you, she was looking good. She started flirting and—to be honest—I was having a tough time with it."

George lowered the magazine. "What're you, queer?"

"Just let me finish the story."

"Well, then, tell the damn thing."

"All right, take it easy. So we drank a couple of beers, then some tequila, and I start thinking, *Shouldn't I leave now?* I mean, I was getting myself into some serious trouble. She was pretty drunk by then, and she says, 'You sure you're ready to get married? You ready to have sex with just one woman for the rest of your life?' I say, 'Yeah, I guess so.' And she says, 'Wouldn't you like to have one last fling?' *Then,* she drops her skirt to the floor, takes off her blouse, and walks into the bedroom."

Colby shook his head and waited.

George asked, "What the hell'd you do?"

"I got up and walked right out the front door."

George let out a snort of derision. "Goddamn, I knew it. Friggin' faggot."

"I'm not done yet. I stepped outside, and her *father*—who's about six-four—is standing there on the porch. He starts laughing and clapping me on the back and says congratulations, I passed his little test. Wanted to take me out for a beer to celebrate."

Now George was looking at him again, his eyes in slits. "For real?"

"Yep."

"That son of a bitch. Pretty damn smart."

"Yeah, I guess so," Colby said. "You know what the moral of the story is?"

"Hell no. What?"

"Always keep your condoms in your car."

For some reason, Marlin calmed down a little bit when he pulled into David Pritchard's driveway and spotted Brooks's car sitting in front of the house.

Everything had to be okay, right? It was a nice, sunny day. Nothing seemed out of place.

He and Tatum stepped from the truck.

Nicole drove one shoulder squarely into Pritchard's midsection, and she felt the air rush out of his lungs as their bodies collapsed to the floor.

He grabbed a fistful of hair and jerked her head back. His other hand clenched her exposed throat.

She was on top of him, clawing at his face, trying to sink her fingers into his eyes.

"You bitch!" he roared, turning his head side to side to avoid her hands.

She got hold of an ear and twisted with all her strength.

The high-pitched scream reminded Nicole of a wounded animal.

Marlin glanced at Tatum when he heard the scream, and both men scrambled up the front steps.

Marlin rattled the knob, found it locked, and pounded on the door. "Nicole!"

"Let's take it down," Tatum said.

Marlin stepped back, raised a foot, and drove the sole of his boot into the door.

It didn't give.

* * *

Nicole heard someone yell her name outside—and then there was a pounding on the door—but Pritchard wasn't giving up.

He released the hold on her throat and managed to flip her sideways, toppling the end table, and now he was straddling her, trying to cover her face with his hands.

She was losing strength and knew she couldn't fight much longer.

She turned her head sideways to avoid his hands, and she saw the letter opener lying on the carpet.

As she reached for it, Pritchard's hands again encircled her neck, throttling her. She couldn't breathe. The ends of her fingertips danced across the cool metal. It was amazing how quickly the lack of oxygen got to her. She was already fading.

She pawed at the letter opener, dragging it closer with her fingernails, until she was able to wrap her hand around it.

Marlin's third kick did the trick, and the door crashed inward. He burst through the doorway, Tatum right behind him, both with their guns drawn.

"Two guys were driving out in the country," George said, "and they saw a sheep with its head stuck in a fence."

Colby nodded, feigning interest, even though he'd heard this one a hundred times.

"So the driver pulls over," George said, "drops his pants, and starts humping that ol' sheep. The other guy just sits there in the truck, watching. Finally, the first guy finishes up, and he hollers, 'You want some of this?' The second guy says, 'Hell yeah,' and he runs down and sticks his head in the fence."

Colby faked a pretty good laugh, and he thought things were going pretty well. But George suddenly sprang from the couch and said, "Shut up!" He cocked his head, listening. "Someone's coming."

Now Colby could hear a vehicle navigating the rutted road up to the cabin. Then the engine abruptly stopped. It sounded as if somebody had entered the property and parked somewhere between the cabin and the road, maybe a hundred yards away.

George walked to a window and peered out.

She was aware that people—who knew how many?—had just burst into the house. She heard a shout.

Her vision was dimming.

Pritchard's flushed, angry face loomed over her, still choking her, and she swung the letter opener toward his torso with as much strength as she could muster.

She felt it sink in. His grip loosened.

Then there was a swirl of violence around her—the sound of a fist hammering flesh, a tremendous grunt of pain—and Pritchard was suddenly gone. Just gone. She sucked in as much oxygen as her lungs could hold.

John Marlin was kneeling beside her now, speaking in soft tones, asking if she was okay.

31

"I'D SAY THIS looks like a pretty good spot," Red said. "What do y'all think?"

"It's fine," Lucy snarled, starting to lose her patience with these two boneheads. She couldn't help thinking, *If Vance was still alive, I wouldn't have to be dealing with all this shit.* Lucy had had a soft spot for Vance right from the start—ever since she'd met him at his father's place. There was something about the man. Charisma, raw sexuality, something. God rest his soul, he was a hell of a guy. Liked to party, too, and once he got started, look out! Hornier than a billy goat.

The other cool thing was, she and Vance had thought alike. When he got booted from that hunting club, he had realized—with a little nudging from Lucy—that it was an opportunity, not a setback.

It happened when they were in bed together, and Vance started going off again, mad as hell, badmouthing Chuck Hamm, Lance

Longley, and all the others. Then he said something about "that pervert Herzog."

"Who?"

"That senator they got in their pockets."

"What about him?"

Vance laughed. "We had a meeting at his office one day—this was last fall—and, well, I ended up getting to know his secretary a little bit. Anyway, what she told me is, Herzog likes to be spanked."

Lucy couldn't believe what she was hearing. She propped herself up on her elbows, a scheme already forming in her head. "Spanked?"

"Yep."

"This guy got any money?"

There was a pause—just a short one—as Vance figured out what Lucy was driving at. "Hell yeah," he said. "Tons of it."

It took them no more than a minute to decide that the esteemed senator deserved to have a few candid photographs taken. Wouldn't the guy be willing to shell out a big wad of cash to keep those photos from the media? Damn right he would.

Then Lucy had one of those rare moments when a decent scam blossoms into something so brilliant, it has the potential to become a classic. The kind of con job that has early retirement written all over it. "This senator does things for your hunting buddies, right?" she asked.

Vance snorted. "Writes the laws just the way they want 'em."

"Okay, good. So what would happen—this is just an idea—if we asked each of them to kick in some cash, too?"

Vance mulled it over. "That's a tough one. They'd probably just throw Herzog to the wolves and wait for his replacement."

Lucy shook her head. "But not if we don't ask for money right off the bat. What if we ask for something else instead? Like some sort of ridiculous change in the hunting laws, something that would screw all of them up real good. Then, by the time we tell them we're willing to settle for money, Christ, they'll be *relieved.*"

She had never seen Vance get so excited.

"How we gonna do it?"

"Just tail him till we catch him fooling around."

"Then what?"

"Nothing fancy. Drop some pictures in the mail, follow it up with a phone call."

But Vance was nervous, talking about how powerful his hunting buddies were, asking what would happen if they figured out who was doing the blackmailing. "What if they trace the call?"

"How they gonna do that?"

"What about caller ID?"

"There's a code you can use to block it. Nobody knows who's calling."

"But come on, the phone company would know. They could get them to tell."

"Jeez, relax. We'll call from a pay phone."

Vance was still uneasy. "Man, all it would take is one person saying they saw me using that phone and I'd be dead meat."

"Then hell, drive to Austin if you're that worried. Use a pay phone there."

Then that mischievous smile of his creased his face. "I got something better. I know a jerk who absolutely hates high-fencers. I'll call from his house. If they manage to trace the call—well, this guy deserves whatever they do to him. I win either way."

"Fine," Lucy said. She didn't give a rat's ass where he called from.

So they'd mailed the photos, Vance had snuck into the guy's house to make the phone call, and that was as far as it got before Vance was killed. The truth was, Vance's death scared the snot out of her. Maybe the men in that hunting club really were as powerful as Vance had said. Lucy figured she wasn't in any danger—slim chance that anybody could connect her to the photographs—but she didn't want to push her luck. Forget the negatives, just get the cash.

Red climbed out from the driver's side, and Lucy followed after him, telling him to hurry up and unload the safe.

Both ambulances were gone now. Nicole hadn't wanted one, but Marlin and Tatum had insisted on it. The EMTs had checked her over, then agreed that she should have her neck examined. She had given Marlin a weary smile, squeezing his hand firmly before she climbed through the rear doors.

"I'll see you at the hospital," Marlin said.

"Good," she replied.

Good. Yes. Yes, it was.

Now Marlin and Tatum were sitting on David Pritchard's front steps, stunned by what had just taken place.

"Hell of a job," Tatum said, for the fourth time.

Marlin looked at the knuckles on his right hand. Swollen and red, but he didn't think anything was broken. Except maybe Pritchard's skull. "What now?" he asked.

Tatum pointed a thumb back over his shoulder. "We'll get a warrant for his place and see what we can find. But I think I'll hold off on that until tomorrow."

"What for?"

Tatum grinned at him. "Because I think Brooks deserves to lead the search."

Marlin nodded. "I think that's a hell of an idea."

Colby could hear voices in the distance.

George turned and pointed a long finger at him. "You don't make one fucking sound, you hear?"

Sitting on the floor, Colby made a gesture with his hands: *Who, me?*

"If you do, those people out there are dead. You understand that? It'll be on your conscience."

Colby was truthful in his reply. "I won't say a thing, I promise. Just don't shoot anybody."

George snuck another peek from the edge of the window. "Who the fuck is out there?"

He moved toward the front door.

Red couldn't remember ever feeling as excited as he did right at that very moment. This was a bigger rush than poaching!

Now the safe was on the ground, nestled in some tall weeds, the door facing up toward the sky.

He used a piece of duct tape to strap the stick of dynamite to the handle.

He glanced at Lucy and Billy Don, who were hiding behind the truck, thirty yards away.

"Get on with it!" Lucy hissed.

Colby didn't know what would happen next, but he sure didn't expect a blast so loud it would shake the small cabin like a dollhouse.

"Jesus Christ!" George said, flinching. He had the door cracked about six inches, and he was peering through the opening. Colby was watching.

Please step outside, George.

Colby was edging toward the plank against the wall. *Please step outside, just for a moment.* Colby was *willing* it to happen.

He reached toward the plank, getting ready, and the chain around his arm dragged across the wooden floor, as loud as hail on a metal roof.

George still had his back to Colby. He didn't turn around.

Colby slipped his fumbling fingers around the plank's protruding nail.

Then it happened. George opened the door wider and stepped outside.

Colby swung the hinged plank upward and peered into the hole.

Red staggered up to the safe, his ears ringing, and looked past the jagged metal into the interior.

What he saw was . . .

Nothing. Absolutely nothing.

No, wait. There was something. One small envelope, blackened and tattered.

Billy Don and Lucy were at his side now.

"I can't believe it!" Lucy screamed. And she let out a wail that pierced Red's soul.

"Let's get outta here!" Billy Don said.

Red could hardly hear him.

Lucy was moaning now, and cussing Vance Scofield with all the rage of a drunken sailor.

"Let's go!" Billy Don pleaded.

Red grabbed the envelope and headed for the truck. Then he stopped, pulled his shirt off, and turned to wipe the safe clean of fingerprints.

It was there. The old Krag was in the hiding spot. Colby stretched—and the damn chain wasn't long enough for him to reach the rifle's rusty barrel.

Standing on the porch, watching through the trees, Buford was having a tough time figuring out what the hell was going on. First, these rednecks come bouncing up the road in a junked-out truck. Okay, fine. Then they unload what appears to be a safe. Getting interesting. Then the one skinny little dude straps a stick of dynamite to the door and blows it sky high. They all rush up and gather round, then there's a bunch of hollering and shouting, followed by all three of them piling back into the truck and flinging gravel on their way out.

Moe, Larry, and Curly, right here in Blanco County.

Buford was tempted to take a closer look, but he figured the safe must be empty, which was what the hoopla was all about. Plus, he didn't want to leave Colby inside for that long by himself. He stepped back into the cabin.

Marlin could hear Darrell calling his unit number over the radio, so he stepped to his truck and keyed the microphone. "Go ahead, County."

"Yeah, John, we just had a call about a possible explosion over near Wade Morgan's hunting cabin." Darrell sounded skeptical.

"You're thinking a rifle shot?" Marlin asked.

"Ten-four."

Poachers, most likely. There had been trouble over there in the past. "I'll check it out."

He glanced at Tatum, who said, "I don't want to leave this place unmanned. Not until we search."

"Yeah, Darrell," Marlin said, "I'll be en route momentarily. Meanwhile, can you send someone over to spell Bill Tatum?"

"Ten-four."

"Why are you sweating?"

"I'm not sweating," Colby replied. But he could feel the dampness on his brow. The plank above the rifle hadn't seated flush with the other floorboards. It was higher by an inch or so.

George stared at him long and hard. "Thought those guys were your ticket outta here, didn't you? Got you all worked up."

Colby nodded, looking anywhere but the plank.

"Well, they're long gone," George said.

"What was the explosion?" Colby asked.

"Nothing for you to worry about."

Yeah, but it might be something for you to worry about, Colby thought. Because it was loud enough, someone was bound to call it in. Especially after what had happened at Lucas Burnette's house.

George took a seat on the couch, but he didn't look comfortable at all.

Marlin kept it at a steady eighty miles per hour heading north on Highway 281. No sense in getting in a wreck over a poaching call. Seemed like small potatoes after what he'd just been through at Pritchard's house.

He turned west on Miller Creek Loop and goosed it to forty.

Passing the entrance to the Circle S Ranch, he decided he'd make a quick stop to check on Phil after he had a look at Wade Morgan's cabin. Then he'd go to the hospital to see how Nicole was doing.

Three hundred yards farther, Marlin slowed to take a right, noticing that the bluestem grasses in the driveway had recently been trampled by tires. Yeah, poachers. Probably come and gone.

George stood and paced the floor, stopping to look out the front window. Colby could tell he was nervous, maybe thinking about abandoning the cabin.

"There are shots out in this area all the time," Colby said. "Poachers usually. Happens so often, I doubt anyone even noticed."

"Shut the hell up."

George stepped to his right and peered out the side window. His left foot was inches from the raised plank.

"The game warden around here is pretty lax," Colby said. "He might make a pass down the county road, but he won't pull in here."

George turned toward him. "I said shut up!"

That's when it happened. The plank, now under George's foot, fell into place with a thump. George looked down at the floor. "What the hell?"

He slowly dropped to one knee for a closer look. His hand skimmed the surface of the floor and found the raised nail.

Then Colby heard it again. An engine. A vehicle coming up the driveway. But this engine sounded completely different than the one before. He *recognized* it.

"Maybe I was wrong," he said.

George stood abruptly and returned to the front window. Then he faced Colby. "Just like last time!" he roared. "You make any noise, this guy is dead!"

32

MARLIN SAW SPORADIC tire marks across the caliche, but no vehicles. The cabin was tucked behind some oak trees, looking as peaceful and empty as usual.

He grabbed his microphone. "Seventy-five-oh-eight to Blanco County."

"Go ahead, seventy-five-oh-eight."

"Darrell, I'm here at Wade Morgan's. Everything looks quiet, but I'm gonna have a look around."

"Ten-four."

Marlin maneuvered the remainder of the rutted driveway and parked in front of the cabin. He killed the engine and stepped from his truck.

He listened.

Nothing out of place.

Birds in the trees. The faint sound of traffic four miles away on the highway.

But there were shallow tire tracks all the way up here, leading around the side of the cabin.

He noticed that his heartbeat had picked up. Still rattled from the encounter with David Pritchard. He stepped gingerly to the edge of the front wall and glanced around the side of the structure.

Nothing.

Except more tire tracks.

He followed them, moving slowly, his palm resting on the butt of his revolver.

Maybe kids had been up here, merely exploring. Or a poacher had driven in, looked around, and left. Whoever it was, it wasn't anything to get nervous about.

Marlin was to the side of the cabin, moving toward the rear. He took another step forward, and then a bumper came into view. Another step, and now he saw the back end of an old Cadillac convertible.

A man wearing a Stetson stepped from behind the cabin.

Marlin instinctively unsnapped his holster.

"Whoa. Take it easy," the man said, smiling, holding up both hands. "Got hit with a sudden urge, if you know what I mean. Had to find a place to go to the bathroom."

Marlin stepped closer. "You shouldn't be up here, sir."

"Yeah, I know," he said, still grinning. "But you know how it is when nature calls."

Marlin walked to within five feet. "I'd like to see some identification, please."

"I don't blame you a bit." The man's eyes fell to the small nameplate on Marlin's chest, and his expression changed. "Marlin, huh? Like the fish, I guess. Or the rifle."

Colby lifted the plank again and stretched as far as he possibly could. His fingertips grazed the edge of the rifle, but he couldn't get a grip. Son of a bitch!

There was nothing he could do except wait for a gunshot. Or, if things went well for George, Marlin would simply give up his gun. Then they'd both be stuck in here, chained to these stupid eyebolts in the floor.

Oh, Christ. The eyebolts. Now the answer was obvious. He'd been too exhausted and shaken up to realize it. All he had to do was walk in a circle, unscrewing the eyebolt out of the floor. The same way George had sunk the bolt into the floor, but in reverse. He couldn't have done it with George watching, but there was nothing to stop him now.

Marlin held a palm out. "Your driver's license."

The man didn't move. "You must be Wade. I've heard about you."

Wade? Why did he call me Wade? Marlin felt an overwhelming urge to pull his weapon, but he didn't understand why. The man didn't appear threatening. He was just standing there, a lazy smirk on his face. Now he was reaching into his back pocket for his ID.

He called me Wade. Just like Phil did. Because Phil was sending me a message!

Marlin pulled his .45 out of its holster, but the man's hand quickly reappeared with a small revolver, which he aimed directly at Marlin's face.

"Slow down, partner," the man said. "I want you to drop your gun on the ground. Right there at your feet."

Marlin hesitated.

"Drop it!" the man barked. "Now!"

Marlin bent slowly to one knee, placed his revolver on the ground, then stood up. He sensed movement directly behind the man.

"Now remove your handcuffs from your belt."

"My handcuffs?"

"Give 'em to me."

"Before I do that," Marlin said calmly, "you should know that

Phil Colby is right behind you. And he's pointing a rather large rifle at your shoulderblades."

The man's expression froze for a split second, but then he smiled. "Bullshit."

There is a condition known as "buck fever," and it's the scourge of hunters around the world. It happens this way: A hunter dreams all season long—if not for his entire life—of getting a shot at a humongous trophy buck. He adjusts his hunting tactics to make such an encounter as likely as possible. He'll monitor the phases of the moon. Try different deer calls and antler-rattling techniques. Experiment with every type of deer attractant or food source that comes on the market. Mask his scent with everything from cedar shavings to skunk piss. And then . . . it happens. The planets line up right, or Orion smiles, or all that planning and strategizing actually works, but it happens. One fateful day, a buck—not just any buck, but the kind of massive, strutting animal that the hunter has heretofore seen only on videotape—emerges out of the brush like a ghost.

And the hunter immediately becomes a quivering mass of jelly.

His breathing becomes labored. His ears ring. His fingers turn into numb, useless stubs. The scene before him takes on a surreal, dreamlike quality, one in which he seems to be watching from above, or behind, or anywhere except his own treasonous body.

That's how Phil Colby felt.

This would be the most important shot of his life, and he didn't know if he could do it. His arms were clumsy and heavy. His vision was patchy and indistinct. The rifle felt foreign in his hands.

Was there even a round in the chamber? He hadn't had time to check.

Marlin slowly took a step back from his handgun.

"Quit moving!" the man yelled.

"Relax. I'm not going anywhere."

Again, Marlin bent and dropped one knee to the ground, then the other. Then he laid flat on the dirt.

"What the hell are you doing?"

"Just getting out of the way," Marlin said. "Bullets have a nasty way of going through people."

Now there was genuine concern on the man's face. His eyes darted to the side, but he still didn't glance backward.

"Stand the fuck up!"

Marlin ignored him. All was quiet for a few seconds as the man pondered this strange turn of events.

Then Phil Colby jangled a length of chain that appeared to be attached to his wrist. "Hello, George. Forget about me?"

The man called George was rigid now, defeat in his eyes. But he still did not turn. He aimed his gun at Marlin. "I'll shoot him."

"And then I'll blow you right in half."

Marlin and George stared at each other for an eternity.

Then the grin returned to the man's face, and Marlin knew it was almost over.

He'd drop the gun, or he'd try to wheel and shoot it.

Five seconds.

Ten.

It happened fast. The man twisted his torso, leading with the pistol.

But he wasn't quick enough.

The rifle in Colby's hands roared.

Back at his trailer, Red studied the contents of the envelope.

"Negatives of what?" he asked again.

Lucy was sitting at the kitchen dinette, her head hanging low. "Nothing. They's worthless. At least, they are to me. I'm done with it."

"Done with what?"

She didn't answer, just took a big swig from the can of beer on the table.

Red held one of the negatives to the light and studied it closely.

Couldn't make heads nor tails out of it. Might be a couple of people in the photos, maybe a guy wearing baggy white shorts. Then again, maybe it was a couple of monkeys at the zoo. Impossible to tell.

He tossed the negatives onto the table. "What about the damn money?"

Lucy snorted. "He musta burned through it all."

"Scofield?"

Lucy glared at him. "Yeah, Scofield. Who the hell else would I be talking about?"

Red felt the trailer shift as Billy Don struggled out of the recliner in the living room and walked into the kitchen. He eyeballed Red for a few seconds, then Lucy. "I'm hungry. Anybody else hungry?"

Red didn't answer. Lucy took another drink.

Billy Don walked to the pantry, removed a can of Cheez Whiz and a box of Triscuits, then returned to the living room.

Red didn't know what to think. All that effort, for nothing. Well, he did get laid a couple of times, but he wasn't entirely sure it was worth the trouble.

Marlin had his .45 in his hand now, and he stood over the man. Prodded him with his toe. No movement. No reaction at all. Not even a fluttering eyelid.

He looked at Colby, who was still cradling the rifle. Wade Morgan's old Krag. Marlin recognized it now. "You all right?"

Colby shook his head. When he spoke, Marlin heard a tremor in his voice. "You saved my ass."

"I'd say it was the other way around," Marlin replied. "Why don't you put that thing down?"

Colby bent and laid the rusty weapon gently at his feet. Then he decided to sit on the ground beside it. Marlin noticed that Colby's face was ashen and his eyes were glazed. Could be mild shock.

Marlin was feeling sort of lightheaded himself. "I'm sorry if I was a jerk." He felt better for saying it.

"You? A jerk? Never." Only Phil could manage sarcasm like that moments after shooting a man. Then, a moment later, he added, "Yeah, me, too."

Nothing more needed to be said. Marlin stared at the body. "Any idea who this guy is?"

"Not a clue."

Darrell. Marlin had to radio Darrell. "Wait right here."

As Marlin walked toward his truck on shaky legs, Colby said, "See how much excitement you'd miss if you moved to San Antone?"

Marlin turned. "You think so?"

"Yeah," Colby said. "You'd go nuts down there. On top of that, there might actually be a couple of people around here who'd miss you if you left."

Marlin nodded. "I'll keep that in mind."

As he rounded the corner of the house, he heard Colby call after him, "Not me, of course."

Marlin couldn't help but smile.

33

THE NEXT MORNING, Red woke to the sound of cartoons again. Shit, with cable TV, cartoons were on the air every day of the week. Billy Don's favorite channel was Nickelodeon, and it nearly drove Red up the wall. The good thing was, hearing those moronic high-pitched voices meant his hearing was almost back to normal.

He opened one eye and saw that Billy Don had taken root in the recliner again and was eating another bowl of Froot Loops.

Lucy, apparently, was still asleep in the bedroom. She hadn't even given him the option of sleeping with her last night, and—Lord help him, maybe he was turning sissy or something—he hadn't wanted to. That woman could go from zero to bitch in six seconds flat.

Red swung his feet to the floor and sat up straight. He stood up, still feeling a little wobbly from the explosion, and scratched a few important places. He tiptoed toward the bedroom to check on the Dragon Lady.

The door was open just enough for Red to peek inside.

Lucy was gone.

Marlin intended to remain quiet during the questioning of Chuck Hamm, chiefly because he was afraid he would be tempted to reach across the table and rip the man's throat out. He wasn't altogether certain Bobby Garza and Bill Tatum would be able to refrain from such behavior themselves. Time would tell.

Sunday afternoon. They were in the interview room at the sheriff 's department, the four of them around one small table.

Hamm did not appear at ease. But he also appeared cocky. He didn't know what was waiting for him.

"Mr. Hamm," Garza said, "we asked you here to talk about . . . well, hell, I'm not even sure where to begin." Garza opened a manila folder and placed a photograph on the table. "Let me start by asking if you know this man."

Hamm picked up the photo, studied it, and placed it back on the table. "Sorry. Never seen him before."

"Sure about that? His name is Joseph Taggart. Goes by the name of Little Joe?"

"No, sir. Don't know the man."

"He was found dead in his motel room this morning. He'd been shot."

Hamm shrugged. "Wish I could help y'all out, but I don't know anything about it."

"The thing is, when we checked Taggart's sheet, we saw that he spent some time in jail—just one night, actually—with a man named Buford Rhodes." Garza cocked his eyebrows. "I believe you know Mr. Rhodes."

Hamm wanted to deny it—it was plain from the look on his face—but to do so would have been an obvious lie. "My ex-wife's nephew. Her sister's boy."

"You keep in touch with him?"

"Now and again."

"When was the last time you talked to him?"

"Actually, it was just last week. Talked to him a couple of times."

"What about?"

"Nothing much. I asked him if he wanted to come out and do some turkey hunting."

Garza nodded, as if that were a perfectly acceptable answer. "Did he take you up on it? Was he in the area lately?"

Hamm was starting to squirm, and Marlin loved every minute of it. "What's this all about? You mind telling me that?"

Garza had managed to keep the events of the day before away from the media so far. "I'm afraid I have some bad news. Your nephew was killed yesterday in a hunting cabin on Miller Creek Loop."

Perhaps the surprise on Hamm's face was real—or maybe he was an excellent actor. "Jesus Christ. That's terrible. What happened?"

Garza let that question hang in the air for a long time. Then he said, "Mr. Hamm, I suggest that you think long and hard about how you want to play this. Now's the time to be straight with us and minimize the damage you do to yourself."

Again, Hamm did his best to appear perplexed. "I've got no idea what you're talking about. You tell me that Buford's dead, and then you—"

Now Tatum stepped in. "We've already talked to Lance Longley, Barry Yates, Tyler Hobbs, all of them. They gave us a pretty good idea of how it all went down."

Hamm opened his mouth, but closed it without speaking. His eyes were feral and angry, like a trapped animal's.

Tatum placed three photographs on the table. "We found these in the hotel room with Joseph Taggart. They pretty much tell the story."

Marlin hadn't been to the crime scene at the motel, but he had seen the bizarre photographs earlier, and he had heard the details that had been shared by the members of the Wallhangers Club. Those men had scrambled to avoid the oncoming legal massacre, and when Tatum had warned each of them not to speak to Chuck Hamm, they had readily agreed.

Hamm crossed his arms and stared at Tatum with defiance. He glanced at the photos but made no attempt at shock or surprise. "Man's a damn pervert, that's all I've got to say."

Tatum tapped the photograph in the center—a senator named Dylan Herzog. Wearing a diaper. A woman identified as his executive assistant was preparing to spank him with a riding crop. "You want to tell us exactly what happened when you saw these? Or should we rely on what Senator Herzog told us?"

Hamm's eyes darted from the photographs to Tatum's face.

"That's right," Tatum said, "Herzog was more than willing to talk to us. First thing he said was the photographs were fakes. After that, though, he told us how upset you were about it all. You said, fakes or not, those photos could really hurt the senator in the election this fall. Next thing he knows, he gets a visit from Rhodes and Taggart. According to Herzog, you hired them to find out who the blackmailer was. He said he thought they were merely private investigators, and he had no idea that they'd resort to violence. Longley and the rest of them said the same thing."

Garza chimed in. "If they're stretching the truth a little bit, maybe you'd better tell us your side of the story. I'd hate to see this whole thing land on your shoulders."

Marlin hoped Hamm would talk. After all, there was a question that none of them had been able to puzzle out: Why Phil Colby? What had led Rhodes and Taggart to believe that Colby was the blackmailer? Last night, Colby had described in detail how Rhodes had abducted him at gunpoint, then taken him to Wade Morgan's hunting cabin. But when Garza asked Colby why Rhodes had thought he was the blackmailer, Colby had no explanation for it. Garza didn't ask him again. He believed him the first time.

Perhaps Hamm had the answer. Maybe he'd break down and explain the entire fiasco. But Hamm wasn't ready to go down so easily. He let out a sigh, drummed his fingers on the table, and said, "I want to talk to my attorney."

That was it, then. Maybe they'd never know what really

happened. Marlin could live with that, because he was looking forward to the next few minutes.

Garza said, "John, you want to do the honors?"

Marlin smiled. "Love to." He rose from the table and addressed Hamm for the first time. "Stand up, you dumb son of a bitch. You're under arrest."

After Marlin booked Chuck Hamm, he drove to David Pritchard's house. Yellow tape blocked the driveway, so he parked in the street, behind Ernie's and Nicole's cruisers.

Homer Griggs, the reserve deputy, was posted at the front door, looking official. He held a clipboard. "Gonna have to sign you in, John. You know how this works."

"Tell you what, Homer—I'll wait outside. Will you let Nicole know I'm here?"

Homer nodded, as if it were the most important task of the day.

A minute later, Marlin was leaning against a tree in the yard when Nicole emerged from the house. Marlin had never kissed this woman, never even held her hand, and yet his heart danced in his chest when he saw her coming. She was smiling, and it was enough to make his knees weak.

"Hey," she said, slipping her hands into her back pockets, looking as carefree and happy as a college coed.

"Hey back," he said.

They both stood in silence for a moment, and it was as comfortable as a favorite sweater.

"How'd it go with Hamm?" she asked.

"About like we figured." He nodded toward the house. "How's it going in there?"

"Let's see—where do I start? Found a baseball bat in a closet. Looked clean, but it tested positive for blood."

Marlin remembered what Pritchard had said: He and Scofield had played on a softball team together. "Nice job."

"That and a box of panties on the upper shelf. Twenty-three pairs."

Marlin grinned at her. "Man's gotta have a hobby."

She pointed at Pritchard's SUV in the driveway. "His tires? Same brand as the ones on Phil Colby's truck. Plus, there's a credit-card receipt from the Exxon. The idiot bought a gallon of gas two hours before Lucas's house went up."

All Marlin could think was *Thank God.* Lucas was in the clear on the arson. He'd still have to deal with the charges on the stolen Corvette, but Marlin figured—under the circumstances—the prosecutor would be inclined toward leniency. When they finally tracked Lucas down.

Meanwhile, Rita Sue had admitted that her confession was a fake. She had been willing to take the fall in Lucas's place, and Marlin thought that was noble. Stupid, but noble. She also revealed a second lie: Stephanie had never phoned to report that she was in Colorado. That was just Rita Sue's way of throwing Marlin and the deputies off the runaway couple's trail. Marlin hoped the prosecutor would go easy on Rita Sue, too, because she was a neat old gal. Marlin couldn't find it in himself to blame her for what she had done.

Nicole continued, "We also found some stubs from the money orders Lucas's landlord received for rent. According to Stephanie, Scofield promised to talk to the landlord and get Lucas out of his lease. But instead, Scofield paid the rent himself."

"So he could run the meth lab there instead of his own house," Marlin said. "Pritchard burned the house down after he killed Scofield because his fingerprints would've been all over the place."

"Sure looks that way. Of course, we'll see what he has to say about it. For all we know, he'll recant everything he told me. That is, when he can talk sensibly again."

"What's his status?"

"I think the puncture wound I gave him was the least of his worries."

Marlin laughed. "You kidding me? You collapsed his lung."

"Yeah, but you gave him a concussion. Hell, you knocked him unconscious. By the way, did I say thank you?"

"Yeah, you did. But I think you had it all under control."

She rolled her eyes but didn't respond.

"How's your neck?"

She rubbed it self-consciously. "A little sore, but not too bad. Didn't bruise as bad as I thought it would."

There were light purple streaks in the shapes of fingers around her throat. Some women might have worn a higher collar, or perhaps a turtleneck, to conceal them. Nicole did not.

"How's Phil Colby?" she asked.

"Well, considering that he killed two men, I guess he's taking it all right."

"I'm glad." She smiled again, and Marlin wondered what it would be like to see that smile every morning. A man should be so lucky.

"Have we heard anything from Henry this morning?" she asked. "Did he get anything from the safe?"

That was another odd detail that nobody had been able to figure out—the ruptured safe that had been found in some high weeds on Wade Morgan's property. It had to be Vance Scofield's, but how it ended up at Morgan's place, nobody had a clue.

"No prints," Marlin said. No money, either, which jibed with what Stephanie had told the deputies. She said that Scofield had burned through the cash from the raffle as quickly as it had come in.

"Okay, then, I'll let you get back to it," Marlin said. "I just wanted to see if y'all were making progress."

"Yeah, we're almost done. I guess I'll see you back at the station."

"Sounds good."

Marlin paused briefly, reluctant to let the moment end, then began walking toward his truck.

Nicole called out, "Hey, John." He turned to face her, and she had a mischievous grin on her face. She said, "Yesterday, at my place?"

"Yeah?"

"We never got a chance to finish those beers."

34

TWO DAYS LATER, Dylan Herzog held a press conference to tackle the bad press head-on. After a brief prepared statement, he fielded the first question.

"So you're saying the photographs are fake?"

It came from the third row—a smart-ass female reporter who worked for the *Austin American-Statesman.* Dylan Herzog had dealt with her before on other issues, and he gave her the same patient smile he always did.

"Absolutely. You know how advanced some of these software programs are nowadays. Somebody constructed them from his own sick imagination, it's that simple. Whoever it is, the poor man needs professional help. Either that, or he needs a job in Hollywood."

A few laughs here and there.

Then a reporter from the *San Antonio Express-News:* "Senator, the photos are now part of the public record, and they're already appearing on the Internet. Any comment?"

Herzog spread his hands in a magnanimous gesture. "Why let the Democrats get all the bad press? As long as people remember that the photographs are purely fabrications. Frankly, I'm flattered that all of you would think I have, uh, such a creative libido."

More chuckles, just as Herzog had hoped. This was going fairly well. With any luck at all, he could emerge from this ordeal unscathed. So far, he hadn't received any more anonymous calls about the photographs.

Another hand went up. "How has your wife reacted to all of this?"

Herzog grinned and lied through his teeth. "Oh, come on, she wasn't fooled by those silly pictures for a minute. She's been right beside me, getting a good laugh out of the whole thing."

"Any reason why she's not here today?"

What should he say? The truth? That she fled the country in embarrassment? "We agreed that it wasn't even worth her time. This whole thing is just so preposterous."

"And there is no improper relationship between you and Susan Hammond?" That damn *Statesman* reporter again, using some of the same language that had been used on Clinton. Intentionally, no doubt.

"There isn't now and there never was. Period."

"Any comment on Chuck Hamm? He was one of your biggest supporters, and now he's facing charges for attempted murder."

This was touchy ground. Herzog's lawyers had advised him not to comment, but he couldn't help it. "The man acted completely of his own accord and without my knowledge. He was a dear friend of mine, but I am appalled at his behavior. I can only hope that the court system will deal with his transgressions appropriately."

Herzog continued for ten more minutes, handling each question with practiced eloquence, deflecting insinuations and pooh-poohing anything that came remotely close to the truth. The reporters finally seemed to accept that the blood in the water was nothing but an illusion, and the questioning came to an end.

Herzog was in his office an hour later when the phone rang.

It was one of his fellow committee members. "We're behind you, Dylan," he said. "You need anything, just give me a call."

That was a fabulous sign. His brethren were rallying behind him!

Herzog thanked him graciously and hung up.

The phone rang again. A senator from East Texas—and a Democrat at that! "You handled that perfectly. Don't let 'em get you down."

Herzog was beside himself. He was touched that a man would actually cross party lines to offer words of support. It was unheard of!

The phone warbled yet again. It was the governor himself! "I hate that kind of smear campaign," he said. "You just stand tough and hold your ground, pardner."

This was incredible! It appeared as if the scandal might actually *increase* his popularity!

Herzog was indeed in a buoyant mood. Why, he might even have to call Susan and line up a little celebration.

Red wasn't going to lie to himself. He was a big boy. He could handle the truth. Lucy wasn't coming back.

Billy Don was in the recliner, thumbing through the TV channels. Red was lying on the couch.

She'd been using him and Billy Don to get into that damn safe, that's all there was to it. She scammed him just like she scammed everybody else.

Billy Don stopped on a Faith Hill video, and Red felt a pang in his heart. "I don't wanna watch that shit," he said.

Billy Don kept surfing. Some corny movie with that chick from *The Bionic Woman.* An infomercial about a food dehydrator.

Red felt kind of stupid about it all. Falling for a woman like that. Jesus. He should've seen it coming.

Billy Don paused for a moment on ESPN. A rerun of a NASCAR race.

Red was going to be damn careful next time. Not get suckered in by a pretty face.

Billy Don cruised through the news channels—CNN, MSNBC, Fox News—not even stopping to hear what the stories were about.

Red decided it might even be best if he didn't date at all. Just go cold turkey on the women altogether. That way, he'd—

Wait just a minute.

What the hell had he just seen?

"Billy Don, flip it back to that other channel."

"Which 'un?"

Red sat up. "Just go back. I'll tell you when to stop."

Billy Don put it in reverse.

Fox News.

MSNBC.

CNN.

"Stop!"

There it was, just over the anchorman's shoulder. A photo of a man in a diaper. Some big scandal about a senator in Texas. The senator, according to the guy talking, was claiming that the photos were fakes.

Red smiled at first.

Then he started laughing—so damn hard that he couldn't hardly breathe.

Billy Don was looking at him, then looking at the screen, not putting it together at all.

Red could hardly get the words out, but what he said was "Billy Don, go dig those negatives outta the trash."

In John Marlin's empty kitchen, the phone rang four times and the answering machine picked up.

This is Marlin. Leave a message.

After the beep, a man spoke:

Hey, John, this is Max Thayer calling you back again. Seems like we're playing a lot of phone tag these days. Anyway, I got your message this morning, and I wanted to get back to you. I think you'd do real good down here in Bexar County, but, well, I understand your decision completely. Blanco County's lucky to have you. Let's catch another Spurs game this summer, you hear? I'll talk to you later.

READ ON FOR A HILARIOUS EXCERPT FROM

BEN REHDER'S NEXT MADCAP BLANCO COUNTY MYSTERY

(available in Summer 2007)

GUN SHY

Log on to www.benrehder.com for a second installment of Ben's hilarious new Blanco County mystery

Saturday, June 20
National Weapons Alliance Rally
Houston, Texas

FIFTY-TWO YEARS AGO, at the tender age of nine, Dale Allen Stubbs fell head over heels in love. He simply couldn't help himself. The object of his affection was slender and hard, blessed with understated curves that begged for the caress of his young hand.

It was a bolt-action Remington .22 given to him by his grandfather Atticus Stubbs on Dale's birthday. Christ, what a gun! Oil-finished walnut stock. A twenty-inch barrel with the same blue-black sheen as a raven's wing. A true thing of beauty. Stubbs's palms were sweaty with anticipation the first time he cradled that marvelous weapon. For the first week or so, he actually slept with it, the barrel rising up between his legs, little Dale having no understanding of the Freudian implications.

Now, half a century later, the white-hot love affair continued, though Stubbs was by no means monogamous. He'd amassed an arsenal over the years, nearly fifty weapons in total—handguns, rifles, contemporary black-powder muzzleloaders, antique flintlocks and muskets—all housed inside twin burglarproof safes, with a certified fire-protection rating of more than sixteen-hundred degrees. Had to protect his babies, you know.

Of course, like a father with many children, he had his favorites. His Winchester Model 70, a pre-1964 specimen, chambered in .357 H&H magnum. His L.C. Smith side-by-side twelve gauge with rear oval lock plates, manufactured in 1898. Monogram grade. Extremely rare. And the centerpiece of his collection—a pair of Colt Model 1849 pocket percussion revolvers, inscribed to Major C. Smith.

Yes, he loved each and every one. A lot. More than his six-bedroom home with its state-of-the-art security system. More than Dexter, his five-thousand-dollar bird dog. More than his brand-new fully loaded Chevrolet crew-cab pickup. Yes, even more than sex—with Margie, his wife of twenty-five years, or with Tricia, his twenty-four-year-old secretary, who captured Stubbs's heart when he discovered that she carried a snubnose .38 in her handbag.

The only thing that maybe, just maybe, stirred Dale Stubbs's passion more than guns was speaking to other people who held the same convictions he did. Preaching the gospel of Truth gave him a sense of satisfaction more profound than dropping a charging Cape buffalo (which he had done on three separate occasions).

And now, as he strutted onto the dais, preparing to address a crowd of four thousand—true patriots, every last one of them—Stubbs was feeling an all-time high. Adrenaline flowed through his heart like water through a hose. The audience rose to its feet, clapping and cheering wildly.

It was amazing, really, he thought. A simple country boy had managed to reach dizzying heights, turning his fondness for guns into not just a lucrative career, but a higher calling. He was making a *difference* in the world, by God. He was president of the Texas chapter of the National Weapons Alliance, the most powerful lobbying organization in the world. As such, he *lived* for moments like this.

As the applause slowly ebbed, Stubbs adjusted the microphone. The opening line of a speech was always the most important one, and Stubbs was up to the task. Using the deepest, most charismatic voice he could muster, he said, "I wanna welcome y'all to Houston . . . where great Americans still recognize the value of freedom!"

The crowd went berserk.

Right on cue, thousands of red, white, and blue balloons dropped from the rafters. Someone backstage cranked the music to a deafening level. Men in Stetsons proudly waved flags and banners. The pandemonium lasted a full minute. Stubbs simply waited, beaming, enjoying every last moment of it.

Finally, just as the auditorium began to settle down, a buxom blonde girl wearing miniscule shorts, a tight NWA T-shirt, and a cowboy hat yelled, "We love you, Dale!"

"I love you, too, sweetheart," Dale replied cheerfully.

That elicited a booming round of good-natured laughter, followed by more hearty applause.

"In fact, I love *all* of you," Stubbs continued, taking the microphone in hand like a television evangelist. "Each and every one of you is a soldier in the battle to keep our great country strong."

Another eruption, almost as long as the first. He expected it; he'd carefully crafted his speech to draw reactions at various key moments. You had to control the audience, just as you controlled your pacing and your content. Sometimes, though, you needed a little help, and that's why Stubbs had asked one of his assistants to plant the blonde girl in the third row. Just a little parlor trick to get him off on the right foot. Now Stubbs raised one hand, palm outward, and the audience grew silent. It was as impressive as Moses parting the Red Sea.

"It's apparent that we're all in a great mood this morning, and for good reason. The National Weapons Alliance, I'm proud to say, is stronger today than it has ever been. Granted, we've faced treachery on many fronts in the past decade. In the nineties, a weak-minded and short-sighted president attempted to usurp the power of the American people."

Boos all around. Stubbs nodded sympathetically.

"More recently, misguided cities and counties, and even a few states, tried to sue the gun manufacturers out of existence. But were we daunted or discouraged or defeated? No sir! We did what our daddies would've done. We persevered! We fought back, using the second-most effective weapon we have: our God-given right to vote. From state capitals around the nation, all the way to Washington, our voice was heard as one—and that voice said THE RIGHT OF THE PEOPLE TO KEEP AND BEAR ARMS SHALL NOT BE INFRINGED!"

The audience sprang to its feet. A standing ovation! Quoting the Second Amendment was always a sure-fire winner. This outbreak was the longest one yet! Stubbs basked in the glow and waited for the calm before he proceeded.

"Now, it seems, we are in a position to ensure liberty for generations to come, for our children and our grandchildren. We have a friend in the White House—a great man who understands that we, the common citizens, must always remain vigilant as we stand guard against tyranny. He's one of us, my friends, and you have yourselves to thank because YOU PUT HIM THERE!"

Applause for ten seconds. About what Stubbs had expected because, let's face it, the president did have certain flaws. His intelligence was questionable. His diplomatic skills were suspect. He was often nervous and clumsy in front of a camera. Plus, to get picky, he didn't even have a gun rack in the truck he used on his ranch. What kind of message did that send? Ah, well, you did your best with what you had, and one of Stubbs's jobs was to make the NWA's strengths appear indomitable.

"But, as we have all learned over the years, we cannot become complacent. We cannot rest on our laurels and our accomplishments. The anti-gun zealots and the liberal media are quick to jump on even the smallest crack in our armor. Take the incident last month in Springfield, Massachusetts, where one of our members—Zelda Grimby, a retired algebra teacher—mistakenly thought her postman was a burglar and shot him in the groin. Did the reporters mention that Zelda was fully licensed to own a handgun? No, they did not. Did they mention that Zelda lived in a high-crime area? Somehow they overlooked that. They focused solely on the fact that the mail carrier lost a testicle, and the second one was badly damaged. Yes, it's unlikely that he'll ever father children, but"—Stubbs paused for effect, then came back stronger than ever—"I'd say that's a small price to pay for a strong and well-armed republic!"

Wild cheering proved that Stubbs was right. He had the audience eating out of his hand. Time to wrap this up and get out on a high note. Move on to the barbecue and a cold beer.

"The point is, we must keep up the good fight, and that is the reason we are all here today. We have gathered to show our unified support for a man who, with our help, will be elected the next governor of the state of Texas. I'm speaking of a man who will push to fully expand our Second Amendment rights, making it legal for law-abiding citizens to carry a concealed weapon anywhere in Texas without a permit. I'm referring to a good friend of mine by the name of Congressman Glenn Andrew Dobbins!"

This was the moment the crowd had been waiting for. They quickly began a chant: *Daw-bins! Daw-bins! Daw-bins!* They waved placards and hand-painted signs. Khaki-clad men kissed khaki-clad women with joyous exuberance. Somewhere in the back, someone played "Deep in the Heart of Texas" very poorly on a trombone.

After a minute, Stubbs tried one of his usual settle-down gestures, but even that didn't work. He simply had to wait it out, and he didn't mind at all. If this was any indication, the NWA's candidate was a shoo-in come November. Finally, after nearly two minutes, the ruckus began to subside.

"Unfortunately," Stubbs said, "Congressman Dobbins was unable to join us today. But as you know, this is only the first of many rallies to be held in the next few months. Fort Worth. San Antonio. Midland. Abilene. Not Austin, thank you very much."

Stubbs waited for the chuckles that line merited, and he was amply rewarded. No, Austin, the liberal bastion of Texas, would not be hosting an NWA rally. No way. Not a city that had more anti-gunners than the remainder of the state combined. The rest of Texas—that's where the NWA intended to spread its message.

"In fact, two weeks from today," he said, "on Independence Day, we'll be convening in the heartland of our state . . . in Blanco County, just outside Johnson City, and I know Congressman Dobbins fully intends to be there to thank each of you for your support. Because make no mistake—it is you, the rank and file, the front-line troops—who are the backbone of our organization!"

Pure pandering, but they ate it up. Audience members slapped each other's backs and exchanged high fives.

"Speaking of the Blanco County rally," Stubbs said, switching to a folksy delivery for a moment, "I have a very special announcement to make, and this just tickles me to death." He paused again to build the drama, studying the crowd with what was meant to come across as genuine affection. "We've been holding the location of the rally back as a surprise, and now I can share it with you."

A buzz was starting to build. This was going to be big, Stubbs had no doubt of that.

"I'm pleased to say that it will take place at a ranch owned by—hold on to your hats, friends!—none other than our newest spokesman, star of our latest radio and television ads, country music superstar Mitch Campbell!"

The audience responded with an outburst unlike any Stubbs had ever seen or heard. Even the gleeful cheers for Dobbins paled by comparison. Stubbs did his best to speak over the uproar.

"Mitch Campbell, I think we'd all agree, is a fine representative for the NWA. His smash-hit song, 'My Cold, Dead Hands,' has brought in a quarter-million new members nationally in the last six months alone!"

Was anyone even listening at this point? It was hard to tell above the melee.

"Mitch offers a powerful new voice for responsible gun ownership!"

Lusty female shrieks ascended to the heavens.

"He is a man of ethics!"

Men whistled and stomped and shot imaginary pistols into the air.

"A man of virtue!"

An overweight woman near the front swooned and cracked her head on a speaker assembly.

"A man of strong moral fiber and good old-fashioned Christian values!"

The hall was now a full-on madhouse.

"The kind of man the NWA can be proud to call its own!"

The crowd had taken up a new chant—*Campbell! Campbell! Campbell!*—and Grazer knew, without question, that the NWA was about to enter its golden age.

Two hours before Mitch Campbell pumped a two-hundred-grain forty-five-caliber slug into an innocent man, he was in bed, struggling with a massive hangover, trying in vain to remember the names of the naked twin sisters sleeping next to him.

Too much whiskey. Too much cocaine. Too much of, well, whatever those pills were that had made the rounds last night. Mitch hadn't planned for the party to happen—he'd only invited a handful of his new friends over—but these things had a way of snowballing, everybody wanting to rub elbows with the hottest male vocalist on the country charts. By midnight, the house had been crawling with people. Mitch knew he should've thinned it out and toned it down, but damn, where was the fun in that? Hell, he'd *earned* it, hadn't he? Sixty shows in seventy days, and now he deserved a little R&R, right?

But, Christ, this morning he was paying the piper. His brain throbbed like he'd just had cranial surgery. His mouth tasted like a hamster had camped out in it overnight. His memory of the evening's festivities reminded him of one of his trendy music videos: lots of quick cuts and fades, vignettes that lasted mere seconds, bathed in shadow. He had fragmented flashbacks of nude people in the hot tub. White lines on the glass-topped coffee table. Sucking tequila out of some babe's navel. Had it been one of the twins?

Kathy and Kelly? Lisa and Leslie? Something cutesy like that, he was pretty sure. The girls were still snoozing, or passed out, really, one on either side of Mitch in his king-sized bed. He propped himself on his elbows, trying to ignore the drumbeat in his skull, and surveyed the room.

Three pairs of boots and jeans were scattered on the floor. Panties. Blouses. He looked for telltale condom wrappers—expecting two or three—but spotted none. Was that a good sign or a bad one? Had he gone in completely unprotected, not even a thin layer of latex between him and a paternity suit? Or had he managed to control himself this time, to refuse the bounty that was so lovingly offered?

It brought back a recent conversation Mitch had had with Joe, his manager.

"You cain't keep humpin' everything on two legs, Mitch," Joe said with that harsh East Texas twang Mitch still hadn't gotten used to. Sounded so damn ridiculous.

Mitch laughed. "Wanna bet? I take vitamins."

"What I mean is, you shouldn't."

"Why the hell not?"

"Damn, son, you're a *country* star, not a *rock* star. I know the ladies love you and all, but take it easy on the one-nighters, will ya? You got an image to maintain. No more buckle bunnies."

"But I—"

"Besides, you're getting married, remember?"

"Yeah, I guess."

"And dope, too. Steer clear of that shit. Nothing stronger than beer, ya hear?"

"Ryan Buckley does it," Mitch pointed out. "Sleeps around *and* gets high."

"Now, see, Ryan Buckley is an entirely diff'rent product. He's the bad boy of the industry. Why d'you think he wears a black hat?"

"Well, then, maybe I should get a black hat. Maybe we should shake things up a little and—"

"Too late. You're white hat all the way. You're supposed to be *wholesome*, Mitch. All-American. God-fearing. The boy next door, 'cept better looking. You're lucky they even let you keep the goatee."

"What about this whole gun gig? The boy next door carries a gun?"

Scroggins shook his head, like he was dealing with a slow child. "Down here they do. As far as country fans are concerned, ain't nothin' more American than guns. Ain't you been paying attention?"

"I still don't understand why I can't just be myself," Mitch whined.

"You do that," Scroggins replied, "and we'll both lose a got-damn fortune. That want you want? Hot one week, out on your ass the next?"

So, yes, all in all, it had taken some getting used to, this whole hat-wearin', boot-scootin', gun-totin', good-ol'-boy act. That's because Mitch Campbell's real name was Norman Kleinschmidt, and he'd been born and raised in Middlebury, Vermont. His father was a highly paid industrial chemist, his mother a stay-at-home mom. Back when he was known as Norman, he'd never shot a deer, roped a calf, or chewed tobacco. He'd never done the two-step, and he didn't know the first thing about tractor pulls, stock-car races, bass fishing, or any of that other redneck crap.

Norman, in fact, had attended private prep school, followed by four years at Dartmouth, where, between pot-smoking parties and Ecstasy-induced orgies, he occasionally attended class. His grades were appalling, but generous donations to the school by Norman's exasperated father ensured that he wound up with a degree. After graduation, Mitch worked on Wall Street for two years. Wore a thousand-dollar suit every day. Made big bucks. Absolutely hated it. Assholes everywhere.

What he needed, he decided, was something a little more creative. A career where everyone wasn't so damn uptight. So, to his parents' dismay, he switched gears and signed on at an advertising agency as a junior-level copywriter. Here, he thought, he could use his brain and his sense of humor. This would be fun and rewarding and glamorous.

His first assignment was to write a thirty-second television commercial for a feminine-hygiene spray called *Spring Mist*. The project brief specified that the spot should feature "two middle-aged Caucasian women" who were having a "genuine and frank discussion" about "neutralizing feminine odor, not just covering it up."

Holy Christ.

Norman left for lunch, had five Manhattans instead, and decided not to return.

Two days later, stoned out of his gourd on some outstanding herb, listening to a group called Canker Sore, it finally dawned on him. Of course! It had been so obvious all along. He had never enjoyed anything more fully than the garage band he'd had in high school. They called themselves Pus Bucket, a mixture of rock, neo-punk, and fusion. As far as talent went, they were plenty loud. But Norman *did* have a voice. Despite his cushy and privileged upbringing, Norman always managed to sound as hauntingly poignant as Kurt Cobain or Alanis Morissette.

I'll write some new songs! he thought. *I'll cut a demo!*

And so he did, ignoring the fact that the odds of making it in the music industry were astronomical. Norman got hold of some wicked meth and wrote ten songs overnight. When he finally had a clear head, he narrowed it down to the best three—"Sweet Love Weasel," "Say Hello to Woody," and "Binge and Purge."

Then he hired some awesome session players and they were in the studio three days later. The recording went flawlessly. He felt certain he had genuine platinum on his hands. The next day, Norman sent press kits—a CD, a bio, and a head shot—to two dozen producers, record-label heads, and managers. Norman was feeling giddy as he dropped the promotional packages into the mail.

Then reality set in.

A month passed. Nothing. Two more weeks. Not a word. Norman made some calls, but he couldn't get past the iron wall of front-office stooges and peons.

Two months later, finally, a response! A man named Joe Scroggins had scribbled a note across the bottom of Norman's head shot: *You got a face for Nashville. Ever written any country?*

Country? Norman thought. *Sappy songs about broken hearts and beer joints? Fiddles and steel guitars? You gotta be fuckin' kidding me.*

He tossed the note in the garbage can.

Another month passed. Norman sent out more press kits and got nowhere. He was being completely ignored, and it pissed him off. *Don't these fuckwads recognize talent when they hear it?* he wondered. He should do the music industry a favor, he thought, by tracking these jerkoffs down and putting a bullet into each one of their heads.

That's when he decided to write a country song after all. A catchy little ditty about guns. It started out as a joke, really, just goofing around on his acoustic guitar. Something he noodled around with to make himself feel better. It was full of black humor and bitter revenge fantasies. He mailed it out for no other reason than to give all those assholes a piece of his mind. Nobody could possibly take it seriously.

Nobody, that is, except Joe Scroggins. Joe heard something more. He had a vision. He saw the potential for this tossed-off novelty song to become an American classic.

"It's a winner," Joe said over the phone. "But it needs help. Maybe a bit of redirection."

"What do you mean?" Norman replied, a little stunned. And a little stoned. Was this guy for real? The song was mostly a gag. But Norman decided it wouldn't hurt to play along.

"I'm thinking it needs to be a tad more patriotic and a bit less, well, homicidal."

"Yeah?"

"Instead of hunting down record producers, for example, make it terrorists. Then you'll have something."

"Terrorists?"

"Got-damn right. They's big right now. Now, I don't mean come right out and say 'Let's all kill Mohammed' or some shit like that. Ya gotta be subtle. And pro-USA. Wrap a flag around it, as they say. Guns are what make us strong. Guns prevent crime and keep our country safe. That sorta thing."

"Anything else?"

"Change the Kalashnikov to a Remington or a Colt. American-made product. Now I realize that'll gum up your rhyme scheme, but I think it's for the best. Just rework that whole section. And down in the chorus, where you're talking about writing epitaphs in blood—make it something about the Constitution instead."

"You serious?"

"As a swollen prostate."

Norman had never been to Nashville, so, three days later, he decided to fly down and present the revised lyrics in person.

Joe read them twice and said, "Damn, boy, now we're getting somewhere."

"You like it?"

"Got-damn, I love it. This could be huge. The time is right for this kind of message. 'Mericans are nervous, maybe a little scared. The world's in turmoil. Song like this makes 'em feel safe and secure. Like we're all in it together, ready to kick ass and take names."

Norman couldn't help himself. He was starting to get excited by the prospect. Country music? Really? Who would have guessed?

"One other thing," Joe said. "You're gonna need a new name."

"What?"

"And a dialect coach."

"Seriously?"

"No offense, son, but you talk real funny."

Norman laughed. "*I* talk funny?"

"Glad we agree. And I notice you got a little hitch in your gita-long."

"A what?"

"A limp, son."

"Oh, that's an old snowboarding injury."

"Snow what?"

"Snowboarding."

"The hell's a snowboard?"

"It's, um, kinda like a surfboard, but smaller. You ride it. On snow."

Joe gave him a puzzled stare. "Well, forget that crap. Cowboys don't snowboard. Anyone asks, you done that riding a bull."